THE MAIDEN AND THE DRAGON

Ivy walked along the path. It was darkening now, and the trees were turning ugly. She ran and tripped over a root that lifted to snag her toe. She skinned her knees in the fall and got dirt in her face.

That was too much. Ivy sat down in the path and wailed. She was, after all, only three years old.

Something heard the noise and came toward her, half-slithering, half-whomping through the under-brush. It had six legs and green, metallic scales. It steamed—and it was hungry.

Ivy heard it and looked up in time to stare into the horrendous countenance of the rejuvenated Gap Dragon!

By Piers Anthony
Published by Ballantine Books:

THE MAGIC OF XANTH

THE APPRENTICE ADEPT

DRAGON ON A PEDESTAL

Piers Anthony

A Del Rey Book

BALLANTINE BOOKS • NEW YORK

For my nephew Patrick Jacob Engeman,
who, people say, resembles me

Contents

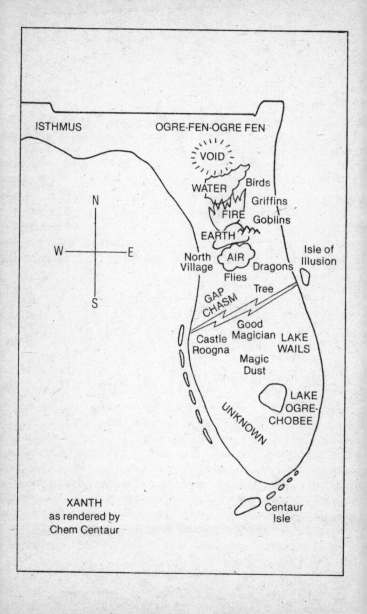

Chapter 1. Ivy League

Irene held her little girl snugly before her as they rode the centaur. They were approaching Castle Zombie, and she didn't want any problems about sliding off. Ivy, only three years old, had not encountered a zombie before and might react in an unfortunate manner.

Suddenly Irene experienced a terrible vision. She screamed and almost fell off the centaur herself.

Chem Centaur spun her front section about, trying to catch woman and child before they fell. Simultaneously, Chet jumped close, reaching out to steady them. "What happened?" he asked, his free hand reaching for the bow slung over his shoulder. "I didn't see anything."

"You didn't; *I* did," Irene told the centaur, recovering. They had been friends for a long time. "A vision. It appalled me."

King Dor, riding Chet, glanced obliquely at Irene. He evidently did not know how serious this might be, so he limited his comment to practicalities. "Let's get on inside the castle. Then you can tell us about it." He didn't say so, but he might have been nervous about having his daughter riding with a person who screamed without apparent reason, for he reached

1

across and lifted Ivy from Irene's arms. Irene stifled a flash of anger and embarrassment, but did not resist the transfer. She could hardly explain her reaction herself.

They rode on in slightly awkward silence, the two centaurs choosing the path. Irene glanced at her husband and child. Dor had been young and gangling when she had arranged to become engaged to him, and still somewhat unprepossessing when she had finally managed to marry him five years ago, even though he was a full Magician. She remembered their nuptials with a certain fondness; they had been in the zombie graveyard at Castle Roogna. Most of those zombies were gone now, having perished at the brutal hands of the invading Mundanes. It was difficult for a zombie to die, since it wasn't really alive, but it could be hacked to pieces. However, the newer zombies here at the Zombie Master's own castle in the uncharted wilderness of southern Xanth had not been subjected to such indignity.

She closed off that subject in her mind, as she was not partial to zombies, useful and loyal though they might be. She returned her thought to Dor. The assumption of the throne of Xanth had abruptly matured him, at least in her eyes, and the arrival of their darling child two years later had matured him again. Now, at age twenty-nine, Dor seemed quite solid and respectable. In a few more years he might even look kingly!

Ivy, in contrast, was a bundle of squiggle. She was large and agile for her age, with fair hair that bore just a tinge of green and eyes with more than that. She was insatiably curious about the whole of Xanth. That was natural with any child, of course; Irene's parents, who had ruled Xanth before Dor, had remarked on her own propensities for mischief at an early age. Irene's magic talent was for growing plants, which was probably why her own hair was green, and it seemed that talent had manifested early. Before she had learned to talk, she had caused all manner of weeds to sprout around Castle Roogna. Blue roses were all right, but skunk cabbages were awkward, particularly when they got upset.

Ivy's talent, though, was of a different nature. They had had to readjust palace life when she was around, because—

"Halsh!" It was a zombie centaur guarding the approach to the castle of the Zombie Master. Zombies came in all varieties;

most were—or had once been—human, but some were animal or crossbreed. The Zombie Master could reanimate any dead creature, giving it perpetual half-life. This one's hide was mottled with mold and its face was rotting out, but otherwise it was in fair condition.

"We are here for the twins' debut," King Dor said, just as if he were addressing a living creature. "Please let us pass."

"Ssurre," the zombie said. Evidently it had been told to be accommodating for this very special occasion. Zombies had rotten brains, but could comprehend and remember simple instructions.

They moved on toward the castle. It was a truly grotesque specimen of its kind. It had a moat filled in with thick, greenish sludge, populated by corrupt monsters. Its stones were degenerating slimestone. It looked centuries old, though it had been built less than a decade ago. That was the way the zombies liked it. They had made it, and their ichor stained every surface.

The Zombie Master's twin children were alert. Both hurried out to meet the incoming party. They were just sixteen, lanky and fair-haired, about the same height and almost identical from a distance. But as they approached, their distinctions manifested. Hiatus was male, with developing shoulders and the first traces of a beard; Lacuna was female, her hair framing a rounder face and her clothing arranged to set off contours that were evidently not entirely to her satisfaction. Irene smiled to herself; some girls filled out early, as she herself had done, while others were late. Lacuna would get there in due course.

"Welcome to Castle Zombie, your Majesties," Hiatus said formally. The two were on their good behavior; no mischievous magic occurred.

"Good to be here," Dor responded. The truth was, the King had come on business; the twins' debut was merely a pretext so that citizens of Xanth would not be concerned that something was wrong. For something was indeed wrong, and this was to be a significant meeting. It was perhaps the first genuine crisis since Dor had assumed the throne on a regular basis, and Irene worried that he might mishandle it. Her father, King Trent, had been fully competent to deal with anything—but Trent had retired and moved to the North Village so as not to interfere with the policies of his successor. Irene would have preferred to have her father closer by, just in case. She loved Dor, and always had, especially when she was furious with him, but knew he was not the man her father was. Of course, she never displayed that sentiment in public; her mother Iris had long since impressed on her that it was not politic to be too open about the inadequacies of men, particularly husbands, especially those who also happened to be kings. It was better to run things behind the scenes, the old-fashioned way. That was where the real power was.

"We cleaned up the zombies for you," Lacuna said shyly.

Irene glanced at the zombie centaur, which had followed after them as a kind of honor guard. Gobbets of decayed flesh fell from its body as it moved and plopped sickeningly to the ground. But the creature had a bright red ribbon in its tail. "We can see that," she said diplomatically. "That was very nice of you." Zombies did take some getting used to, but they were, in their putrescent fashion, decent folk. It was hardly their fault that they had died and been reanimated as walking dead.

They crossed the moat, using the warped wooden drawbridge. Irene couldn't help glancing down into the green fluid coated by slime and wrinkling her nose against the terrible smell. No enemy in his right mind would storm this sewer!

A zombie water monster lifted its largely defunct head, but did not bother them; it was used to the frequent passages of the lively twins. Such a creature would not be very good for real defense because it had lost most of its teeth, but naturally it would not be polite for a visitor to remark on that. Zombie monsters, like husbands, required careful management.

The interior of the castle was quite different, for this was where Millie the Ghost held sway. The stone floor was clean, and pleasant draperies covered the walls. The zombie centaur did not go inside, and no other zombies were in evidence.

Millie stepped forward to welcome them. She was dressed in a soft pink gown that fitted her very well. She had been in her teens for eight hundred years, as a ghost in Castle Roogna, but since then had had another twenty-nine years of real life, just about tripling her mortal age. She had been an amazingly supple creature, as Irene well remembered, and Irene had always been secretly jealous of that. But now Millie was plumping out in the manner of a pampered housewife.

She still had her magic talent, though; Irene could tell by the way Dor reacted. She felt a stronger tinge of jealousy. Millie had been Dor's first love, in a fashion, for she had been his governess while his parents were away for extended periods. But Millie affected every man that way—and Millie's own love was only for her husband the Zombie Master. So Irene's jealousy was mainly a perfunctory thing, and she controlled it rigorously. She had come to know Millie better in adult life, and liked her personally. Millie was really very sweet and permanently innocent. How she managed to be so after bearing and raising two children was a minor mystery, and Irene was also a bit jealous of *that*.

There was a small commotion outside, and the twins dashed out to get in on the action. In a moment they escorted Arnolde Centaur to the interior. Arnolde, no zombie, was much older than Chet and Chem and showed it; he walked with a certain stiffness and wore spectacles, and parts of his hide were turning gray. He was a Magician, which magic had gotten him banished from his original home on Centaur Isle, but his talent did not manifest in Xanth itself. He was also highly educated and intelligent, and this did manifest. He had, briefly, been King of Xanth during the Nextwave crisis, and it was generally conceded that his special insights into the situation had been the critical factor in turning the course of the war to Xanth's favor. Irene liked Arnolde; because of him, she herself had been, even more briefly, King of Xanth.

Irene smiled to herself. Xanth custom prohibited any reigning Queen, but did not specifically bar a female King. That had been part of Arnolde's insight, bless him.

After the polite greetings, Chet and Chem went out with the twins to tour the grounds, taking Ivy along, and the Zombie Master made his appearance. He remained as cadaverous as ever, but was neatly dressed in a black, mundane suit, and was actually fairly handsome in his fashion.

There was a pause. Dor turned to Irene. "The vision?" he inquired gently.

The vision! She had almost forgotten it! Now it came back

in its horror. "It—it was a picture, or a still-life scene. A statue. Two statues. And danger."

The Zombie Master's head turned gravely. "Danger—here?"

"She suffered a vision as we approached the castle," Dor explained. "I thought it better to wait for privacy before examining it, as sometimes these things are important."

"Indeed they can be," Arnolde agreed. "There are aspects of the magic of Xanth that remain obscure to us. The predictive visions are a prime example."

"I don't know that it's predictive," Irene said. "It may be just my foolishness."

"This is the best possible occasion to find out," Dor said. "If we can't figure it out, Good Magician Humfrey surely will when he arrives." He reached across and took her hand. "You saw statues?"

"One was Imbri the Day Mare—the statue we made after she saved Xanth from the Horseman."

"Of course," Dor agreed reassuringly. "We all honor Mare Imbrium."

"The other—seemed to be a dragon. On a pedestal."

Dor squeezed her hand. He could be very comforting when he tried. "And that frightened you?"

"No, not exactly. Not the statues. They were just stone."

The Zombie Master's thin lips quirked. "Perhaps the Gorgon is involved."

"I don't think so," Irene said. "But between them—"

She paused, having difficulty formulating what she had seen. "The Void?" Dor suggested helpfully. "Mare Imbri fell into it, and it remains a danger—"

"Not the Void. But something just as terrible. I don't know what."

Dor shrugged, not understanding. But now Arnolde stepped in, applying his fine centaur intellect to the problem. "Why would possible peril to two statues frighten you?"

"It wasn't to the statues," Irene said. "Or from them. They were just markers, I think."

"So there is a specific locale—if we can but fathom it," Arnolde said. "Not here at Castle Zombie?"

"Not here," Irene agreed. "Not anywhere I know of. But definitely a place of danger."

"Is there peril to any of us here?" the centaur asked, shifting to a new line of investigation.

"I don't think so. Not directly."

"To whom, then?"

"I'm not sure," Irene said, feeling her face clouding up.

"I suspect you do know," Arnolde persisted. "If not peril to us, or to yourself, perhaps to someone you love—"

"Ivy!" Dor exclaimed.

That was it. "Between the statues," she agreed heavily.

"Your little daughter, between the statues," Arnolde said. "Was she hurt?"

"No. Just there. She seemed almost happy. But it terrified me. I just knew something awful—that Ivy would—I don't know. It was all in together, in that one scene."

"Night mare, dragon, and child," Arnolde said. "Together in danger. Perhaps that is sufficient warning to enable you to avoid that situation."

"We'll keep her away from statues," Dor said reassuringly.

It all seemed foolish now. The vision didn't necessarily mean anything, and if it did, it wasn't the statues that were responsible. They were just there. Mare Imbri would never bring harm to Ivy, not even a bad dream, and the dragon— that one resembled the Gap Dragon, for it had six legs, but seemed smaller. Such a dragon would be dangerous, for *any* dragon was dangerous—but how could a dragon statue harm anyone? And why would anyone make a statue of a dragon? It made no sense!

Irene relaxed. Now four Magicians were present, and they could settle down to the business of planning the party for the twins' debut.

Which business they promptly ignored. Millie had worked out the plans privately and in an hour would stage a splendid display, buttressed by such props as talking objects and fantastic plants, courtesy of the talents of Dor and Irene.

"Wasn't Humfrey supposed to join us by this time?" Dor inquired, his tone showing mild annoyance.

"Definitely," the Zombie Master agreed. "I can't think what's keeping him."

"Hugo," Irene said succinctly. Hugo was the retarded son of the Magician Humfrey and the Gorgon, his name a combination of theirs: HUmfrey and GOrgon. Well, Irene corrected her thought, maybe "retarded" was too strong a term for Hugo. Certainly the boy was slow, and his magic virtually useless, and Humfrey kept him largely confined to the castle—but perhaps he would improve with age. Humfrey was, after all, well over a century old and so might have had difficulty fathering a completely healthy child, unkind as it might be to think of it that way. Or perhaps Hugo was merely a slow developer; who could tell what he might be when he was eighty or ninety years old?

"Things do tend to go wrong when Hugo is along," Dor remarked. "The boy is a born bungler. Humfrey did mention that he planned to bring Hugo so he could meet the other children here. The Gorgon will be in charge of Humfrey's castle for the day."

"The other children?" Irene asked, lifting an eyebrow. Her brows were modestly green, like her hair, and she had cultivated just the right arch to make the expression effective. Volumes could be conveyed by the small motion of an eyebrow, if one had the talent. "The twins are sixteen, and Ivy is three. Hugo is eight. With whom does he play?"

"We asked Humfrey to bring the boy," the Zombie Master said. "They very kindly shared their castle with us for a decade, but when Hugo arrived, it was time for us to make room. They bore with our children; we can bear with theirs."

"For a few hours," Millie said, smiling from the doorway. Irene had forgotten she was present; Millie still had a certain ghostlike quietness at times!

"We can proceed without him," Dor decided. He was, after all, the King; he could not afford to twiddle his thumbs indefinitely. "Humfrey will know all the details when he arrives. He has already advanced some advice, though we are not sure what it means."

"Which is typical of his advice," Irene murmured. "It's about as clear as a vision is."

"Good enough," the Zombie Master agreed. "The situation is this: a dragon—"

"A dragon!" Irene exclaimed, sitting bolt upright.

"—seems to have moved into this general region and is terrorizing the populace. We have set out the usual warners, and my zombies are currently patrolling, but this is a singularly ornery creature that refuses to be bound by normal conventions. Therefore, stronger measures are in order."

Irene relaxed again. This did not seem to be the dragon of her vision.

"We do have strong spells in the Castle Roogna arsenal," Dor said. "But the Good Magician sent word not to bring any weapon-grade enchantments. That's what mystifies us. Why not use something effective against a rogue dragon?"

"I could conjecture—" Arnolde began.

They were interrupted by a terrible roar that stiffened Irene again. It resounded throughout the castle, making the very stone shake.

Millie the Ghost jumped up. "Oh, I told the children not to tease the monster under the bed!" she exclaimed, almost floating out in her haste to attend to the matter.

"Teasing a monster?" Irene inquired, raising another fine green eyebrow. That roar had really given her a start!

The Zombie Master grimaced apologetically. "There are monsters under every child's bed, but ours is more sensitive than most. The poor thing gets quite upset. The children like to dangle their feet down barely within its range, then yank them up just as its hairy mitt grabs for them. Or they squirt perfume at it. That sort of thing. It really isn't nice to do that. We want them to treat magic creatures with the respect they deserve."

Irene suppressed an illicit smirk. She had always been afraid of the monster under the bed and, in childhood, had tended to leap into bed, not from any joy of sleeping, but to avoid the ankle-grabbing mitt. The monster had disappeared when she grew up, and she came to doubt that it had ever existed, but recently Ivy had claimed to have seen it. When Irene had checked, there had been nothing there, so she knew Ivy was imagining it. Probably the monster had died of old age. The strangest thing was that, though her monster had definitely been real when Irene herself was small, her own parents had pretended not to see it. Why had adults refused to see her genuine monster, while now her child pretended to see it when it wasn't there? Regardless, she had no sympathy for the thing. Monsters under the bed were a species of creature, like dragons and nickelpedes, that she felt Xanth would be happier without.

"Can't it reach to the top of the bed?" Arnolde asked, interested. "Centaurs do not use beds, so I am not conversant with this particular monster."

"That is not the nature of bed monsters," the Zombie Master explained. "They can not depart their lair. It is too bright above, you see. Their domain terminates where the shadow does. They have to travel at night, but only the gravest emergency will lure a bed monster from its lair even then. They just don't feel secure in the open."

Irene could appreciate why. If she ever caught such a monster in the open, she would take a broom to it! "You were about to conjecture about Humfrey's motive," Irene reminded Arnolde.

"Ah, yes," the centaur Magician agreed. "The Good Magician always has excellent reason for his actions or inactions. If there were some special quality about this particular dragon, it would be unwise simply to slay it. We might thereby do irreparable harm to Xanth."

"By eliminating a rogue dragon?" Irene asked incredulously. "Dragons are common in Xanth!"

"But there are different types of dragons," the centaur pointed out. "Just as there are different types of humanoids, ranging from the giants to the elves. Some dragons are intelligent."

"Not this one," the Zombie Master said. "Or if it is, it doesn't care to show it. It just blunders along, rampaging randomly."

"Strange," the centaur said. "I suppose we shall just have to wait for the Good Magician to enlighten us. Is it usual for him to be so late to a meeting?"

"Nothing is unusual for Humfrey," Dor said with a smile. "He does things his own way and can neglect or forget routine details."

"Such as meeting with other Magicians of Xanth to work out a program to deal with a crisis," Irene said wryly. "A crisis that has been exacerbated by his refusal to let us use effective measures."

"I understand he had some errands to attend to on the way," the Zombie Master said mildly. "Some magic potions he can harvest in this vicinity. He is always collecting magic artifacts."

"Well, he ought to know where they are," Irene said. "He *is* the Magician of Information."

Dor twiddled his fingers against his knee, obviously impatient with the delay. "Should we make our decision without him? We can't wait too long, or the children will—"

There was a crash, followed by horrendous mixed noise. "Speak of the devils!" the Zombie Master said. "Now they're playing their music box."

"That's music?" Irene inquired, both brows raised.

"It's some sort of Mundane device called a jerk box," he explained. "Teenagers associate with it."

"Juke box," Arnolde corrected him gently. "My friend Ichabod the Mundane arranged to import it, and Humfrey found a spell to make it operate here. I am not certain they exercised good judgment in this instance."

"If that's Mundane music, I'm glad I live in Xanth," Irene muttered.

"Wasn't there another problem?" Dor inquired of the Zombie Master.

The dour man nodded. "Yes. People have been turning up at the castle with amnesia."

"Amnesia?"

"They have forgotten who they are and where they're going," the Zombie Master explained. "It is as if they have just been born—but they possess all their faculties. We can't send them home, because we don't know where they belong. Animals, too—they just wander aimlessly."

"That sounds like a forget-spell," Arnolde said.

"Like the one on the Gap Chasm?" Dor asked.

"No," the Zombie Master said. "That spell makes people forget that the Gap exists, once they depart from it. It doesn't make them forget who they are themselves."

"It hardly makes them forget the Gap itself, these days," Irene put in. "We are all able to remember the Gap now."

"Still, this could be a spell," Arnolde said. "It is unfortunate the affected people are unable to remember what happened to them."

"Did anyone follow their tracks back?" Irene asked.

"Yes, of course," the Zombie Master said. "We have several excellent zombie hounds. We traced the tracks some distance through the forest—but there seemed to be nothing of significance. The tracks just wandered randomly. We did trace a couple back to their origins; one came from the South Village, and his wife recognized him—but he neither remembered her nor was able to say what had happened to him. There was no evidence of misplay anywhere along his route. It seemed he had gone out to fetch a pine needle for his wife to sew with and never returned. We retraced his route several times, narrowing down the region where his progress became aimless, but there was nothing. No one else was affected, and there was no sign of the passage of any unusual animal or plant."

"At least he was able to rejoin his family," Irene said.

The Zombie Master smiled briefly. "Fortunately, she is an attractive woman, or he might not have chosen to exercise that option." He waved a thin hand in a gesture of negation. "But a number of other cases remain unsolved, and in any event, we don't want this complaint to spread. Especially not while a dragon is rampaging."

"Good Magician Humfrey will have the Answers," King Dor said. "He always does."

"Take care he doesn't charge us each a year's service for it," Arnolde said with a faint smile. Humfrey normally did not charge other Magicians, as a matter of propriety or caution, but the Good Magician was often absent-minded. All the other Magicians of the senior generation had retired, but Humfrey seemed eternal. Irene wondered what his secret was. She also wondered if they had not become too dependent on him for Answers. How would they manage if the Good Magician were no longer around to give advice? That was not a pleasant thought, but it would be foolish not to prepare.

Millie reappeared. "I had to pack them off outside," she said. "But we had better finish the meeting soon, or they'll be in trouble again."

"All we need is the Good Magician," Arnolde said. "We have defined the problems; he must define the Answers."

"It's not like him to be this late," the Zombie Master said. "Not when the matter is important. He doesn't like to leave his castle, but he keeps a pretty strict schedule once he does. Perhaps I should send a zombie out—"

"He could be traveling by magic carpet," Irene pointed out. "Or by direct conjuration. He wouldn't bother with a footpath."

A zombie in a ragged tuxedo appeared at the door. "Yes, Jeeves?" the Zombie Master inquired. It seemed there were a few indoor zombies, performing necessary chores.

"Carpish ashoy," the creature announced, spitting out a decayed tooth in the effort of speech.

"Well, open a window," the Zombie Master said.

The zombie dropped a chunk of sodden flesh from somewhere on its anatomy within the tux and went to a window. After some struggle, since its muscles were mostly rotten, it got the window open. Then it shuffled out.

Just in time! A flying carpet glided in, supporting two figures. The Good Magician had at last arrived.

The carpet landed on the floor with a bump. Humfrey and his son sat there. The Good Magician was a small, wrinkled gnome of a man with a bare pate and thick-lensed glasses. Hugo was evidently following the pattern of his father; though his skin was smooth, his head fair-haired, and his face innocent, he was very small for his age and already somewhat gnarled. By no stretch of euphemism could he be called handsome, and he was all too likely to grow into a man no prettier than Humfrey.

Too bad, Irene thought, that Hugo had not taken after his mother, for the Gorgon was as tall, stately, and good-featured as a human being came. Of course, few people ever gazed on the Gorgon's features, and those who did were likely to pay a rather severe consequence. There were still a number of statues of Mundane invaders placed around Castle Roogna, souvenirs of the Gorgon's part in that last great battle.

There was over a century between the ages of Humfrey and Hugo, but they were obviously two of a kind, physically. Alas, not mentally! Humfrey was a special kind of genius, while the boy—

"Come and sit down," the Zombie Master said, rising to welcome the Good Magician. "We have been waiting for you."

"I *am* sitting, Jonathan," Humfrey grumped. As he spoke, the wrinkles around and across his face seemed almost to ripple. "I had other business."

"Hugo can join the other children," Irene said diplomatically. She knew the adults would not talk freely while the boy was present, though Hugo was unlikely to comprehend anything significant.

"No, we have another chore, and I'm behind schedule," Humfrey said. "Your problems are these: the Gap Dragon is ravaging the country; you must not hurt it, for it is necessary to the welfare of the Gap, especially now that the spell is breaking up."

"Spell?" King Dor asked.

"The forget-spell, of course," Humfrey said, as if impatient with dullness. He probably had a lot of practice with that, traveling with his son. "It received a fatal jolt in the Time of No Magic twenty-nine years ago, and now is fragmenting and mutating. Forget-whorls are spinning off and causing mischief; they can incite partial or complete amnesia. Spray each whorl with this liquid to neutralize it temporarily, then move it out of Xanth to the Mundane regions where it has no effect." He grimaced, remembering something. "Not much effect, at any rate; it does cause the Mundanes to forget that magic works— not that that is very much loss for them." He handed the Zombie Master a small bottle of translucent fluid with a nozzle and pneumatic bulb on it. "Take it up, Hugo."

The carpet lurched into the air toward the wall. "No, out the window, idiot!" the Good Magician snapped, out of patience before he started. "Straighten out and fly right!"

"Wait!" Dor cried. "How can we spray and move—"

The carpet straightened out, wobbled, then sailed through the window. The Good Magician was gone.

"—a forget-whorl we can't even see, hear, or feel?" Dor finished, frustrated.

The others exchanged glances. "So much for our business meeting," Irene said. "We got the business."

"The amnesia," the Zombie Master said. "So it *is* from the Gap's forget-spell! Mutated—I never thought of that! No wonder we couldn't trace the source of the problem; the whorls would be undetectable and leave no trace except the wipeout of memory!"

"That was my question," Dor said. "Invisible, silent, no smell—how will we know one is near, until it is too late?"

"That is indeed a problem," Arnolde agreed. "It had not occurred to me that such a fragmentation would be so undisciplined, but I suppose that if the forget-spell now lacks its primary object—"

"Undisciplined," Dor said. "That describes the Gap Dragon, too! The breakup of the spell must have enabled it to remember a way out of the Gap, and it doesn't have any limit to its marauding, up here in regular Xanth."

"But to follow it to its secret exit," the Zombie Master said. "That will be dangerous. The Gap Dragon is one of the largest and most savage creatures we know, and no person in its vicinity is safe."

"We shall have to plan a strategy of procedure," Dor said. "We must deal with both the dragon and the forget-whorls, somehow."

"At least now we know the cause of our problems," Arnolde said. "Humfrey was not here long, but he did cover the essence. Perhaps we should proceed to the twins' party before they become more restive, so that we are freed from that distraction. Then we can meet again and try to work out—"

He was interrupted by commotion and screaming from outside. Something dramatic was going on!

"I fear they are already restive," the Zombie Master said wryly.

They hurried to the window the Good Magician had used. It offered a fair view of the moat and the surrounding countryside. Irene saw a cloud of smoke approaching through the forest. "I'm not sure the children are doing that," she said.

No, it wasn't smoke, exactly. It was steam, or condensing water. It was puffing from—

"The Gap Dragon!" Arnolde Centaur exclaimed. "It is raiding *here*!"

"And we're not supposed to hurt it," Dor said with disgust. "What does Humfrey expect us to do—tie a yellow ribbon on its tail and follow it home?"

"The children!" Irene exclaimed, appalled. "The children are outside!" She charged through the castle and out the front portal, oblivious to all else. Her vision, the dragon— "Ivy! Ivy!" she cried.

Lacuna was sitting by the edge of the moat, forming words, sentences, and paragraphs on the slimy surface of the water. That was her talent; she could cause print to form on anything and could change it at will. She was so engrossed in her composition that she was obviously unaware of the approaching menace. "Ivy's all right, your Majesty. She's enhancing the zombies. They like her."

"The Gap Dragon's here!" Irene cried. But even as she spoke, the monster appeared, a great cloud of steam enclosing it.

Irene tried to run along the moat bank to get at Ivy, but the child was on the other side. So was the Gap Dragon. It was bearing down on them.

Irene screamed. Ivy looked up and saw her. The child was facing away from the dragon.

Then one of the zombies saw the dragon. For a long moment it paused, a thought churning through its sloppy cranial matter, while the dragon steamed rapidly closer. The thought was lucky; it made it through to the zombie's action-command center.

The zombie picked up the child and lumbered along the moat, out of the dragon's path. It was an act of remarkable relevance for this type of creature.

The dragon steamed right up to the moat—and hunched its foresection across it. A large moat monster attacked, being too far gone to harbor either fear or common sense, but its teeth were mostly caries and could not make an impression on the steel-hard scales of the Gap Dragon. The dragon shook off the zombie and plowed into the outer wall of the castle, snoot-first. Such was its impact that the stone crumbled inward.

The dragon stalled at last, head buried in the wall. But it wasn't trapped; it wrenched its head up, and a larger section of the wall crumbled out. Slimestone simply had not been designed to stand up to treatment like this!

Zombies rushed up to defend the castle, bearing rusty swords and rank clubs. They sliced and bashed ineffectively at the dragon's side and back. Irritated by this nonsense, the dragon brought its head about and issued a blast of steam that entirely obscured the zombies.

When the cloud cleared, the zombies were in a sorry state. Portions of their decaying flesh had melted away, leaving steamed bones, and much of what remained was too cooked to function well. Zombies were generally immune to physical damage, other than being cut to pieces, but there were limits. These ones staggered and fell into the moat, annoying the other moat denizens but enriching it with their substance.

The dragon, having breached the castle defenses, seemed to lose interest. It turned toward Irene.

The Gap Dragon was low-slung, with a triple pair of legs, exactly as in her vision. Its metallic scales shone green in the shade and iridescent in the sunlight. One ear perked up; the other was merely a stub, evidently the casualty of one of its many battles. Indeed, there were scars all over its tree-trunk-thick torso. Its eyes were bright with the malevolent delight of the rampage.

Now Irene became aware of her own peril. She had been standing more or less transfixed by the action, oblivious to personal danger. The Gap Dragon was one of the most for-midable monsters of Xanth. Ordinarily it was no threat to people outside the Gap Chasm. That hardly mattered now!

The dragon took a step toward her, as if deciding whether she was worth going after. It was time to act.

Irene brought out a pincushion seed. "Grow!" she directed it and tossed it in front of the dragon.

The plant sprouted immediately, forming a button that swelled into a cushion that sprouted a score of sharp pins, their points jutting sharply out.

The dragon paused to sniff at it. A pin stuck in its nose. The monster shot out a jet of steam, but the pins didn't melt. The cushion continued to grow.

The pin in the nose tickled. The dragon sneezed. That sent pins and steam flying out from the cushion. The steam floated up into the sky, while the pins rained down into the moat, sticking the moat monsters. Pins didn't bother zombies, but there was an angry squeal from the denuded cushion.

The Gap Dragon, of course, had not been hurt. It was armored against swords; pins were beneath its notice. It peered again at Irene, still trying to decide whether she was worth the trouble of gobbling. She did not wait any undue time for its decision. She reached for another seed.

The dragon decided to explore in the opposite direction. It turned about and moved off. Ironically, Irene found herself angry; wasn't she good enough to eat?

More zombies rushed up, armed with pickled stink bombs. Evidently the Zombie Master was getting his defenses organized. The zombies lofted these bombs at the Gap Dragon, who snapped the first out of the air with easy contempt and crunched it into a foul mass.

Now the Gap Dragon made a sound that resembled its initials. It was not particularly intellectual, but there was nothing wrong with its perception of smell or taste. It could distinguish a foul stench quite as readily as could the next creature. It coughed out another cloud of steam, but the odor clung to its teeth.

Really irritated now, the Gap Dragon lunged and snapped up a zombie. But the rotten creature didn't taste much better than the stink bomb. The Gap Dragon spat it out with another utterance of its initials.

At last, with poor grace, the dragon gave it up as a bad job and humped back across the moat and galumphed away into the jungle. The raid was over.

"You would have done better chomping me!" Irene called after the dragon snidely. "*I* don't taste like a stink bomb!"

She breathed a sigh of relief nonetheless—then remembered Ivy. *She* was the object of the danger in the vision! Where had the zombie taken her?

Irene hurried across the drawbridge and around the outside of the moat, following the route she had seen the zombie take. She tuned out most of everything else, intent on this one thing. Along the way she saw the devastation left by the Gap Dragon, with broken trees and pieces of zombie, but not the thing she most sought: her darling daughter. *Where was Ivy?*

In moments others joined her, searching the entire area. "Which zombie took her?" the Zombie Master asked. "I can question that one."

"I don't know one zombie from another!" Irene replied, the ugly clutch of apprehension tightening about her rib cage. That vision was becoming more real!

"Then I will question them all," the Zombie Master decided. He brought out a battered horn and blew a blast that sounded like the final wail of a dying buzzard.

Immediately the zombies converged from the entire area, shuffling up so hurriedly that they left pieces of themselves all over the premises. It was amazing the number that appeared; soon there was a dense and grotesque crowd of the things. Irene knew that each one was a person who had died and been reanimated; a lot of people had died in the past few years!

And would one more die in the next day? *No!* she cried mentally. She could not even think of that!

"Which one of you carried Ivy?" the Zombie Master demanded of the motley throng.

There was no answer.

"Which one of you knows who carried Ivy?" he asked next. Three fetid hands hoisted.

"Tell me who carried Ivy," the Zombie Master said, pointing to one of them. Irene realized that it took a special technique to question zombies; they reacted literally, like inanimate things.

"Zzussch," the indicated zombie replied, losing part of its lip in the effort of speech.

"Zush, where are you?" the Zombie Master called.

Another zombie shuffled forward.

"Where did you take Ivy?"

The zombie shrugged, dropping a piece of bone from its shoulder.

"I fear it does not remember," Arnolde said. "Perhaps a forget-whorl . . ."

"But then Ivy—" Irene began, horrified. The horror of the vision—had it been forgetfulness? That would explain its undefined nature.

"May be lost in the jungle—without her memory," the centaur concluded for her.

Now everyone understood. There was an appalled silence. Into what league of incapacity and peril had Ivy been thrown?

Chapter 2. Humfrey's Horror

"I'll have to go to the Good Magician for advice," Irene decided. "He must be home by now; I can reach him in half an hour. That will be faster and better than casting aimlessly about the wilderness. The rest of you can do that."

Her husband looked at her with a certain familiar resignation. He knew she would do things her own way, regardless of his preference, so he didn't set himself up for embarrassment by opposing her openly. It did not seem to occur to him that her way was best; men were not very practical in some respects. "I will organize a search party here, to range farther into the local jungle," Dor said. "Ivy can't be far away." He did not seem unduly concerned, but that was just his way; Irene knew he would leave hardly any local stone unturned.

"You'll probably find her before I get back," she said, though she had a sick premonition that this would not be the case. That vision had been no passing fancy; it had hinted at a terrible ordeal and danger as yet unglimpsed. She gave Dor a quick, distracted kiss, then turned to the more important business.

She brought out one of the seeds she had planned to use to entertain the twins. Now she had a better use for it. This was a bird-of-paradise plant seed. "Grow," she commanded as she flipped it into the air.

The seed obeyed with alacrity. Irene had always been able to make plants grow, so that in minutes one of them would complete a life cycle that would normally have taken months or years. When Irene had been a child, the Elders of Xanth had judged her magic talent to be excellent but beneath Magician level, to her frustration. Her mother Iris had been privately furious, suspecting sexual discrimination; but the fact was that her talent was not as versatile as those of her parents. During the crisis of the Nextwave invasion of Mundanes, five years ago, when Kings of Xanth had been falling like Mundane dominoes, Arnolde Centaur had assumed the throne and decreed Irene's talent to be Magician level. Her mother had not been partial to centaurs before then; her attitude had suffered a remarkable change. Since that time, as if in response to that promotion, Irene's talent had intensified, so that now she could grow in seconds what had required minutes before. She had become, indeed, a full Magician. Perhaps it was the result of the birth of her unusually talented child. Ivy caused the qualities of those near her to intensify, and this applied to both physical and magical aspects. Irene had always been nearest her child, and yes, the enhancement of her talent had manifested during her pregnancy. Funny she should realize this just now, when her daughter was lost.

Her comprehensive chain of thought was compressed into a very brief span because the seed was sprouting in the air at the same time, sending out tendrils that radiated large, smooth, flat, oval leaves that became wings that flapped and supported the swelling mass of the body before it fell to the ground. Another shoot became the ornate tail of the bird, and another the head, which was actually a phenomenal flower with lovely petals spreading delicately.

"More," she said, and the plant renewed its effort and increased its growth, becoming much larger than it would ever naturally have been. In moments it had a wingleaf span of twice Irene's height and a massive if convoluted twisted-stem body. Brown roots became legs and feet and claws. The down-draft of its beating wings flattened the grass beneath and stirred up a cloud of dust. The bird-of-paradise plant was ready to fly.

The zombies were watching with dull interest, never before having seen this type of magic. Perhaps they wondered why only one seed grew, instead of all the plants in range of the sound of her voice. The answer was that it was more than her voice that did it; it was her concentration. She could have made any of the surrounding plants put on sudden new growth, had she wished to; but she had addressed only the one seed. How-ever, there was no point in trying to explain such matters to zombies; they could hardly understand ordinary things, let alone magic.

"I'll be back in an hour, dear," Irene promised Dor as she mounted the bird. She always took care to remind him in little ways how much she cared for him, because she knew men were in constant need of such reassurance. If they didn't receive it, their attention could wander, and that was not necessarily wholesome for a marriage.

There were many footholds and handholds amidst the vines of the plant, so she had no concern about falling. She settled herself in the saddle area and blew Dor a kiss.

King Dor nodded. Her magic with plants was old stuff to him; his own magic was more than equivalent, and he was as concerned as she by the peril to their child. He would turn new leaves and old ones in the search for Ivy, rough as that might be on the trees of this region.

She nudged the bird-plant with her knee and it took off. For a moment it faltered, for this was its first experience carrying a load; then its beat strengthened and it forged aloft. It circled, gaining altitude, while the zombies watched with another surge of dull curiosity. Irene tucked her green skirt in close about her knees, aware that the view from below differed from that above. In her younger days she would have reacted more strin-gently, as she had been very sensitive about people trying to see under her skirt in their chronic effort to discover what color her panties were. Now she knew that they didn't really care about that sort of thing, and certainly zombies didn't, but old reflexes died hard.

The bird-plant rose above the highest decaying spire of Castle Zombie, above the tattered and slimy zombie flag, and above most of the trees of the region. From this vantage, the zombies below looked like squashed slugs. It was an improvement.

The Good Magician's castle was northeast of here. By foot the journey would have been next to impossible, for most of the jungle here remained unexplored. No telling what horrors lurked in uncharted wilderness! But by air it was easy enough to—oops.

Clouds were headed this way, mean little gray ones with tentacle-tendrils of dark vapor. They were obviously up to no good. The inanimate could be perverse in the wilder regions of Xanth, and clouds often liked to soak down passersby just for the electric thrill of it. Thunderclouds could get a real charge from such mischief; they huffed and puffed their delight and crackled their merriment. Irene decided to get above these nuisances.

She nudged the bird-plant, and made it another upward loop. But these annoying clouds were not so readily avoided. They reared up new layers and projected longer contrails, trying to enclose her in fog. They blew out gusts of wind, and the chill drafts made her shiver; water coalesced on the slick wingleaf surfaces and caused the bird to gain weight and lose tractions. Oh, fudge! she thought angrily.

Irene had little patience with this. She had never put up with much guff from the inanimate, having been exposed to the smart remarks of rocks and furniture and even water when Dor was present. His talent was making inanimate things talk; that was fine, it was an excellent talent, and because of it he was now King and she was Queen—but why did those things have to have such mouthy attitudes?

She brought out six more seeds from the bag she always carried with her. "Grow," she ordered them, and flung them out.

The seeds sprouted, sending out roots and vines. In midair they flowered and fruited, forming swelling, gourdlike masses. They were watermelons, and required immense amounts of water to complete their cycles. They normally drew this water from the air—and the air was filled with clouds, which were, of course, composed of water droplets. This was sheer delight to the melons. Because they were growing magically rapidly, they drew their water fast. The first cloud touched by a sprouting seed was sucked dry in an instant; it shrank and shriveled and disappeared with a breezy sigh. The others suffered similarly.

One larger cloud, with a silvery crown above, made a fight of it. This was evidently the leader of the pack. The king cloud reached out and enclosed the watermelon plant in vapor, so that it disappeared. But the watermelon only took in more water greedily, its tendrils threading through the cloud, and soon the embrace was reversed. The cloud disappeared, and a monstrous melon formed and plummeted to the distant ground.

One fragment of cloud tore free at the last moment and scudded away, its contrail between its legs. "I'll get even!" it seemed to mouth before it floated over the horizon. "You haven't seen the last of me, solid creature!"

Irene smiled. It would be a long time before that survivor harassed travelers again. "Dry up, King Cloud!" she called mockingly as it disappeared behind a hill. She had gotten into the habit of talking back to the inanimate, because of the way it talked back to her when she was with Dor. Rocks and other things on the ground could be especially obnoxious when she stepped over them.

There was a splat from below, and a bellow. The melon had struck a firedog basking below and very nearly put out the poor creature's fire.

The scattered remaining clouds had learned their lesson; they no longer intruded on Irene's flying space. That was just as well; her long association with Dor had taught her how to deal with the inanimate, but she was now out of watermelon seeds and wasn't sure what she would have done for a follow-up. After all, this had been a business and pleasure excursion when they had set off for the Zombie Master's castle; she had left most of her weapons-grade seeds behind.

She flew directly to the Good Magician's castle without further interruption. Trees and lakes and hills passed by below; it was pretty enough scenery, but she knew there were a number of unpretty monsters lurking in it. That made her nervous again for the welfare of her daughter. The jungles of unexplored Xanth were no place for a three-year-old child!

Her steed descended, becoming uncertain. Irene's brow furrowed; what was the problem? The turret of Humfrey's castle showed clearly in the vale. She nudged the plant onward, going for a landing on a convenient parapet.

The castle looked different from its configuration of the past—but that was normal. It always changed. How Humfrey managed this she had never discovered; it was just part of his magic. As the Magician of Information, he obviously had information on how to revise castles periodically. The talent of a Magician was always impressive, once the full extent of it was known. Too bad there were so few of that caliber! Her daughter's talent had not yet been classified by the Elders, but Irene had the depressing feeling that it was not Magician level. Ivy's presence tended to enhance the qualities of others; that was nice for the others, but what did it do for Ivy herself? Now if Ivy could enhance her own abilities, what a creature she might become! But that was a foolish daydream.

Daydream? "Hello, Imbri!" Irene said and fancied she saw the flick of the day mare's tail as a return greeting. Irene had come to know Mare Imbrium as a night mare, but now Imbri had become the bearer of the dreams of the day, which were much more pleasant. The mare was invisible; most people never knew when she was present. It didn't occur to them that dreams of any kind had to be formulated somewhere and be brought by someone. Dream duty was an often thankless task.

"Thank you for the dream, Imbri!" Irene called belatedly. But the mare had already gone. A creature had to be constantly on the move to keep up with the delivery schedule for daydreams, since so many people had them. A human carrier would have been unable to keep the pace, but horses were designed for running.

They glided to the turret, the bird-plant still trying to balk. Annoyed, Irene kneed it harder; plants were not usually very smart, so often they were not able to obey well, but this was a simple landing procedure. There was no excuse for holding back.

The leg- and foot-roots touched—and made no contact. The bird-plant continued on down into the stone. "What?" Irene asked, startled to see her own legs disappearing into the castle rampart.

Then they were all the way in it. The Good Magicians's castle was nothing but fog! She nudged the bird, and it ascended rapidly, drawing out of the darkness, glad to get away from this. Now she knew why the steed had balked; it had realized something was wrong.

Irene looked down. There was the castle, exactly as before. "Illusion!" she exclaimed. "The castle doesn't exist!"

Then she had a second thought. "It *has* to exist! I need Humfrey's advice, in case Dor fouls up the search!"

She nudged the bird down again, cautiously. Again the two of them intersected the castle—and found nothing of substance. The Good Magician's castle simply wasn't there.

Irene shook her head. "Some joker is playing games, and I'm sure it isn't my mother." Her mother Queen Emeritus Iris was mistress of illusion, but she seldom used her talent now, and never for mischief. It was a sad fact that age was softening the senior Magicians of Xanth, all except Humfrey, the oldest of all. Irene wondered again what the Good Magician's secret was. He had been old before Irene herself was born and he remained old—but no older than before in appearance. Maybe he had achieved the ultimate age, the plateau beyond which the years became meaningless. But she couldn't ponder that at the moment; she needed to find him and quickly, so as to learn how to save her child. Dor might or might not find and rescue Ivy, though he would certainly try; Humfrey's advice would make that rescue certain.

"If the castle isn't here, it must be elsewhere," she decided. "I know I'm in the right general region." For she had flown here before and was familiar with the lay of the land. She nudged the bird and it flew on northeast.

Now an unrelated thought struck her. She should have asked Mare Imbri about the vision! After all, Imbri's statue had been in the vision; maybe—but no, Imbri no longer brought bad dreams, so she should not have done this. Still, the next time the mare showed up, Irene would inquire. Imbri might know, or be able to find out, who had brought the vision, and why, and what it signified.

Soon another castle hove in view. They glided down, touched—and passed through. "Another illusion!" Irene exclaimed in disgust. She slapped at the fog that formed it, without effect, wishing she had another watermelon seed to dry it up. Then she nudged her mount to zoom onward.

Very soon she came to a third castle. Again she approached cautiously, and again it was illusion.

Irene uttered an unladylike word. The bird-of-paradise plant, startled by the expletive, shed several tendril feathers. It derived from a line of creatures which associated with a far loftier realm than that described by such a word, and so the shock was formidable.

Irene was getting downright annoyed, but sealed her erring lips. The bird was getting tired; no sense hurting it this way. She had to find the correct castle soon, before the bird wilted, for she had no other flying seed with her. Oh, the hazards of unpreparedness! Had she but known what was to happen—

Maybe that dreadful vision had arrived late. Had it come to her before she left Castle Roogna, she would have packed some devastating seeds! A foul-up in scheduling for visions—

But such bemoanment was useless, and Irene was a practical woman. She directed the bird back the way they had come, a new suspicion teasing her mind. Sure enough, there was no castle visible where the last one had been. It had faded out after she had left it. The illusion was moving from site to site— or from sight to sight—so as always to appear before her, leading her in the wrong direction. She had caught it by surprise by backtracking suddenly, but all that accomplished was the proof of its nature. She had to get rid of it before she could spot the real castle.

But how could a person abolish an illusion? That was like removing something that wasn't there.

Irene concentrated her thought. Obviously she couldn't eradicate the nonexistent; there had to be another way to deal with this. It was no use to get rid of the illusions after she saw them; she needed to stop new ones from forming so that she could find the real castle.

She snapped her fingers. Suppose she stopped the illusion literally? By fixing it in place so it could no longer move ahead of her?

She brought out a new seed, then guided the tiring bird-plant back to the location of the third phantom castle. It was still there, because she had not yet passed all the way out of sight of it. Evidently the illusion remained in place as long as someone was watching it; it would have very little effect if that were not the case. Imagine an illusion that disappeared while being watched; it would very rapidly lose its credibility! "Grow!" she directed the seed and flipped it out.

The seed landed and bounced and sprouted into a black-eyed pea. The black eyes focused on the castle, for such plants were always watching things. The illusion castle would be intently watched for weeks, until the pea grew old and withered and its vision failed.

She flew on. If this worked, the illusion would be pinned in place because it was still being watched. It would not be able to move to new locations to bother her.

In moments she experienced the dismay of defeat. There was the castle in front of her again! She had another black-eyed-pea seed, but what was the use of planting it if her ploy wasn't working? Meanwhile, the bird-of-paradise plant was failing rapidly, unable to remain aloft much longer. It was really designed to be pretty rather than strong. It dropped toward the phantom ramparts.

Crash! They collided with a wall. The bird spun down, shedding more feather-leaves. Irene barely righted herself in time to land on her feet. This illusion had teeth! Now she was without her steed and could not look for the—

She clonked her head with the heel of her hand, as if to knock out the dottle. This was no illusion! This was the real castle! The pea ploy had worked. She didn't have to search for Humfrey any more.

She tucked herself together and walked around the bank inside the moat, toward the front gate. Soon she would be able to rescue Ivy!

As she walked, she fished in her bag for another seed. She

had located the castle, no thanks to the illusion, but she would surely need—

There was a loud, booming squawk. An enormous shape lifted from an alcove in the castle wall, spreading wings that seemed to block half the light of the sun. It was a truly monstrous bird.

Irene's fingers, questing in the bag, closed convulsively on a seed. She was so surprised that she made no other motion. She just stood there, seed pinched between thumb and finger, watching that gargantuan bird.

The bird swooped down, extended a foot, and grasped her in its claws, lifting her from the ground. She wasn't hurt, for the claws were like heavy metal bars that confined her in a cagelike embrace, rather than squeezing her. She found herself aloft again, and not by her own choosing.

Finally she acted. She threw the seed down. "Grow!" she cried. But she didn't even know which seed it was.

This was a roc, the largest of all birds! What was it doing with her? Rocs normally did not prey on human beings; they required larger morsels to sustain them, like dragons or Mundane elephants.

The roc, having attained an awesome elevation in seconds, now plummeted. It swooped low, banked, and hovered for a moment, releasing Irene just above the ground. Then it hurled itself upward again with a downdraft of air that shoved Irene back several steps and ruined her hairdo.

"Birdbrain!" she shouted after it, disgruntled. "May a giant feather stick in your craw!" Of all times to be subjected to such pointless mischief! Just when she was going in to see Humfrey.

She paused, annoyed by a new realization. This wasn't coincidence! This was the castle defense system! All newcomers had to struggle through three types of obstruction in order to get inside and see the Good Magician. That was because Humfrey didn't like to be bothered by trivial concerns. Anyone who really wanted to see him would persevere until he got inside. At least that was the theory. Humfrey was a taciturn gnome of a man with his own ornery ways of doing things. No one really understood him, except perhaps the Gorgon, his wife.

But Irene was the Queen of Xanth. She wasn't supposed to be subjected to this indignity! The traveling illusion, the roc— those were intended for lesser folk.

She paused. Lesser folk? Beware the arrogance of royalty! She was just the woman who had married the King, and her present concern was a personal one. She could not presume to deserve favors that the least of the denizens of Xanth could not.

She would darn well conquer these challenges herself. She had already handled one, the illusion. Now she would deal with the second.

Obviously the roc was assigned to pick up all intruders and dump them well away from the castle. She had to nullify that big bird. But how? The roc was far too powerful for any plant short of a tangle tree to conquer, and she didn't want to hurt it. It had not hurt her, after all. This was really a kind of game, a challenge, not warfare.

She checked through her collection of seeds. Purple turnips—no good. Soda poppies—no. Night lilies—no.

Suddenly she brightened. She had a rock garden kit with her! That just might do it.

She heard a putrid sound in the distance. Her nose wrinkled. That was the belch of a stink horn! That must be the seed she had dropped, back at the castle. She could use that foul signal to locate the castle immediately.

She marched back toward the castle. It took her a while, for the huge bird had covered a lot of distance during the brief flight. When she came to the moat, she dropped her seeds on the ground. "Grow!"

The rock group sprouted. Rock moss spread across the ground, forming a carpet. Colored stones expanded in pretty crystalline patterns. Sand formed in miniature dunes, and tiny streamlets of water appeared. From the whole issued the sound of strange music, reminiscent of the noise of the twins' jerk box but harsher. Irene didn't understand rock music, but of course this was not for her benefit.

Now she grew a water lily in the moat. It formed a series of sturdy wide leaves, stepping-places across the water. She started crossing.

Immediately the roc appeared again. This time she was ready for it. "Look over there, bird," she told it. "A roc garden."

The bird looked, listened—and almost plummeted into the moat. "Rawk!" it squeaked.

"That's right, bird—rock," Irene agreed. "Pattern and music—all yours."

The roc landed by the garden and stared at it, fascinated. It cocked its head, listening. Rocs loved rock gardens! Irene knew she would have no more trouble with the big bird. She proceeded on across the moat. She knew there would be one more hurdle.

The stone walls of the castle were imposing. They were fresh and firm, unlike those of the zombie castle, and were buttressed by a wooden lattice, though they hardly needed it. No normal person could scale this barrier. Of course, she wouldn't have to; she would have a climbing vine to do it for her, if the front door was locked.

Now she arrived at that door. It was solid wood. She knocked politely. There was no response. She knocked impolitely, with no better result. She looked for a knob or latch, but there was none. She pushed on the door, but it was firmly in place. She couldn't even find a lock; it was probably barred on the other side. She had expected as much. This was unusual wood; she had a general familiarity with many types of trees, but did not recognize this particular kind. It seemed almost as solid and hard as stone, but it wasn't rock maple or ironwood.

Very well; she would use her talent. She brought out a clinging-vine seed and set it at the base of the wall. "Grow."

Nothing happened. She stooped to check the seed but could not find it. That was funny; that hadn't happened in years. It must have been a bad seed.

She took out a climbing bean and held it in her hand. "Grow."

The bean shriveled up and disappeared.

Irene stared at her empty hand. This was definitely peculiar! Her climbing bean had changed to a has-bean.

Experimentally, she set out a firecracker plant seed. This was another of the ones intended for the twins' party; too bad that party had been so brutally broken up. This plant wouldn't help her cross over the wall, but it would verify that her talent was in order. "Grow!"

The seed shrank until it disappeared. There wasn't even the faintest of detonations. It had done the opposite of what it was supposed to do.

Then she caught on. "Reverse wood!" she exclaimed. "When I exert my magic, it acts backward!" Her father-in-law Bink had once spoken of wood like this, found in the hinterland of Xanth. Evidently the Good Magician had harvested some of it. What a devious ploy!

Now she had a problem. If her talent worked backward near this wood, how could she grow anything to help her?

She considered the castle wall and door again. Irene was a healthy woman, but this sheer barrier was beyond her. She could neither scale it nor break it down without help. She might carry stones and pieces of fallen wood to lay against the wall and build a ramp she could use to surmount it, but that would take many hours—while Ivy might be gobbled by a jungle monster any minute. She needed to get inside the castle *now*.

Humfrey had set up this challenge, and she intended to conquer it. But she was doing a slow burn at this delay.

Burn? Could she set fire to the wood and destroy it? No, because her flame-vine would only put itself out instead of burning. She didn't know how to start a fire without magic.

"Darn it!" she swore, stamping her foot in a fury of frustration. "I've just got to get rid of that blankety reverse wood!"

She put her hands on the nearest section of the lattice, trying to rip it free, but it adhered tightly to the wall. Now she knew why the lattice was there—to prevent her from using her magic on the wall. All the wood, the whole door included, was made of this stuff.

Maybe she could move away from the castle, grow something useful, and use it to surmount the wall. The reversal did not apply to magic already completed, it seemed, for the bird-of-paradise plant had not suffered until it cracked into the wall, and that was a straight physical shock rather than a magical one. But this process, too, would take time she might not be able to afford.

There was natural grass growing between the wall and the

moat. Maybe that was immune to the reversal. "Grow," she told it.

The grass shriveled back into the ground, leaving a bare spot. So much for that. Her talent worked—but not the right way. Shrinkage was no good for her.

But what about the stink horn? She had made that grow! No—now she saw it, on the far bank of the moat. It had grown some distance from the wall. No exception there.

Too bad her talent could not also shrink plants, because then she could try that, and when the wood reversed the thrust of her magic—

A pear-shaped flash of light illuminated the inside of her head. Shrink plants? The reverse wood was from a plant, wasn't it? If the stuff retained any life of its own, which it might, since it retained its magical effect—

"Grow!" she commanded the reverse wood.

Immediately the wood shrank, reversing her magic. The lattice diminished to thin lines, and the massive door warped and pulled away from its moorings, becoming smaller.

The wood had reversed its own growth.

Irene pushed the dwindling remnant aside and entered the castle. "Serves you right, wood," she said ungraciously. "You shouldn't have messed with a person with Magician-caliber magic." Her husband had more than once accused her of always insisting on having the last word; it was a true charge, and she gloried in it. No word was better than the last word!

She walked down the main entry hall. A heavily veiled woman hurried up. It was the Gorgon, whose direct gaze could petrify a person. "Oh, Irene, I'm so glad you made it!"

"You wanted me to come in?" Irene demanded. "You knew it was me? Then why didn't you turn off the castle defenses? I may have ruined them all!"

"I couldn't! Only Humfrey can do that!"

Irene was in no mood for games, not even with so formidable a figure as the Gorgon. "Why didn't he, then? The last thing I wanted to do was waste time!"

"Oh, it's terrible! I don't know what to do! I wish I could change it, but I can't!"

"Change what?" Irene snapped.

"Oh, you don't know, of course," the Gorgon said distract-edly. "You couldn't know!"

"Know what?" This was not only annoying, it was getting peculiar, for the Gorgon was normally the most sensible and self-possessed of women.

"Here, I'll have to show you. Come to the playroom."

"The playroom? Look, Gorgon, my child is—"

"So is mine." The Gorgon was already leading the way. Frustrated, Irene followed.

The playroom was nicely set up with padded floor and walls and brightly colored toys. A diapered baby sat in the middle, chewing on a dragon doll. He seemed to be about a year old.

"I didn't know you had another child," Irene said, surprised.

"I don't," the Gorgon responded grimly.

"But that's obviously Humfrey's offspring! There is the same—" She hesitated.

"The same gnomelike features?" the Gorgon asked.

"Well—"

"You have no need to be embarrassed. I loved Humfrey from the first for what he was. His physical appearance was never important to me. But his mind, his talent—there has never been another like him in Xanth!"

"Yes, of course," Irene agreed, discomfited. "No reason not to have another—"

"That is not my baby."

"Not—?" Irene felt a slow flush creeping rebelliously along her neck. Had Humfrey sired a baby by another woman and turned it over to his wife to raise? No wonder the Gorgon was beside herself! "I just can't believe—" She found she couldn't even utter the suspicion. "Humfrey's too brilliant and honest to—that's why I came to see him—"

"You have seen him."

"I have to get his advice!" Irene flared. "Why are you showing me his baby?" Then she bit her tongue; she hadn't meant to say that!

Yet the Gorgon hardly reacted. "That's not Humfrey's baby. I assure you, he would never step out on me."

Not if he wanted to remain flesh instead of stone! Was that what had happened? No, it couldn't be!

Irene's brow furrowed. This was too much for her. "What are you saying?"

"That's Humfrey."

Irene laughed. Then she stopped, perceiving the serious expression under the Gorgon's thick veil. "I must be misunderstanding all this in several crazy ways!"

"Let the mirror show you." The Gorgon fetched a magic mirror and propped it up against a wall. "Replay the scene," she directed it.

A picture formed in the mirror. It became, as it were, a window to a jungle scene. There was a deep spring in a hollow, the water not flowing out but rather keeping to itself. By the spring's edge there was only sand; vegetation appeared in a peculiar concentric progression outward from it, becoming larger the farther away it was, until at a fair distance the trees were full grown. It occurred to Irene that someone or something must have taken a lot of trouble to trim this region, clearing the spring, but now the vegetation was growing back. Odd that it was not growing fastest nearest the water, however.

A man tramped into view, old and gnarled and small. "Humfrey!" Irene exclaimed. "When is he coming back to the castle? I must talk to him in a hurry!" All manner of nasty private suspicions were allayed by the sight of him, as hale and healthy as a gnome his age could be. But she was aware that this picture did not jibe with what the Gorgon had just told her. What was the explanation?

"Just watch," the Gorgon said tersely.

Humfrey approached the spring with exaggerated caution. He extended a bottle fixed on the end of a pole, carefully dipping from the spring. When it was full, he shook it so that the flip-top lid on it snapped closed.

"Poison!" Irene exclaimed. "The opposite of healing elixir—"

"Not so," the Gorgon said.

His sample complete, the Good Magician shook it dry, then brought the bottle in to himself and wrapped it in a voluminous cloth. He retreated from the spring, and the view of the mirror followed him.

Now he came to the magic carpet. There sat his son Hugo,

looking as dull as usual, a pile of soggy fruit before him. It was really a pity, Irene thought, about the boy's inferior talent; a really excellent talent could have redeemed most of his other inadequacies. Hugo tried, but simply couldn't conjure decent fruit. As it was, Hugo had to be a severe disappointment to his illustrious parents. Small, ugly, stupid, and without useful magic—what was there to say?

Humfrey took time to put away his pole. He handed the wrapped bottle to Hugo with a warning—the picture conveyed no sound, but none was needed—in order to free his hands for the job. His bag of spells was resting on the carpet beside the boy. Humfrey toted spells around the way Irene toted seeds.

The pole, evidently supposed to telescope into a smaller form, balked. With a grimace of irritation, Humfrey braced its base against the ground, took a two-handed grip, and shoved down. Reluctantly, the pole contracted. Irene knew that if her husband Dor had been doing that, the pole would have complained loudly about getting shafted. The inanimate was always as perverse as it thought it could get away with. Humfrey took a new grip, forcing the shaft to shorten again. He was getting there.

The job took him some time, for he was small and old, while the pole exhibited a splendid diversity of resistances. It tried to bow and twist out of the man's grip, and it made itself slippery, and it tried to spring back to full extension while Humfrey was taking a new grip. But finally he got it compressed into a cylinder, and then to a disk resembling a Mundane coin, and put the disk in his pocket.

There was a shaking of the ground. Hugo covered his ears, reacting to some horrible sound. Good Magician Humfrey whirled about to face the sudden threat. The view in the mirror swung to bring into sight—

"The Gap Dragon!" Irene exclaimed in horror. Her memory of that monster was fresh from her own recent encounter. "That's where it went after it left Castle Zombie! While I was looking for Ivy—"

The dragon bore down on Humfrey and Hugo, steam jetting from its nostrils. Words were shouted, still silent in the mirror, and the magic carpet abruptly took off. Hugo, sitting unbraced, lost his balance and fell off. The carpet sailed into the sky, carrying Humfrey's bag of spells away. In a moment it was out of sight.

"Oh, no!" Irene exclaimed. "He's lost his magic!"

The Gorgon nodded grimly. "I should have been there," she said, touching her veil meaningfully. "Men are so inadequate by themselves. But someone had to tend the castle while he went for the water from the Fountain of Youth."

Irene suffered another shock. "The Fountain of—!"

"Oh, I shouldn't have let that slip!" the Gorgon fussed. "It's a secret."

In the mirror, the action continued. The Gap Dragon bore down on the man and boy. "A secret?" Irene asked, distracted by the significance of the Fountain despite the horror of the scene. Actually, it wasn't a fountain, just a pool or spring; perhaps it only fountained at certain hours of the day or when the water level dropped and needed replenishing. Many people, over the centuries, had looked for the Fountain; maybe its poollike aspect had caused them to miss it. Anyone who happened on it unaware and drank deeply, not knowing its property, would have been put out of business by an overdose of youth. "Don't you realize what that water could do for the people of Xanth? My father—"

The Good Magician was yelling at his son. Hugo fumbled stupidly with the wrapped bottle he held. The sequence seemed to take forever: dragon advancing, blowing steam, man retreating, boy extricating bottle.

"Don't you see, it has to be secret," the Gorgon was explaining. "Humfrey uses it judiciously, to keep himself not much over a century old, and the Zombie Master uses it to improve the performance of his zombies—he knew about it in the old days, in his prior life, and told Humfrey. It used to be a literal fountain, but it wore down over the centuries—but if it were available generally in Xanth, no one would ever die of old age, and some things have to—soon things would be so crowded—"

Irene tuned her out, watching the mirror. Finally the boy got the bottle out and the lid off. Responding to instructions, he swung the bottle in an arc so that its magic water flung out toward the dragon in a spreading stream.

"Watch out!" Irene cried uselessly, realizing what such an undisciplined splash could do.

The water struck the charging dragon, who immediately began to shrink into youth. It also doused the man.

Irene watched, dumbfounded. The water of Youth was a weapon, for an overdose would rob a creature of all its adult powers. It seemed that it did not have to be imbibed; the mere touch of it on a person's skin sufficed. But a weapon could be turned against friend as well as foe. Both dragon and Magician were helplessly youthening.

The Gap Dragon became a smaller monster, with brighter green scales and thicker steam. The Good Magician became a halfway handsome gnome of age fifty or so, with a straighter body and a solid head of hair. But the trend did not stop there. Both progressed, or regressed, to childhood.

"They both OD'd," the Gorgon said. "I suppose we're lucky they didn't youthen into nothing. Both are over a century old; that's probably all that saved them. I used the emergency spell Humfrey left me to conjure him back—"

The baby Magician disappeared from the image. Irene quelled her shock, realizing that this was not youthening into nonexistence, but simply the operation of the conjuration-spell. Humfrey vanished from the scene in the mirror because he had appeared here in his castle.

Hugo, dismayed and confused, began to cry. The baby dragon shook itself, looked about, spread its fledgling wings, and scooted away, terrified.

The mirror image faded out. Irene turned to look again at the baby in the playroom. "It really *is* Humfrey!" she breathed.

The Gorgon sighed. "It really is. And Hugo is still out there. He didn't seem to get any of the water on himself, but that's about the only bright spot. I can't tune in on him with the mirror, because it is set on Humfrey and I don't know how to retune it. As soon as it realized Humfrey was gone from the scene, it quit the image. I can't even go out to search for my lost son, because—"

Irene realized that the Gorgon was crying under her veil.

She had been devastated in the last hour and needed help. Irene knew exactly how that felt—but was surprised to discover that the Gorgon, older and more experienced than Irene and the most formidable woman in Xanth when she lifted her veil, was in fact less well equipped to handle such calamity than was Irene herself. Physical or magical power did not serve as well at this moment as did emotional stability.

"Come, sit down, and we'll work this out," Irene said, taking the Gorgon by the elbow. "My child is out there, too. That's why I came here." But obviously her mission had been in vain; there would be no help from Humfrey now.

The Gorgon suffered herself to be guided. Soon they were in the kitchen, the most comfortable place for married women, sharing cups of T sweetened by the product of B's.

Irene eyed a plate of cheeses. One piece was huge, with a mottled rind, and when she reached for it, it growled menacingly. "Don't take that," the Gorgon warned. "It's monster cheese, reserved for muensters—I mean monsters. Try this instead." She turned the plate to present another type.

Irene took a piece and chewed delicately. "It's good. What kind is it?"

"Gorgon-zola. I make it myself. I stare at it through my veil until it's half petrified."

Irene had to smile. This was a useful incidental aspect of the Gorgon's dread talent.

Now they got down to business. "First we must get a good baby-sitter for Humfrey. Uh, is there any known cure for magic youthening?"

"Only time—the same as for the victim of a love spring," the Gorgon said sadly. "But I'm willing to wait, knowing that in due course he will regain his full powers and be in the prime of life. But what a wait that will be, even if I get hold of some Fountain of Youth water myself so I can rejoin him in middle age. And who will fill the role he does for Xanth?"

The outlook did look dismal. "Usually there is some countercharm," Irene said. "If there were some substance or spell to reverse the effect, to age him more rapidly—"

"Only Humfrey would know where to find that," the Gorgon said. "And he is the one who *doesn't* know, now."

It was an unfortunate irony. Irene shrugged and chewed her cheese, unable to offer any other suggestions.

"But I've got to rescue Hugo!" the Gorgon exclaimed. "Did you say someone could come here and care for Humfrey while I'm going out to find my son?"

"Lacuna, the Zombie Master's daughter, will do nicely. She's just sixteen and good with children." Irene suffered a retroactive regret that the twins' debut had been so rudely shattered; instead of a party, there had been disaster.

"Oh, yes, I know Lacuna. A perfect imp of a child. She used to print messages all over the castle. Things like NEVER PUT OFF TILL TOMORROW WHAT YOU CAN DO TODAY. It seems funny in retrospect, but it was annoying at the time."

Irene's brow furrowed. "Annoying?"

"It was printed on the toilet."

Irene swallowed her chuckle. "I won't even inquire what Hiatus did to the bathroom." Hiatus' talent was growing eyes, ears, noses, and mouths from walls and other places. "Lacuna was taking care of Ivy, and I believe it was no fault of hers that Ivy got lost. The Gap Dragon—" It was hard to speak so objectively, but it was necessary; time was of the essence. "Lacuna lived here as a child; she surely knows how to stay out of trouble and where the facilities are. She won't poke into the Magician's spells." Irene had divided the Good Magician, in her mind, into two aspects: the century-plus old man he used to be, and the baby who now existed. The presence of the old Humfrey would always be felt here, no matter how long he was away. "You can give her any special pointers she needs; the rest will come naturally. That will free you to go out and fetch Hugo with a clear conscience."

The obscure countenance behind the thick veil brightened. Now the Gorgon had a positive program of action! "I don't know why I didn't think of that myself!" she exclaimed.

"We'll have to get Lacuna here quickly," Irene continued. "That wilderness jungle is dangerous for children." But there was no need to remind anyone of that ugly reality; best not to dwell on it. "The carpet's lost; we don't know how to use Humfrey's stocked spells; is there anything else?"

The Gorgon considered. "The roc," she said. "It will obey you now, since you got past it. It can fly very fast."

"I'm sure it can," Irene agreed, not much liking this idea but aware that it was probably best. "I will have to return to Castle Zombie to tell Dor what has happened here, then go after Ivy myself."

"I'll help you!" the Gorgon said. "We can go together, combining our searches!"

"No use. Your son's lost at the Fountain of Youth; my daughter's lost near Castle Zombie. I don't know how close the two are to each other—"

"I don't know either," the Gorgon admitted. "Only Humfrey knew the location of the Fountain. But it has to be somewhere in that region."

"What about the Zombie Master?" Irene asked. "You said he knew—"

"Eight hundred years ago, he knew. But in his long tenure as a zombie, he forgot. All he remembered was that it did exist, and somewhere in that area; Humfrey worked from there to pinpoint it precisely."

"But Humfrey must have told—"

The Gorgon shook her head. "That was not his way."

All too true. The Good Magician had been notoriously tight-fisted with information of any type, to the frustration of others, even kings.

"Since both Ivy and Hugo are in peril," Irene said, "we'll have to look for them separately. You rescue yours, I'll rescue mine—and pray we're both successful."

"Yes," the Gorgon agreed faintly, and Irene realized that the woman had really wanted to make the search together. Probably she needed the moral support in this hour of crisis. But it just didn't make sense in the circumstance; they might find one child and lose the other.

"Will you be all right, alone in the jungle?" Irene asked solicitously.

The Gorgon touched her veil suggestively. "Who will challenge me there?"

Who, indeed! The Gorgon had less to fear from monsters than did any other person. "Then it's agreed. Let me use the roc to return to Castle Zombie, and then it can bring Lacuna here, and then you can have it take you to the general region of the Fountain, which I think must be north of the castle; that's the way Humfrey went when he left."

"Yes," the Gorgon agreed. "Oh, Irene, you've been so much help! I didn't know what to do until you came!"

Irene patted her hand reassuringly. But inside, she was not at all assured. She had come here for help—and there was none. Humfrey's horror had been added to her own.

Chapter 3. Yak Talk

Ivy looked around her. She was in a nice jungle with many interesting things, so she inspected each one in turn.

She realized something was in her hand, and she put it in her pocket so it wouldn't distract her.

Closest was a plant that smelled like a pickle, but its branches and leaves were so hard as to be metallic. "What are you?" she inquired, but the plant didn't answer.

She pouted. She didn't like unresponsive things. She walked on, looking for something that would talk to her.

She heard a noise in the brush and discovered a large animal grazing. It had horns like those of a sea cow, a tail like that of a centaur, and silky hair along its sides like that of a beautiful woman. In short, it was a strange, composite creature.

But Ivy was too young and inexperienced to realize how strange this animal was or to know proper fear. She marched right up to it. "What are you?" she asked. She had always found this question useful, because, when her father was near, things always answered.

The creature raised its head and stared down at her with a huge and lovely eye. "I thought you'd never ask! I'm a yak, of course, the most talkative of wild creatures. I will talk your ear off, if you don't figure out how to stop me."

Ivy put a hand to her delicate little ear. It seemed to be securely fastened, so she relaxed. "How do I stop you?" She was rather pleased with her ability to assemble a question correctly; after all, she wasn't very big. But she had discovered that she could do a lot more than she thought she could, if she only believed she could. She had decided to believe she could talk as well as a grown-up person, and now she could, almost. But she didn't do it when her folks were present, in case they should object. Grown-ups had funny notions about what children should or should not do, so she had learned caution.

The yak shook his head. "Not so readily, cute human child! That is the single thing I won't tell you! It is my nature to talk as long as I have a receptive ear—an indifferent ear will do in a pinch—regardless how anyone else feels about it. You can't shut me up unless you know how. What do you think of that?"

Ivy looked up at him. "You're a real pretty beast. I like you."

The yak was taken aback. "You aren't annoyed?"

"You talk to me. Most people don't. They don't have time. My folks don't know how well I can talk, fortunately."

The yak seemed uncertain whether she was joking. He twitched his horns. "Well, I have time. I have nothing better to do than talk. I'd rather talk than eat."

"Eat." Ivy realized she was hungry. "I want to eat."

"I will talk about eating, then. But first we must introduce ourselves more formally. What is your given name?"

"Ivy. I'm King Dor's child."

The yak's mouth curved into a tolerant smile. "Ah, royalty! You will surely have royal tastes!" He was humoring her, not believing her parentage. "What do you like?"

Ivy considered. It was not that it took her any great cogitation to come to a conclusion, but that she enjoyed this particular type of consideration. "Chocolate cake."

"I never would have guessed! As it happens, there's a chocolate moose in the vicinity, but it doesn't like getting nibbled. Once a bunch of ducks started nibbling, and it said—"

"I don't want to hurt anything," Ivy said, sad for the moose. "Now I don't know what to eat."

"Then we'll just have to explore. There's lots of succulent grass in this glade; do you like that?" By way of illustration, the yak took a mouthful of it.

Ivy bent down and took a similar mouthful of grass. She chewed a moment, then spat it out. "No. It's too much like spinach."

"There are also leaves," the yak said, reaching up to pull down a leafy branch. Ivy took a leaf and chewed it. "No. Too much like cabbage."

"You are hard to please!" the yak lamented cheerfully. "Let's look around more widely."

They walked back the way Ivy had come. "What's that?" she asked, pointing to the metallic plant with the pickle smell that had refused to identify itself before.

"Why, that's an armor-dillo," the yak said. "It grows the best armor, but it stinks of the brine used to store it. Some creatures like the odor, though."

Ivy wrinkled her cute little nose. "Ugh. They must be dillies."

"They are indeed! They get pickled every night."

They moved on to a plant whose huge limbs terminated in delicate human hands, each finger manicured and with bright polish on the nail. "What's that?"

"A lady-fingers plant, naturally," the Yak said. "You have hands; you can shake hands in the typical human fashion if you wish."

Ivy tried it, extending her right hand toward the nearest branch. She could tell her right hand from her left because her hands lined up the same way her feet did, and her shoes were marked *R* and *L*. The nearest lady-fingers grasped her hand immediately. But then all the other hands clamored for attention by snapping their fingers, and she had to shake them all.

At length she drew away, resolving to be more careful thereafter. She started toward a somewhat vague bush. "What's that?"

"Don't go near that one!" the yak warned. "That's a trance plant. It doesn't belong here at all."

"Why not?"

"It grows elsewhere. Probably someone carried it here and set it on the ground and it rooted. Anyone who gets too close to it gets dazed."

Ivy considered. She was a pretty smart little girl when she tried to be, especially when she thought she was. Her father's friend Smash the Ogre had said she might have had an Eye Queue vine fall on her head; Smash knew about jungle vines. But that was their secret. Smash took her for walks sometimes, and he had been quick to discover that she was smarter than she seemed, sometimes, because he was that way himself, but he had promised not to tell her folks so she wouldn't get in trouble. In fact, it was because of Smash that she wanted to explore the jungle; he had told her how fascinating it was. Now she had her chance! "How did they carry the trance plant?"

The yak paused. "Why, I never thought of that! Anyone carrying it would have gone into a trance. Yet I happen to know that all trance plants grow elsewhere, and are moved to new locations. It seems to be their lifestyle. They must have some additional magic to enable them to travel." He looked ahead. "Ah, there's a foot-ball."

As he spoke, the foot-ball rolled into view. It was a sphere formed of feet. Every kind of extremity showed in it—dragon talons, bird claws, griffin paws, human feet, centaur hooves, insect legs, and so on. The feet tramped down a path wherever it rolled, so that it was easy to tell where the ball had been, but not where it was going. With so many feet, it was able to travel quite swiftly and was soon out of sight.

However, the path it left made their route easier, since there were no brambles or pitfalls in it. It didn't matter to Ivy where it led, as long as there were interesting things along it.

Ivy spotted a glittering glassy ball the size of her two fists, not round but carved with many small, flat facets. She strayed from the path long enough to pick it up. Beams of light coruscated from it as she held it in a stray shaft of sunlight. "What is this?"

"That is a very precious stone, one of the gems distributed by Jewel the Nymph," the yak said. "Crystallized carbon in spherical form: a very hard ball. Specifically, a baseball diamond."

"What's it for? It's pretty."

"People play stupid games with it. I understand the main game is very tedious—a bunch of players spread themselves out around the diamond and simply wait, and someone else throws the ball, and another stands with a stick resting on his shoulder and watches the ball go by him three or four times, and then either he gets mad and quits trying, or he runs around the diamond. Then they start over."

Ivy's smooth little brow furrowed in a fair emulation of her mother's expression at times like this. "That's no fun! Who does that?"

"Mundanes, mostly. They are strange creatures and, I suspect, not too bright. Otherwise they would take more of an interest in magic, instead of pretending it doesn't exist. What can you say about a person who refuses to believe in magic?"

"That he deserves his own dullness."

"That's a most astute remark!" The yak glanced ahead, hearing something. "Hark! I think I hear a game now!"

They walked on toward the sound. Two centaurs were doing something. "No, that's not a baseball diamond they're throwing. It must be some other game."

Indeed it was. Two wooden stakes had been pounded into the ground, and the centaurs were taking turns hurling shoes from a nearby shoe tree at them. They were the type of shoes human folk used, with shoelaces and all. One shoe would land leaning up against a stake, but the next one would knock it away. Finally one centaur managed to hang a shoe up on the stake, whereupon he clapped his hands and the other grimaced.

"Oh, that makes you look so sick you'll need a new croggle-test!" the winner teased the loser.

"Equines need regular croggle-tests," the yak explained privately to Ivy. "To make sure they haven't been infected by magic. It is very bad to be croggled."

Ivy felt a little croggled herself, though she was not an equine. Some of her best friends were magic-infected centaurs, but she knew that most centaurs rejected magic as determinedly as the Mundanes did. "What are you playing?" she called to the centaurs.

"People-shoes, of course," one of them responded absently, then trotted off to pick up his collection.

The yak shrugged. "There's no accounting for tastes," he remarked. "Some folk like to talk, some like to throw shoes."

Ivy agreed it was a strange world. She walked on.

The marvels of the Land of Xanth continued, and the little girl spent all afternoon exploring them, with the yak's helpful commentary continuing incessantly. A passing milksnake gave her a bottle of milk to slake her thirst, and she plucked a lollypop from a pop-sickle plant. Her only bad moment came when a big B buzzed her and she stumbled off the footpath. The yak also stumbled, for it was a bumble B, causing creatures to become clumsy.

Ivy wound up at the base of a large tree, feeling terrible. "Oooh, ugh!" she exclaimed. "What hit me?"

The yak looked none too sanguine himself, but he peered about, seeking the answer. He found it. "The tree!" he exclaimed painfully. "It's a torment pine! We must get away from it!"

Ivy hobbled away, and the farther from the tree she got, the less worse she felt. Finally she got back to the footpath she had bumbled from and felt well again. She would be alert for any more B's, so she would not stumble into any more trees.

But night was nigh, and she was tired. Usually her mother Irene curbed her long before her explorative instincts were sated, so she got frustrated but not tired. This time it was the other way around. "I want to go to bed," she said and paused in momentary shock, realizing she had spoken heresy. No child ever wanted to go to bed! So she qualified it. "I don't want the monster under the bed to be lonely."

"Then you should go home," the yak pointed out.

"Home?" she asked, baffled. "What's that?"

The yak looked at her in perplexity. "That would be the place where your mother lives. And your father, the—" Here the yak paused to smirk. "—the King of Xanth. Where you stay when you don't have anything better to do. Where your bed is."

Still her little brow furrowed. "Where?"

The yak was puzzled. "You mean to say you don't know? How can you remember your mother and your bed without remembering your home?"

Ivy shook her head, confused.

"Where did you come from before you met me?"

She pondered. "Don't remember."

"How could you forget your own home?" the yak persisted.

"I don't know." She began to cry.

The yak was disconcerted. "Here, I'll find a bed bug. They make very nice beds." He began to cast about, looking for a bed bug.

There was the faintest of swirls in the air, not so much a breeze as the mere suggestion of motion. Ivy almost remembered being near something like this before, but not quite. The yak, intent on his mission, walked right through that swirl.

He stopped, looking perplexed. "What am I doing here?" he asked, switching his tail.

"You're my friend," Ivy said, her sniffles abating for the moment. "You're looking for a—"

"I don't remember you!" the yak exclaimed. "I don't remember anything! I'm lost!" Alarmed, he galloped off.

Ivy stared after him. It seemed she had found the way to shut him up—but she was not pleased. She had lost her only immediate friend.

She walked along the path, trying to catch up to the yak, but he had forgotten her and was already out of sight. Once she thought she saw him, but it was only the chocolate moose, who was going in the opposite direction and didn't wait for her.

It was darkening now, and the pleasant trees were turning ugly. She ran and tripped over a root that lifted to snag her toe. She skinned her knees in the fall and got dirt in her face.

This was too much. Ivy sat in the path and wailed. She was, after all, only three years old.

Something heard the noise and came toward her, half slithering, half whomping through the underbrush. It had six legs and green, metallic scales, and it steamed, and it was hungry.

Ivy heard it and looked up in time to stare into the horrendous little countenance of the rejuvenated Gap Dragon.

Chapter 4. Zora Zombie

Irene was fuming. She had, as it turned out, wasted precious time traveling to the Good Magician's castle, and now she was losing more. Of course, she had helped the Gorgon, and that was worthwhile—but what was happening to Ivy meanwhile? The Xanth jungle was no place for a three-year-old child alone!

She glanced at the little plant perched in an upper pocket. It was a miniature variety of ivy, enchanted to relate to the child Ivy. As long as the plant was healthy, so was Ivy. If the plant wilted, that meant trouble or illness. If the plant died—

Irene shook her head. The plant was healthy; no point in worrying about what might be. She knew her daughter was all right and had known it all along. It was the future that worried her. All she had to do was *find* her daughter—soon.

The roc deposited her at Castle Zombie. "Wait here," she told it. "There'll be a return delivery." She hurried inside.

Millie the Ghost came to meet her. "Listen carefully," Irene said without preamble. "Good Magician Humfrey has been turned into a baby, and his son Hugo is lost. The Gorgon will look for Hugo, but needs a baby-sitter for Humfrey. A roc is waiting outside to take Lacuna there. Is that all right with you? Good. Go tell Lacuna. Where's Dor?"

"Out looking for Ivy," Millie said, taken aback by the rush

of information. "They all are—but there's so much jungle to search—"

"I'll find him myself," Irene said impatiently. "You see to Lacuna." She hurried back outside, leaving the older woman to her confusion. Actually, she was sure Lacuna would be thrilled to get roc-transport; that was a most unusual mode of travel for ordinary people.

"Where's Dor?" Irene demanded of the nearest zombie.

The mottled face worked, trying to assemble an answer. A hand came up to scratch the nose, and the nose fell off. "Wwhhooo?" the creature whistled.

"My husband!" Irene snapped. "Dor. The *King*, you imbecile! Where's the King?"

Decayed comprehension came. "Kkemmm," the thing said, and pointed a skeletal extremity to the north.

"Thaankss," Irene said, mimicking it, though what scant humor the action might have had was wasted on a thing whose brain was glop. She rushed north.

Soon she encountered a centaur. It was Chem. "Hello, Irene!" the filly called.

Chem was a few years younger than Irene, but centaurs aged more slowly than human beings did, so she was now in the flush of nubility. In human terms, Chem would have been about the age of the twins, Hiatus and Lacuna, or a little older. She was certainly an attractive specimen of her kind now, with fair hair falling from her head to touch the equine shoulder, and a full and bare bosom of the centaur kind. Of course, Chem's appearance was nothing new to Irene; she had ridden the centaur from Castle Roogna to Castle Zombie, a journey of several hours by hoof and longer by foot. But she gained a clearer picture of Chem, seeing her standing alone in the forest. This filly was currently well worth the attention of a male of her species, but as far as Irene knew, there was no immediate prospect. There were not many of the magic-performing centaurs, and the other kind would not have anything to do with them. This meant, unfortunately, that Chem had a quite reasonable chance for spinsterhood, attractive though she was.

"Oh, ouch, no!" Irene exclaimed, making a connection. "That zombie said, 'Chem,' instead of 'King.'"

The centaur frowned. "What's the matter?"

"I was looking for my husband!"

"Aren't we all," Chem murmured, frowning again. But in an instant she smiled. "He's searching southside, with Chet. I can take you to them. Grundy says Ivy's not in this region anyway."

"Grundy?" Irene asked blankly.

"Me—Grundy the Golem," the little creature said from the foot of a tree, insolently pretending she did not remember him. Grundy seldom did anything politely that he could do impolitely, and prided himself on being obnoxious. But he did care, and was a reliable aid in emergencies. "I came to help search. Chem's taking me from glade to glade, and I'm asking all the local flora." He ran to rejoin Chem, who reached down to pick him up. Grundy was so small he could sit comfortably in her hand.

"Well, take me to Dor," Irene said, mounting the centaur behind the golem. She had never really liked Grundy, but had to concede that he could be useful at a time like this, and it was nice of him to volunteer.

Chem galloped south, dodging around trees and boulders and hurdling ruts. Centaurs liked to run, and they were good at it. Soon the threesome located King Dor.

Irene rattled out her story about the fate of the Good Magician. "So I've got to find my daughter myself," she concluded. She didn't even need to ask whether Dor had found Ivy; she knew he had not. She had known at the outset of this crisis, in her heart, that only she could handle it properly. Why else had she suffered the horrible vision?

"That doesn't necessarily follow," Dor said with his annoying masculine reasonableness. "Our search pattern should in due course succeed—"

"I'm her *mother*!" Irene cried, refuting all further argument.

The familiar look of male bafflement and resignation passed across his face. "Well, if you ride Chem, with Grundy along—"

It hadn't occurred to Irene to join forces more permanently with the centaur, and certainly not with the golem; but actually, that was not a bad idea, especially if it allayed Dor's hesitancy.

Irene glanced at Chem to see if she were amenable. She was. "Of course," Irene agreed, as if that had been the intent from the start.

"And take a zombie—"

"A zombie!"

"They know the area," he pointed out. "And you can send it back to the castle if you get in trouble. That is, if you should need to send a message back." He was correcting his slip; naturally, she would not be the one to get in trouble. "Then the Zombie Master will know where to send assistance."

"You're not objecting to my going?" Irene asked, just to make quite sure he knew he did not.

"Dear, I know you work best in your own way. I'll return to Castle Roogna and consult with Crombie and check the arsenal. There should be something that will help, in case you don't find Ivy soon. Meanwhile, with Humfrey out of business, I had better be available at home so you'll know where to get in touch with me. There is also the matter of the forget-whorls to handle."

This did make some sense, she had to concede. She had anticipated more argument from him, but evidently he was learning the uselessness of that. He really would not be able to help locate Ivy from Castle Roogna, because, though Crombie the soldier's talent lay in pointing out the direction of anything, Crombie was now so old and frail that his talent was unreliable. But with Dor safely back at Castle Roogna, she would not have to worry about anything happening to him and could concentrate completely on the immediate mission. "I'll keep going until I find Ivy," she promised. "It shouldn't be long. She can't have wandered far."

"True," Dor agreed wanly. Suddenly Irene realized what his real motive was—he was half afraid Ivy was in deeper trouble than mere separation from her family and he wanted to locate some magic means to confirm or deny this without alarming Irene herself. He had an ivy plant of his own, so knew the child was healthy—but this disappearance was already more serious than it had first seemed. With the forget-whorls moving through the area, taking out people randomly . . .

Dor was letting her keep her hope as long as possible. She would let him keep his. Irene kissed him in silent thanks for what he hadn't said, then remounted Chem. "You," she said, pointing to the nearest zombie. "Come with us." Anything to satisfy her husband, who was trying so hard to do what he thought was right. The zombie would be a nuisance, but maybe she would find Ivy soon, so it wouldn't matter.

The centaur started walking. Irene waved good-bye, then turned her face forward, knowing Dor would be watching her as long as she remained in sight. The designated zombie shuffled along behind.

"Hey, you plants!" Grundy called. "Any of you see a little girl pass by this afternoon?" This was for the others' notice; actual plant language was largely inaudible and wholly incomprehensible to the human ear. The golem would repeat the message in the dialects of any plants and animals he saw.

After a pause, Grundy shook his head. "None here," he reported. "But I guess we already knew that. We'd better circle around the castle until we pick up Ivy's trail. It's got to be here somewhere."

"Let's see a map of the area," Irene told Chem. "We can pick the best route for circling the castle."

Chem projected her map. It formed in the air before her, a three-dimensional representation of Castle Zombie and the region around it. But portions were fuzzy. "What's wrong with your picture, horserump?" Grundy asked, his normal lack of diplomacy evident.

"I'm not familiar with this region," the centaur explained, unruffled. Centaur stallions, like human males, could have bad tempers, but the fillies were femininely stable. "I didn't have time to explore much of it before the Dragon came. I have to see it before I can map it."

"Then what good is your talent, marebrain?" Grundy demanded. Irene felt a tinge of ire at his insolence but kept her mouth shut; Chem could take care of herself.

"I never get lost, ragbrain," Chem said evenly. Actually, the golem's original head had been wood, not rag, but it was a fair insult. Now, of course, Grundy was alive, with a living brain. "Once I've been to a place, I've got it on my map. So I can always find my way back."

The golem, realizing that insult would be met with insult, shut up and concentrated on his business. They circled Castle Zombie clockwise; three-quarters of the way around, Grundy picked up the trail. They had actually spiraled out somewhat and were now a fair distance from the castle.

"This armor-dillo plant saw her pass!" Grundy exclaimed. He pointed east. "That way."

Irene controlled her thrill of joy. They hadn't completed the rescue yet.

"Odd direction to go," Chem remarked. "Didn't you say you saw the zombie carry her west, not east?"

"That's right!" Irene agreed, her gratification at finding the trail tempered by this surprise. "She couldn't have wandered all the way around the castle!"

"Ask the 'dillo how Ivy arrived," Chem told Grundy.

The golem queried the plant, using a series of rustlings and creakings and pickle-crunching sounds. "She just toddled up from the direction of the castle," he reported. "She didn't look as if she'd walked far."

Irene hesitated, athwart a dilemma. She wanted to recover her lost child as soon as possible, but knew that in the Xanth wilderness it was best to take no mystery on faith. If she found how how Ivy had traveled this far, she might have an important clue to where she was going.

"We'd better check this," she decided, hoping she wasn't wasting critical time on something irrelevant. "Go back and trace how Ivy got here."

"You know it's late," Grundy reminded her. "If she's caught out here at night—"

"I know," Irene agreed. "I dread that. But this may be important. There's a mystery here that may have bearing. However she got from west of the castle to east of the castle, she may do it again to get somewhere else, while we are looking in the wrong place."

The golem shrugged his tiny shoulders. "It's her funeral."

Irene suppressed the urge to hurl the miniature man into the nearest tangle tree. "Just ask the plants," she said between her teeth.

Chem moved toward the castle. Grundy queried the vegetation along the way. "They haven't seen her here," he reported.

The group backtracked, checking more closely. The zombie, who had been dutifully trailing the centaur, did its best to help, peering into the bushes on either side.

Ivy's trail commenced near the armor-dillo. The plants there said she had walked from the west, but the plants to the west did not remember her.

"Something extremely peculiar here," Chem said. "She can't be traveling intermittently."

Irene spotted something in a nearby field. It was a large animal. For an instant her chest tightened; then she saw it was a grazing creature, not a carnivore. "Maybe that—whatever it is—saw Ivy," she said.

Chem looked. "That's a moose. A vanilla—no, a chocolate moose. Harmless."

They went over, and Grundy questioned the moose. The animal looked up warily. "It wants to know if we're ducks," Grundy said with disgust. "It doesn't like ducks who nibble."

"Tell it to stop ducking the question," Irene said.

After a moment, the golem reported that the moose had seen a child of the proper description, but not here; she had been some distance to the east, going the other way.

"Farther along," Irene said. "At least we know she was all right then. We'll go there soon; right now I want to know why her trail is intermittent *here*."

They resumed the backtrack. Grundy narrowed it down to two blades of grass. The east one remembered Ivy and said she had come from the west; the west blade denied it. Soon the two were in an argument, and then in a fight. One blade slashed at the other but was parried and countered. In moments the surrounding blades chose sides and joined the fray. The field became a battlefield.

"This is getting us nowhere!" Irene protested, dancing about to avoid getting slashed on the ankles. "One of those gay blades must be lying."

"No, grass is inferior," Grundy said. "It doesn't have the wit to lie. It just stands tall and defends its turf."

"But their stories directly contradict! They can't both be true!"

Now Chem's fine centaur mind came into play. She suffered less distraction from the blades because her hooves were invulnerable. "They could—if a forget-whorl passed."

"A forget-whorl!" There was the answer, of course. It had blotted out the trail, for the plants it had affected had no memory of events preceding the passage of the whorl. "But that means—"

"That it could have touched Ivy, too," Chem finished. "I had hoped that wouldn't be the case."

"But without memory—" The prospect was appalling, though Irene had also thought of it before. She just hadn't wanted to believe it. "Not even to remember the dangers—"

"But the whorl could have passed after Ivy did," Chem pointed out. "So it didn't hurt her, just wiped out a section of her trail."

"Yes . . ." Irene agreed, relieved. "Or maybe it just grazed her, making her forget a little, such as how to get home, without really hurting her." That was stretching probability somewhat, but was a better theory than nothing. It *was* possible, Irene reminded herself fiercely.

"We shall trace her quickly," the centaur reassured Irene, cutting off the questionable speculations. They all knew how deadly the wilderness of Xanth could be, even when a person's memory was intact.

"Let me try one more thing," Grundy said. "That buckeye over there is to the east of the forget-line, and those bucks eye everything that passes them, especially if it's in a skirt. Maybe it saw Ivy come in and wasn't in the path of the whorl."

"Good idea!" Chem agreed. "Ask it!"

The golem sent out a mooselike honk at the tree. In the distance, the chocolate moose looked up, startled, then realized this call was not for it. The tree's antlerlike branches twitched. Eyelike formations in the trunk blinked. It honked back.

Grundy became excited. He honked again. The tree responded with a considerable passage of rustlings and wood noises.

The golem translated: "The buck says he eyed this region four hours ago and saw a magic carpet glide in, carrying a bag and a child."

"That's no way to refer to a woman!" Irene snapped.

"A bag of spells," Grundy clarified, and Irene blushed. She had waded into that one!

"A carpet!" Chem said. "That could only be—"

"Humfrey's carpet!" Irene exclaimed. "It escaped when the Gap Dragon attacked him!"

"It must have come down near Ivy," Chem said. "These carpets may spook, but they always return. They don't know what to do by themselves. But why didn't it return to Humfrey?"

"He was gone!" Irene said. "The Gorgon conjured him home. Hugo must have wandered away, so the carpet simply went looking for them. When it spied Ivy—"

"It dropped down to see if she was its owner," Chem finished. "And Ivy took a ride on it, just for fun."

"She would," Irene agreed grimly. "She has very little sense of danger when she gets interested by something. She inherits that from her father."

The centaur glanced askance at Irene, but did not comment.

"And she picked up a good-luck charm," Grundy added. "The buckeye saw that happen, too."

"Good-luck charm?" Irene asked. "Then how could she have gotten caught by the forget-whorl?"

"The tree didn't see that," Grundy said.

"Naturally not! The whorls are invisible!"

"But the whorl may have missed her," Chem pointed out. "We know only that it passed here, perhaps soon after she did, not that it got Ivy. The good-luck charm could have fended it off, or at least diminished its effect, depending on how strong the charm was. If her continuing trail remains purposeful, we can assume that she wasn't really hurt by the whorl."

"I don't know," Irene said, worried. "Things don't always happen the way they should, here in Xanth. Dor's father

Bink—" But that was another subject; Bink had always been amazingly lucky, needing no charm.

"We do know a whorl got the zombie who carried her from the path of the Gap Dragon," Chem said, glancing at the zombie who patiently followed them now. This was a different zombie; the patterns of rot were dissimilar, not that it mattered. One zombie was very much like another. "There must be a number of whorls around, striking randomly."

"Probably the whorls followed the dragon from the Gap," Irene agreed. "The dragon should be immune to them, having lived in the ambience of the original forget-spell for centuries. There could be an affinity because of that long association. Anyway, we seem to have solved the riddle of Ivy's departure; she flew the carpet to this side of the castle. But she's on foot now; the carpet evidently took off again when she got off it, and is lost. We need to catch up to her before—"

"Before nightfall," Chem supplied diplomatically.

They followed the trail more quickly now, the golem eliciting a report from a lady-fingers plant that used hand signals to describe a human child and a huge animal.

"Animal?" Irene asked, alarmed.

"Perhaps the chocolate moose," Chem suggested.

Grundy conversed further with the local plants, while the lady-fingers wrung their hands in distress at not being able to identify the creature. But another plant recognized the type. "A yak," the golem finally reported. "They like to talk. They're generally harmless, unless they talk your ear off. Stroke of luck her running into that particular animal."

"The good-luck charm," Chem said. "Obviously she had it with her, though she may not have recognized its significance. It brought her a fortunate wilderness companion."

"After fending off the forget-whorl, or most of it. But those charms only last a few hours when used," Irene said worriedly. "They only have so much power, and each intercession of good luck depletes their charge. Ivy must have needed a lot of luck out here, so the charm will be exhausted by nightfall."

The centaur glanced at the sky. "We have another hour yet. We can move faster than she could. We'll find her."

"Fat cha—" Grundy started to remark with his normal calculated insensitivity, but was interrupted by a coincidental cough from the centaur that almost dislodged him. "Uh, yes, sure."

They went on, tracing the trail along a footpath and past a centaur-game region. "If only the centaurs had realized Ivy was lost," Chem said. "I know they would have carried her right back to the Castle Zombie!"

"The lucky charm was fading," Irene said grimly.

There was a warning rumble of thunder. A storm was headed their way. They hurried.

They passed a torment pine. Then, just beyond it, the trail stopped. No plant remembered anything.

"Another forget-whorl!" Irene exclaimed. "Or maybe the same one, rolling along. It blotted out everything's memory!"

"Those whorls don't seem to be large," Chem said. "We should be able to pick up the trail on the other side of it. I'm sorry we didn't think to bring along some of that whorl-nullifying potion Humfrey gave you."

"Haste always does make waste," Irene said.

The thunder rumbled again, louder. It sounded like the cloud Irene had disciplined with the watermelon seeds, and that could mean trouble. The inanimate wasn't very smart, but it was very ornery. The cloud must have rounded up reinforcements and returned to the fray.

Soon they found the trail—but it was only the yak. "Do yaks leave their companions?" Irene asked.

"Not while those companions are still able to listen," Chem said. "A yak will never voluntarily stop talking."

"Yeah, you have to know how to shut it up," Grundy put in.

"How do you do that?" Irene asked.

The golem shook his little head. "No one knows."

"Ivy surely didn't know—and even if she did, she wouldn't. She likes conversation." Irene frowned. "I only wish she were willing to talk more herself. She listens to me, but she doesn't say much. Sometimes I worry about her being retarded, like—"

"Like Hugo?"

"Not that bad, of course," Irene said hastily. "I'm sure Ivy will talk when she gets around to it. She's only three years old, after all." But that tinge of uncertainty remained.

"Something must have happened to her," Grundy said.

"The forget-whorl!" Chem interjected before Irene could get more upset. "It must have touched the yak, and the animal forgot Ivy and wandered away."

Irene relaxed. "Yes, of course. We must backtrack, then cast about for Ivy's trail."

There was a detonation of thunder that made them all jump, then a stiff gust of wind, and the rain began. This was definitely the fragment of the King of Clouds, restored to power by the moisture of the evening and a host of satellite clouds. Now it was getting even with Irene, and she was not in a position to do anything about it. She ground her teeth in private ire—she didn't like being bested by water vapor.

"The trail will have to wait a little," Chem said. "We aren't going to be able to trace anything in the storm."

"Yeah, it'll be a real drenchpour," Grundy said enthusiastically. "I wonder who antagonized that cloud? They don't zero in like this for no reason."

With bad grace, Irene took out a seed. "Grow," she directed it, and an umbrella plant sprouted. Its broad leaves spread out in an overlapping pattern, creating a watertight shelter. Soon it grew large enough to protect the three of them.

Just in time, for this was indeed a drenchpour. Water came down in traveling sheets, doing its best to blow in sidewise. Oh, that cloud was angry! Irene had to grow a wallflower to wall it off, but they were soaked before the flower completed its growth. Rivulets washed across their feet. Chem excavated channels with her hooves to drain the water, but now the ground was so soggy that it was no pleasure to stand on. Irene grew rock-roses in lieu of chairs for herself and Grundy. But then itch-gnats swarmed in, as they did when people were vulnerable, and she had to grow a giant toad plant to snap them up. The trouble was, the toad also snapped at dangling curls of Irene's green hair and Chem's blond tail, mistaking them for flies or spiders dangling on threads. All in all, it was an uncomfortable situation.

The zombie stood just outside the shelter, having no need

of it and knowing that its kind wasn't wanted inside. The sluicing rain carried bits and pieces of the creature away, but it never seemed to lose mass. That was the thing about zombies; they were forever shedding their spoiled flesh, yet always had more to shed. It was one of the less appetizing types of magic in Xanth. But Irene knew how loyally the zombies had defended Castle Roogna through many crises, freely sacrificing whatever sort of lives they had when any trouble came. They were the ultimate selfless creatures. And she remembered how a zombie justice of the peace—maybe that was "piece," because of the way he had been falling apart—had agreed to officiate when she married Dor. Zombies were good people, despite being rotten.

Still the rain came, settling in for a long seige. Obviously the storm meant to pin them down for the night. Hell had no fury like that of an angry cloud, she reflected, for Hell was full of fire, while the cloud was full of water. Irene didn't like being pinned down; the wilderness was especially dangerous at night. Maybe the king cloud hoped something bad would happen to her while she was pinned. But she couldn't go home as long as Ivy was out here alone.

Something had to be done; Irene's teeth were chattering with developing chill. That cloud had reached high in the cold sky to find icy water! She used the last remaining light of day to grow a candle plant, lighting it with a small flame-vine. That provided enough artificial light for her to grow a few staples. Most plants wouldn't grow in the dark; they required the energy of sunlight. But her talent could force the issue with a few, with the artificial light.

She managed to grow a towel plant, with fine dry towels for all, so they could dry off and abate the chill. Since Irene had to strip to use her towel, she grew a curtain plant to give her some privacy. Actually, she wasn't sensitive about being seen by Chem, as centaurs had little personal modesty; and anyway, Chem was female. She showed all the time what Irene was showing only now. But Grundy was another matter. He would make obnoxious remarks, not because he had any real interest, but because that was his nature. He would feel in-adequate if he let such an occasion pass by without some observation about cheesecake or the erosion of birthday suits. And his big mouth would be active when he encountered other males subsequently. Irene knew it was foolish of her to pay any attention to such nonsense, but she did.

Once dry, she wrapped two towels about her and pinned them with pins from another pincushion plant. The towels would have to do as clothing till morning, when she could grow a sunflower to dry her regular clothing and a lady-slippers plant to replace her sodden footwear. She grew a cheese plant and a breadfruit and a chocolate plant before the last natural light faded; these would suffice for supper. It was a miserable situation, but they could endure it for one night.

Irene hoped her husband Dor wasn't worrying too much. He seemed to think she would not survive by herself; it was one of the halfway charming male notions he retained. She missed him already, there in snug Castle Roogna with the dry floor and friendly ghosts and the continuing entertainment of the magic tapestry.

But she missed Ivy more. That sweet, innocent, inexperienced child lost in this jungle! *Her* child! Irene touched the ivy plant she wore; only its continued health reassured her that her daughter remained well. Without that assurance, Irene would have been forging through the night, regardless of the danger, desperately searching for what she might never find. She was none too sanguine as it was, but the ivy made the situation bearable.

She saw the zombie at the fringe of the flickering candlelight. It looked miserable out there. Of course zombies were always miserable-looking, with one foot pretty much in the grave. A zombie would rest literally in the grave; some of them slept for centuries, quietly decaying, and only roused themselves to throw off their blanket of dirt when summoned by some strange awareness of need for their services. Still, the sight of this one bothered her. "Are you hungry?" she asked it.

"Hhunnggh?" the thing said.

"Hungry. Eat. Food." Irene extended a piece of cheese, not knowing whether such things ever ate.

The zombie reached a gangrenous hand to accept it. Irene

forced herself not to flinch away from the contact. "Ffooodh," the creature said.

"Yes, to eat." Irene illustrated by taking a delicate bite of her own piece of cheese, though now her appetite had diminished considerably.

The zombie tried it. Three teeth crumbled, and a segment of lip fell off. The firm cheese was impervious to the creature's feeble effort at mastication.

"I suppose not," Irene said, controlling the roiling of her stomach. "I really don't know much about zombies."

"None of us do," Chem agreed. "They are not like us, if that is not a ludicrous understatement."

"Easy enough to find out," Grundy said, perceiving an opportunity for mischief. "I can talk to the things as readily as to anything else, though they aren't strictly alive. It's one place where King Dor's talent overlaps mine; he can talk to them because they aren't quite alive, and I can talk to them because they aren't quite dead." He smiled with happy malice. "What intimate girlish secrets do you wish to exchange with this one?"

"Well—" Irene discovered that she really wasn't very curious about zombies. They were such appalling things! Part of the horror was the thought that someday she could find herself animated as a similar creature if she happened to die in the vicinity of Castle Zombie. Death was never fun to contemplate, and this kind of half-death was worse.

There was a low hissing roar from the damp darkness beyond the shelter. "That's a bonnacon!" Grundy exclaimed with alarm. "I'd know that noise anywhere."

"Sounds more like a dragon to me," Chem said, swishing her tail nervously.

"The bonnacon *is* a dragon, horseface," the golem responded. "It has the horns of a bison—that's a mythical Mundane animal—and the posterior of—well, let's just say it's worse going than coming."

"Dragons eat people!" Irene reminded them. "And I can't grow many plants in the dark. We're in trouble!"

"You'd better grow *some*thing, because the thing has winded us," Grundy warned. "The bonnacon is too big and fast for us to escape it; we have to fight it off."

"With pieces of cheese?" Irene demanded. "We need a weapon, and I doubt my knife will—"

Chem unslung her bow. "Pinpoint its location, and I'll shoot it," she said.

"No good, ponytail," the golem said. "Your arrows would only annoy it. We've got to have a tough plant, like a boxwood or tangler."

"Not at night," Irene said. "Right now all I can grow is night bloomers."

"Then grow the night bloomers!" Grundy cried. "The monster's almost upon us!"

Irene heard the most horrendous rasp of the dragon's breath. She was not the most timid of women, but now she was terrified. Her mind numb, she tossed down a seed. "Grow!"

"Maybe we can make a lot of noise and scare it off," Chem said.

"No good," Grundy replied. "When the bonnacon retreats, it blows out its whole quantity of digestive refuse—in simpler language, its—"

"Spare us your vernacular," Irene said. "We understand what the stuff is."

"Right into the faces of its pursuers," the golem continued with a certain enthusiasm. "The stuff not only stinks to high heaven, it's so strong it sets fire to trees."

"But if we can't escape the monster, and we don't scare it off—" the centaur said, understandably concerned.

"That's why we need Irene's fighting plants. Something that will balk the dragon without really frightening it, so it will go away peacefully. That's the key: we must discourage it without annoying it."

"Lots of luck," Irene muttered. "Look at them!" She moved the candle to illuminate what she had grown. "My night bloomers!"

There they were—several sets of delicately tinted feminine bloomer-panties, the kind worn at night or under voluminous skirts.

Grundy worked his little face in an effort not to guffaw. "Now if we can just get them on the dragon—" he said. A smirk was obviously scrambling around in his head, trying to get out through his face.

Bloomers to prevent the dragon's voiding from splattering them! The notion was ludicrous; the people would be eaten long before the bloomers could do any such thing, and the dragon's refuse would burn out the bloomers on the way by. Yet the idea had a certain foolish appeal. A dragon in bloomers! That was almost as nonsensical as Irene's vision of a dragon on a pedestal.

Now the huge horned head of the bonnacon became dimly visible in the fringe of candlelight. There were flickering highlights on every giant tooth. Irene saw immediately that, though this dragon lacked steam or fire, it was far too formidable for them to fight. Even its eyes had metalbone lids that would probably stop Chem's arrows. They were helpless before it. Irene got ready to scream, though she detested this sort of useless feminine reaction. Sometimes there was no alternative.

The dragon nudged forward. The zombie interposed itself between the sheltered party and the monster. "Schtopf!" it cried, blowing out a piece of tongue. Speech was not easy for zombies.

The bonnacon never even hesitated. It snapped up the zombie. The huge and awful jaws crunched together. The zombie squished, and putrid juices squirted out.

The dragon paused. An expression of distaste spread slowly across its chops, in much the same manner as a like expression had spread across the face of the Gap Dragon when it crunched the stink bomb. Then the bonnacon spat the zombie's body out. "Ugh!" it groaned, understandably. There was nothing delicious about a squished zombie.

The zombie landed under the umbrella, a sorry mess. The dragon turned and tromped elsewhere, looking for better food. It did not spray out its fire-started refuse, since it was not frightened; it just departed in disgust.

"The bonnacon thinks we're all zombies!" Irene breathed.

"You do sort of look like one," Grundy informed her helpfully. "In a towel, yet."

Probably true. Irene's hair was plastered to her head and body, and the towels could be mistaken for ragged clothing.

There were so many zombies in this region near Castle Zombie that the confusion was natural. The zombie had saved them by discouraging the dragon.

But at what cost? Irene was not exactly partial to zombies, but she did appreciate the sacrifice this one had made. If it weren't for the zombie, Irene herself would have been crunched by the jaws of the monster. The creature had acted with courage and dispatch when all other hope was gone—and had paid the terrible price.

She knelt to inspect the zombie. It was in a sad state—but *all* zombies were in a sad state. They were the walking undead, perpetually decaying without ever quite collapsing. Usually it took complete dismemberment to put a zombie all the way out of commisssion. If this one were typical, it might survive. "Are you—?" she asked, balking at the words "alive" or "dead." Zombies, as Grundy had clarified, weren't exactly either.

"Hhurrtsh," the thing replied faintly.

"It's still functional!" Chem said, surprised.

"She says it hurts!" Grundy translated for the zombie.

"Of course it hurts!" Irene snapped. Her diffidence vanished, and she grabbed a spare towel and used it to mop up the pus and saliva and juice that covered the body. "She's just been crunched by—" Irene paused. *"She?"*

"Sure, she's your kind," the golem said. "Didn't you know?"

"No, I didn't realize," Irene said, taken aback. "She's so, uh, far gone it wasn't obvious." But now, as she wiped the torso, she saw that it was true. There were what once had been female attributes there.

"I hadn't realized either," Chem said soberly. "Naturally, there would be females of their kind as well as males. The Zombie Master can reanimate anything that once lived."

The zombie tried to sit up. "Hey, don't do that!" Irene protested. "You've just been terribly crunched by a dragon. Your—your blood spurted out! Your bones must be broken! You're lucky you're—animate!"

"Ah, you can't kill a zombie," Grundy said. "You can hack it to pieces, but the pieces will slowly draw together and reassemble. Magic makes a zombie function, not biology."

"Maybe so," Irene said grimly. "But this one just saved our

lives, and she's not so far gone she can't experience pain and human sensitivity. We've got to do something for her."

"I agree," Chem said. "But what *can* be done for a zombie?"

"Ask her, Grundy," Irene said.

"And ask her name," Chem added.

It had not occurred to Irene that a zombie would have a name. Now she chided herself for the way she had dehumanized them in her mind. Zombies were, after all, people—or had been, before dying and becoming undead.

The golem issued a series of slushy syllables and decaying particles. The zombie responded with coughs and chokes and noises that sounded like garbage being sucked down a half-clogged sewer drainhole.

"She says her name is Zora," Grundy reported in due course. "She killed herself about fifteen years ago when her true love was false. Her folks took her body to the Zombie Master, and he animated her. She's been serving him since. She would prefer to be all-the-way dead or fully alive, but neither is possible, so she just muddles along. She says it's a living. Well, that's not precisely it, but the term doesn't translate well."

Surely it didn't! What an awful thing it must be, Irene thought, to be forever half dead! "Yes, but how can we help her?" she demanded of the golem. "There must be something."

The golem interrogated Zora Zombie again. "The only thing that brings her kind closer to life is love," he reported. "Some living man must truly love her, to counteract the evil of the one who did not. Then she would be almost human, as long as his love lasted."

Chem whistled. "That is a difficult thing! Nobody loves a zombie. Most men prefer their women young and, er, wholesome."

"Yes, I know," Irene said. "I was that way once. Then I got married." She smiled, but it wasn't entirely a joke. Marriage had brought new responsibilities—and Ivy. Marriage had been the end of her nymphly existence and the beginning of a matronly one, but she wouldn't trade it. "Well, we'll try to help Zora Zombie somehow. She certainly deserves it!"

Irene put her hand to the zombie's bony shoulders, no longer repelled by the contact, and helped her sit up. Whatever healing processes occurred in zombies were operating now, and soon Zora was back on her feet and stumbling about in her normal fashion. She moved out into the falling rain, where she seemed to be the least uncomfortable.

"If there is anything I, personally, can do—" Irene called to Zora, still feeling inadequate.

"I believe you have already done it," Chem murmured.

"Done what?"

"Extended a little human caring. That's why she mended so rapidly—and may continue to improve, if such treatment continues."

Irene was taken aback, and hardly pleased with herself. She knew she had been treating the zombie with contempt before. Could any amount of decent treatment make up for that?

Well, she would find out.

"I suppose we'd better sleep," Irene said. "We can't do anything now, and we're probably as safe here as anywhere."

The others agreed; they lay down on towels and bloomers and tried to sleep. Zora flopped on a wet rock outside the umbrella shelter. Irene was not at all comfortable, physically or mentally, but she was a realist. She would endure what she must to get her child back alive. No price was too great.

She thought she would lie awake all night, but somehow she didn't. Not quite. She thought if she did sleep, she would have bad dreams; however, it seemed the local night mare was not paying attention, and no bad dreams came.

Chapter 5. Coven-tree

The baby Gap Dragon was only a fraction of its adult size and not much more than triple Ivy's mass. But its primary features were intact; it had six legs, a sinuous tail, a set of wings too small to enable it to fly, and a horrendous head full of teeth. Its scales were metallic, a rather pretty green with iridescent highlights, and the tip of its tail was knifelike.

The dragon eyed Ivy. It slavered. Its tongue slopped around its face, moistening its teeth and making them gleam. A jet of pure, clean, white steam issued from its throat. Big creatures were now too much for the dragon to tackle, but Ivy was little and succulent. It was ready to feast.

Ivy looked the dragon in the snout. She clapped her hands with girlish glee. "Oh, goody!" she exclaimed in delight. "A playmate!"

The dragon paused. This was not, it suspected, the proper reception accorded its kind by lone human beings of any size. Its memory of its adult life had been excised along with its age, so it could not remember any prior encounters with this life form; but its basic instincts were more important than its memory anyway. It was geared to chase down a terrified and fleeing morsel, to steam it into a tasty, half-cooked state, to crunch it into digestible chunks soaked in delicious blood, to swallow the delectable pieces, then to burp afterward and take a pleasant nap. It was also geared to flee anything larger than itself or more dangerous, such as a man with an enchanted sword. Creatures of approximately its own size and ferocity it would fight, establishing territorial prerogatives. It was vaguely aware that it had once possessed an excellent private territory, but it had no idea now where this was. That hardly mattered here, because it faced prey, not a monster similar to itself. But the Dragon lacked experience and instincts relating to friendly receptions. What was the proper response?

Ivy walked up to it fearlessly. "My very own pet dragon!" she cried. "Green, like Mommy's hair! To be my friend and companion and to guard me when I'm afraid." She reached out to pat the ugly snout. "What a lovely creature!"

The dragon was not at all reassured. In fact, it found itself athwart a dilemma. Chase, flee, or fight? None of the signals matched a pattern. No one had ever called it lovely before or patted it on the snout. So it remained stationary, taking no action. A nervous waft of steam puffed from it.

"Nice steam!" Ivy said. "You're a steamer, so your name is Stanley." She had been told tales of strange, funny Mundania, where impossible things existed, such as metal machines that traveled on wheels and people who had no magic. She wasn't good at comprehending impossibilities, but she had an apt memory for names. "Stanley Steamer," she repeated. "You're wonderful!"

Ivy was indulging in a simple but subtle process of identification and transference. First, she was a creature of love, for love had always abounded in her family, so naturally love radiated from her. She bestowed on her toys and pets and friends the kind of unquestioning love she received herself. Also, she was aware of the way men treated women, as exemplified by her father's handling of her mother. King Dor placed Queen Irene on a pedestal. Irene complained about it often but was privately rather pleased. Ivy had spent many hours of many days searching Castle Roogna for that pedestal, but it seemed to be invisible, like the ghosts. Finally she had realized that it was magic, like the monster-under-the-bed that only she could see. King Dor was able to put Queen Irene on the pedestal that no one else could see or feel, and Irene could not get off it, complain as she might. It was a special enchantment he could perform. Ivy liked enchantment, so she had tried to develop her own invisible pedestal on which she could place her friends. She had by diligent effort perfected it, but had lacked a suitable friend for it. Smash the Ogre was really too big to fit on it. But now she had a suitable prospect, and so she placed her new friend Stanley on it. He was the very best of all the little dragons she knew!

Stanley, like Ivy's mother, was not entirely comfortable on that pedestal; but again, like her mother, he was not entirely displeased. There were things to be said in favor of pedestals, and he was the right size for this one. What made Ivy's pedestal especially effective was her talent of enhancement. Whatever traits a person or creature possessed, in her eyes, became more pronounced, powerful, durable, and good. When she had noted how well her mother grew plants, her mother had grown them even better. When Ivy had met the friendly, talkative yak, the creature had become more friendly and helpful. Now Ivy perceived how handsome and nice Stanley Steamer really was.

Stanley suffered a period of disorientation, as was normal for creatures abruptly discovering themselves on pedestals. He hadn't known his name was Stanley. He hadn't known he was wonderful. Certainly he hadn't known he was lovely. Then the full power of Ivy's magic took over, for it was Magician-caliber sorcery, the kind of power few mortals comprehended, and the dragon became exactly what she perceived him to be—her handsome and loyal friend, playmate, and pet. Like many a male before him, he succumbed to the enchantment of a sweet little female, without even knowing the nature of her sorcery. He was not aware that he had lost a battle of remarkable significance; he didn't even know there had been a battle. Because his natural instincts had no guidelines for this role, he had to accept hers. He was precisely what she wanted.

Ivy, because she was what she was, a creature of love and innocence and unsuspected power, had in an instant tamed one of the most formidable monsters of Xanth—the Gap Dragon. No one had ever done that before. Some people might have considered it a miracle, but it was not; it was merely an early indication of Ivy's own formidability, which was allied to that of her grandfather Bink.

"You must have very hard scales," Ivy said, tapping the scales of Stanley's neck; and now they were metal-hard. "Such pretty colors, too!" And the colors intensified, manifesting as elegant shades of green and blue and gray with iridescent sparkles. Stanley was now so pretty as to smite the unwary eye. "Oh, you're such a *nice* dragon!" She hugged him about the neck and kissed his green ear.

Bemused, the dragon accepted her embrace. Had he not been so hard-scaled and pretty-colored, he might have melted right into the ground, for Ivy's affection was a very special thing, quite apart from her magic.

"And such nice, hot steam," she continued. Stanley jetted a superheated jet, much hotter than he had ever managed before.

Ivy's attention soon wandered, for she was, after all, only a little girl without any great store of attention. She hardly needed it. "I'm hungry! Aren't you?"

Stanley agreed that he was hungry by nodding his head, making the scales of his neck glitter nicely. In fact, now he was ravenous.

"Then we must find some food," Ivy decided. "For supper." She looked about.

Stanley sighed privately. Ivy herself was the most delicious possible morsel, but he could no longer even think of that without wincing. No one would consume her while he was on guard!

Nearby was a crabapple tree, with quite a number of ripe crabs. "Gee, I bet those are good," she said, reaching for one. But the crab snapped at her with its huge pincer, and she hastily withdrew her hand. She had learned the hard way about things that pinched, back at Castle Roogna.

Still, those crabs looked awfully good. "I know!" she decided, for she prided herself on her ability to solve problems when she tried; indeed, that ability had intensified to do justice to her pride. "Mommy cooks crabs in hot water. Then they don't snap!" She had not realized, before this moment, *why* her mother went through the ritual with the water, putting hot peppers into the pot to bring the liquid to the boiling point, then dumping in the crabs. It was a significant revelation, worthy of Ivy's effort.

But she didn't have any hot water. In fact, she had no water at all and no hot peppers to heat it. Ivy pondered, and in a moment she came up with a solution, for she was trying to be a precocious child. "Stanley, your hot steam can cook them! Then we can both eat!"

Stanley looked at the crabapple tree, not understanding. He did not need to steam crabs; he could crunch them raw without difficulty. Their meat became his flesh, and their shells became his scales, in the natural order of assimilation.

"Oh, come on," Ivy said encouragingly. "I know you're smarter than that!" The dragon discovered he *was* smarter than he had thought, and now he understood her notion. *She* could not crunch crabs live and raw.

Stanley positioned himself before the crabapple tree and sent forth a jet of sizzling steam. It touched a crab, whose greenish shell instantly ripened to bright apple red, and the creature fell to the ground. Ivy picked it up—and dropped it, for it was hot. She stuck her fingers in her mouth, unscorching them. Then she made do; she used a section of her ivy-green skirt to protect her fingers and picked the crab up again. It smelled delicious.

But she didn't know how to crack open the shell, as she had no nutcracker. Then she looked at Stanley's gleaming teeth and had another bright idea. "You can crack it!" she exclaimed.

She poked the cooked crab into the corner of the dragon's mouth where the chewing teeth were. Stanley crunched down slowly until the shell cracked. Then he eased up, and she took the crab back. The problem had been solved.

She picked out the meat and chewed it. "Yes, it's very good," she said. "Cook some for yourself, Stanley."

Stanley shrugged and steamed several more crabs and chewed them up, shells and all. He discovered that they were good this way, too. His horizon had been broadened; now he knew how to eat cooked as well as raw meat. In due course, both girl and dragon were satisfied.

But now night was closing more insistently. "I guess Mommy hasn't found me yet, and Daddy's busy with something more important," Ivy remarked, unconcerned. She knew Queen Irene would show up when it suited her convenience. It wasn't often the woman forgot about bedtime, though. "We must find a good place to sleep."

The dragon, of course, normally slept anywhere he wanted to; no other creature would attack him. But he was much smaller and less experienced than he had been, and was daunted by the threat of darkness. How would he escape the monster under the bed if he had no bed to climb on? So if Ivy believed it was necessary to find a good place to sleep, then it must be true.

They walked on, seeking a good place. They came to a tree on which grew not crabs but small men. Stanley wafted an experimental cloud of steam at it, in case the men were edible, and a number of them turned red and dropped off.

They had been steamed, but they were not cooked. Each fallen man bounded to his feet, and a company of them gathered below the tree. "Oh, babies!" Ivy exclaimed, perceiving that each wore diapers. "This is an infant-tree!"

These were pretty tough babies. Each had a helmet and a little sword or spear. Now they scowled and marched, their weapons extended threateningly. Stanley wafted more steam at them, but the troops of the infant-tree forged on, using little shields to deflect the steam. Their red color was that of anger, not of ripening or cooking.

"I think we'd better run," Ivy said intelligently. "Your scales are tough, Stanley, but my skin is tender, because I'm a cute little girl. Anyway, it's getting too dark."

Stanley wasn't certain of the logic of all this, but knew he wasn't as smart as she was, since thinking wasn't normally the prerogative of dragons. Yet he understood what she wanted.

They found the trunk of another tree. This one was huge; it would have taken Ivy some time just to walk around the base, climbing over its monstrous, buttressing roots. The foliage was dense, an impenetrable mass that spread out almost horizontally near the bottom. "We'd be safe up there," Ivy decided. "But how can we get up?"

They were in luck. Behind the tree was a crane. The bird had long, thin legs and a long, thin neck and a long, thin bill. It was a large bird, so that when it stood up straight, its head disappeared into the leaves of the tree. Indeed, it was engaged in lifting stones from the ground to the foliage, cranking up its head in slow, measured stages.

Ivy paused, watching this procedure. She concentrated, and finally figured it out: the bird was practicing rocky-tree.

The troops of the infant-tree were in hot pursuit, delayed only by the shortness of their stride and by their need to detour more widely around the projecting roots than Ivy and Stanley had to do. Ivy didn't waste time. "Mister Crane, will you lift us up into the tree?" she asked. "I'll give you—" She hesitated, searching about herself for something to offer, for she knew that it was proper to give favors for favors. She found a metal disk in her pocket and brought it out. "This."

The crane peered at the disk. The disk gleamed in the last slanting beam of daylight. The crane was charmed, for it liked bright things. It accepted the disk, then hooked its bill into Ivy's skirt-band and hoisted her up into the foliage. She spun dizzily with the sudden elevation, but grabbed the branches as they came within reach and scrambled up into the soft darkness of the leaves.

The crane's bill descended, hooked onto Stanley's tail, and hoisted him up similarly. Soon he was with her again, which was just as well, because she was nervous about being alone in the dark.

It was almost completely night in the tree, but there were many soft leaves, so Ivy arranged a bunch of them by feel into a bed that was comfortable enough. She couldn't see the ground, so she didn't worry about falling. Stanley formed a nest of his own and curled up snout to tail in the fashion of his kind. In moments they were both asleep.

There was a terrible storm during the night, but the massed leaves channeled the water around, so that Ivy and Stanley did not get wet and were only dimly aware of the deluge. Ivy drew her leaf-blanket more tightly about her, and Stanley snorted a waft of steam. Both were glad to be high and dry; few experiences are cozier than being nicely sheltered from bad weather.

In the morning it took Ivy a little while to remember where she was. At first she thought she was home in bed, but the color wasn't right. Her bedroom was pink, with climbing ivy plants that her mother had grown for her. This place was green, with faint pink swatches of light where a few bold sunbeams poked through. And, of course, she had no pet dragon at home.

"Stanley!" she exclaimed with joy, reaching across to give him a hug. "You're such a *nice* dragon!"

The baby Gap Dragon woke with a startled snort of steam, switching his tail. His middle set of legs fell through the foliage, and he had to scramble for a moment to recover secure footing. They were, after all, up a tree. But he was also much nicer than he had been.

"I like this tree," Ivy decided. "Let's stay up here!" Stanley, who had discovered that he liked being hugged by a cute little girl, agreed.

Ivy looked for a bathroom, but found none. She discovered, though, that anything she did dropped harmlessly through the floor of foliage and out of sight and out of mind, so that was no problem. Birds did it, after all; no wonder they found trees so convenient!

Next she looked for a kitchen, with no better success. But there were assorted fruits and nuts dangling within reach, so she plucked and ate them. Stanley wasn't sure about this form of sustenance, but at her urging he consumed a bunch of red-hot pepper fruits and found them delicious. He liked hot stuff; it helped heat his steam just as effectively as it heated Ivy's mother's water. Then he ate some of the more juicy fruits, for he also needed liquid from which to generate his steam.

Now they moved on through the tree, exploring. Foliage was everywhere, making this a jungle in itself, but there was a certain pattern to it. The branches twisted generally upward, and the layers of leaves became firmer at the higher levels. This was vaguely like an enormous house, with many floors and walls and ramps; it seemed to extend forever. Stanley had no trouble, for his body was long and low and sinuous, but Ivy felt nervous on the smaller branches.

Finally they reached the highest level, where the sun shone down, and here the network of branches was so thick and so intertwined, and the leaves so many and strong, that the visitors could safely walk anywhere. The top of the tree was roughly level, with the mounds of individual branches resembling hills; the outermost boughs rose higher to form a kind of retaining wall that prevented them from falling off. The leaves were of varied colors here, too, so that it was more like a regular landscape.

There were some large, individual leaves projecting from the nether mass of the treescape, with black patterns on them. The nearest one was marked WELCOME TO COVEN-TREE, and below it a smaller leaf was marked DO NOT LITTER. Ivy was too young to read, and the Gap Dragon had never learned how, so they ignored these leaves.

Ahead was a series of leafy cages containing strange animals. The sign-leaf by the first said GI-ANTS. Inside were several huge and strange insects, each as big as Ivy herself. Their bodies resembled those of ant lions, but their heads were strange. Ivy pondered a moment, then managed to remember where she had seen creatures like these before. "In a picture!—" she exclaimed. "In a book of weird Mundane monsters. Mommy called them 'ants.' They must be a crossbreed of ant lions and, and—" But here she stalled; she could not figure out what could account for the changed heads. "But I thought they were smaller."

Stanley peered at the odd creatures, as fascinated as Ivy was. One of the huge ants snapped its mandibles at the Dragon, and Stanley jetted some steam back at it. The ant waved its long antennae, and Stanley switched his tail. Mundane monsters made him uncomfortable; they simply weren't natural.

The next cage was labeled MA-MOTHS. Inside were the biggest night butterflies Ivy had ever seen, with furry antennae and folded dark wings. They carried no butter, however. They seemed to be asleep, though it was day.

Another cage contained an ENOR-MOUSE crunching up a huge chunk of cheese. Others had TREMEN-DOES, which were large, split-hoofed animals, vaguely like the yak, eating leaves; GIGAN-TICS sucking on a big bloodroot; STUPEN-DOES, even larger than the other does; and IM-MENS, which were ogre-sized men.

Ivy paused at the last exhibit. It didn't seem right to her for any type of men to be imprisoned like this. Her mind was small, so her thoughts translated to action very quickly. "Stanley, let's let these creatures go," she said.

The dragon was willing. He jetted so fierce a shot of steam at the leafy lock in the IM-MENS cage that it melted, and the gate swung open. The mens crowded out, pleased with their new freedom.

Ivy and Stanley went back along the cages, melting each lock, having found out how easy it was to free the exhibits. Soon all the confined creatures were free, charging about madly. There was such pandemonium that Ivy and Stanley were daunted. They retreated to the very edge of the coven-tree, climbing the retaining wall. This wall intersected the wall of an adjacent tree where things were less hectic, so they jumped across, leaving the confusion behind.

This new tree was very pretty. WELCOME TO PAGEAN-TREE, its leaf-sign said, and of course they ignored it. They were too interested in all the pretty colors of the foliage, much brighter than the leaves of the last tree, and in the remarkable forms this new foliage assumed.

There were also marching bands, each band a strip of cloth or cord or rubber with little legs that tramped along at a measured pace, somewhat the way the tough babies of the infant-tree had marched. Ivy was entranced, and Stanley became interested, too, since she thought he would be.

But after a while, even the splendors of the pagean-tree palled, for life was more than pageans, and they jumped to the foliage of still another tree. This was, its sign said, a DATE PALM, its fronds representing all the days of the year. Day lilies grew in little cups of earth, but only one bloomed each day, so that the precise date was always marked. In the very center grew a large century plant, its thick, long, green leaves spreading out in a globe, spiked along the sides and tips.

In the middle of the century plant was something really fascinating. It seemed to be another plant with straight stalks clothed by many small, round, bright leaves that glittered in the sunlight like golden coins. "Ooooh, pretty!" Ivy exclaimed. "I want one!" Little girls resembled big cranes in this respect; they liked pretty things.

She tried to get in to the coin plant, but the spurs of the century plant prevented her. The spurs were very sturdy, so she could not simply push them aside. Stanley helped, steaming each spur so that it turned soft, which enabled Ivy to pass. But progress was slow, for there were many spurs. Stanley had to stay right with her, because as soon as the two of them passed, the spurs became hard again. Stanley tried to chew off a leaf, but its juices were like those of a zombie, and he quickly desisted before he got sick. So they wriggled and scrambled their way through the many thick leaves with Stanley expending much steam, until at last they arrived at the bright plant in the very center.

Ivy reached for a coin, a smile of innocent delight on her face. But the moment her little fingers touched the golden leaf, there was a flare of light from the plant that bathed both girl and dragon, making the entire scene glow eerily. It was a glow Ivy's mother had seen in a vision but had not quite understood, for it was only an incidental part of the vision.

The two of them froze exactly as they were, becoming living statues, unmoving, unbreathing.

They had been caught by one of the least dramatic but most powerful plants in Xanth, the one that ultimately governed and brought down almost every other living creature: thyme.

Chapter 6. Xanthippe

The storm had cleared by morning, but it had had its revenge on Irene by wiping out all conceivable tracks and traces and so battering the vegetation that it could not remember the events of the day before. The trail was now thoroughly cold and wet.

In addition, the sun was laggard about penetrating the cloud cover, so Irene couldn't dry her clothing properly. She grew new bloomers and slippers, and from dry towels fashioned a skirt and jacket, cut and buttoned appropriately. She wasn't entirely comfortable, but she set out bravely enough, making Grundy query every plant in the region, just in case. None of them remembered Ivy.

"I hesitate to suggest this," Chem began, "but—"

"Then *don't* suggest it!" Irene snapped. She knew what the centaur was going to say—that something had captured Ivy and taken her away, so that the little girl might never be found. But the ivy plant remained green, signaling the child's health, and Irene would not rest until she rescued her.

They searched for hours. At one point a griffin spied the party and swooped down for a closer look. Griffins were among the most feared creatures of the wilderness, as they possessed the bodies of lions and the wings of eagles and were always hungry and ferocious. But Irene gave this one no shrift. She hurled down a boxwood seed and ordered it to grow.

The plant grew into a small tree with many hard, wooden gnarls. It moved these gnarls about, boxing at the griffin. The boxwood was aggressive; it liked physical contact. Only a few of these attacks were necessary before the animal fled.

Finally Grundy got a lead. "This anchor plant saw her! It's very hard to dislodge, so the rain couldn't wash out its memory. But—"

"But what?" Irene cried, dashing over.

"But she had a companion," the golem said reluctantly. "Not the yak."

"But she's all right!" Irene said, as if daring the golem to deny it.

"Yes. But the creature she met—"

"It didn't attack her!" Irene said with the same defiance. Her ivy plant remained vigorous, reassuring her.

"Not exactly . . ."

"Perhaps I had better question him—" Chem offered.

But Irene would have none of the centaur's levelheadedness. An uncomfortable night, physically and emotionally, had shortened her fuse, and she had never been especially noted for her patience. "Out with it, knothead! What creature?"

"It sounds like the Gap Dragon."

Now Irene reacted. She had been braced for anything. Anything but this. She fell back against Chem, almost collapsing. The centaur grabbed her to support her. "The—Gap—?"

"Reduced," Grundy said quickly. "Remember, you told us it got doused with Youth elixir and youthened into babyhood, just like Humfrey."

"But the G-Gap Dragon!" Irene protested. "The most vicious monster in Xanth! No matter what size it is now!"

"Yes. The same."

Irene nerved herself. "What happened?"

Grundy queried the anchor plant. "They seem to have made friends," he reported doubtfully. "They walked away together."

"The Gap Dragon has no friends!" Irene said, perversely arguing with him. "It's a loner. It eats everything it catches."

"That can't be entirely true," Chem said. "Unless the dragon is immortal, it must have had parents, and it will have to breed to reproduce itself. So there must be a place in its scheme for companionship. And now it has been rejuvenated. It could indeed be immortal, if it uses the Fountain of Youth regularly— but I doubt that is the case. Regardless, it could be lonely, as a child in that situation would be."

"Some child!" Grundy exclaimed.

"Children do differ from adults," the centaur insisted. "They are more impressionable, more open—"

"More likely the dragon just didn't happen to be hungry at the moment, so it saved her for the next meal," Grundy suggested helpfully.

Chem aimed a forehoof at the golem but missed. Irene, just beginning to believe that her child might possibly be all right, suffered a renewed pang. The Gap Dragon was a scheming, canny creature, smarter than the average dragon. "We had better catch up to them soon!" she said grimly.

They traced the youngsters to an infant-tree. Several of the tough babies remembered the pair. "'Sure we chased 'em,'" Grundy translated. "'The beast really steamed us! We don't take that shift from anyone!'"

"But where did they go?" Irene demanded.

"What's it to you, old dame?" another baby asked, hanging loose as the golem translated.

"Just answer the question, you little swinger," Irene said sternly.

The baby paused in its swinging. "They fled beyond the witch's tree," it said. "By the time we made a forced-march there, the trail was cold. We've got better things to do than hunt for dummies."

"One of those dummies was my daughter!" Irene exclaimed angrily.

"Tough shift, sister," the infant retorted.

"I'll tough-shift *you*, you fat brat!" Irene cried. She threw down a seed. "Grow!"

The seed sprouted into a cowslip plant. In moments it was depositing slippery and smelly cow-chips all around. Next time the infants marched, they would find themselves slipping in truly shiftless stuff.

"That wasn't nice, Irene," Grundy said smugly. He appreciated dirt, no matter who flung it.

"Just tend to your business, golem, or I'll grow a wart plant on your head!"

Grundy shut up and tended to his business.

But the trail was indeed cold. The witch's tree was distracted by an infestation of large bugs or wild animals in its foliage and wouldn't answer Grundy's query. Apparently the bugs had been confined and recently released, for they were raising havoc in the upper foliage. The grass below the tree was washed out. So the party simply had to go on, casting about as before, hoping to find a plant or tree that remembered a child and a little dragon.

They got beyond the region where it had rained, but still there was no clue. Irene was too stubborn to admit they had lost the trail entirely and were probably going in the wrong direction. Her daughter had to be out here somewhere!

They came to a bleak area, yellowish overall, where normal trees gave way to strange, thick-trunked growths from which grew long, thin, grasslike leaves with upright spikes at the top bearing whitish flowers. Grundy queried one and discovered it was a grasstree named Xanthorrhoed.

"Now this is interesting," Chem said. Centaurs were chronically fascinated by unusual fauna and flora. "Xanthorrhoed is one of the really primitive, fundamental plants of Xanth, as can be told from its name."

"Xanth-horrid?" Irene asked. "I don't have any seed for that."

"Perhaps you should add some to your collection. I believe this type of plant is associated with—"

"Witches," a new voice said. Irene looked around to see a sallow, yellow, old woman. Distracted by the grasstree, she had not seen the woman approach. "What are you creatures doing in my garden?"

"I'm looking for a child," Irene said shortly. "Have you seen her? Three years old, perhaps accompanied by a small dragon—"

"Ah, so," the witch said. "I just may have news of those. They belong to you?"

"My daughter," Irene said. "Where is she? I must reach her before—"

The witch looked Irene in the face. The witch was an ugly old crone, hunched and dirty, with a wart on her nose. "Go to my hut yonder, enter the cage there, and lock yourself in," she said.

Irene tried to resist this ridiculous directive, but found herself compelled. The witch's talent was instant hypnotism, or something stronger; Irene had to obey.

She walked to the hut, entered it, and found the cage inside. She got into it and drew the door closed, hearing the click of its lock.

Now that she had done the witch's bidding, Irene found the compulsion relieved. She was in control of herself again. But she was locked in, and the wooden bars of the cage were too strong for her to break. She had a knife, but knew it would take a long time to saw through one of these bars.

Well, she could cope with that! She dropped a seed on the floor. "Grow!"

The seed sprouted brightly. It was a fire fern. In moments it had set fire to the cage and was burning through several bars.

While she waited, hunched in the corner farthest from the blaze, Irene kept busy. She grew an octopus plant, which she knew would do her bidding. When the witch entered the hut, she would become captive herself. As an added precaution, Irene sprouted a club moss so she could arm herself better.

A few minutes later, the witch entered the hut. The octopus wrapped its tentacles about her, and Irene menaced her with a club. "Now, you illicit creature, I want to know—" Irene began.

The witch looked her calmly in the eye. "Put down the club. Tell your creature to release me."

"Oh, fudge!" Irene swore. "I forgot about the hypno-stare!" But she put down her club, then directed the octopus plant to release the witch. She had some limited powers over the plants she grew, though she still had to be careful with the most aggressive ones. A tangle tree, for example, did not take many orders from anyone. She resolved to turn her back to the witch as soon as the compulsion left her, so that she could not be hypnotized again.

But before that happened, the witch *did* hypnotize her again. "Sit down, woman. Listen to what I say."

Irene sat down on a rickety wooden chair and listened, seething. She had made such an obvious mistake, letting the witch look her in the eye a second time!

"I shall introduce myself," the witch said. "I am Xanthippe, the wicked witch of the wilderness. I associate with the Xanthorrhoed trees, the root plants of Xanth, as their name suggests. You have intruded on my property and you are in my power. I see you are a sorceress yourself, and that pleases me more than you may presently appreciate, but you remain subject to my will. Because I have your daughter."

Irene could not speak, since she had been ordered to listen. But the news electrified her, and she strained forward attentively.

"She and the little dragon are captives of my thyme plant," the witch continued. "They intruded on my premises, as you did, and indulged in much mischief before they were restrained. They loosed my collection of gargan-tuons. There are tuons rampaging all over my coven-tree, where I keep my most valuable exhibits. So they had to be punished. They will remain enchanted forever, until I decide to free them, or at least a century, whichever comes first." She eyed Irene speculatively.

"Oh, to be sure, with your clever control of plants, you could free them, too—but only I know where my thyme plant is hidden and what menaces are guarding it. I can have your child destroyed before you can rescue her. You must have my co-operation, if you wish to save her—and you shall have that only at my price."

Now Irene could speak. "You have the nerve to hold my daughter hostage? Do you know who I am?"

"No," the witch said. "Who are you?"

Irene suddenly realized that this old crone could be much worse to handle if she learned she had the Queen of Xanth in her power. Better to leave her in ignorance. Irene found that the old hag's power could compel her actions but not her words— except when words *were* actions, as in directing her plants to grow or let someone go—so she didn't have to say more than she chose. "I am—Irene. What do I have to do to get my child back?"

The witch studied her appraisingly again. "That's the proper attitude. You strike me as a fine, healthy young woman, with good magical power and some practical skills, such as making your own clothing from towels. You should make an excellent mate for my son, and your talent with plants would assist my own collections."

Irene was aghast. "A m-m—!" She couldn't get the word out. "But I'm *married*! I have a child! That's why I'm out here looking for her!"

"Yes, I want a woman who can breed. I want my son to settle down, to be a family man. To be under the influence of a competent woman and a proven breeder. You'll do."

"I will *not* do!" Irene flared. "You may be able to make me do something for five minutes, but you could never get me to stay with a man I don't love!"

"There is much a knowledgeable woman can do with a man in five minutes, with or without love," Xanthippe remarked. "I can see that you do that, and do it again on another day, as many times as are necessary—and once you carry my son's child, you may not be quite so eager to leave him."

Irene was shocked again at the witch's directness and un-scrupulousness. "This is impossible!"

"I assure you it is possible. How do you think I got my son?"

How else, indeed! Even when young, Xanthippe must have been too ugly to attract a man. But her magic made attraction unnecessary; the man would perform at her behest.

Irene tried again. "I mean my husband would—"

"What would he do, after he learned you carried another man's child?" the witch inquired.

Irene didn't like to contemplate that, so she didn't. "You can't be serious! The moment you aren't watching me, I'll destroy you!"

"And what, then, will happen to your daughter, who remains in my power?" the witch asked. "You may have her back only after a sibling is on the way."

"A sibling!" Irene found it hard even to grasp the enormity of the witch's design. "I'll never—"

"You were unable to locate your daughter before; can you do so now?"

Irene was silent. She couldn't stand the thought of putting Ivy into any unnecessary jeopardy. She couldn't risk wiping out the witch until she had gotten Ivy out of danger.

"I will introduce you to my son Xavier," Xanthippe said. "Perhaps you will like him, though that really doesn't matter. It would simply make it easier for you. Come this way."

Numbly, Irene followed the witch. She had no further thought of harming Xanthippe directly. Ivy was hostage; the witch was in control, for now.

Xanthippe led the way to an orange tree. The trunk and all the leaves were orange, making it distinctive. Chem Centaur was tethered to it by an iron chain fastened to a hind foot, and Grundy Golem was locked in a small mesh cage. The witch had captured the whole party, except for the zombie.

"Wait here," Xanthippe said. "I will bring my son to you." And Irene had to obey.

"Go soak your warty snoot, hag!" Grundy called from the cage.

The witch ignored him and walked on to a dilapidated yellow barn.

"She hypnotized you?" Irene asked Chem.

The centaur nodded grimly. "I closed the cuff on my own leg," she admitted. "I couldn't oppose her, though I desperately wanted to. And Grundy climbed into the cage himself. She just looked each of us in the eye—"

"I know. Too bad the Gorgon wasn't traveling with us."

Grundy doubled over with laughter, though Irene's remark had been serious. She *could* have had the Gorgon in the party, had she but known.

But their time for any exchange of information was limited. "What happened to Zora Zombie?" Irene asked.

"The witch's power didn't work on her," Chem said. "I think the zombie doesn't have enough of an eye or mind to be hypnotized. She wandered off. There's nothing she can do anyway."

"I suppose not," Irene said, testing the chain that held the centaur. It was far too strong for her to break herself, but she knew she could do the job with the right plant.

"Quick, grow something and spring us!" Grundy exclaimed. "Before the old dame gets back. She told you to wait here, but she didn't tell you not to help us."

True, as far as it went. "I can't," Irene said sadly. "She's holding Ivy hostage."

"Oops, that *is* trouble," Chem agreed. "What does she want from us?"

Before Irene could answer, the witch returned. Behind her was a hippogryph carrying a young man, evidently the witch's son.

The remarkable thing about both man and animal was their matching color. Both were golden yellow. The hippogryph had the forepart of a griffin, with a great golden bird-of-prey head and splendid yellow-feathered wings, now folded back along his body; the rest of him was equine, with powerful horse muscles and flashing yellow tail. The man, too, was yellow, at least in his clothing, with vibrant blond hair and beard and a tan that almost glowed like polished gold. He was actually quite handsome.

"What a creature!" Chem breathed with reluctant admiration. Irene wasn't sure which creature the centaur meant, but suspected it was the equine one.

The party arrived. "Get down, Xavier," Xanthippe said. "I want you to meet a woman."

"Aw, Maw," the man said. "Xap and I were just going flying!"

"You ungrateful yellow-bellied wretch!" the witch screamed, showing instant ire that startled Irene because of its contrast to her prior manner. "Get down from there!"

Xavier, the dutiful son, grimaced and dismounted. He seemed to be in his early twenties, and his bronzed muscles bulged. Irene was privately amazed that a woman as ugly as Xanthippe could have a son as robust as Xavier. It must have been some man she compelled to sire her child! But why not? She could afford the best! The witch evidently had excellent taste in human flesh. That thought almost made Irene blush, for the witch had chosen *her* to—never mind.

"See this woman?" Xanthippe said to her son, indicating Irene. "Do you like her?"

Xavier hardly glanced at Irene. "Oh, sure, Maw," he agreed. "She'd be real pretty if she got out of them towels. Now can I go flying?"

"Not yet, son. Notice the body on her. Good legs, good front, nice face. A sweet one to hold."

"Sure, Maw. She's great, if you like that type. Now can I—?"

"Shut up, you imbecile!" the witch screamed at him, and the powerful youth was cowed.

"What a sharp tongue you have, Granny!" Grundy called from his cage.

"I can make her take off the towels so you can see—" Xanthippe continued in her reasonable tone.

"Naw, that's too much trouble, Maw. Me an' Xap was just going out—"

"I think she would make a good wife for you," the witch told her son firmly.

"Aw, Maw, I don't want a wife! I just want to fly." Xavier turned again to his steed, ready to mount. Irene didn't know whether to feel relieved at the youth's evident disinterest, or affronted. She wasn't *that* far over the hill!

"Freeze, you pea-brained creep!" Xanthippe shrieked, and he froze. "You will marry this woman, what's-her-name—"

"Irene, you old hen!" Grundy called helpfully.

"Quiet, you pea-brained creep!" Irene snapped at him in a semiperfect fury.

"This woman Irene," the witch concluded. "She's a good match for you. She's a plant Sorceress, she's got spirit, and she can breed."

"Aw, Maw, I don't know anything about—"

"You don't need to know! This woman has had experience. I'll just give her an order, and she will take it from there. You will find it very easy, even pleasant, to do what is necessary. After that you can go fly."

Aside from the horror of her situation, Irene found a moment to marvel at the naïveté of the young man. Was he really that ignorant of the facts of life? Then she remembered that Dor had been almost as innocent at first. Men seldom knew as much about life as they thought they did; perhaps Xavier merely had a better notion of his ignorance than some did.

"Aw, Maw, I want to fly *now*!" he protested. "Can't it wait for a rainy day or something?"

A rainy day! Irene bit her tongue. It would be just her luck that the fractious cloud would spot her again and make that day come true.

The witch perceived a problem. Obviously she didn't want to be too harsh with her handsome son or to introduce him to the facts of life too abruptly. Irene noticed that Xanthippe did not use her power on Xavier, but employed persuasion instead. She did seem to care about him and genuinely wanted what she thought was best for him. That hardly excused her complete callousness about other people, but did show that she wasn't all bad. Irene would have had more sympathy if her own welfare were not in peril.

Xanthippe tried another kind of coercion. "Your steed needs a good mate, too. I'll breed him to this filly centaur, what's-her-name—"

"Chem, old trot," Grundy filled in.

"Shut up, you imbecile!" Chem snapped, swishing her tail fiercely.

"This filly Chem," the witch finished. "She's young, but centaurs are smart animals; she'll produce a fine foal. Maybe it will have the brains of a human and the wings of a gryph. Wouldn't you like that?"

The hippogryph, no dummy, backed away nervously and half spread his splendid wings. He didn't want to be bred to a centaur!

"Aw, Maw," Xavier said. "Now you've scared Xap. He don't want any foal! Can't we go flying instead?"

"No, you can't, nitwit!" the witch shrieked. "I'm going to breed you both to these fine females. I want to be a grandmother before I kick off. Now let's get on with it!"

Irene, shocked by the whole business, had been silent. Now she realized that she might, after all, have a common cause with the witch's son. "Xanthippe, Xavier doesn't want to marry, especially not an old married woman like me. You can't force your son into a commitment like this and hope to keep his love."

"He'll do what I say!" the witch snapped.

"Maybe so. But you will inevitably alienate him, and the moment you pass away, he'll do what he wants. Can't you see, it's no good! He doesn't want me, and I don't want him. These things never work out unless they're voluntary. Love is one thing you can't compel with your stare. You really have nothing to gain, and considerable to lose."

"Oh, I don't know," Grundy said. "A smart, spirited, golden grandchild who can breed—"

Chem, closest to him, stomped the top of the golem's cage with a forehoof. The sound was like a minor crack of thunder. The golem took the hint and shut up.

"Confound it, I can't wait for him to get around to it," the witch complained. "All he wants to do is fly! A wife and family will make him grow up and settle down."

Irene had to agree with that analysis. Her husband Dor had settled down considerably after their marriage, and that made him a better King. But the witch had decided on the wrong matchup!

"Aw, Maw, I don't want to—"

"Quiet, you moronic child!" Xanthippe shrieked.

"That's telling him, crone!" Grundy called.

Irene cast about desperately for a way out of this. The witch might be wrongheaded, but the witch had the power. "Maybe I could do something else for you," she suggested. "I could grow you a nice tree, even an orchard, with plants that would otherwise take years to mature—"

"I've got trees galore," the witch said. "Your brat messed up my coven-tree exhibits something awful!"

"I'll try to get them back for you!" Irene said.

"No, I was about ready to get some new exhibits anyway. But I planned to do it in an orderly fashion. You have nothing I want except your body for my son."

"Then I'll fetch him a nymph!"

"Nymphs don't breed. They're playmates, not reproducers. He's already had more than enough play time."

There seemed to be some justice in that statement. Irene cudgeled her brain for some other notion that might appeal to the single-minded witch, but nothing offered.

"There must be something!" Chem said. Her fate was on the line, too. "Witches always need strange things for their collections."

"The only other thing I want, you could not get," the witch said shortly. "But as mates for my son and his steed, you are, as it were, birds in the hand."

"Try us," Chem said. "We might surprise you."

"Yeah, try them, battle-axe," Grundy agreed.

"Quiet, you runty rag snippet," the witch told him. "I am just about to try them! Xavier, come stand before this woman, so I can give her the order—"

"I meant the alternative service!" Chem cried.

"Nice choice of terms, mare-mane," Grundy remarked.

"What is the one other thing you want?" Irene cried, picking up on Chem's lead.

"Aw, Maw don't want nothing else—" Xavier began.

"Quiet, you moron!" Irene snapped at him.

Xanthippe considered. "Very well, I will mention the other matter, so that you can see it is useless to consider. All my long and angry life I have wanted three seeds from the Tree of Seeds—"

"Seeds!" Irene exclaimed. "I know about seeds!"

The witch paused, reappraising her. "Why, so you do! You do have a way with plants. However, these are not ordinary seeds, and I seriously doubt—"

"What is this Tree of Seeds?" Chem asked, more cautious about an unknown commitment than Irene was. "I don't believe I have information on it."

Irene realized that it had to be an extremely rare tree, for centaurs were well educated, with a great bent for taxonomy, and Chem specialized in geography. Indeed, she had mapped most of Xanth as part of her course of centaur research. Because of her, the once-unknown regions of the Elements in northern Xanth were now known. She would be aware of the most significant things in Xanth.

"It's on Mount Parnassus, hidden in the illiterate wilderness," the witch explained. "Only my son's hippogryph knows how to reach it from here. And the Tree is guarded by the Simurgh."

"The Simurgh!" Chem explained. "That's the wisest bird alive! It has seen the destruction of the universe three times and has all the knowledge of the ages! I didn't realize it remained in Xanth; I thought it had departed centuries ago. How I'd love to interview it, even for an hour!"

"Which relates to the rest of my desire," Xanthippe said. "What I'd like is a feather from its tail. Those feathers have magical properties, and can cure wounds. But the way to Mount Parnassus is so dangerous—"

"This Tree of Seeds," Irene said. "What kind of seeds does it have?"

"All the seeds produced by all the wild plants that exist," the witch said, her wicked old eyes turning dreamy for a moment. "The seed from which my own coven-tree sprouted came from there centuries ago. Likewise the pagean-tree, geome-tree, infant-tree, indus-tree and psychia-tree."

"I would very much like to see that psychia-tree," Chem murmured. "I suspect that would be a mind-affecting experience."

"There are seeds on the Tree of Seeds that no longer exist

anywhere else," the witch concluded. "Seeds no ordinary person can even imagine!"

"I'm sure a centaur could imagine them," Chem said.

"Such as the ex-seed, the pro-seed, and the inter-seed," Xanthippe said.

"All the seeds that exist!" Irene breathed. "How I'd like to see that Tree!"

"You can't reach it," the witch asserted. "Parnassus is guarded by the Python, who consumes anyone who sets foot there. No one of any intelligence has ventured near Parnassus in decades."

"But we aren't that smart," Grundy said. "We might venture."

For once the big-mouthed golem was correct! "Suppose we make you a deal," Irene said. "We'll fetch your three seeds and one feather, and you'll return my child and let us go."

Xanthippe shook her head. "It's too much of a gamble. You might never return."

"But of course I'll return for my child!" Irene exclaimed.

"Not if you die on the way."

Oh. There was that indeed. Yet if the alternative was to be involuntarily mated to the witch's son—

"We'll do it," Irene decided. "We'll fetch your feather and seeds. If we don't return, you lose. But if we do return, you will have the items you have always wanted that you can get in no other way."

"Double or nothing, bag," Grundy put in.

"I'm not sure—" Xanthippe said, wavering.

"Just tell us how to reach Parnassus."

"I can't tell you," the witch said. "Only the hippogryph knows the way, and only my son can control that beast."

Irene perceived another reason Xanthippe was halfway careful about the feelings of her son. Xavier did have some leverage. Xap would be dangerous indeed, were he not under control.

"So Xav and Xap come along, frump," Grundy said. "No problem there."

Irene winced. No problem? The last thing she wanted was to associate closely with the witch's son, and she doubted Chem was any more sanguine about the hippogryph. Yet it seemed to be the only feasible way to reach Parnassus, and Parnassus seemed to be the only route clear of their present predicament. So if she had to conquer Parnassus to get her child safely back, she would do it. "This time Grundy is right," Irene agreed reluctantly. "They must come along."

"What do you mean, 'this time'?" Grundy cried.

"Quiet, you nitwit!" Chem snapped, poising her forehoof above his cage.

"Xavier and Xap can lead the way, and we'll follow—" Irene began, then broke off, for she saw the zombie. Zora was making her way toward them, carrying something.

Irene sighed inwardly. She had forgotten about Zora! Of course she couldn't neglect the zombie, who had saved them from the monster of the night. Yet Zora would only be a hindrance on this special quest.

The zombie shuffled up. She held out the thing she carried, showing it to Irene. It was a scale from a fish or reptile, apparently broken off in the course of some quarrel or accident. "Gaftsh," she said, blowing out some of her epiglottis.

"This zombie is one of our party," Irene told the witch. She was determined to do the right thing, though she didn't enjoy it. "She will have to come, too."

"How will she travel?" Xanthippe asked. "That hippogryph moves fast; only the centaur will be able to keep the pace, even if Xap keeps to the ground."

"So she'll ride the gryph, old snot," Grundy said.

"Aw, Maw, Xap don't want to carry a living corpse!" Xavier protested.

But the notion of actually getting the seeds had captured Xanthippe's imagination. "Good enough," the witch decided. "The gryph can handle one more. Bring me back my feather and seeds, and I'll free your brat from my thyme." She touched the shackle on Chem's foot and it fell open, freeing the centaur. Then she opened Grundy's cage similarly.

"Which three seeds do you want?" Irene inquired as she and Grundy mounted Chem.

"The seeds of Doubt, Dissension, and War," the old witch said with gusto.

"Doubt, Dis—" Irene started, shocked. "You can't possibly mean—"

"You do want your daughter back?" Xanthippe inquired with a wrinkled smirk.

Chem trotted across to lift Zora up behind Xavier. Neither man nor steed seemed enthusiastic about this companion, but the witch glared them both quiescent. Irene hoped the zombie could ride well enough to stay on.

The hippogryph took off, literally. He spread his wings and launched into the air. Zora started to slide off, but flung her rotten arms around Xavier and kept her seat—though possibly part of that did fall off. Irene twitched an inward smile, wondering how the golden young man was reacting to this embrace.

Chem moved out, trotting to follow below the hippogryph. "See you later, old heifer!" Grundy called back to Xanthippe.

Xap spiraled up at an angle, his wings spreading hugely, their beat so strong that the ascent was steep, despite the considerable mass of the animal and two riders. The flight was magic-assisted, of course; such a creature could never get off the ground in Mundania.

Chem had to break into a canter to stay in range. "That's one healthy animal!" she said, obviously impressed.

Irene had to agree. The witch might be a shrill and ruthless hag, and her son a muscular dunce, but the hippogryph was a phenomenal specimen of its kind. Burdened by the weight of two people, it nevertheless sailed up as if carrying no weight at all. Griffins were impressive, but the hippogryph was more impressive because it had the body mass of a horse, rather than that of a lion.

Then Xap got his bearings and glided southeast. Chem followed, varying her route to pick up decent running terrain. "Did you catch the significance of Zora's find?" she asked as she ran.

"A dumb fish scale?" Grundy demanded slightingly. "Trust a creature whose brain is sludge to think that's worth anything!"

"A small, bright dragon scale," the centaur corrected him. "Zora's brain must be fairly high-quality sludge, for she recognized what was important. I am something of a scholar in the fauna of Xanth, so I know the different types of scales by sight. That variety is unique to the Gap Dragon, but it is too small. So it must be from the rejuvenated dragon."

"Who is with Ivy!" Irene exclaimed, suddenly making the connection. "Did Zora find them?"

"She must have found evidence of their passage, at least," Chem said. "That's why she brought the scale to you. She was trying to say 'Gap.' I was hoping the witch wouldn't catch on."

Grundy clapped his tiny hand to his forehead. "So she was! I heard it and didn't notice!"

"If we fail in this quest and survive, Zora can still help us rescue Ivy, maybe!" Irene said, greatly relieved.

"So it would seem," Chem agreed. "But let's do our best anyway. We have made a commitment, and Ivy's trail may not be easy to pick up, even with that hint—and I really would like to meet the Simurgh."

"But those seeds! Doubt, Dissension, War! How could I deliver that sort of mischief to a person like that? Think of the harm she might do with them!"

"I don't have the answer," the centaur admitted. "I think we shall simply have to let events take their course."

Irene nodded reluctant agreement. She had consented to fetch the seeds for Xanthippe, and she always honored her agreements, even when she regretted them. Her father King Trent had taught her the importance of that.

Chapter 7. Hugo Award

Ivy was a little Sorceress, though not yet recognized as such. Her magic talent was one of the select few that extended beyond the normal limits and had ramifications that would not have been credible anywhere except in Xanth. This was the gift of the Demon X(AN)th, whose enormous magic permeated the Land of Xanth, though the Demon had no interest in the affairs of Xanth. At the behest of Chem's mother Cherie Centaur, the Demon had bequeathed to the descendants of Bink and his wife Chameleon the status of Magicians. Thus, their son Dor was a Magician, destined from birth to become King of Xanth, and their granddaughter Ivy was another, similarly destined. However, the Demon had not bothered to inform anyone of this, allowing each person to find out in due course.

Throughout the volatile history of Xanth, it had always been awkward to mess with Magicians. The hag Xanthippe should have realized this, but she was out of touch with events and did not know with whom she was messing; she would surely pay a price.

Ivy had been trapped by the thyme and held helpless by its timelessness. There were only three ways to escape this trap: to suffer a general holocaust that destroyed the entire region, to be freed by the witch, or to wait for the century plant to bloom. The holocaust was not advisable, for it would destroy Ivy and Stanley, along with the thyme and much of the rest of Xanth and part of Mundania, too. As for the witch, she was not about to free the child before obtaining one feather and three potent seeds, so that wasn't a worthwhile prospect either, because the chances of her obtaining those artifacts were small. And the century plant still had ninety-three years to go before it bloomed.

But Ivy was a Sorceress, which was a sexist definition of a female Magician. Her power was her ability to intensify the qualities of things about her. Thus, though she was ensorcelled by the thyme, she also acted upon it in her curious fashion. The timelessness of thyme became concentrated to an extraordinary degree—and this affected the century plant in which it rested. The century plant thought it was aging at the rate of fifty-two weeks per year, give or take a day or so; or, failing that, at twelve months per year. But the intensification of time near the thyme warped and curved the environment in a manner that possibly only a brilliant Mundane expert might theorize about, and now the century plant was actually aging at the rate of one year per minute.

Thus, in just ninety-three minutes from the time Ivy touched the thyme and fell into its power, the thyme fell into her power. The century plant completed its cycle and bloomed. It shot up a central stalk which branched and flowered. The stalk sprouted right under the thyme, for that was the center of the plant. The witch had put the thyme there because she knew it would not be disturbed for a hundred years, by which time she would no longer be concerned with it—and indeed, it had been all right for the first seven years. Thyme was very important to a person as old as Xanthippe.

Now the flower-stalk ascended, carrying the thyme up with it. The stalk didn't bother with the entranced girl and dragon, who were extraneous to its design. Thus, in due course, the contact between thyme, girl, and dragon was broken. It was a small thyme plant, and its range was limited; this was perhaps fortunate, for otherwise all of Xanth and a smidgeon of Mundania would have experienced the acceleration of time, and that would have been a complication of another nature. When the contact ceased, so did the spell of timelessness.

Ivy and Stanley woke together. They did not yawn and stretch, as they had not been asleep. To them it seemed that no time had passed. They had not aged even ninety-three minutes, since the thyme did not affect all things identically, especially not Sorceresses and their companions. They didn't notice how the sun had jumped an hour and a half ahead in the sky, for it happened to be behind a cloud at the moment.

"Hey!" Ivy complained. "I was just going to get a pretty disk—and it shot up out of reach! That wasn't nice of it!"

The dragon snorted steam, agreeing. He didn't like to see his friend distressed. He tried to climb the flower-stalk, in order to fetch the disk for her, but the stalk was too narrow for him to get a proper grip, and too tough for him to pull down.

"Oh, never mind, Stanley," Ivy said, disgruntled. "I didn't really want it anyway." This was known as the sour grape ploy, and it was adequate for the occasion. "I'm tired of these big trees; let's go back down to the ground."

Stanley happened to be a ground creature himself, so was glad to oblige. They made their way cautiously out of the century plant, which was now larger than it had been, though they hadn't seen it grow. Stanley steamed the spines soft, as he had done before. Then they paused to eat some fruits. Finally they climbed down the big branches of the pagean-tree until they were able to poke their heads below the foliage and see the ground.

Now there was a problem. They were too far from the ground to jump down safely, and the massive trunk of the tree was vertical—too difficult for them to climb.

But Ivy remained a reasonably smart child, just about as smart as she thought she should be, and she soon came up with a notion. "We must call for help. Someone always comes when a damsel calls for help." Someone always had come before, at any rate. "A Night in Shiny Armor, I think."

Stanley wasn't sure about this, but since his specialty was not rescues, he let Ivy handle it.

Ivy took a deep, small breath and screamed: "HELP!"

In a moment something stirred below. It was a person, obviously coming to the rescue. Ivy was delighted.

She peered down, favorably disposed toward her benefactor, whoever or whatever he might be. Sure enough, the Night was a handsome young man with an intelligent face. He seemed to have left his shining armor behind, but perhaps it had been too hot for this warm weather; that didn't matter. She fell instantly in love with him, for this was what rescued damsels in the company of dragons did.

Now it was time for introductions. These things had to be done according to protocol. "Hello, Night-out-of-Armor, what's your name?" she called.

The rescuer looked up. "Hugo," he said after a pause for reflection.

"I'm Ivy. This is Stanley. He's a dragon," she said, completing the formula. "Help get us down, handsome."

Hugo pondered again. The truth was, he had never been considered a bright boy, and certainly not a handsome one, so he wasn't certain what this meant. He looked down at his clothes, which were dirty and ragged. But somehow they didn't seem as disreputable as expected. What he didn't realize was that Ivy's talent was working on him already. She considered anyone who came to rescue her to be a model of intellect and appearance and courage, by definition, so he was assuming these attributes, like them or not.

Indeed, his dull wit was brightening and beginning to function as never before. He needed to help them get down. What was the best strategy? A light bulb appeared above his head, shining its light all about before fading out. "Something to fall on," he said. "Something soft. Like a pile of squishy fruit!"

But Ivy wasn't quite sure about that. "I don't like squishy fruit." Her mother had fed her that when she was a baby, not long ago, and Ivy had made a horrendous face, spat it out, and disliked it instantly and permanently, exactly as any sensible person would.

"Oh." Hugo considered again. He didn't really like squishy fruit either. Unfortunately, that was all he was able to conjure. He looked around.

He was in luck. "A bed bug!" he exclaimed, spying one sleeping nearby.

Ivy remembered that the friendly yak had said there were bed bugs in this neighborhood. "Oh, goody!"

Hugo hurried over, gripped the bug by the headboard, and hauled it across to the pagean-tree. The bug dragged its four little roller-feet but was otherwise passive; it really wasn't constructed for exercise. This was a good one; it had excellent springs and fat pillows.

Ivy approved. She dropped down and bounced on the mattress with a little squeal of joy. There was hardly a more enjoyable pursuit for a child than bouncing on a really soft and springy bed, though the monster under the bed complained about the noise and vibration. But this bed didn't have a monster, so it was all right.

She bounced a few times, then got off so the dragon could come down, too. He did, following her lead. But Stanley had never bounced on a bed before and wasn't as good at it as Ivy was. He flipped tail-over-snout and missed the mattress on the rebound. But that fall was from a lesser height, and he was a tough breed of creature, so he wasn't hurt. One scale did get knocked off, though. Well, he would grow a new one in due course; that spot would be tender for a while, but a dragon learned to cope with such discomfort.

Hugo gazed upon the dragon with a certain dismay. He had spent a day and a night hiding from monsters, and this was certainly a monster, albeit a small one. He was sure he had seen it before.

The dragon for his part, did not really appreciate the appearance of a human being. He had had Ivy all to himself until now. Obviously she liked this boy, and that meant Hugo was a rival for her attention. Once Stanley had come to accept Ivy's attention, he didn't want to share it. So he growled, turned a deeper shade of green, and heated up some steam. One never could tell when a good head of steam might be useful.

Hugo, in turn, got ready to summon some really squishy fruit; the one thing that was good for was throwing it at monsters. Dripping pineapple was especially nice.

Fortunately, in the way of women of any age, Ivy realized there was a problem. She acted with instinctive finesse to alleviate it. "Don't quarrel!" she cried. "You two must get along together, for you are both my friends. Hugo is my boyfriend—" At this, Hugo was freshly startled. "And Stanley is my Dragon friend. So you're friends to each other, too."

Neither boy nor dragon was quite certain of the logic—but this, too, was typical of such situations. Ivy wanted it that way and she perceived them to be friends, so that aspect of their psychology was enhanced, and they were friends. It would not be fair to say it was a completely tranquil friendship, but it would do. Sorcery, as always, was a marvelous thing.

"Now we must go home," Ivy decided. "Where are your folks, Hugo?" She had never been to Humfrey's castle and indeed did not know Hugo was the son of the famous Magician of Xanth.

Hugo considered. "My father's a big baby, and my mother's face turns people to stone," he announced.

"Mine too," Ivy agreed. "Especially when I've been bad. Where's your home?"

Hugo pondered again. He wasn't used to being as smart as this, so it took some reorientation. He did have a fair sense of direction, when he thought to use it. "That way," he said, pointing roughly northeast.

"Okay. We'll go that way." Ivy faced northeast, getting it set in her mind. She had not thought to ask how far it was. It did not occur to any of them that they would have been better off proceeding west to Castle Zombie.

Ivy started marching, and so Stanley and Hugo marched with her.

They entered a deep, dark section of forest where the sunlight did not penetrate and the wind was chill. Ivy felt nervous, since she did not like dark, cold places, but she forged on. The others forged with her.

They soon tired, for they were all young, and rested on a sodden log in the gloom. "I'm hungry," Ivy said. "How can we get food?" She believed she didn't need to be smart now, because, of course, Hugo was smart and he could do the thinking. He was, after all, the Night in Shiny Armor.

"Well, I can conjure some fresh fruit," Hugo said. "But—"

"Oh, goody! I like fresh fruit!" That was quite different from the squished fruit she hated.

"But it isn't very good."

Ivy refused to believe this. "I just know anything you do is good, Hugo, because you're such a handsome, wonderful, talented person. You'll bring perfect fruit. Not that squishy stuff grown-ups use to punish babies with."

She did have a point. But Hugo had less confidence in his ability than she did. "You won't like it," he warned and conjured an apple.

The apple appeared in his hand. It was a fine, large, red, fresh, firm fruit, and looked absolutely delicious. Hugo gazed at it with amazement. All his prior apples had been more like applesauce enclosed in wrinkled bags formed of peel. What had gone wrong?

"Goody!" Ivy exclaimed, accepting it while Hugo stood frozen. She opened her little mouth and took a big bite. The apple crunched wholesomely.

"Scrumptious!" she pronounced around her mouthful. "Bring some more!"

Hugo shook his head as if clearing it of dottle. Disbelievingly, he conjured a banana. It appeared in his hand, big and firm and yellow. He made a motion to peel it, but his belief failed, so he offered it to the dragon instead.

Stanley had only learned to like fresh fruit since encountering Ivy, and this was the first banana he had met. He set it on the ground and steamed it. The fruit cooked and split open, smelling delicious. The dragon decided he liked it and he slurped it up complete. The skin wasn't as chewy as bone, but would do.

Hugo conjured a plum, taking courage. It seemed as good as the other fruit. He nerved himself and took a small bite. The fruit was juicy and tasty. "I can't understand it," he said. "Usually my fruit is as rotten as a zombie."

"Zombies are fun," Ivy said. "They know all kinds of games, like hide-in-the-grave and yuch-in-the-box."

Hugo hadn't thought of it quite that way before, but realized it was true.

"You're a good conjurer," Ivy continued confidently. And of course, in her presence, he was. His talent had been enhanced into competence.

After that, reveling in his newfound power, Hugo conjured fruit freely, so that all of them could feast. He produced a whole pile of beefsteak tomatoes for the dragon, as Stanley preferred meat when he could get it. For the first time in his life, Hugo felt competent.

They resumed their travel, more slowly now because of darker and more scary terrain and their tiring legs. None of them had ever realized just how big Xanth was. Always before, they had been carried from place to place on carpets or on centaurs, so that long distances seemed short. Walking was a different matter. But they were confident they would arrive where they were going if they just kept at it.

Ivy's mind wandered, as there certainly wasn't much for it to do around here. She thought of her nice room in Castle Roogna, with the magic tapestry that showed scenes of the fabulous history of Xanth. She thought of the nice cherry trees of the castle orchard, with the exploding red fruits. She thought of the friendly ghosts of the castle. She did not think of Millie as a ghost, for Millie had returned to life long before Ivy was born, but fun-loving Jordan was still there. Jordan had helped save Xanth from the Nextwave, she had been told, so he was now in excellent repute and was sometimes allowed to baby-sit her when her folks were out. It was amazing how much more interesting home became when she was far away from it!

Ivy paused in her thoughts. Was that the ghost-centaur she had glimpsed? Maybe not, since there was no sign of it now.

But Hugo paused too. "Hey—Imbri's here!" he exclaimed.

"Who?"

"The day mare. She brings me daydreams all the time, back home."

"Is she a centaur?"

"No, she's a horse, of course. A mythical animal with the front end of a sea horse and the hind end of a centaur. She used to be a night mare, and would carry bad dreams to sleepers. But now she is a day mare and she brings good daydreams. I like her because she visits me a lot when I'm lonely and she never says anything bad to me—to clean up my room or wash behind my ears. But I didn't think she could find me out here in the jungle."

"Oh, I guess it was me she found. Can we ride her?"

"No, dummy. She's a phantom horse."

Ivy had not heard the term "dummy" before, as it was not used in her home, and she took it to be an endearment because that was the kind of term Nights in Shiny Armor used on rescued damsels. She formed half a flush of pleasure. "Can she tell our folks where we are?"

"My father, maybe. He can talk to mares when he uses a spell. But he's a baby."

"Oh." Ivy didn't quite understand this figure of speech, so she ignored it.

"But I can talk to her a little, because she brings me so many dreams. Sometimes I spend whole days alone in my room, and Imbri keeps me company. She's a great companion."

"Can she show us the best way home?"

"I don't know. Her job is to bring dreams; she gets sort of invisible any other time." Hugo concentrated. "No, she says she's not allowed to show us where to go. But she says be careful, because there's something awful bad ahead."

"Something awful?" Ivy asked, worried. "Oh, I don't like awful things!"

The dragon had another opinion: he loved awful things! He perked up his ears and fired up his steam.

"That's right—Stanley will protect us," Ivy said with happy revelation. "He can fight anything!" She patted the little dragon's hot, scaly head, and because she said it, it almost seemed possible.

They went on. Sure enough, something awful appeared. At first Ivy thought it was the monster under the bed, but its hands weren't big, horny, or callused, so it couldn't be that. It had multiple bug-legs and wings and feelers, and a huge, horrible mask of a face.

"A bugbear!" Hugo cried, appalled.

If this monster was related in any way to the other bug they had encountered, the bed bug, it certainly wasn't letting that show. It wasn't large, as monsters went, but it didn't need to be, for it specialized in snatching children, especially naughty ones. Since naughtiness was part of the definition of childhood, every child who ever existed was vulnerable.

The bugbear advanced on Ivy, who knew she was naughty

because she had gotten herself lost. Its bug-eyes glared malevolently at her, and its bug-mandibles gaped slobberingly.

Ivy screamed, and not merely because that was what a damsel in distress was supposed to do. She wasn't really afraid of dragons; they were distant adult creatures, except for Stanley, who was her friend. But the bugbear was her size, and it was close; it knew exactly how to terrify her. It grew larger and worser as it tromped toward her.

Hugo conjured a ripe tomato and hurled it at the monster. His aim was better than usual, because Ivy believed Nights had good aim, and the fruit splattered on the bugbear's face. This made the face only slightly less ugly than before. Still the thing advanced, hairy bug-arms reaching.

"Bug off!" Hugo cried, throwing an even riper tomato. But the monster merely sloughed the squish from its nose and grabbed for Ivy.

Now Stanley acted. He aimed his snout, pumped up his pressure until his safety valve whistled, and let fly a searing jet of superheated steam. His steam had become much fiercer since he had started associating with Ivy.

The steam struck the horrible mask-face and ricocheted off. But the heat and moisture were so intense that the bugbear's face began to melt. Dripping different colors, the thing retreated.

Stanley pursued, pumping up another burst of steam. The bugbear turned tail and fled. Its tail was not fearsome at all. Such monsters had all their fear in front and became next to nothing when retreating. Indeed, this one shrank visibly with each step it took, and soon it vanished entirely.

"Oh, Stanley, you're so wonderful!" Ivy exclaimed, hugging his neck. She polished up the pedestal, which was higher and prettier now, though still invisible. The dragon discovered again that he liked getting hugged by a cute little girl, and the pedestal was actually a pretty comfortable place to rest on his laurels. He made a low, purring growl. It was fun saving damsels from bug-eyed monsters.

Hugo was not entirely satisfied, however. He felt that more attention was being lavished on Stanley than the dragon warranted. In fact, he was a mite jealous, which was odd, because it was the dragon who was green.

They ate some more of Hugo's conjured fruit, and proceeded with greater confidence. They had met and conquered an enemy!

The jungle thinned as the land rose. Soon they were climbing a fairly hefty hill. The dragon puffed naturally, but now Hugo and Ivy were puffing, too. "Oh, it's hot!" Ivy complained. Actually, the air was normal temperature; it was Ivy who was heating.

Then the air cooled as they came to a region of mist. The wet air brushed by them, coating them with moisture. The dragon didn't mind, for he was a steamer and drew on mist to replenish his water supply. Mist was rather like cold steam. True steam, like true water vapor, was invisible, so it could hide magically; but water droplets tended to form from it, giving its presence away. Had the mist been able to maintain its invisibility, Stanley would not have been able to tap it for his own purpose. But the two children did not appreciate this advantage and were uncomfortable.

"Oh, let's rest," Ivy said. "My legs are like noodles!" Indeed, they seemed to bend under her, forcing her to flop on the ground. The others were glad enough to rest.

But they were not fated to rest long. There was something in the mist behind them, and it was not pleasant. They couldn't see it, or hear it, yet they were aware of it. Stanley fired a jet of steam back in its direction, but with no effect. The problem with steam was that its range was limited; if a thing was out of sight, it was also out of reach.

Then thunder rumbled, increasing their nervousness. Ivy and Stanley were not safely ensconced in the coven-tree this time; they could get wet. That bothered Ivy more than it did Stanley.

A bolt of lightning scorched into a rock nearby. "Oh, I don't like this at all!" Ivy said, jumping up.

They hurried away from the thunder and lightning, going on up the hill. This was just as well, for the thunder continued to rumble behind, punctuated by more shafts of lightning. Breathlessly, they scrambled toward the top of the hill.

At last they broke out of the top of the mist. It was, in fact, a sunken cloud. There were other clouds above, but the intervening layer was clear.

They looked around. The top of the hill was like an island in the nether sea of cloud, poking up through it. As far as they could see in each direction, there was the wavy, white surface. The effect was rather pretty, in its fashion. Ivy was quick to appreciate prettiness wherever it occurred. That was the way she had been raised.

"Do you think Imbri will bring us a daydream of being carpet-wrecked on this island, and we can't leave it until the fog goes down, so we have to stay here forever and just eat fruit?" Ivy asked.

Hugo shrugged. "I doubt it," he said. There was the merest flicker of something disappearing, like a black horse's tail; the daydream had been canceled at the last moment and the mare had to depart.

But now a small gray cloud floated down from the upper layer. It formed a malevolent face under its pointed crown. The mouth opened, and a small roll of thunder came out.

The day mare reappeared. This time Ivy could see her clearly. She was a black equine, hardly more than a shadow, with flaring mane and tail.

"It wants to know who on earth you are," a centaur said in Ivy's mind.

Surprised and confused by this development, Ivy did not answer.

"That's how Imbri talks," Hugo explained. "She gives you a dream, and the dream figure speaks. Imbri can't talk herself, 'cause she's a horse. But the dream figures can. Just answer it back."

Ivy was glad Hugo was so smart and knew all about such things. "The centaur?"

"No, dummy, the cloud! Imbri's translating for it."

Ivy blushed again with pleasure at the endearment. This was all new to her, but she decided it was all right. It was nice of Mare Imbri to help out like this.

"I'm Ivy," she said to the cloud. "Who are you?"

The mare must have projected a talking dream to the cloud,

for it paused a moment, then scowled darkly and blew out another piece of thunder. Ivy was a little frightened when it did that, but tried not to show it because she wasn't sure Stanley could make this thing go away.

"He says you're supposed to recognize the King of Clouds when you see him and perform abject obeisance," the centaur-dreamlet said.

Ivy looked at the ground and dug a toe in the dirt, trying to fathom what "abject obeisance" meant.

"That's better," the centaur said. "The cloud sees you are bowing and/or curtseying. He says he is his Majesty Cumulo-Fracto-Nimbus, the Lord of the Air. He says you remind him of someone he doesn't like—a female with green hair."

Ivy realized that would be her mother Irene. She was about to ask where the cloud had seen her, but Hugo spoke first. "Aw, Fracto's just a bit of scud," he said depreciatingly.

The cloud heard that, and evidently needed no translation. He swelled up and turned purply-black. Lightning speared out of his Majesty's nose, followed by a belch of thunder and a smattering of rain-spittle. Hugo had to jump to avoid being scorched. It seemed clouds were sensitive about name calling.

"How dare you refer to the Lord of the Air as 'scud'!" the dream centaur translated. "He wants you to know he hails from a long and foggy line of lofty meteorological effects, from Cirrus through Stratus. His relatives process the water that grows all the plants of Xanth and fills all the lakes! He advises you that, without his kind, the whole land would be a dust bowl and you would be ashes! He is Fracto the King, a real Thunderhead!"

"Dunderhead," Hugo agreed, with uncommon wit. Nights were noted for that.

The cloud turned so black he was almost a Black Hole. He blew out such a blast of fog admixed with thunder that he nearly turned himself inside out.

"Oh, now Hugo's done it," the dream centaur said. "The King of Clouds is very volatile and tempest-headed. Flee before he strikes!"

"But there's more thunder down there!" Ivy protested, looking at the roiling layer of fog below.

The Fracto-King shaped himself up enough to take good aim at Hugo. Now he looked like a towering anvil. But before he could hammer out a devastating thunderbolt, Stanley stepped forward and shot a fierce jet of steam into the spongy nether region.

This would have sent any ordinary monster sailing high with a youp of pain, but the steam had little visible effect on the cloud. Clouds were composed of water, as was the dragon's steam; the jet only added to Fracto's strength.

Then Ivy had a bright-bulb notion. "Hugo!" she cried. "Conjure some fruit!"

Hugo conjured a watermelon and heaved it at the cloud. Cumulo-Fracto-Nimbus recoiled, but then saw that this was only a fruit, not a plant, and surged back. When the melon passed harmlessly through the cloud and splatted against the ground, the moisture only added to the cloud's strength.

"No, Hugo," Ivy clarified. "A pineapple!"

Hugo caught on, for Nights were very quick to grasp battle strategies. "Yes, I can do it now!" he cried. A huge, firm, potent pineapple appeared in his hand. Just before Fracto spat out his next lightning bolt, Hugo heaved the fruit.

The pineapple disappeared into the mouth of the cloud just as the lightning bolt emerged. The two collided—and the pineapple exploded. The blast was phenomenal. It blew the King apart. Fragments of Fracto fog shot out in an expanding sphere, jags of sundered lightning radiated out like a sunburst, and thunder crashed into the ground, bounced, and lay quiet.

"Ooo, you destroyed him!" Ivy exclaimed, nervously chewing on a finger. She wasn't accustomed to such violence.

"You can't destroy a cloud that way," the dream centaur said. "Fracto is somewhat like a demon. He will recoalesce, worse than before, in a few minutes. Flee!"

Ivy saw that it was so. Already the mean little scud-clouds were globbing together, forming larger fragments, each with a single spike of Fracto's crown. This was no safe place!

"Conjure some fresh cherry bombs!" Ivy cried to Hugo. "We'll beat a strategic retreat!" She almost surprised herself with that word "strategic"; it had been beyond her comprehension before, though she had heard her father use it when dis-

cussing the ancient War of the Nextwave, which had happened
two years before she was born. But now she was in a battle
situation, and the meaning of the term was manifesting clearly
enough.

"Gotcha," the boy agreed, with the excellent grammar of
the typical Night. A huge bunch of cherries appeared, a double
handful. He flipped one cherry at the northeast side of the
island, and when the bomb exploded, the layer of cloud there
was disrupted. It started closing in again immediately, but
obviously the fight had been temporarily knocked out of it.

Hugo marched down, clearing the way with a series of
detonations. Whenever thunder threatened, Hugo threw a cherry
at it, and the effort dissipated explosively.

Before long they emerged below the mist. The cloud had
suffered enough concussion. It lifted high in the sky, out of
reach, and floated away in a gray dudgeon.

Ivy was thrilled by the victory. "You defeated Fracto!" she
exclaimed. "Oh, let me award you, Hugo!" She flung her arms
about him and planted a fat kiss on his left ear, in the way she
had. She might have had her terminology a trifle confused, but
the boy was quite satisfied with his award. It was the first such
thing he had ever earned. He began, almost, to believe that he
might be worthwhile.

Stanley might have had a different opinion, and his pedestal
seemed somewhat cramped, but he was so glad to get away
from the clouds that he didn't bother to develop that opinion.
He did rather like the cherries; they were his kind of fruit. The
pineapple, too; that had been a real blast!

They continued on through the valley. But the jungle remained thick with recognizable menaces like tangle trees and
hanging vines—an unfortunate animal caught in one of the
latter was not a pretty sight—and unrecognizable ones like
sections of ground that were suspiciously still. The shadows
were lengthening, where they showed at all. It was obvious
the three of them needed a safe place to spend the night.

Stanley sniffed the ground. He had excellent reptilian per-
ceptions. Little drifts of steam puffed up between sniffs. He
picked up some kind of scent and followed it to the side. Ivy
and Hugo trailed after him.

The valley narrowed here, becoming a kind of chasm. Suddenly the side of the chasm opened into a hole—a large cave. In the fading light, they could see that it was a fine, dry place, with warm air wafting from it. It seemed to be the shelter they were looking for.

They entered, found a convenient ledge, and hauled in some fragrant brush to make a comfortable nest for the three of them. Hugo conjured several kinds of fruit, and they feasted and tossed the seeds on the floor below. Then, in the dark, they settled down to sleep.

In what seemed like the middle of the night, something huge and sweaty loomed in the entrance of the cave. They couldn't see it, but the ground shook with its tread, and the air stank with its body odor, and its great rasping breath stirred breezes near the top of the cave.

Abruptly wide awake, the three young travelers cowered in their nest, aware that they had camped in the lair of a monster. The very worst place!

The monster didn't spot them. It had brought something in with it, evidently a dead animal. They heard the crunching of flesh and bones as the monster consumed the animal. Then the creature flopped down across the cave entrance and snored. The sound was like the distant roaring of Sphinxes with indigestion.

They were trapped inside the monster's cave, and the coming of the light of dawn would expose them to the monster's view. How were they going to get out of this picklement?

Chapter 8. Tisi, Alec & Meg

They traveled southeast into the depths of Unknown Xanth. Chem was delighted, for it was her personal mission to map all of the peninsula she could find, especially what had never before been recorded. Periodically she projected her magic map, adding the new features and marking their progress with a neat, black, dotted line.

Grundy, true to his fashion, irritated her by finding minor fault with the details. "Your stupid line-dots are covering up key features," he said, pointing to a section of the line. "There's a tiger lily squished under this dot!" He pointed to one of them.

"Serves it right," Chem retorted. "It snapped at my tail as I passed it."

Irene looked up, keeping track of the flying hippogryph. She was half afraid the beast would disappear entirely, but evidently Xavier was taking his mother's directive seriously and was guiding them correctly. It was obvious that the gryph could have flown much higher and faster than it was doing, had it so chosen. At least those two were getting their desire: to go fly. Even if they did have to carry a zombie along.

"Hey, that's nice," Grundy said, reaching out to grab a small flower from a plant growing on a close bank.

"Don't touch it!" Irene warned.

Naturally the golem touched it anyway.

"Eeeek!" the flower shrieked piercingly, wrenching itself away.

Startled, Grundy looked back at the protesting flower. "What was that?"

"I *told* you not to touch that touch-me-not," Irene said complacently. "They are delicate plants, and don't like to be handled by clumsy oafs."

The golem started to say something, then thought better of it.

They continued on through a field of creature plants, generally harmless but sometimes startling. Duckweed quacked, an alligator pear ground its teeth at them—naturally it had two jaws for the purpose, an upper and a lower, making the pair—a windmill palm rotated its great blade-leaves, causing wind to gust past them, a pig lily oinked, a pussy-foot crept away on little fog-feet, fish grass swam away, several toad plants croaked with great displays of mortal agony, and a money plant waved green papery leaves at them. Then the air was filled with the frozen petals from a giant snowflake plant; the petals settled in a maidenhair tree, much to her annoyance. She took a brush from a bottle-brush plant and brushed off the snow, then plucked a powder-puff to restore her complexion.

Chem, distracted by the novel plants, stumbled against a rock. Fortunately, it was a sham-rock, so her hoof wasn't hurt. A real rock would have been much worse. A running myrtle, spooked by the noise, ran off. A nearby punk tree laughed, making the sound by cracking its wooden knuckles and creaking its limbs.

"Yeah?" Grundy demanded, always ready for an argument. "You ain't so hot yourself, punk!"

A short distance away, a pencil tree was making busy notes on a paper plant. Irene smiled; apparently to these plants, the sight of a centaur, woman, and golem was worthy of note. The visitors were as strange to the plants as the plants were to the visitors. But notes weren't really necessary, as there were several forget-me-not flowers around to remember.

Near the edge of the field, a spider lily was hot in pursuit of a butterfly flower, while silver bells rang a warning. That startled a zebra plant who was grazing on some unlucky clover. Chicken corn squawked as the zebra ran past, and a curiosity plant craned its stem to see what was going on.

They must be getting closer to the Tree of Seeds, Irene reflected, for all these unusual plants had to have sprouted from seeds scattered from an unusual source. The thought of that Tree excited her. She would try to fetch the witch's three bad seeds, but she also hoped to garner some exotic specimens for herself. All the seeds of the wilderness would be available!

As they re-entered the deeper jungle, Grundy reached for a feather fern, surely intending some ticklish mischief with it, but a fan palm fanned it aside. The golem slapped at the palm, but it drew back, closing its fingers about itself, and all Grundy struck was a section of a neighboring crown-of-thorns. That plant dropped its thorny crown on the golem's head. What the golem said as he wrenched the prickly crown off was not comprehensible, since it was in plant language, but a bleeding-heart vine blushed, a trumpet lily sounded a retreat, an artillery plant fired off a salute, and a never-never plant wilted.

They halted for a snack, as traveling made them hungry. Xap and Xavier came down; company might not appeal to them, but the food certainly did, and they knew they could separate from the zombie when they landed, at least for a while.

Irene grew a custard-apple plant, a honey plant, and a swiss-cheese plant for Xavier, Chem, and herself; a hot red pepper for Xap; and a genuine has-bean for Grundy.

Evening was nearing. "How much farther do we have to go?" Irene asked Xavier.

"Oh, Xap could be there in an hour," the yellow man replied cheerfully. "But I guess you'll need more time."

"Yes," Chem agreed succinctly. It was evident she was tired from the long run through such varied terrain. Wings were definitely an asset for this sort of excursion.

"So we'd better make camp," Grundy said. "And move on to Parnassus in the morning."

"Yes, I think that's—" Irene started. Then she froze, absolutely horrified.

There, at the base of a barrel cactus, lay the battered body of a child. It looked like a girl, and Irene knew with a sick and awful certainty whom it had to be, for the hair had a green tint.

Her vision, when they approached Castle Zombie—had it come true?

She forced her frozen limbs to move, and ran to the body—and there was nothing. Just undisturbed forest floor.

"Whatever did you see?" Chem asked solicitously. "I saw nothing out of the ordinary."

"It must have been—my mistake," Irene said faintly. "I saw—Ivy. She was—she looked dead!"

"But your ivy plant remains healthy," the centaur pointed out. "So whatever was there, it could not have been your daughter."

"Yes, of course," Irene agreed, touching the ivy plant. "I should have realized. But it had green hair—"

"Oh, that's the fetch," Xavier said. "Don't pay that no mind, miss."

"The what?" Irene asked dazedly.

"The fetch. It's around our place all the time. I told you, it don't mean nothing."

Chem switched her tail nervously. "I'm sure that is the case, Xavier. But what exactly is the fetch? An apparition?"

"Naw. It's when you see a live person, only you see him dead. Maw likes the fetch; it suits her sense of humor."

"It would," Grundy put in.

"The person you see dead—is really alive?" Irene asked, her horror abating. It was not like her to be so destabilized by such a minor event, but this vision had reinforced her prior vision, reviving a deeper horror, and that was hard to shake.

"Sure. Always," Xavier said. "It ain't no fun for the fetch to show a real dead person."

"Fun!" Chem exclaimed indignantly.

"I don't like the fetch," Xavier confessed. "It used to be death to see it, in the old days when Xanth was new; now it's just bad luck. Maw likes bad luck, but I don't."

Irene glanced sidelong at the handsome young man, liking him better despite his backwardness. "You don't get along with your mother?"

"Oh, I get along. She tells me what to do, and I do it, so she don't use the eye on me. But I'd rather fly."

Irene could appreciate why. Any normal person would seek an excuse to spend time away from such a witch. "Thank you for the information about the fetch," she told him. "It's a great relief to me."

"Well, you're a pretty gal, real pretty, even if Maw does say so," he said, as if that related.

Irene considered the ramifications of that minor comment before responding. His mother the witch had wanted to match the two of them, and both Xavier and Irene herself had resisted. So he had complimented her, despite the negative phrasing. She rather liked, at the age of twenty-eight, being called a "pretty gal." Her days of girlhood were long past, and sometimes she missed them. She had been a showoff and a tease a dozen years ago, and though it embarrassed her to remember it, she had to admit it had been fun. So if someone saw her as that sort now, she was not really displeased. Even if he was an ignorant lout and she was a devoted wife to her distant husband and mother of a precious child. So she behaved recklessly and returned the favor. "And you're a handsome lad."

"Aw, don't start on that mush stuff," he said, disgusted.

Irene smiled privately. Xavier was truly a boy at heart! The witch must really have sheltered him from life.

Grundy chuckled, though theoretically he had not been listening.

Xavier grimaced. "Maybe I better clear up a misunderstanding," he said. "I don't need no help from Maw to figure out what to do with a nymph, when it comes to that. It's just that something like marriage is too important to be done offhandedly. I aim to make my own choice of women—and when I do, it'll be forever. Maw don't understand that; maybe you do."

Irene appraised him again. He made a good deal more sense than she had thought him capable of. "Yes, perfectly," she agreed. "I wish you well."

"And the same goes for Xap. He knows his own mind; he just hasn't found no fem-gryph he likes yet."

Irene didn't comment; she was satisfied to let it stand exactly at that. It was not, after all, so bad traveling with this pair of males.

She grew a nice tree house and some cushion cactus for bedding—that kind had spines so soft they hardly even tickled—and swept out the house with some broom she sprouted for the purpose. Xavier watched her at work with open admiration. "You sure are good at that," he exclaimed.

"I should be," Irene murmured. "It's my talent." Then, to distract his interest, which she judged to be getting possibly too personal, she asked: "What is your talent, Xavier?"

"Oh, I zap things," he said nonchalantly. "It ain't nothing much."

"Xap? Your hippogryph?"

"Not Xap. Zap. With a Z-snore sound."

Irene couldn't distinguish the distinction of pronunciation but concluded that one was the animal, the other an action. "You zap things," she repeated.

"I don't ever do it to friends," he clarified. "I don't like hurting folks. But when I'm hunting or something, or if a monster comes after me—" He shrugged.

That sounded like a weapon. Irene's interest increased. They were deep in unexplored Xanth, and monsters could appear at any time. Xavier had evidently traveled through this region and had no fear of it, so his zapping must be effective. Of course, the hippogryph represented considerable protection for him, so maybe his talent didn't matter. "Could you demonstrate?"

"I guess so." He looked about. "See that cobra plant getting ready to strike the filly's leg?"

Irene looked, startled. Sure enough, the plant was rearing its flattened stem, with two thorn-fangs glistening from its flower. When a cobra plant spread such a cape, the prudent person vacated the region quickly. But Chem was in dialogue with Xap, Grundy translating. Chem wanted to determine a good mappable route to Parnassus, so that the mountain would no longer be unattainable. She did not see the dangerous plant, and Irene was afraid to call out to her for fear that would trigger the strike. It was a delicate situation. "I see it," she murmured.

Xavier pointed his right forefinger. Something shot out from it at about the speed of light, possibly a little faster, and zapped right through the lifted cobra head. The plant hissed and expired, bleeding poisonous sap.

"Why—" Irene said, astonished. "You can kill with that!"

"Oh, sure. Anything, any time. But I don't like to hurt creatures. I mean, they got feelings and things, same as I do. So I just go fly with Xap and I zap at the clouds. It don't hurt them none, you see, and it sharpens my aim. That's fun. 'Course, there's this one cloud, King Fracto, who don't like it; he zaps back with lightning jags. Xap lost some tail feathers once— well, he don't have tail feathers, but same place. Fracto's always looking for a fight."

"I think I've met him," Irene said, remembering the cloud she had encountered on the way to the Good Magician's castle. "He has a bad attitude."

"I don't mind zapping Fracto. But I wouldn't zap a bird."

Or a person, she trusted. "That's very good, Xavier," she said carefully. "Certainly you don't want to hurt any friendly creatures."

He looked at her more squarely. "Gee, you sure *are* pretty, miss. You got a shape on you like a nymph."

And he had told her he knew what to do with a nymph. It seemed that, though he resisted his mother's influence and was determined to make up his own mind, that mind had not yet excluded Irene from consideration. She could not afford to have his interest fix on her in that manner. Even if he were more innocent than he claimed, it was a fact that innocent youths did not necessarily remain so indefinitely. "I'm an old married woman, looking for her child," she said quickly.

"Oh, sure, you'll get the kid back safe," he agreed encouragingly. "Too bad Maw caught you, the way she does everyone, or you'd probably have found the tot by now."

Very likely true, Irene reflected ruefully. The distractions of this quest to Parnassus had blunted her concern somewhat, for immediacies always came first, but she knew she could never really rest until Ivy was safe again.

What she had learned about Xavier was important, too. Before this conversation, it had not occurred to her that this backwoods hick could be dangerous. He was a powerful man, his talent was deadly, and his steed was one of the most formidable creatures of Xanth. If he had shared his mother's temperament, or if for any reason he turned against Irene—

She had a fine line to walk. She could not afford to have

Xavier become either too friendly or too unfriendly. It would be best if he and Xap flew elsewhere, as soon as Parnassus was reached.

Chem turned about and came over, carrying Grundy. "Xap says there is some bad terrain between us and Parnassus," she said. "He can fly over it, but I can not, so I've got to scout it out. Then I'll be able to thread my way through it safely. He says there's a knoll not far distant from which we can see the mountain, a good place from which to map the intervening terrain. If we go immediately, we can reach the knoll before dark. So if you don't mind, Irene—"

"You want us all to go?" Irene asked, dismayed. "I can't finish growing the tree house after dark—"

"No, I can move much faster alone," the centaur said.

"But you're tired—"

"Not any more."

"You don't need me along, do you?" Grundy asked. "I want to rest."

"Yes, naturally you will remain here," Chem said, smiling obliquely. "I will not require translation on this foray."

"Good enough," Grundy said, jumping down.

"But are you sure you want to—to go alone with such a creature—?" Irene asked worriedly.

Again that oblique smile. "I am sure."

An amazing notion pushed at Irene's consciousness as she glanced at the powerful bird-horse standing a short distance away. Xap was as fine a specimen of creature as she had seen in a long time, all muscle and feather and gleam. Could Chem want some private time with the hippogryph? Impossible! And yet centaurs were crossbreeds, and so were hippogryphs, with a common heritage through their equine ancestry. Chem had found no suitable male centaur, and Xap had found no female of his kind. Could Chem want a foal who could fly?

Irene shifted her thoughts. It was none of her business. "I'm sure we can get along here until you return. We do need to find a good route to Parnassus." Among other things, she added silently.

"Excellent." Chem turned about and trotted back to Xap.

She did indeed seem to have lost her fatigue. Then the two shifted into a gallop and were quickly out of sight.

Irene shook her head. "And I thought I understood centaurs!" she exclaimed to herself. It seemed the witch's notion of breeding had fallen on fertile soil, after all.

Xavier stared after the two. "Well, I'll be jiggered! She's grounded him! I thought he didn't go for landbound fillies!"

"Never underestimate the power of a filly," Irene murmured. She remained astonished at this development, but cautioned herself that it was mostly conjecture. She could be misreading it all.

She wished Chem well, in whatever the centaur had in mind, but was now doubly nervous about her own situation. She was virtually alone with a man who could zap holes in creatures. Of course she could grow plants to protect herself—but she didn't want to do that unless she was quite certain of the need. The manner in which Xavier had zapped the cobra plant unnerved her, now that she thought about it. She would not be able to handle him with mere pussy-willows!

Of course Grundy was here, and Zora Zombie, but she really would have preferred Chem. However, the centaur had her own affairs, if that was not putting it too bluntly.

The tree house was almost complete. It would have been done before now if Ivy had been here, Irene knew. Her power was diminishing in the absence of her daughter. The loss would not be critical, but it was noticeable. She had allowed enough time, for the daylight had not yet faded. She would plant some sword ferns around the base of the tree to prevent intrusion by nocturnal predators; the fern would not grow any more by night, but wouldn't need to; any foot stepping on it would get slashed.

Now there was the problem of sleeping. She hadn't thought of it before, being concerned with her mission and the unusual social interactions this party was experiencing. She had once supposed that the trip to Parnassus could be completed in a few hours, perhaps a day. A foolish notion, obviously. So they had to camp along the way, which was routine. There was room for four in the tree house. But when the four were a woman, a golem, a zombie, and a strange man . . .

She could take precautions, however. She climbed into the

tree house and planted a monkey-puzzle tree. She knew what its grown configuration would be, so she would be able to crawl in and out of its cagelike puzzle readily, while others would not. She sprouted a few saw ferns at the entrance; they would not saw at her, but would at others, and she would have a fairly secure, fairly private chamber within the tree house, without having to make an issue of it. A lot could be done with plants when a person had the talent, as well as a little foresight.

But oh, she wished she were back with Dor and Ivy at Castle Roogna! She worried how Dor was getting along without her. He really didn't have much of a head for governing; few men did, aside from her father. That was why women were essential.

Well, that was hardly the only reason women were necessary! Nonetheless, men had their uses, too.

Irene jumped down from the tree house, then lifted her head, hearing a noise. It sounded like the screeching of a wounded hydra.

Xavier was listening, too. "Hey, I don't like that," he said. "Could be a covy of harpies. If it comes too close, I'll have to zap it."

Now Irene was glad about his talent, for the sounds were raising hairs on her neck. So far, they had been fortunate and had not encountered anything bad; that luck was evidently about to change.

"It's coming close," Grundy said. "Irene, you'd better grow a plant quickly."

But darkness was closing rapidly, inhibiting her power. Also, until she knew the precise nature of the threat, she could not select an appropriate seed—and she feared by then it would be too late. "I think we'll have to depend on Xavier," she said reluctantly. It wasn't that she doubted the young man's competence or courage; she just didn't like the notion of having to depend on any man other than her husband for anything.

The screeching came closer. Not harpies, she decided, but perhaps something related. Then, in the gloom, three shapes appeared—hooded, cloaked old women, crying to one another in raucous, whining, ill-tempered tones.

"If I didn't know better," Xavier murmured grimly, "I'd

swear that was my mother Xanthippe. But she's yellow, and there's only one of her."

The last of the light showed their faces. "They're real dogs," Grundy said.

He was speaking literally. The faces of the three creatures were strongly canine, with projecting snouts, furry ears, and bloodshot eyes on the sides of their heads. Long, red tongues licked canine teeth between screeches, as if moistening them for the next effort.

But that was not the oddest thing about these women. Their hair twisted in coils like the bodies of snakes, their exposed arms and legs were so dark that they reflected almost no light at all, and their cloaks turned out to be not cloth but huge, batlike wings. Each female carried a kind of stick with several thongs dangling from it.

"There you are, you ungrateful urchins!" one of the creatures cried, spying them. "We shall scourge your sins from you! Prepare to die in torment!"

"Now, wait!" Irene said, alarmed. If only it were full day, when her power was strongest! She felt so defenseless. "Who are you, and why do you come bothering innocent travelers?"

"Innocent travelers!" the canine crone screeched, sounding worse than a harpy. "You, girl who was such a trial to your lonely mother the Sorceress for nigh thirty years and now neglects her entirely! What illusion can she spin to shield her own awareness from the serpent's tooth of your ungratefulness? With what solace shall she die, away and alone, while her daughter murders her with uncaring?"

Irene rocked back, scourged indeed. This was the last kind of attack she had expected, and it was cruelly accurate. She *had* been neglecting her aging mother! How could this vile dog woman know?

"Don't talk to the lady like that, you miserable spook!" Xavier said angrily. "She asked you a question! Who the hades are you?" He lifted his finger, ready to zap the crone.

"And you, you sniveling excuse for a son!" the second crone screeched, advancing on him with her scourge raised. "When did you ever obey your mother the witch without forcing her to threaten to compel you with her eye, a thing you knew she did not want to do? All these one-score years she labored to raise you right—what thanks did you ever give, you careless and callous lout? When she sacrificed her very pride to put another woman in your worthless life, to cause you to marry and settle down and become a useful person, what did you do? How deep is her sorrow, while you neglect all obligations of responsible life to *go flying?*"

Xavier stepped back in the way Irene had, his face frozen in shock and guilt, his zap-finger stifled. The hag had scored on him as readily as her sister crone had scored on Irene. How did they know so much?

But now Grundy spoke up. "You talk pretty big, you bundles of bags!" the golem cried. "But I know you! You are the Furies, trying to blame everyone you meet for parricide—for killing his parents! But you can't get me! I know your names—Tisiphone, Alecto, and Megaera! You are the daughters of Mother Earth, as old as the world. You call yourselves the kindly ones, but it's a lie! You're the vicious ones! You're creatures of vengeance and ill-conceived retribution. But you can't blame me for neglecting *my* mother, because I never had a mother! I was made from sticks and cloth, animated by magic, and rendered to life by greater magic. What do you say to that, dogface?"

So that was the story on these wretched harridans! They were the fabled Furies! Irene had thought Xavier would be the one to defend the party, but it turned out to be Grundy, with his knowledge of the nature of these women.

The third Fury stepped forward, threatening with her scourge. "Golem, do you think that because you were made, not born, you owe nothing to your creator? What were your sticks and rags and string before the Good Magician animated you? What thanks did you ever give him for that inestimable service of awareness? Did you not flee the moment you woke, refusing to serve the purpose for which you were made? Did your neglect not cause him to lose several valuable days devising alternate means to converse with animals and plants so he could complete his project? Did you not return only after you discovered there were no others like you, so you wanted to become real? Only then did you return to serve, in exchange for the Magician's

Answer, which he never owed you in the first place but gave out of the generosity of his heart! And did you care? Did you care for anyone or anything except yourself? How many times did you abuse the Magician, calling him gnome? How many other innocent people has your foul rag mouth wronged? How many times has your perjury of translation caused mischief to those who trusted you? Where were you when the Good Magician needed you to warn the Gap Dragon away, to avoid the disaster of the Youth elixir? He helped you in your infancy of awareness; what favor did you return in his own infancy? Should he not have reason to curse the day he made you and gave you consciousness and self-determination? O, cower, wretch, for surely the scourge must fall most heavily on your deserving hide!"

Indeed, Grundy did cower, for the Fury had bested him with the terrible justice of her accusation. These were three awful creatures of retribution, their words as devastating as their weapons. They bore down on the three chastened people, their deadly scourges ready to draw more than physical blood. Irene knew now that none of her plants could have stopped these terrible old women, whose voices echoed the complaints of all neglected parents, and that Xavier's zapping would not have touched them. Even Grundy's sarcastic tongue was powerless here! She had never heard the golem so accurately set back! Yet Xavier had been cowed, too, and she herself humbled.

All three of them were retreating now—Irene, Xavier, and Grundy. In moments the scourges would cut into them, and somehow Irene knew those whips were poisonous. Their mere touch would draw copious blood and inflict extraordinary agony; the wounds would fester and refuse to heal, until the victims wished ardently for a clean and honest death. Now Irene remembered stories about the Furies punishing errant children; it was bad luck even to mention their names. Tisi, Alec, and Meg—the three horrors of guilt, sorrow, and suffering! And the worst of it was, Irene could not claim with any certainty that this savage retribution was wrong. She had always thought other people would and should suffer for their callousness, but had never realized that she was as guilty as they and deserved similar treatment.

She tripped over a root and fell on her back, unable to retreat any more. Tisi loomed over her, the canine snout drooling spittle, the animal breath rasping out in what seemed like a fiery fog. The black wings were half spread, and the scourge was lifted high for its devastating strike, each thong glistening hungrily for its share of blood.

Yet even worse than this physical threat was the emotional one. Irene realized that she would never get to tell her mother how important she, the Sorceress Iris, was and had always been to her daughter! Irene would never have the chance to make up for the years of neglect. This was the cruelest portion of her punishment—the denial of absolution.

Oh, Iris, dear mother, forgive me! she cried in her heart as the scourge came down at her face, knowing that plea would never be heard. She no longer had even the will to turn her face aside; she was doomed.

But the scourge did not land. Startled by the reprieve, Irene looked up—and saw a shape interposed.

It was the zombie! Zora had taken the blow intended for Irene. Strips of Zora's decayed flesh were dangling, ripped off by the lash of the thongs, but it seemed the zombie hardly felt them. Zombies were always losing flesh.

Tisi looked into the rotten face of the zombie and retreated. "You are undead!" she shrieked. "I can't punish you! The poison can't hurt you, the whip can't draw your blood, the truth can't sear your mind!"

Zora went on to intercept the next Fury, Alec, catching the blow intended for Xavier. The second crone recoiled similarly, not knowing how to handle an undead person. "Even if you lived, I could not flay you!" the Fury protested. "You never neglected your parents!"

Then Zora rescued Grundy, pulling him out of the way while she absorbed Meg's blow and sacrificed more shreds of flesh. "It is wrong, it is wrong!" Meg screamed in frustration. "You have suffered more, for less reason, than any living creature! I can add nothing to it!"

But now the crones rallied, reorienting on their original targets. The zombie had caught them by surprise but could not stop them if they acted in concert.

"Ffiiee! Ffiiee!" Zora cried, losing some lip and showing extraordinary animation for her kind. Generally the emotions of zombies were as atrophied as their bodies. "Theesh nocht yyoors!" The three formidable Furies hesitated, daunted by the scolding of the undead and spiritually unsoiled woman. They had neither physical nor moral power over her.

The three drew together in a huddle, conferring in unintelligible shrieks and woofs. Then, deciding on a new strategy, the Furies turned, faced the victims, and lifted their left arms in unison, as if to hurl something. But those three left hands were empty.

"Look out!" Grundy yelled. "It's a curse! The hideous hags are going to throw a—"

The three arms descended, each making a throwing arc. Irene and Xavier hunched down, their shoulders colliding. Zora flung herself back, again interposing her body between the Furies and their victims.

Something like a wind stirred in the grass around them. Irene found herself on the ground, half embracing Xavier, with the body of the zombie against them both.

The vicious Furies had been partially foiled again. Their curse had struck Zora instead of its intended objects. But evidently one curse was all each hag could throw. In moments the three turned and departed, huddling within their wing-cloaks. This horrible siege was over.

Irene got up and dusted herself off. That had been a remarkable escape! She saw Xavier staring up at Zora as if he had never seen her before. "It—the zom—she took the strike meant for me!" he exclaimed incredulously.

"Twice," Irene agreed. "For me too. Zombies are immune to physical pain and very hard to hurt. They are undead—the revived corpses of once-living people. They're not bad folk at all, if you can bring yourself to get to know them." She was speaking for herself as much as for him. This was the second time Zora had saved her, perhaps the second and third times, if she counted the scourge and the curse as separate items.

Zora seemed not to hear them as she unhunched herself and stood more or less erect. The impact of the curse was not visible, but it had to be considerable.

"She must have been some woman when she lived!" Xavier said. "A better person than any of us!"

"Probably so. I never knew her alive. But I gather from what the Furies said that she led a blameless life and was cruelly wronged by one not worthy of her."

"A man," Xavier said grimly. "A worm of a man!"

"Yes." Zora wobbled on her feet, and Irene moved over to take the zombie's flaccid arm to steady her. "Are you all right, Zora?" she asked solicitously.

"Ccurrsh . . ." the zombie said.

"You took our curse," Irene agreed. "What was it? What is supposed to happen to us—to you?"

"I can tell you that," Grundy said, climbing to his own feet. "I got caught by it."

Irene realized that was true. The zombie had blocked off the punishment from two of them, but Grundy had been behind her. He had had no protection this time. Yet he seemed functional, so the curse couldn't be something like instant, total collapse. "Is it—maybe we can nullify it—?"

"It's a curse of misfortune," the golem said. "One bad thing is going to happen which will make the victim wish he were dead. I interpreted their screeching; that's how I knew what they were up to."

"We'll protect you from it!" Irene said.

Grundy shook his little head. "I doubt that's possible, now that the curse has tagged me. The best I can hope for is that you'll find a way to abate it, once it strikes. And it will be twice for the zombie, because she took your two curses."

Irene hadn't thought of that aspect. Of course a curse was not a thing to be sloughed off like a tatter of flesh! "What would make a zombie wish she were dead?" she asked.

"I don't know," Grundy said. "But I guess we'll find out when the misfortunes strike."

All too likely true. Irene looked at Zora with mixed regret and puzzlement. The zombie had been—was *still* a truly nice person, completely self-sacrificing. But what possible penalty could she pay for her kindness?

Irene put the matter out of her mind for now, as there was

nothing she could do about it. She checked the tree house. "Let's sleep; Xap and Chem may be late returning."

Xavier agreed wordlessly. Evidently he was not certain how he felt about what his steed might be doing. Possibly he wasn't entirely pleased to see someone else tame the hippogryph.

"There's room for you in the house, Zora," Irene said. "Can you climb the ladder?"

The zombie hesitated. She was in bad condition, even for her kind, because of the savagery of the Furies. Decayed bone showed where her flesh had been scourged away, and her dress was so tattered it would have been indecent on any other female. "Nnosh nneedth—" she began.

"Not need shelter?" Irene asked. "Do you stay outside because you want to—or because your kind usually isn't welcome inside?"

Zora stood there, not attempting an answer.

"You have helped me and my friends twice," Irene said firmly. "Maybe you saved my life—from the bonnacon and the Furies. It would be wrong for me to treat you like—" She broke off, unwilling to say *like a zombie*.

"You know, it's just about dark now," Xavier commented. "I can hardly see her. She looks sort of slender and shadowed. She don't seem half bad, this way. And the smell's not bad, neither. More like soil."

As compliments went, that wasn't much, but Irene realized the youth meant well; he had not had much experience with this sort of thing. Considering his background, that was not surprising.

"The scourge would have torn me apart," Grundy remarked. "Literally. There's worse things to be next to than a zombie."

Irene addressed Zora again. "So come join us inside the tree house. You'll heal better under cover. You need sleep, don't you?" That was a guess, but it had become important to Irene to make this gesture. It might be some transference from her guilt about neglecting her mother Iris—oh, the Furies had scored there!—but it was also simple gratitude. Zora had saved her from the bonnacon, and Irene had allowed herself almost to forget about that; now Zora had saved her again, and this time there would be no forgetting. This zombie was no longer an unpleasant thing to be tolerated, and no necessary evil; this was a friend. Zora must indeed have been, as Xavier surmised, some woman when she lived; she was some woman *now*.

Zora accepted the invitation and shambled to the ladder leading up to the tree house. She tried to climb, but her body was less functional than usual because of the scourging, and her clumsy, skeletal hands slipped off the rungs. Irene winced to see the scourge wounds, knowing that her own flesh had very nearly suffered similarly. Obviously the poison of the whips was interfering with even zombie regeneration. Maybe in her healthiest state, Zora could have made it; not now.

Xavier stepped behind her, put his two large hands at Zora's somewhat sloppy waist, and lifted. Once again Irene noted how strong a man he was; though he hardly seemed to put forth any effort, the zombie rose like a feather. Xavier resembled his steed in this respect, being the finest of physical specimens. With this considerable assistance, Zora was able to scramble to the top of the ladder, fortunately within the young man's reach, and get her balance on hands and knees at the house portal. She disappeared inside, dropping some slivers of skin behind.

"I never touched one of them things before," Xavier murmured, half to himself. "Not with my hands. 'Course, she was hanging on to me, riding Xap, but I just sorta tuned her out. As if she were a bag of garbage going to the dump. But now, after she took that scourge for me—if I had been hit, I guess *my* flesh would be dropping off and showing my bones." He shook his head. "I never had no one do me a favor I didn't do back. But how do you give back the favor of a life when—I mean, she lost her life long before I ever knew her." He clenched his fists in a frustration Irene shared. He was a decent man, facing an insoluble ethical problem. "It's not so bad, touching her. No worse than entrails from some monster I killed. Touching stuff—it really don't mean nothing. It's how you feel about it. She sure don't weigh much."

Xavier was, in his crude but honest fashion, voicing sentiments similar to those Irene had privately entertained, to her half shame. His reassessment parallelled hers. There was no prejudice in Xanth greater than that relating to zombies, and she had shared it, though she knew better. Even Millie the Ghost, who had loved a zombie for eight hundred years, until he was at last restored to his living self as the Zombie Master— even she did not permit many zombies in their castle, although zombies had built that castle and now defended it. Castle Roogna had always been defended by zombies, yet they were not permitted inside it. Nobody wanted to be close to a zombie.

But if zombies were not properly alive, neither were they properly dead. They did have feelings, loyalty, and courage, as Zora had so dramatically shown. Zora had done more, and had asked less in return, than anyone else on this odd excursion.

"She's a decent person," Irene said, knowing this to be an understatement so gross as to be obscene.

"Yeah. Too bad she's dead."

And there was the ultimate tragedy of it. How could anyone repay a person who was not alive? That was the wall against which each notion smashed.

Irene climbed on up and into her monkey-puzzle chamber. Xavier and Grundy got settled.

Irene lay there in the dark. There was certainly a smell from the zombie like rotted leaves or a small, dead animal left in the sun. But Xavier was right; it wasn't too bad, especially when one remembered what Zora had done.

Chapter 9. Parnassus

Xap and Chem were back by morning. Irene heard them arrive and decided not to inquire; it really wasn't her business. That was why she was so infernally curious!

Maybe it was her imagination, Irene thought, but in the light of dawn, Zora looked improved. The scourge gouges had filled in so that bone no longer showed, her flesh no longer hung in tatters, and her eyes seemed restored to the point where they were capable of normal vision. Even her dress was whole now, apparently renovating itself as part of the zombie process. Her hair was longer and fuller and less straggly, with some of its original fair color showing. It seemed that rest and shelter did mend a zombie somewhat.

This was the first case Irene knew of in which a zombie had become less, rather than more, rotten with the passage of time. But of course she had never before interacted this closely with a zombie for several days. What had she ever really known about them? Little more than jokes: How many zombies does it take to plant a light bulb? She could no longer remember the punch line and didn't care to; she was sure she would not find it very funny now.

There was one other factor, she recalled: human consideration and caring. That was one thing that was supposed to help a zombie—and the one thing few if any zombies received. But all of them had welcomed Zora into their group after the episode of the Furies. Perhaps they had, after all, returned part of the debt they owed her.

Irene's original clothes were quite dry now, so she no longer had to wear the towels or other substitutes. That improved her outlook. She grew milkweed and eggplant for breakfast, for those who wanted it. Xap and Chem were not hungry; presumably they had eaten on the run during the night.

Chem projected her map. The scenery ahead spread out in miniature. "Here is the mountain of Parnassus," she explained, indicating a large, irregular area. It was as if they were looking down on it from above; she must have questioned Xap closely about the details he perceived from the air, in order to fill out what she saw from the knoll. "It has two peaks. The one we want is here, to the south. The nine Muses live on it; the cave of the Oracle is over there, but we'll skirt around that to reach the peak where the Tree of Seeds grows. It's quite a climb, but we can handle it, if—"

Irene didn't like the smell of that hesitation. "If what?"

"If nothing interferes," Chem said reluctantly.

"What might interfere?"

"Well, Xap says there are things on the other peak of Parnassus that—of course, we won't be traveling on that side of the mountain—"

"But we'd better be prepared," Irene finished. "Especially with that curse." She had told Chem about the visitation of the evening, of course, and the part Zora had played. "What affects Grundy and Zora is likely to affect the rest of us, since we're traveling as a group. So let's have the worst. What's on that other peak?"

"I'll have to give a little background," Chem said apologetically. Unlike some centaurs, she hesitated to show off her extensive classical education.

"Spit it out, horsefoot," Grundy said. "Anything bad will probably hit me first."

"The shrine of the Oracle was originally guarded by the Python, who had a keen insight into the fallibilities of man. But the huge reptile was attacked and severely injured and driven out; it survived only because it fled to the other peak of Parnassus, where the Tree of Immortality was, and ate one of its leaves. Now the Python is barred from the Oracle's cave, but it is a most sagacious reptile and would do anything to return. So it slithers about, seeking some avenue. If we were to stray into its present territory—"

"We won't," Irene said firmly. "Not with your map to guide us. What else?"

"The maenads. They are the wild women of wine. They dance ritually on the north slope, tearing apart and consuming any creature they catch. Once they served the god of fertile crops, but the old gods are gone now and the maenads serve no one except the Tree of Immortality, which keeps them alive and youthful."

"They sound like nymphs," Xavier remarked.

"They may be related, but their personalities are more like those of harpies or ogresses. They are predators, not prey, though they are naked and beautiful."

"I see," Irene said, frowning. She tended to be foolishly jealous of eternally young, beautiful, naked wild women. Once she herself had been—but she stifled that thought. "So wild women roam the slopes of Parnassus. We'll stay clear of them, too." For sure!

"So here is the appropriate path," Chem concluded, pointing out a dotted line on the map. "We'll have to stay right on it to be safe. It is too bad you can't use Xap to fly directly to the Tree of Seeds. But the Simurgh allows no one to enter Parnassus by air, because every so often dragons and griffins try to raid. A hippogryph vaguely resembles a griffin in flight, so Xap knows it isn't safe for him to fly there. Nothing larger than a small bird can risk it. Xap can handle just about any airborne creature he might meet, but the Simurgh is something else."

"I'm sure it is," Irene agreed, getting more curious about this notorious bird.

"We have to approach slowly, by foot, so the Simurgh has time to study us and see that we are not raiders but serious visitors."

"Parnassus seems very choosy," Irene commented.

"Yes. A select and strange group of creatures abides there. We have to follow their rules, or we will get nowhere. That's why the witch Xanthippe could not go herself; the Simurgh would know her for what she is and would never let her get near the Tree of Seeds."

"It is not a mission I would have chosen myself," Irene admitted grimly. "But we must do what we must do."

They set off on the final stretch to Parnassus, as delineated on Chem's map. Zora rode behind Xavier on Xap again, while Irene and Grundy remained on Chem. They trotted southeast, but with more certain impetus, for Chem had traveled this route before. Xap now stayed on the ground, and not because he was tired. Whether he wished to avoid the attention of the Simurgh even this far away, or simply to keep Chem company, Irene wasn't sure. But she suspected the latter.

Those two semi-equines must have had quite a night of it, Irene reflected. Xap spoke only in squawks, but Chem seemed to understand him perfectly now, and he understood her. Irene remained surprised that Chem should show such interest in a non-centaur, yet human beings were non-centaurs, too, and she associated with them all the time. Was a human person any more worthy than a hippogryph person? A smart centaur certainly ought to be able to judge. But Irene suspected that Chem's dam Cherie would not entirely approve. What would the Furies have said to Chem?

In due course they came to the base of Mount Parnassus. The jungle halted as if in deference to the great mountain, so the view was clear. There were indeed two peaks; on each one, half hidden in mists, was a large and spreading tree. They would avoid the Tree of Immortality on the north peak; too much mischief had already been wreaked by the water of the Fountain of Youth, which was surely related magic.

"Doesn't look like much," Grundy said.

"Let's hope you're right," Chem said. "I want to talk to the Simurgh—nothing else. And Irene wants to get those seeds."

They crossed the channel at the foot of the mountain. This was a dry creekbed filled with rounded stones. It wasn't comfortable footing for hooves, so Xap spread his wings and leaped across, risking this tiny bit of flight, while Chem picked her way carefully. Even so, the stones tended to turn under her feet, slowing her down further.

"Here, tenderfoot, I'll find you a solid path!" Grundy said impatiently. He jumped down and began shoving at stones, testing for solidity.

Something struck at the golem. Grundy jumped back. "It bit me!" he exclaimed indignantly as a small snake slithered quickly away.

"Hardly the Python," Irene said. The golem was touching his little leg, but did not seem to be crippled.

Chem stiffened, her four hooves firmly in place. "That snake looked very much like a dipsas. I hope that's a misperception."

"The cursed thing bit me!" Grundy repeated, pressing at the flesh of his leg. "I'm not a true golem any more, you know; I'm flesh now. I hurt!"

That was true. Grundy, like Millie the Ghost, had for some time been fully alive, because of very special magic. The Furies had known. Too bad, Irene thought, that no similar magic was available to restore Zora Zombie! But Good Magician Humfrey had been involved in the other case, and he was no longer available.

But she had better concentrate on the immediate problem. "What's a dipsas?" she asked Chem, who was now picking her way forward again.

"Cursed thing," the centaur mused. "Maybe not just a figure of speech."

"I don't understand," Irene said, annoyed.

"Hey, got anything to drink?" the golem asked.

"It *was* a dipsas!" Chem said, horrified. "I hoped I was wrong or that the snake's reputation was exaggerated. Its bite makes a person unquenchably thirsty."

"Curse," Irene repeated, catching on. "The Furies' curse of misfortune!"

"Yes," the centaur agreed. "You told me how the Furies came while Xap and I were away and how Grundy caught their curse. This bite of the dipsas does seem to fit the description. Perhaps if you had caught the curse, you would have been the one bitten—or me, if I had been there to meet the Furies. I was certainly vulnerable."

All too true! "Zora has my curse," Irene said. "She did not get bitten, so I think this one was intended specifically for Grundy."

"I'm starving of thirst!" Grundy exclaimed. "Find me a lake, somebody!"

Irene looked around. "There's a beer-barrel tree behind us." She dismounted, picked her way through the treacherous stones of the riverbed, keeping a nervous eye out for snakes, and went to the huge, swollen barrel of the tree. Now she realized why the streambed was dry—the magic snake had caused all creatures here to drink until the water was gone. Too bad that had not been obvious before!

She used her knife to punch a hole in the bark. Yellow beer spouted out. This might not be the best liquid for the golem to drink, but there was plenty of it, enough to quench the thirst of a hundred golems.

Grundy hurried up and put his little mouth to the stream of beer. He gulped the stuff down insatiably.

Irene watched with growing amazement as the golem swallowed more than his own mass in beer and kept on drinking.

The stream seemed to be flowing into a bottomless hole. His body swelled up like a watermelon, but still he drank.

Finally the barrel ran dry and the flow stopped. "More! More!" Grundy cried, though he was bursting out of his clothing. Irene had never seen a smaller, fatter man. "I'm ravenous with thirst. Hic!"

Irene glanced again at the dry stream, then at the empty tree. This thirst was truly ferocious! Mere liquid obviously wouldn't abate it. "I don't know where there's more."

"I'm drying up!" Grundy cried, popping a button. "I wish I were dead!"

That was another aspect of the curse, of course. "What we need is not more liquid, but a cure," she said. "Otherwise Grundy will drink until he explodes."

Chem had made her way across the riverbed and was now safely on Mount Parnassus. "As I recall, the only natural cure is a draught from a healing spring, and I don't know where—"

Xap squawked.

"He says the winespring of the maenads quenches all thirst," the centaur said. "That's fairly close."

"But that spring must be—"

"On the north slope of Parnassus," Chem said grimly.

"The very place we don't want to go." Irene sighed. "Yet Grundy is dying of dehydration, or of swelling. We can't ignore that!" Indeed, the golem was chewing up the local vegetation, trying to squeeze water out of the leaves.

Irene dropped a seed and ordered it to grow. In a moment a water hyacinth sprouted, bursting with water. The golem grabbed its leaves and flowers and crammed them into his mouth. But plants couldn't hold him long. Already his swollen limbs looked shrunken, as if dehydrating. He had the worst of both conditions.

"I'd like to have Fracto the Cloud here now," Irene muttered. "Grundy would swallow him whole."

"Maybe Xap and me can take him to the winespring," Xavier offered.

"But Xap doesn't dare fly here," Chem protested, concerned for the welfare of the hippogryph.

"Yeah, but he can gallop good."

"True," Chem agreed, with one of her obscure smiles. "Perhaps we should separate, and rejoin farther up the mountain when Grundy is cured." She projected her map. "The spring should be about here," she said, making it glow in the picture. She had really learned a lot of geography from the hippogryph! "If you follow this route—" The dotted line progressed to intersect the glow. "—you can rejoin us farther up the mountain—here." The line intersected the line of their route to the southern peak.

"I really don't like breaking up our party," Irene said. "But I suppose we have little choice at the moment. We can't let Grundy die of thirst, or whatever, and Xap is best able to avoid the maenads."

So it was reluctantly decided. Zora got down from the hippogryph, and Grundy took her place. Xap galloped away, around the northern curve of the mountain.

"There go three fairly brave and foolish males," Chem murmured as Zora mounted behind Irene.

"Let's hope we fairly sensible and timid females can complete our mission," Irene said.

They moved up the slope. Parnassus was not a smooth mountain; it was riddled with ridges, gullies, crevices, and caves, and the vegetation was odd. Strange seeds had sprouted, probably from the Tree of Seeds. There was a proliferation of paper trees and ink plants, and secretary-birds zipped among them in seemingly pointless activity. Irene wondered what natural place a community like this had in the larger scheme of Xanth, for things generally interrelated, but she could see nothing worthwhile. Parnassus seemed pretty much wrapped up in its own concerns, which hardly related to those of the world beyond.

There was a loud and sinister hiss ahead. Chem skidded to a halt, all four hooves making grooves in the dirt. The path ran through a small gorge here, with sliding rubble on the slopes, so it was not at all convenient to change the route—but she didn't trust what was ahead. Chem unslung her bow from her shoulder and nocked an arrow; like all centaurs, she was an excellent archer. She walked slowly forward.

There, around a curve, was a monstrous serpent. Its head

was half the size of Irene's body, carried at human height, and its sinuous body extended back and around another curve.

"The Python!" Irene whispered in horror. "What is it doing here?"

"I am the nemesis and the delight of females everywhere," the serpent hissed. "I made the first woman blush and feel shame for the desire I aroused in her. I will possess the last woman ever to bear a child. Bow down before me, you vulnerable creatures!"

This was more than a mere snake! Irene tried to protest, but the Python's terrible gaze transfixed her. Chem fidgeted on her hooves, caught by the same stare. There seemed to be all the sinister masculine wisdom of eternity in those huge eyes, together with all the masculine promise and threat and a desire, as insatiable as the golem's thirst, that would destroy them long before it was sated; yet neither Irene nor Chem could break the connection.

The Python slid forward sinuously, holding them with his hypnotic gaze. His pale red tongue flicked out. Soon that awful mouth would gape, showing the cruel fangs—

"Wwhaashh?" Zora asked, shedding some epiglottis, as she tended to do when expressing herself with some force. When Irene didn't answer, the zombie craned her neck to peer blankly ahead of the centaur.

Then Zora half scrambled, half slid to the ground, righted herself, and shuffled forward. She took her place in front of Chem just as the head of the Python arrived. "Ffiieee, sschnaake!" she cried.

For a moment, zombie and Python were eye to eye. Now it was the serpent who froze, for the direct gaze of an aroused zombie was a sickening thing.

Irene and Chem snapped out of their trances. The gaze of the Python had been interrupted by Zora, freeing the other two. Irene was appalled and repelled by the memory of her fascination of a moment ago, yet there had been a certain insidious appeal as well. She had not, while caught in the stare of the snake, quite wanted to break it, though she knew it meant doom. Did she have an urge for self-destruction, or was that merely part of the thing's spell?

The centaur spun about so rapidly that Irene had to grab the slender humanoid waist before her to remain mounted. Chem's large rear end swung around to bang into both zombie and Python, knocking them into the rocky bank.

"Grab Zora!" Irene cried, seeing the zombie staggering.

Chem reached out and caught Zora by an arm and hauled her in. Half carrying, half dragging her, the centaur moved down the path, away from the menace. Behind them, the huge serpent thrashed, starting a rockslide that threatened to bury its low body.

Irene knew the monster snake would soon be after them. The Python had been balked, not defeated; it was impossible for mere females to win over him. She felt in her bag of seeds, seeking something that would delay the reptile. She had a tangle tree seed, but that would take too long to grow—Ah! Here was a hedgehog plant seed. She threw it to the ground. "Grow!"

The hedgehog sprouted, sending out quills that pointed in every direction. It was like an oversized pincushion. That would be awkward to pass in any hurry!

But when she glanced back, shielding her eyes with her hand so as to cut off any meeting of the reptile's deadly stare, she saw the Python sliding smoothly past the hedgehog. The plant hadn't had time to grow big enough to block the whole channel.

Hmm. She fetched out two more seeds. The first was false hops; when she sprouted it, it fragmented into a dozen miniature kangaroos who started hopping madly about. They were not real, of course; kangaroos were mythical beasts not found in Xanth. When the Python snapped at one, he encountered only leaves and stem. But this was a distraction that slowed the aggressive reptile.

Next she tossed an alumroot. It wasn't much to look at, but with luck, the snake would snap it up, too, just to get it out of the way.

The Python did. The alumroot was ripped out of the ground and crunched to pieces, its juices squirting. Irene was reminded with horror of the way the bonnacon had crunched Zora. Then the serpent paused, just as the bonnacon had.

Irene smiled. Alum had a special magical effect on living flesh. It was astringent.

The Phyton's mouth shrank as the soft tissues of it drew together. But the hard tissues, such as the teeth, did not shrink. In moments the head was quite distorted, the flesh tightening about the bone. Startled, the Python jerked his head back and tried to spit out the root, but could not get it past his purse-string-tight mouth. Desperate, the reptile tried the other route and swallowed the root.

Irene's smile broadened. Alum was an emetic, too. In a moment the big snake was vomiting as well as it could through its constricted throat and mouth. Bubbles started coming out of its ear slits. The worst thing it could have done was to swallow the alum!

That gave them enough time to stop and get Zora properly mounted. "You saved us again," Irene told her. "You may have absorbed a double curse of misfortune, but you are certainly lucky for us!" For a moment Irene wondered whether being consumed by the Python was one of the misfortunes the zombie had taken on herself, but realized it could not be, for it had not happened.

"I wonder what misfortune is, to a zombie?" Chem remarked, her mind evidently on the same question that was bothering Irene. "It can't be the ordinary type. Not a snakebite or a bad fall . . ."

"That curse might not apply at all," Irene conjectured. "To us, getting hurt or killed would be a misfortune, but a zombie is already dead, or half dead. Many people would consider that the ultimate misfortune—to become a zombie—but Zora is already there." She turned her head to address the zombie directly. "What is misfortune to you?"

"Nnoshingg," Zora replied.

"Nothing," Irene agreed. So she was correct; Zora was already undergoing the ultimate misfortune. The curse had to be meaningless.

But she couldn't be quite sure.

"I think we have gotten away," Chem said. "But now we are going in the wrong direction, downhill."

"We must have been going the wrong way before," Irene

said. "We probably veered too far north and intersected the territory of the Python."

"No, we were on our plotted course," the centaur insisted. "The Python is on the southern peak. He must be testing the boundaries, moving back to his original haunts. We hadn't allowed for that. It was a long time ago that he was banished, and things change."

"Well, now we know," Irene said. "I don't want to meet that gaze again!" There was just a smidgeon of doubt to that, though. She hated that doubt! "We'll have to find another path up the mountain. We can intercept our original route above the Python, who will be looking for us down here, so that the boys can find us."

Chem projected her map. "We can travel past the Oracle's cave," she decided. "That's not too far out of our way."

They picked their way to the alternate path. Irene planted a creeping fig seed in the path they were leaving, to fool the Python, who she knew would be recovering soon from the effects of the alum. It had been a small alumroot, not enough really to hurt the huge snake; and anyway, alum was not generally fatal. The Python's hunger would be greater than ever, because of the loss of the contents of his stomach. The fig would creep on down toward the base of the mountain, making it seem that the party had continued that way. Of course, the fig's smell would be different, but it was still worth the try; maybe the reptile didn't track by smell.

The crannies in the mountain became more pronounced here and finally opened into crevices and fissures from which intoxicating fumes rose. They hurried by, not wanting to experience any more of this than necessary. "The Oracle sniffs the vapors and makes crazy prophecies, as I understand it, that always come true," Chem remarked. "We certainly don't need any of that for our own mission."

"We certainly don't," Irene agreed. "Maybe the powers that be on Parnassus like to go crazy on fumes, but we're more sensible people." She hoped this was true.

They made their way above the cave region, where the landscape evened out somewhat, and were soon close to their original course. They saw no sign of Xap's hoofprints, so they proceeded slowly in order to let the males catch up when they did intersect the path. Irene could not help worrying, however; suppose their companions had fallen into dire straits and did not return?

Then they heard a screaming from the north. "I think that's more trouble," Chem said grimly.

Parnassus was nothing but trouble so far! "The maenads," Irene agreed. "In pursuit of prey. We should have known the males could not touch the winespring without arousing its guardians." But they had been brave to try, she reminded herself.

"We don't dare hide until we know whether Xap and Xavier and Grundy need help."

Irene glanced back. "Oh, no! The Python wasn't fooled! He's after us again!"

"Do you have a suitable plant?" the centaur asked nervously. "I don't want to be caught between two horrors."

Irene checked. "I'm getting low, but these should help." She tossed down several seeds. "Grow!"

Plants sprouted rapidly, spreading across a fairly broad area. "What are they?" Chem asked, glancing forward and back.

"Something to distract each threat, I hope—horehounds and snake plants."

Chem eyed the bristling hound-heads and snake-heads on the plants. "Aren't they as much of a threat to us as to the enemies?"

"No. Snake plants only bite snakes, and horehounds only bite—"

Now the hippogryph burst into sight, running powerfully, pursued by a crowd of naked women. They were young and healthy and, yes, nymphlike, with fine, firm legs, narrow waists, and voluptuous bosoms. But they were also wild-haired and wild-eyed, and awful imprecations spewed from their snarling red mouths. Several of them carried things that most resembled gobbets of raw flesh.

The Python had been sliding slowly close, tongue flicking with anticipation. Now he brightened further. His jaws worked, and slaver dripped. He accelerated toward the maenads.

"I don't know which is worse, the male or the female threats," Irene said, halfway fascinated.

"We'd better gallop!" Chem said, suiting action to word.

They galloped. Chem's course up the mountain converged with Xap's, and they ran side by side until it was evident they were not being pursued. Then they reined in and turned to look back.

The Python and the maenads were not, it seemed, on friendly terms. The giant snake was biting one woman after another, while the wild women were tearing with tooth and claw at the serpentine body and gouging bloody chunks out. The snake did not have time to swallow any morsels, but the maenads were no better off, for the huge reptile's coils were switching too rapidly about for easy consumption. It seemed to be a fairly even battle—the woman-preying monster against the most predatory women. Now and then a woman would stand frozen, caught by the Python's terrible stare, but then three more would cut in between, breaking the spell. The reptile had succeeded in fascinating Irene and Chem, but there were far too many maenads to be similarly held.

Meanwhile, the snake plants and horehounds were snapping indiscriminately at both sides, making the carnage even more bloody. Pieces of flesh went flying up, and blood coursed down the channels of the mountain. This was serious business! Irene found her gorge rising and had to avert her face; she really wasn't much for such violence, however common it might be on Parnassus, and disliked seeing these vicious creatures in action. Their behavior did little for either the masculine or the feminine image.

"Parnassus is a rough place, especially for the natives," Grundy said, echoing her thought. But the golem was enjoying it.

That reminded her. "Grundy! Have you been cured?"

"I think so." The golem paused to belch. He did appear to be normal again; certainly the bloat was gone. "That winespring is potent!"

"Everything was quiet until he drank," Xavier said. "Then the damsels appeared—"

"Damsels!" Irene exclaimed. "Those are bi—uh, bad women!"

"Oh, I don't know," Grundy said. "I understand wild women can be a lot of fun."

Irene stifled her retort, knowing the golem was baiting her. He was back to normal, all right!

"Screaming and waving their claws," Xavier continued. "I didn't want to zap any of those fantastic creatures, they being of the gentle sex—"

"Hardly gentle!" Irene protested, watching another bleeding hunk of meat fly up above the mêlée.

"Like yourself," he said. "I just don't like to—"

"*I'm* like a maenad, a wild woman?" Irene screeched, outraged. Then she had to laugh, knowing she was reacting exactly like a maenad.

"Gentle," Xavier clarified. "And lovely." He squinted at her. "In fact, maybe Maw was right—"

"Let's get on with our mission," Irene said quickly. She should have kept her mouth shut to begin with. Xavier was really a very nice young man, and she remained privately flattered by his perception of her, but this was as far as it could ever go. She had a husband and child to return to, after all.

They resumed the climb, letting the sounds of carnage fade behind them. Soon the way became steeper, until they were unable to progress farther and had to move around the southern slope of the mountain instead.

"Xap could fly on up," Xavier said.

"And maybe get exterminated by the Simurgh," Chem retorted. "That's not a viable option."

They came to a kind of palace set into the mountainside. It did not have high towers but did have ornate columns and archways with curlicues of stone and carvings of animals and people. This was no primitive hideout; it was someone's highly civilized retreat.

In a small court before it, a woman sat at a table, an open chest of books at her side. She wore a floor-length white robe and was of well-kept middle age—the kind of figure of a woman Irene hoped to be when time shoved her into that age bracket.

The woman looked up as the group approached. "May I help you?" she inquired, unalarmed. She spoke with a cultured accent, her voice quiet but thoroughly competent.

Irene dismounted and went to the table, uncertain how much of this to take at face value. The maenads, after all, looked like nymphs, but hardly acted like them. If this were some other kind of trap—but she had to give it the benefit of the doubt. "We are seeking the Tree of Seeds and the Simurgh," she explained. "We can't seem to find the path to the top of the mountain."

The woman nodded. She had curly, dark hair neatly pinned back, and an elegantly straight nose. "And who might you be?" she asked with mild interest.

"I am Irene, and these are my friends Chem, Zora, Grundy, Xavier, and Xap."

"Ah, so you are the current Queen of Xanth!" the woman exclaimed, brightening. "How very nice of you to honor us with a visit."

Irene was startled. "How could you know that? As far as I know, no one from Parnassus has been to Castle Roogna, and this is the first time any of us have—"

"I am Clio, the Muse of History. I am naturally conversant with the significant events of the realm."

"The Muse of History!" Chem exclaimed excitedly, stepping close. "The one who writes the magic texts?"

Clio inclined her head politely. "Some of them, centaur. Most recently I covered the episode of the night mare and the salvation of Xanth from the Nextwave invasion. Your kind has been an excellent customer for such references, and, of course, the Good Magician."

"Not any more," Irene murmured darkly.

"He will recover in proper course; your friend will see to that," the Muse said, glancing at Zora.

"He will?" Irene asked incredulously. "But there's no fast cure for Youth—"

"But her talent compensates, you see."

Irene stared at Zora. "Her talent? But she's a—"

Clio put her hand to her lips. "Oh, my, that's in a future history text, which I have not yet completed! We have a long lead time, and sometimes I lose track. I shouldn't have mentioned it."

A future history text? There was magic of a high order here! How could Zora Zombie relate to the Good Magician, whom she didn't even know?

"And are the other Muses here, too?" Chem asked. "Calliope, Erato, Urania—"

"Indeed," Clio agreed. "This is where we live, here on Mount Parnassus, the home of the arts, the sciences, and memory. The others are resting at the moment, but you may meet them if you wish. We have never intended to be aloof from the public, though we find a certain isolation to be beneficial."

Chem shook her head regretfully. "If I start talking with all the Muses, it will be years before I stop, and I have a more immediate mission. I shall have to be satisfied just putting your locale on my map. Will you tell us how to reach the summit of Parnassus?"

"I regret to advise you that there is no easy way," Clio said. "Talent isn't enough any more. Most talented people never make it; they get consumed by the Python or the maenads, in literal or figurative fashion."

"So we have discovered," Irene said. "And we understand it is not safe to fly. But I must rescue my daughter Ivy, and first I must get three seeds from the—"

"Ivy?" Clio asked. "Let me fetch Thalia." She rose, turned gracefully, and glided toward the palace entrance.

"Who is Thalia?" Irene asked.

"Muse of Comedy," Chem murmured. "And of Planting."

"Planting! Well, I certainly can relate to that! But—"

Clio returned with Thalia. The other Muse carried a face mask that was broadly smiling and a shepherd's crook and wore a wreath of ivy.

"I think the ivy is the key," Chem said. "See if you can enlist the Muses' help."

"No need," Thalia said, overhearing her. "I know of the Sorceress. But why do you seek her here, when she is in the cave of the Cyclops?"

"The Cyclops!" Irene cried, dismayed. "I thought the witch Xanthippe had her captive!"

"No longer," Thalia said. "Xanthippe had already lost possession when you undertook her mission. It is a humorous irony." She lifted the laughing mask to her face momentarily.

"All this—for nothing?" Irene demanded, sputtering. "That witch deceived me?"

"Not so," Thalia said. "Xanthippe thought she had Ivy. But no person of ordinary talent can long constrain a Sorceress. Ivy and the dragon escaped in a manner that only such a person could arrange. They will in due course be in somewhat greater difficulty, however. Your excursion here does relate."

"I've got to get back!" Irene exclaimed.

"We couldn't possibly return in time to be of any use," Chem reminded her. "It shouldn't take much longer to complete our mission than to abort it. Perhaps the Simurgh will give us useful advice, since that bird knows everything."

"Yes, we often exchange information with the Simurgh," Thalia agreed.

"Oh, I hate this!" Irene said, stamping her foot. "I just want Ivy back safely!"

"Easier to save all Xanth," Clio murmured.

"Exactly what does that mean?" Irene flared.

"For a child of that name and that power and for a talent like yours, I will help," Thalia said, touching her wreath. "It was so kind of you to name such a remarkable individual so."

It had been coincidence, since Irene had not known about this Muse. She had needed a name beginning with *I* that related to plants, since the baby had been a girl. Had it been a boy, they would have settled on a name beginning with *D*, after his father, relating to the inanimate. But it did not seem politic to make an issue of that now, and perhaps it was less coincidental than it seemed. There were few true coincidences in Xanth.

Meanwhile, why did Thalia keep referring to Ivy as a Sorceress? And what did Clio mean about saving Xanth? Irene had a nasty feeling that these were not idle fragments of news. But she was sure that she would get no clarifications merely by asking. The Muses were as much aware of the future as they were of the past, and did let slip aspects of each, but it seemed they were not supposed to leak the future to ordinary folk. "How can we get to the top of Parnassus quickly?"

Thalia considered. "Some ride a book to the heights." She indicated one of Clio's texts, which rose out of the chest and hovered in the air before them. "But this method is precarious, for no one knows which book will rise all the way."

Irene eyed the floating tome. It seemed very small and uncertain. "I don't care to trust myself to that, even if the Simurgh permits that sort of flight! I'd soon fall off."

"Most do," Thalia agreed. "They have such high hopes, then fall so low, especially when the climate is adverse. Some make it by promotion." But her too-merry smile suggested that was not a viable option either, in this instance. "Some do it by sheer luck. But the only reasonable route is that of time and persistence."

"We don't have time!" Irene protested.

Thalia paced in a small circle. "Then I suppose you will have to do it the hard way. For you, for this occasion, I think the ivy should do." She lifted the wreath from her neck and set it at the base of the cliff at the edge of the temple. "I must not employ my power for the benefit of a traveler, but you may use yours."

Irene caught on. "Grow!" she ordered the ivy.

The ivy grew vigorously. The wreath sent out several shoots, and these quickly found the face of the cliff. They attached themselves to the surface of the mountain, their little suckers supporting the stems. The vines thickened and became sturdy and continued to reach up the mountain.

"But Xap and I can't climb that!" Chem protested. "Our hooves—"

"I'll get the feather for you," Irene said. "You can wait here and talk to the Muses. We'll have to return this way, and so we shall rejoin you then."

"I suppose that's best," the centaur said without real regret. She had wanted to meet the Simurgh, but she also wanted to talk with the Muses, and the climb was clearly impossible for her. The specialization that made her species fine runners made her a poor climber. "I don't think Zora should try it, either."

Irene glanced at the zombie, remembering the Muse's reference to her. Zora continued to look improved, but this was no minor climb up a ladder to a tree house! "Yes, she would have too much trouble."

"But *I* can handle it!" Grundy said with zest. He was right; his small weight and tight grasp gave him a real advantage here. Too bad; Irene would have been happier without his smart remarks, which could aggravate the Simurgh.

When the ivy growth was solid enough and high enough, Irene, Xavier, and Grundy climbed up it, finding plenty of footholds and handholds in the twining stems. This was a very luxuriant and strong variety of ivy, as befitted the Muse of Planting, and Irene knew it would offer complete support.

She remembered how she had climbed a plant over a dozen years ago, in Mundania, to help Dor use his talent in a castle. That had taken place in the days when she had been young and impetuous and foolish and fun-loving. The halcyon days, when everyone had been desperate to know what color her panties were. Now, of course, no one cared. Her youth had flown.

"Hey, doll, remember that time in Onesti when Dor was embarrassed to see your—" Grundy began, thinking to tease her.

Irene leaned over and kissed him on the top of his little head. "I remember."

The golem blanched. "I must be losing my touch," he grumbled.

It was quite a climb, but Irene was at home with plants, especially this variety, and she kept reminding herself that she was doing it for her daughter. Of course, her daughter was no longer in the witch's power; but still, the sooner she got this mission done, the sooner she could be on her way to rescue Ivy. According to the Muses, this mission did relate, and it seemed they were in a position to know. Anyway, she climbed, mentally repeating the name to herself with each heave upward: *Ivy! Ivy! Ivy!* It helped motivate tiring muscles.

Grundy had no trouble, as he was forever climbing things. He was like a little monkeyshine. Xavier was eternally robust, his muscles flexing smoothly; he seemed to be enjoying the mild effort of the climb. So they made good progress up the steep face of the mountain. Irene looked down to see how far they had come and experienced instant vertigo; no more of that!

They came to a gentler slope near the top and were able to leave the vine, though Irene made sure she could grab onto it again if she happened to fall. She felt less secure on this mountain face than she had when flying the bird-of-paradise plant, because the drop seemed so much more immediate. Her arms were tired but not numb; she was well enough off.

Again she looked back, saw the surface of Parnassus falling away out of sight, and again felt abruptly dizzy. It was much worse looking down from the precarious top than up from the solid base. *Never look back*, she thought, *when at the height*.

Then she looked forward—and saw the Tree.

The Tree of Seeds was absolutely huge. Its roots dug into the domed top of the mountain, its trunk ascended massively, and its branches spread out as if to encompass the whole of Xanth. The foliage was highly varied, for this was the tree of all species, producing fruits and seeds of every kind that existed. To Irene it was the most wonderful tree that ever could be.

She looked north, to the other peak of Parnassus, and saw the Tree of Immortality. From this distance it looked minor, but she was sure it was similar in size to the one on this peak. Proximity made these trees much more formidable!

She returned her gaze to the Tree of Seeds. There, on a large and high branch, perched the Simurgh, a bird the size of a roc, whose feathers were like veils of light and shadow and whose crested head was like fire. It moved, half spreading its enormous wings, and they were like mist over a mountain.

"That's some creature!" Xavier breathed.

It was indeed. Irene had expected to be impressed, but the sheer enormity and beauty of the Simurgh threatened to overwhelm her. If the Tree of Seeds was a monarch among trees, so was the Simurgh a monarch among birds.

"I'll try to talk to it," Grundy said nervously. "That's my job, after all."

DO NOT BOTHER, GOLEM.

Irene looked about, startled, and saw Xavier doing the same, while Grundy was literally knocked off his feet. "That's the bird!" he exclaimed, sitting up. "That's the Simurgh talking!"

SPEAK YOUR NEEDS, the Simurgh said in all their minds.

Neither Grundy nor Xavier was able to formulate anything. Irene was the one with the mission, and as the only woman present, she was the natural leader. She gulped and started to speak. "First, we need a fea—"

A WHAT? the monstrous bird demanded.

"A—" Irene began again.

WHO PUT YOU UP TO THIS, MORTAL WOMAN?

There was something ominous about the way the bird projected the concept "mortal"; life was not necessarily long. Abashed, Irene began: "The—"

I SHOULD HAVE KNOWN! THAT WITCH XANTHIPPE IS A THIEF FROM WAY BACK, ALWAYS WANTING WHAT SHE DOES NOT DESERVE.

"Hey, featherbrain, that's my mother you're insulting!" Xavier protested in the foolhardy fashion of his sex.

One gigantic and brilliant eye shifted to cover him. Xavier was obviously daunted but held his bit of ground bravely enough. He had been stung by the indictment of the Furies; now he was standing up for his mother.

YOU ASK FOR THIS, TASTY MAN? This time the accent was on "tasty."

"Well, sure," Xavier said nervously. "I never did nothing for my mother before, so it's time I—"

YOU HAVE PROFITED FROM THE LESSON OF ALECTO, the Simurgh projected. YOU WISH TO BECOME A DUTIFUL SON.

"I guess so," Xavier admitted. "I know I'm not much, and I can't say I agree with everything Maw does, but she did try to do right by me, and I reckon it ain't never too late to start. Those old crones—uh, the three Furies—they really had something to say, you know? So I—"

FILIAL RESPECT IS GOOD, EVEN WHEN THE OBJECT IS NOT WORTHY, the Simurgh projected. TO MARRY AND SETTLE DOWN IS GOOD. BUT YOUR MOTHER'S DESIGN ERRS IN ONE RESPECT: YOU MAY NOT TAKE A WOMAN WHO IS ALREADY SPOKEN FOR.

Xavier glanced at Irene, who found herself blushing for no good reason. The Simurgh could read a person's thoughts; what had it seen in Xavier's mind? The young man was taken aback. "I may not? But Maw said—"

FIND ANOTHER WOMAN.

"Uh, yes, sir. I—"

YES, MA'AM, the bird corrected him. ONLY A MALE WOULD NOT REALIZE THAT FEMALES ARE THE KEEPERS OF THE SEEDS.

"Yes, ma'am," Xavier agreed, abashed. "Some other woman."

THEN YOU SHALL CARRY THE FEATHER TO XANTHIPPE. The Simurgh flicked a wing, and a tiny feather flew out, sailing through the air toward them. As it approached, it seemed to grow larger; what had appeared small on the giant bird was not small elsewhere. It floated directly to Xavier, who hastily raised his hands to catch it.

The tiny feather turned out to be half the length of a man. It glistened iridescently, a beautiful thing in itself, having all colors and no color.

Xavier tucked it into his belt, where it was suspended like a sword. "Gee, thanks, ma'am. I—"

AND YOU, the Simurgh projected, returning her attention to Irene. WHAT ELSE HAS THE WITCH CHARGED YOU WITH, AND WHY DO YOU ACCEDE?

"She—I thought she had my daughter—" Irene said. She felt as if she were five years old and standing before the grandmother of all grandmothers, trying to justify her foolishness. "Now I suppose I don't have to get those seeds, since—"

WHAT SEEDS?

"The seeds of—"

WHAT?!! The bird spread her wings and half lifted from the branch, flashing light and dark bands of fog out from her person.

"Ooo, now you've done it, greenpants!" Grundy muttered.

NO MORTAL DARE POSSESS THE SEEDS OF DOUBT, DISSENSION, AND WAR! the bird thundered mentally.

"Yes, ma'am," Irene agreed faintly, finding herself relieved. She had had her doubts about delivering such potent seeds to such a person.

"Why not, birdbrain?" Grundy asked, recovering his normal impudence.

"Shut *up*!" Irene and Xavier said together.

AN INTRIGUING QUESTION, the Simurgh responded. Evidently the appelation "birdbrain" didn't bother her, as her bird brain was perhaps the most powerful brain in Xanth. POSSIBLY THE WITCH DOES DESERVE THOSE SEEDS.

"No, there's no need—" Irene started.

SHE SHALL HAVE THEM, the bird decided. She jumped on the branch and the entire tree shook. Several fruits fell down and rolled toward Irene. As they came near, they gained velocity and bounced over the irregularities of the terrain. Irene watched in growing alarm, afraid she would be unable to catch them.

The three fruits landed close and burst apart. Their seeds flew up. One zinged smack into Grundy's stomach, knocking him down again. Another zoomed at Xavier's head; he reached up reflexively and caught it in one hand. The third arced toward Irene; she caught up her skirt, spread it, and captured the seed in it.

"Doubt," Xavier said uncertainly, handing her his seed. Its outline was vague; it was hard to tell for sure exactly what it was.

"Dissension," Grundy continued argumentively, passing along his seed. It had sharp spines, making it difficult to handle without getting hurt.

"And War," Irene finished warningly, fishing the third from her skirt. It resembled a mushroom-shaped cloud.

She put them away carefully in a pocket. She hoped the Simurgh was correct in issuing these. She knew their potential for abuse was staggering.

AND FOR YOU, GOOD WOMAN, the Simurgh projected, ALL YOU CAN CATCH. She spread her wings, flapped with a noise like rumbling thunder, rose briefly into the air, then dropped like a boulder. She bounced on the branch. The Tree of Seeds vibrated so vigorously that all its foliage became hazy.

Seeds flew out in an expanding sphere, already freed from their fruits, so thickly that the light of the sun was screened. Patterns of shadow played across the dome of Mount Parnassus, forming fleeting pictures of birds and trees. In a moment the wave of seeds reached Irene, pelting her like sleet. She screamed, half in amazed delight, half in horror—delight at this opportunity to gain wonderful new seeds, perhaps of types never before grown in Xanth; and horror at the loss of the great majority of offerings. At the same time, she realized now how unusual plants could spring up in places where they had never grown before; the Simurgh must have bounced on a branch and flung them loose from the Tree of Seeds. Who could guess where the present rain of seeds would fall and what oddities would manifest in the coming seasons?

Grundy opened his mouth to say something—and swallowed a seed. That shut him up.

Irene spread her skirt again, catching everything she could. Seeds struck her body and slid down into the basin of the skirt, a pitifully small selection from the mass passing her, yet of incalculable value.

In a moment, the hail of particles was over. Dazed, Irene looked around. No seeds remained anywhere on the top of the mountain; all had rolled or slid over the edge, and somehow she knew they were forever beyond recovery. But her skirt was full. Seeds of every description rested within it. Many were tiny motes; some were like snowflakes; others were like grains of sand; others like puffs of cotton; and others like little pods. They were all colors and sizes and shapes and textures and densities. She recognized some, like chinaberry (miniature teacups), airplant (with tiny wings and propellers), sundrop (shining brightly), gum (blowing bubbles), peacock plant (with pretty spread tails), and blue fern (unhappy expressions); but many others were unfamiliar. What was this one that looked like a pair of crossed bones, or the ones like hairpins? She would have to get them home and look them up in the Castle Roogna classification manuals before she dared grow them. What a fabulous treasure!

"You should look at you!" Grundy exclaimed. "Seeds in your green hair, seeds in your slippers, seeds in your boo—" He caught her fierce glare and modified his term. "Bosom," he concluded.

Now a problem manifested. "How can I carry all these seeds?" Irene asked. "I can't let go of my skirt!" If she tried to use her hands, the skirt would fall, and the seeds would slide out. She knew she would lose any that touched the ground here; the disappearance of all the other seeds made that clear.

The Simurgh had given her a gift, but had not made it easy. She could keep only those seeds she could catch—and hold.

"I'll help you," Xavier said gallantly. He started picking seeds out of her hair and dropping them into her spread skirt. When he reached for the ones caught lower, she had to demur. "Thank you Xav, I'll get the others myself, in due course." She had enough problems without his fishing for seeds in her bosom while she stood with skirt raised, unable to free her hands. He had agreed to find another woman, but there was no sense tempting him.

Grundy was meanwhile picking the seeds off her shoes and depositing them in the dress. "Girl, you sure still got 'em!" he remarked, glancing up under her skirt. Irene glared again— and again he amended himself. "Seeds, I mean. I didn't drop a one."

Now she had most of the seeds in one place—but still couldn't use her hands. What was she to do? She couldn't abide the thought of losing any of them, not even a single seed; it might be the most valuable one of all, whatever it was. Seeds were the most important thing she knew, next to her husband and daughter; she *had* to save them all!

"How you going to climb back down?" Xavier inquired.

Oh, bother! That was exactly the problem. Irene had an embarrassment of riches, and it seemed to have trapped her.

She sighed. The seeds came first. She took several not-too-deep breaths, then faced Xavier. "Xav, would you please undo my skirt? It's a wraparound; it unsnaps at the waist."

The young man gawked. "Oh, no miss! I wouldn't do that! The big bird told me not to—"

"Not to take up with a woman already spoken for," Irene finished. "That is excellent advice, and certainly I am spoken for, so you don't need to worry about that. Now I ask you this favor, as a friend who is going to find some other woman and therefore has no interest in me, to help me get these seeds home. To do that I must wrap them up in my skirt, and to do *that* I must take it off. Since my hands are not free, you and Grundy will have to help me. You must remove my skirt, and Grundy will tie it together. It is all perfectly in order." She hoped she had phrased it properly and that she was not blushing.

This was not a situation she would have cared to explain to her husband.

Xavier pondered. "Uh, yeah, I guess so. But still, it don't seem right."

"The snap is to the side. Undo it carefully and unwrap the skirt slowly, so no seeds get dumped." She spoke firmly, determined to do what she had to do.

"Oh, sure, ma'am." The young man fumbled at her waist. He was not at all good at this; men generally weren't. "You sure got a tight—"

"Watch it," Grundy cut in, grinning.

"—snap here," Xavier finished. Unlike the golem, he had not changed his original thought. Then he got it loose and unwrapped the skirt.

Grundy whistled. "Look at that—" Again he was interrupted by Irene's warning glare. Glares could be exceedingly useful at a time like this! "Pair of ankles," he finished, somewhat lamely.

"You got a seed in your—" Xavier said. "I mean, in the band to your—the green—"

"They're called panties, yokel," Grundy said before Irene could catch him with her eye. "They've never before been seen by human eye."

"Leave the seed," Irene said evenly. "Grundy, you tie the knot." Xavier brought the free side of the skirt around to the front. She continued to hold up the sides of her basin while Xavier held the rest of her skirt, which was now a more or less oblong swatch of cloth.

Grundy climbed up on the bag formed as they folded the skirt up and over the seeds, and tied it in a good topknot. The golem had originally been made of wood and cloth knotted together, so he understood the process. His knot would hold. The bag was complete, and not a seed had been lost.

Now Irene picked the seed out of her panty band. "Still wearing that same pair, I see," Grundy remarked innocently. "Aren't they getting a little old by now?"

"My panties match my complexion," Irene said with what she hoped was humor. She was not about to explain the niceties of maintaining changes of clothing. It had been bad enough

when her present clothes had gotten soaked during the night,
forcing her to grow substitutes while these dried. She did not
normally wear her underclothing several days in a row. The
golem knew that; he just wanted to force her to talk about
titillating things in the presence of Xavier. There were levels
and levels of Grundy's mischief. "Now let's get on down the
mountain." She turned to face the trunk of the main ivy plant,
clinging to the side of the knoll.

This was another problem. She had a good-sized bag to
carry, and it weighed a fair amount. She could heft it with one
hand—but she needed two hands to climb down the vine. She
didn't dare drop the bag down first; it would burst apart when
it struck below, and the seeds would be lost when they scattered. What was she to do now?

Xavier saw the problem. "I can carry the bag for you, miss.
It don't weigh much, for me."

Irene looked at him, considering. He remained a fine, muscular man. But he, too, would need two hands for climbing, so
couldn't safely carry the bag down. He might have held on
to something less bulky with his teeth, but not this.

Fortunately, Grundy came up with the answer. "One of you
go down a bit, and the other hand down the bag. Then the
other can climb below and take the bag again. Stair-step it
down. It'll take time, but the bag will get there."

"Yeah, sure, that'll work!" Xavier agreed, removing his
gaze from Irene's torso. He clambered over the brink and grasped
the vines, readily lowering himself. When his head was just
below the brink, he hooked his left hand firmly in the ivy and
reached up with his right. "Hand it down!" he called.

"He means the bag," Grundy informed Irene. She didn't
bother to glare at him this time; she handed it down. Xavier
had no trouble holding the bag, as long as he didn't have to
move.

Now it was time for her. She didn't relish descending a
vertical vine in her panties, but really, it was not worse than
wearing a bathing suit. When she had been a teenager, she had
believed that the mere sight of those celebrated green panties
would drive men mad, so naturally she had taken every opportunity to proffer fleeting glimpses of them. Now she was

in her—alas—late twenties, and long past such illusions. If only she had known what was coming, she would have come prepared!

Prepared—how? If she had not worn a skirt, she could not have caught these seeds. It would have seemed silly to bring a big bag. So maybe it was just as well, the way it had happened.

No sense dawdling. She swung her legs over the edge and found footholds in the vine. She knew Xavier was looking up at her legs, but that could not be helped; besides, he was worried that she might fall. In moments she would be below him, anyway.

She paused, glancing back up at the Tree of Seeds and the monstrous sapient bird perched on it. "Farewell, Simurgh, and thank you!" she called.

FAREWELL, GOOD WOMAN, the bird responded. REMEMBER THE NATURE OF THE SEEDS YOU CARRY.

Scant chance she would forget! These seeds represented wealth beyond her fondest prior imaginings!

Irene resumed her descent, knowing that she would probably never again meet the like of the Simurgh.

Chapter 10. Cyclopean Eye

In the morning, Ivy and Hugo and Stanley peeked over the edge of their ledge to spy out the worst. It was confirmed. A monster slept across the cave entrance.

They looked about the rest of the cave, seeking some other exit. There was none. This was a one-entrance domicile, and the monster blocked that one.

"Can we sneak out past him?" Ivy asked. "Before he wakes?"

Hugo inspected the monster. It was humanoid, hairy and huge. There was no gap between it and the walls of the mouth of the cave. "We'd have to climb over its legs," he said. "I don't think it would sleep long, then."

"Maybe he'll go away soon," Ivy said.

But as she spoke, the giant rolled over, so that his horrendously ugly face was toward them, and opened his eye.

"Uh-oh," Hugo said.

It was a fair comment, for the giant saw them. "Ho!" he roared with a voice like mottled thunder and scrambled to his feet. The cave entrance was high enough to admit two and a half ordinary people standing on each other's heads, but the hairy pate of the giant barely cleared it. "Midgets in cave!" the gaping mouth roared.

"Run for it!" Hugo cried in a fit of inspiration.

They tried. They slid-scrambled down to the floor—but the only place to run was toward the monster, and his huge, hairy, knobbly legs barred the way. His enormous eye seemed to flash as it watched them, and his gigantic wooden club, formed from the trunk of a medium ironwood tree, hovered menacingly. The three of them lost what little nerve they had remaining and backed away.

But the giant followed them, poking forward with the club. "What you do in cave?" he roared, causing sand to rattle loose and sift down from the ceiling.

Ivy was terrified, but she knew her friends were brave. "We must fight him!" she declared. "We'll make him let us go!"

Hugo exchanged an incredulous glance with Stanley. The logic of women was indecipherable! Then he turned a blank face to Ivy. "Fight him?"

"Throw fruit at him!" she said encouragingly.

"But my fruit is rotten!"

"No it isn't!"

He remembered. "That's right; it isn't any more! But rotten fruit is okay for this!" He conjured a huge superripe tomato and hurled it at the giant. It struck about halfway up, splattering the crude animal-skin clothing with drippy red tomato-brains.

"And you, Stanley, with your superhot steam—you can toast his toes!" she said encouragingly.

The little dragon pumped up his steam. It was indeed superhot now, and he found his courage returning. If Ivy thought he could fight the giant effectively, maybe he could. He braced himself, aimed his snout precisely, and issued a searing jet of white-hot steam that heated the giant's callused, warty, big left toe.

The giant paused, taking a moment to realize that something was wrong. It was, after all, a long way from his toe to his head, and the pain took time to travel through the poorly maintained nerve channels. The aroma of cooking meat wafted up from the affected digit.

The giant sniffed. He licked his lips with a long sloppy tongue. That smelled good!

Then the pain plowed through the sludge clogging the last nerve channel and reached the pain center.

He roared again. Stalactites picked up the impulse, vibrating like tuning forks, and a pile of old fish scales jumped, registering two notches on the earthquake scale. The wind from the roar blew the little dragon head over tail, interfering with his aim; his remaining breath of steam shot up in a vertical geyser and petered out.

Hugo threw another fruit—this time an overripe watermelon. It was too heavy for him to heave high, so it splatted on the giant's hot toe, cooling it.

Ivy realized that they weren't making much progress. "Think of something, Hugo!" she cried. "You're smart!"

"I am?" Hugo still found this hard to believe, especially in the morning. But he discovered he was smarter than he had supposed, and he did think of something. "Cherries!" he cried. After all, they had worked pretty well to disrupt Fracto, the bad cloud, when the three children were fleeing it.

He started heaving cherries, and they exploded all around the giant with fancy red booms. But they were too small to have much effect on a target of this size.

"A pineapple!" Hugo said. It, too, had proved to be an effective fruit in the past, with some sweet results. He heaved one. This was considerably more powerful, and the explosion set the giant's animal skin on fire. The conflagration was closer to the pain center, and the nerve channels had already been reamed out, so the smell of roasting meat hardly got started before the new roar shook the cave. The giant danced about, smashing out the flames with fist and club.

In the course of this activity, the monster bent down. For a moment his eye hovered near the dragon.

Stanley shot out a blast of steam that bathed the eye.

"Owwwgh!" the giant cried, clapping his hands to his face as the club dropped to the floor. "Ungh, smarts!"

"Now we can go!" Hugo cried happily. "Stanley blinded him!"

"Oh!" Ivy exclaimed. She paused to peer up at the tears squeezing out between the monster's fingers. "Poor thing!"

"Hey, we gotta go!" Hugo said. "Before he starts blocking off the door again!"

"But his eye!" she said. She had sympathy for anyone who cried for any reason. Once she had gotten dust in her eye, and it had teared something awful. "Suppose it doesn't get better?"

"So what? Who cares what happens to a mean old monster?"

Her lip firmed rebelliously. "*I* care! I didn't really want to hurt him!"

Hugo exchanged a look of bafflement tinged with disgust with the dragon. They found this feminine sensitivity as bewildering as her Sorceress talent. "You want to help the monster?"

"Well, I guess if he needs it," Ivy said. "Till his eye gets better, maybe."

"And then he'll eat us!" Hugo said.

Ivy couldn't definitely refute that, so she ignored it. She called to the giant, who was now standing silently, blinking his sore eye, from which huge tears were flowing. "Does it hurt bad, giant? I'm sorry."

The giant seemed as surprised as Hugo and Stanley had been. "Me? You talk to me?"

"You see any other gross, awful, one-eyed, hairy giants in here?" Hugo inquired sarcastically.

"I see nothing at moment," the giant said, rubbing his orb with a callused fist.

"Don't do that!" Ivy cried, remembering admonitions by her mother. "You'll get dirt in it and make it worse!"

The giant stopped immediately. It seemed he was responsive to the voice of female authority. "It hurt, but will mend," he said. "I got steamed worse before and mended okay."

"I'm glad," Ivy said. "We didn't mean to hurt you, really. We just wanted to get away, so you wouldn't eat us."

"Why you not say so?" the giant demanded. "I not eat people! Too small, bad taste! I let you go."

"I don't believe you," Hugo said.

"All I ask, what you do in cave," the giant pointed out, blinking his eye. "Why you not answer me?"

Now Ivy and Hugo exchanged glances, then looked at Stanley, who rippled a shrug down the length of his body. "I guess we didn't think of it," Ivy confessed. "We just thought naturally you'd—we're only children, you know."

The giant's eye finally cleared, though it was red around the rim and still rather watery. He sat down with a thump that made the earthquake scales jump again. "I not know, or not have yelled. Get monkeys come in, steal bones—"

"We wouldn't do that," Ivy said quickly. "We just needed a good place to sleep. We didn't know it was your cave." She leaned forward confidentially, for the giant's face was now not nearly so far distant. "There are monsters out there, you know."

"Sure there are," the giant agreed. "Good thing, too. What I eat."

"I don't trust him," Hugo said.

"Hugo doesn't trust you," Ivy informed the giant privately.

"Well, I not trust him neither!" the giant replied, disgruntled. "He fire my uniform!"

"I'm sure Hugo is sorry."

"I am not!" Hugo exclaimed. "It was war!"

"Oh, that different," the giant said. "All fair, love and war."

"Yes!" Hugo agreed, mollified. "My mother says that!"

"She know. Mothers know. What bomb you use?"

"A pineapple." Hugo conjured another and held it in his hand, all bright yellow with a green top. "I conjure fruit."

"That good talent," the giant said. "Wish I do magic."

"Why don't we all be friends?" Ivy suggested, for she was a friendly child.

The giant laughed. "Real people not friends of Cyclops!" he protested.

"Why not?"

That stumped him. Now that she made him consider the matter, friendship seemed more reasonable. He didn't know she was a Sorceress, or that what she perceived tended to become more real. "Just tradition, I 'spose."

"We're too young to know about tradition," Ivy pointed out.

"Oh. well, okay. Be friends. Have some monster." The Cyclops reached across the cave and hauled up the dead griffin he had brought with him during the night. It was half eaten, but considerable mass remained.

Ivy recoiled. "It's all gooky with ick!"

"Blood," the Cyclops explained. "Taste good. I lick off hunk for you. Then it nice and clean."

"Thank you," Ivy said, remembering her manners. "But I guess I'm not really that hungry." She glanced about. "But maybe Stanley would like some."

The dragon agreed immediately. The Cyclops tore off a hind leg and dumped it down before Stanley, who chomped blissfully into it.

"Would you like some fruit?" Hugo asked, feeling neglected. "I can conjure some more."

The Cyclops eyed the pineapple. "Uh, thanks, but that not nice for teeth and burn tongue."

"Oh, I didn't mean *this*," Hugo said, carefully setting down the pineapple. "I meant regular fruit." He conjured a hand of bananas and proffered it.

The Cyclops' eye widened. "Bnans! Not taste in decades! Got big kind?"

"Oh, sure. Anything." Hugo, happy to show off his present power, conjured a hand of plantains. This was, of course, a giant hand, and each finger looked like a monstrous banana, but was too tough for a normal person to eat raw.

The Cyclops tore one plantain off and popped it into his mouth, skin and all. He chomped down. "Oh, slurp!" he exclaimed with his mouth full of squish. "Scrumptious!"

Hugo conjured colored berries for himself and Ivy. He preferred yellow, while she liked blue. They all ate contentedly. Stanley was now cracking bone with his teeth, as happy as he had ever been.

After that they exchanged stories. Ivy told how she had taken a walk with a zombie, and a ride on a carpet, and a tour with a yak, and gotten so turned around she didn't know for sure which way was home. Hugo described how he had accidentally thrown Youth water on his father and the Gap Dragon, then run away when his father vanished, until he met Ivy and started traveling with her. The two explained how they had joined the baby dragon, whom they now knew to be the former Gap Dragon, but who was Stanley now, and how they had fought off the bugbear and King Fracto the Cloud.

"King Cumulo-Fracto-Nimbus?" the Cyclops demanded. "Well I know and not like that airhead!" And he launched into his own story, which naturally enough he called his-story, or simply history.

His name was Brontes, and he had once been one of the powers of the air, along with his brothers Steropes and Arges. They were some of the children of the Sky and the Earth, and they forged thunderbolts for their father. But the Sky grew jealous of them, and deprived them of their powers, and banished them. Their mother Earth gave them sanctuary in her realm but could not do more, for she was not as strong as their father; besides, she liked the Sky. "He gets tempestuous at times," she had conceded, "but he's got such a nice blue eye. Besides, I need the rain he sends."

So Brontes had hidden here in this obscure cave for a long time, afraid to go abroad by day because of the wrath of the Sky, and his power of thunder had been usurped by the self-styled Cloud-King Fracto, who had originally been no more than minor fog. Brontes was alone; more than anything, he missed the company of his brothers, but he did not know where they were and did not dare range too far from his cave, lest he be caught in the open when day came and be destroyed by one of the very thunderbolts he had helped forge so long ago when he was young.

"Oh, that's such a sad story!" Ivy exclaimed. "We've got

to help you find your brothers." She had a very tender heart, because of the way she had been raised.

"How you do that?" Brontes asked, interested but not unduly hopeful. His brothers had been lost a long time.

"There's something about her," Hugo said. "I never was very good with my fruits until she came along, and I don't think Stanley was as hot with his steam."

"All it takes is a positive attitude," Ivy said brightly, pleased with her ability to turn a good phrase. "When I think maybe I can do something, like talking well, then I try it and find I can do it. When Hugo really tried to conjure good fruit, then he did it. And Stanley was able to make hotter steam when he tried. So maybe if you really tried to see where your brothers are, you could do it."

"I've tried to find them ever since we were banished!" Brontes exclaimed. "Why should it suddenly work now?"

As usual, Ivy ignored what she couldn't answer. It was a very effective device. "You have such a fine big eye, I'm sure you can see very well with it. Why don't you look?"

"Very well," the Cyclops agreed, humoring her, for she was an extremely cute child. Light was coming in the cave entrance and retouching her hair to a delicate green tint, and her eyes were the same color.

Brontes peered out of the cave, into the forest beyond. Behind the trees, the gully ascended, so there really was not very much for anyone to view.

Then he sat up straight. "I *can* see well!" he exclaimed. "I can see—right through the trees! I never do that before!"

"He's talking better, too," Hugo noted.

"You just never really, really tried before," Ivy said confidently. She was used to the people she met underestimating their potentials.

Brontes swung his gaze around. "I can see through the cave wall!" he said, amazed. "Through the mountain itself! I've got Y-ray vision!"

Hugo's brow furrowed. He had picked up smatterings of information relating to magic, since that was his father's business. "I think you mean Z-ray vision," he said.

"It's Hoo-ray vision!" the Cyclops said. "Now I can see all

Xanth!" He continued to swing his gaze around, taking it all in. "And there—there's my brother Steropes! Oh, he looks so much older! He's in a cave on the other side of this very mountain! I never realized! And Arges—in the next mountain over! I guess we hunted in different directions! So near and yet so far!"

"I just knew you could do it!" Ivy said, clapping her little hands with joy.

Hugo looked out the cave mouth. "Day is getting on," he said. "We'd better start moving."

"If you wait till night, I can carry you some distance," Brontes offered.

Ivy considered. "No, you must go to meet your brothers then. We like the day; the Sky isn't out to get us. We'll go now." She smiled shyly. "But we'll always be friends, won't we?"

"Friends," the Cyclops agreed. He fished in his uniform and dug out a slightly scorched little bone. "Chew on this if you ever need me at night, and I will hasten to help. It is the one bit of magic I possess. I never had occasion to use it before—but I never had a friend before, either."

"Gee, thanks, I will," Ivy said, accepting the bone. She knotted it into her somewhat tangled hair, where it would not be lost, for nothing was quite as permanent as a tangle. "Now I'm a cave girl!"

With that they parted, the Cyclops resuming his nap inside the cave and the three travelers resuming their journey northeast. Progress was faster now, for they were reasonably well rested and fed, and the day was bright.

Ivy looked up into the patches of blue sky visible beyond the trees, privately surprised that anything so pretty would be so unkind to a nice creature like the Cyclops. But she realized she was too small to understand everything in Xanth yet.

The forest seemed much less threatening than it had the night before. However, appearances in Xanth were generally deceptive. They rounded a tree—and skidded to a pause. "A girl!" Hugo exclaimed, as if he had never seen one before.

It did seem to be a girl. But though the size of the figure was between those of Hugo and Ivy, she was no child. She was a petite, dark, lovely little woman. As she spied them, her hand moved to her hip and drew forth a brightly gleaming knife. "Stay away from me, monster!" she cried.

Ivy realized what the problem was. "That's Stanley," she said. "He's my friend."

"He's a dragon!" the small woman pointed out.

"He's the baby Gap Dragon," Hugo explained.

"The Gap Dragon!" The woman's terror increased. "I thought he looked familiar!" She backed away, knife held ready.

Ivy knew that most women were clumsy with weapons, but this one evidently knew how to use hers. Maybe it was because she was so stunningly pretty, despite her somewhat bedraggled condition. Ivy's mother had impressed upon her that pretty girls needed to be able to defend themselves.

"Oh, come on," Ivy said. "If he doesn't bite me, why should he bite you? You're a people." She patted Stanley on the head.

"The Gap Dragon eats anything, especially people," the woman said. "Anyway, I'm *not* a people. I'm a goblin girl."

Ivy's brow wrinkled. "But goblins are ugly!"

"Not the girls," Hugo said. "My father says the goblin girls are pretty, and he knows just about everything, so it must be true."

"Only the Good Magician knows everything," the woman asserted.

"That's what I said."

She looked at him again, startled. "Yes, the goblin girls are pretty, and the goblin men are ugly," she agreed after a moment. "That's one reason I deserted my tribe to seek romance. Are you quite sure the dragon won't bite?"

Ivy turned to Stanley. "Do you bite goblin girls?"

The dragon puffed steam noncommittally.

"See—he's not hungry anyway," Ivy said. "He's had a good meal of griffin bone and—" She shrugged, not remembering whether Stanley had eaten any fruit this time.

The woman relaxed slightly. "A good meal." Then she stiffened again. "That dragon killed a griffin?"

Ivy laughed. "Oh, no! It was carrion the Cyclops gave him after Stanley steamed his eye."

"The Cyclops!" the woman cried, almost tripping in her effort to retreat farther.

"You misunderstand," Hugo said. "We are friends with the Cyclops. But he never leaves his cave by day."

Again the woman relaxed. "You are unusual people!" She brushed her fine tresses away from her face. "Oh, I'm famished!"

"Famshed?" Ivy asked, perplexed.

"Hungry. I'm about to pass out on my feet."

Hugo conjured a handful of raspberries. "We have lots of fruit."

"I really haven't eaten since yesterday!" the woman exclaimed, as if this were highly significant news. There was a certain flair in the way she spoke; it was part of her beauty.

"Sit down and eat and tell us your story," Ivy invited her. "I'm Ivy and this is Hugo."

The goblin girl accepted the raspberries and sat delicately on a mossy stone. "I'm Glory, daughter of Gorbage, chief of the north-slope Gap Goblins. My story is very poignant."

Hugo and Ivy were perplexed now. "What kind of ant?" Ivy asked.

Glory smiled briefly as she chewed on a raspberry whose juice was no darker than her lips. "Poignant. It means piquant."

"Another kind of ant?" Ivy asked. "We did see some giants in the coven-tree."

The woman frowned, still looking quite pretty. "I meant to say sad," she clarified. "Pointed and sad."

"Oh," Ivy said. "But I don't like sad stories. Couldn't you make it happy?"

"Possibly it will have a happy ending," Glory said.

"Oh, goody!" And Ivy settled back to listen, while Hugo conjured more fruit for their new acquaintance.

Chapter 11. Dread Seeds

Irene was beset by doubt. First she worried that they would drop the bag of seeds in the course of the frequent passings back and forth; when that didn't happen, she was concerned that she would misplace her grip and fall herself. In between, she was nervous about the impression she was making on those below, climbing down the vine in her blouse and green panties. At age fifteen, she would have loved the excuse; now it bothered her considerably. She wasn't certain whether it would be worse to have people admiring her exposed legs and whatever—or to have people condemning them. She had tried to keep trim and firm, but...

They made it safely. Xap and Chem and Zora were waiting, together with several of the Muses.

As soon as she and the seeds were safely down, Irene grew a dress plant and a new pair of lady-slippers, then clothed herself properly. But her worries were only replaced by others. Where was Ivy now? Had the Cyclops eaten her? No, of course not; the little ivy plant—what a contrast between the one she wore and the one she had climbed!—remained healthy. But it would still take at least a day to get back, unless she grew another flying plant and flew back. Chem wouldn't be able to come along, then, or Zora Zombie, and she needed these friends. Also, none of her flying plants could handle the additional burden of the big bag of seeds. Better to ride back as they had ridden in, though the loss of time chafed.

Suppose they encountered the Python again, or the maenads? There were so many hazards between her and her child!

Irene got a grip on herself and checked her big new bag of seeds. She picked out several familiar ones and several unfamiliar ones, just in case. She had used up so many of her regular seeds that she could no longer depend on them.

The Muses were friendly, civilized, intelligent women, and Irene would have loved to visit with them, but she had no time for chitchat. Any delay could be horrendous for Ivy! As it was, there might not be enough time. Everything was so uncertain! "Let's get moving!" she snapped.

The others looked askance at her but didn't argue. They bade hasty farewell to the Muses and set off down the best path.

Still Irene was agitated. Suppose Chem stumbled and broke a leg? So many things could go wrong!

Grundy looked back at her. "Anything wrong, Irene?" the golem asked. "You looked scared."

"Shut up, you little rag blob!" she snapped.

"He only asked if—" Chem started.

"You too, animal rump!" Irene said.

Hurt, the centaur was silent. Irene had never before addressed her in such manner, and the language was undeserved.

"The seeds!" Xavier exclaimed. "The big bird said to remember what they were!"

Suddenly it connected. "Doubt, Dissension, and War!" Irene exclaimed. "I've been doubting ever since I got them!"

"That isn't all," Grundy muttered sullenly.

Irene realized that it wasn't enough just to know the cause of her problem. She had to find a way to eliminate the bad effects of the seeds.

"We can carry them," Xavier said helpfully. "Pass them out, one to a person, so it won't be too bad for none of us."

Despite her doubt, irritation, and growing inclination for violence, Irene saw the merit in the suggestion. The lout was actually pretty smart. She handed the seed of Doubt to Grundy, the seed of Dissension to Xavier, and the seed of War to Zora. She didn't want the two steeds to have them; they were too important for transportation, and Xap would be too dangerous if he developed warlike notions.

Irene felt immediate relief as the seeds left her. Confidence and equilibrium returned. They would make it.

"Lot of bad things on the way," Grundy said. "Maybe we should take another route."

That was the seed of Doubt. It helped to know that; she could ignore the golem.

"Come on, Xap, get your gait straight," Xavier said irritably. "You're bouncing us all over the place, you birdbeak!"

"Don't let the seed of Dissension govern you!" Irene warned, having felt its effect herself so recently.

"Shut your yap, you middle-aged broad!" he snapped at her.

Irene felt the color cruising up her neck and face. She knew the cause of his language, but it was all she could do to hold her tongue.

She looked apprehensively at the zombie, who now rode behind Xavier again. Zora seemed as sanguine as only a zombie could be, despite the fact that zombies had very little blood. Apparently the seeds did not affect the undead. "Give your seeds to Zora," Irene called. "She can handle them." At least Irene hoped so.

It was done. The problem seemed to be solved.

One thing Irene now realized—the three dread seeds would do Xanthippe little good! That must be why the Simurgh had decided to send them to the witch.

With the seeds under control and the route known, the travelers should be able to make good progress back to the region where Ivy was lost. Irene began to feel faintly confident. With luck—

Luck was not with them. The Python lay coiled in their path. The huge snake was bruised and had patches of skin missing, but had survived the onslaught of the wild women. The deadly head lifted and the huge jaws gaped.

"We ain't off Parnassus yet!" Xavier muttered.

Quickly Irene fetched out her new dragon seed and threw it down before the Python. "Grow!" she cried.

The seed sprouted vigorously—but something happened to Irene's head. She put her hand to her hair—and discovered plants growing there. She had missed three seeds hidden in her hair, and her command had started them off! Normally only the seed she directed her attention to grew, which was why the big bag of seeds wasn't sprouting; but there was some peripheral effect, and seeds actually in contact with her body could also be set off, though at a slower rate. She was starting a garden in her hair!

Worse, there was another seed hidden in her bosom. It must have fallen there during the original spray from the Tree. It was growing inside her blouse, curling around an unmentionable area. She plunged her hand down her neckline, fishing for the plant.

"What a place *this* is!" a sneering voice exclaimed from inside her dress. "Are these mountains, pyramids, or bags of sand?"

Worse and worse! That was a devil's tongue plant! She had to catch it and get it out before the others noticed.

"I've heard of cushy locations," the tongue said, slurping around some more. "But this is entirely too much of a good thing! I can't get my roots properly grounded in all this cheese-cake."

Irene finally got her fingers on the tongue. It was slimy and slippery, but she yanked it out. The thing flapped about in her hand, but could not get free.

"What you got there?" Xavier inquired, glancing at her.

"What's it to you, you son of a witch?" the devil's tongue demanded. Irene hastily threw it away. It landed in an elephant bush, which trumpeted angrily. "Oh, go pack in your trunk!" the tongue said.

Now Grundy looked at her. "Hey, you've fixed up your hair!"

Irene touched her hair again. The tongue had distracted her, but now these other three plants were the main concern. She identified each by touch: a centipede plant, a fiery love flower, and a bird's-nest fern.

The Python hissed and slid forward, tired of waiting for this party to get moving. The half-grown dragon tree snapped at it. Her hair would have to wait a little longer!

Xap reared and charged, eager for the fray.

Irene grabbed another seed—this one for a snowball plant. "Grow!" she told it, and tossed it into the Python's opening mouth. The reptile, naturally enough, swallowed the sprouting seed.

For an instant nothing happened; the plant was still growing. Then the huge serpent became cold. A segment of its body turned blue. The mouth opened again, and freezing fog came out. Icicles formed on the upper teeth.

The dragon tree pounced on the frigid snake, but found only ice. It would be a while before the creature thawed. Xap and Chem trotted past, unmolested. One hazard was out of the way!

But already the next hazard manifested. The maenads, who, it seemed, were still pursuing the Python, swarmed up the path. Blood was in their eyes and on their claws; probably some of it was their own, for several were limping. But they remained as vicious as ever.

Irene fished for a suitable seed. She had an African violent that she wouldn't have used on any man, but these wild women were another matter. She grabbed it and threw it forward. "Grow!"

The seed sprouted in air, sending out green-backed foliage and silvery stalks. Gold disks fruited, gleaming in the sunlight. Brightly shining stones appeared, decorating the vines.

The maenads shrieked and pounced on the fruit. They plucked the golden coins and hurled them at the oncoming party. They tossed the greenbacks in the air.

"What kind of plant is that?" Grundy asked.

Irene looked more closely and groaned. She had thrown the wrong seed! "That's a treasure vine!"

"These creatures of Parnassus sure like money," the golem remarked. "Look at them play with it."

Indeed, the wild women were throwing the bills and coins around as if they were splashing water. They formed piles of money and reveled in them. They fought over particular bills with big figures printed on them; it seemed women were partial to that kind. But those who had not amassed enough of a fortune were turning again toward the visiting party, their predatory eyes glinting. Irene knew there was nothing quite so dangerous as a hungry wild woman.

She got her fingers on the correct seed and threw it. "Grow, violent!" she cried.

The plant obeyed with alacrity. Purple clubs appeared, smashing at anything in reach. "Ow!" a wild woman screamed as a club clobbered her toe. She danced away on one foot.

"Oof!" another cried as another club whomped her bottom.

"Hooo!" a third screeched, sailing into the air, and a club sprouted right underneath her.

"You sure fight mean!" Xavier said admiringly as they skirted the mêlée and went on down the mountain.

"And you thought women were gentle," Grundy reminded him snidely.

Xavier looked nonplused. "Well, the centaur filly here is—"

Xap made a squawk of negation tinged with humor, and Chem blushed. It seemed there were some aspects of centaur private life that were sensitive. Startled, Xavier shifted his statement. "A mighty healthy one," he concluded. With that both hippogryph and centaur were satisfied.

Irene nodded to herself. That must have been some night exploration those two mixbreeds had!

Xavier brightened. "Zora!" he exclaimed. "She's gentle! She don't have a violent bone in her body!"

"All her bones are rotten," Grundy agreed. "It's easy to be gentle when you're dead."

"Undead," Irene said, coming to Zora's defense. "That's not the same." It occurred to her that even Zora had not seemed gentle when she faced down the Furies and drove them away. But that was not an issue she cared to argue; she owed too much to the zombie. "I agree; Zora is a nice girl."

"If you like that type," Grundy muttered.

"She sure helped us," Xavier said. "Right now she's carrying the bad seeds for us! If she had any doubt, dissension, or war in her, she'd be a zombie tigress by now!"

"Yes, that's right," the golem agreed, glancing across at Zora. Irene glanced, too, to see how the zombie was taking this discussion. Zora seemed blissfully unconcerned; in fact, she even looked healthier. Her flesh now seemed more soiled than decayed, all the features of her face were in place, and her hair swung as if recently cleaned and brushed, with only a few patches missing.

"But some zombies are violent," Chem remarked. "During the War of the Nextwave, the zombies fought like maniacs." She seemed happy to have the subject be Zora instead of herself. "So it must be Zora who is peaceful. Even the Furies remarked on it. She must have been awfully nice when she lived."

It hadn't actually been peacefulness that the Furies had remarked on, Irene remembered, but Zora's loyalty to her parents. Chem was only going by what Irene and the others had talked about, since she herself hadn't been there at the time; it was a minor misunderstanding. "And the heel who caused her to suicide must have been an unutterable slob," Irene concluded with some feeling.

"She suicided?" Xavier asked, surprised.

"Heartbreak," Irene told him. "Her true love was false."

Xavier scowled. "You know, I never zapped a living man. I guess that's one I would. A man's got no business making no commitment he don't keep, ever."

Again, Irene was impressed with the young man's crudely expressed values. She herself had absolutely no romantic interest in him, but she could appreciate that if she had, that interest would not be misplaced. Xavier was true to his values, and they were decent ones. No woman would commit suicide because of him.

Zora, riding behind him, still said nothing. Irene realized with another surge of shame that all of them continued to treat the zombie like an unfeeling thing. What almost made it worse was that none of them did it intentionally; it just was very easy to treat a zombie like a zombie, a thing.

"I wonder what misfortunes she's cursed with," Xavier said after a moment. "The Furies' curses, which she saved us from?"

"Either they haven't affected her any more than the three bad seeds do," Irene said, "or they haven't occurred yet. We've had some close calls, but nothing's happened to her."

"It's really too bad about those curses," Xavier said. "I should have taken my own, like a man."

Irene found she could neither agree nor argue with that, so she let it pass without comment. After all, she also had been spared the curse of misfortune because of Zora's intercession. It was possible that a misfortune that would kill Irene would have little or no effect on Zora—but it was also possible that it would be equally devastating for human or zombie. She simply didn't know, so didn't know how to feel. She owed so much to Zora and had no idea how she could ever repay it.

Once it had been possible to restore a zombie to life, but only two people had known the formula for the necessary elixir—the Zombie Master and the Good Magician. The Zombie Master had forgotten it in the course of his own eight hundred years as a zombie; the information had probably been in one of the portions of his brain that got sloughed away. The Good Magician was now hopeless. So there was no such reward possible for Zora—and if there had been, she would not have wanted it, since she had no reason to live. Irene tried to imagine a greater tragedy than that, but could not. Why was it that sometimes the best people suffered the worst fates? Was there no inherent justice in Xanth, despite all its magic?

They reached the base of the mountain and crossed the rolling creekbed. This time Irene took the precaution of growing an action plant, which sent its roots throughout the bed and caused all the loose stones to vibrate and roll. Any snakes or other dangerous or annoying creatures would depart in haste! Crossing was now no problem; all they had to do was set their feet where nothing was active, because the action plant guaranteed that anything that could move was already doing so.

Now they were in a more normal region of Xanth and moved rapidly. Irene was glad to leave Parnassus behind; it was no place for civilized mortal creatures, except perhaps at the top. Xap remained on the ground, running beside Chem. It was evident that the hippogryph's squawked comment about ungentle centaurs had been a compliment, not an insult. He liked her very well.

In gratifyingly short order, they were back where they had made camp last night. It was now late in the day, but they didn't want to sleep in this particular spot. They had hardly passed it before they heard the screaming of the three Furies.

"We sure don't need this again!" Xavier said grimly. "They were right about me and Maw—I'll give the old crones that!—but I'll take care of it my own way without no other lesson."

Irene agreed, remembering her own guilt about her mother.

"I'm not sure the Furies are strictly fair about their charges," she said. "Or their curses. If so—I mean, if they're more interested in cursing and hurting people than in improving their behavior—then they are to some extent hypocrites. It happens I have a seed that should stop them." She located it and held it ready. "Just charge on by when you see them."

The three Furies appeared. Irene nudged Chem with her knee, and the centaur swerved toward the dog-faced trio.

"Ho, you vile equine!" Tisi cried, spreading her wing-cloak threateningly. "Does your dam Cherie know what you have been doing with—"

Irene threw down the seed. "Grow!" she cried.

The seed sprouted before the three hags. "What's this?" Alec cried, alarmed.

"Argh!" Meg screamed. "I know that one! 'Tis an honesty plant!"

"So how have you three harridans treated *your* mothers?" Irene called back.

"That's awkward," Chem said. "The Furies never had a mother. They sprang from the blood of their murdered father. That's why they're so concerned with—"

The Furies were appalled as they came into the spell of the honesty plant. "Ah, oh!" one screamed. "In truth we have neglected our sire's grave!"

"We were so busy punishing the sins of others, we neglected our own!" another agreed.

"And we must pay!" the third cried, waving her brass-studded scourge.

"Ooo, what you did!" Grundy said happily. "They'll have to flog and curse themselves!"

"Honesty does awkward things to people," Irene remarked smugly. "Yet I'm sorry if they never knew a mother." It was, she found, difficult to condemn anyone once that person's situation was understood. The Furies, too, were creatures of tragedy.

They left the Furies behind, then found a secure place near a pleasant stream and made their camp. Irene grew a chain fern around the perimeter, so that any intruder would trip over it and set the sweet-bells plants to ringing a warning. Then she grew several food plants for them to eat and a blanket plant from which to make beds. She didn't worry about protecting herself from Xavier during her sleep; she now understood his nature well enough to know that he took seriously the warning of the Simurgh not to mess with a spoken-for woman. He would turn his attention elsewhere as soon as this mission for his mother was complete, and whatever girl he found would be fortunate.

How she wished she were back with her husband Dor, who was surely quite worried about her! But he could, if he thought of it, get hold of a magic mirror that would show him she was all right.

Too bad, she thought, as she wound her way toward a troubled sleep, that Dor could not similarly verify exactly where Ivy was. Good Magician Humfrey had been able to tune the mirrors on to anyone or anything, but they would not obey other people as readily. There was a mirror at Castle Roogna that would show either Dor or Irene, whoever happened to be away from the castle, but no one else. They had assumed that Ivy would always be with one parent or the other—indeed, she always had been before, or at least within calling range— so they had not worried about tuning to her separately. That could have made an enormous difference this time! But at least the little ivy plant Irene carried offered its continuing assurance. Without that, she would have been driven to distraction long since.

They resumed travel at dawn, eating halfway on the run. Irene just wanted to deliver the three seeds and the feather to Xanthippe, return Xavier and Xap to her, and get on with the business of locating and rescuing Ivy. They had been lucky so far that nothing serious had happened to any of them, but luck was a fickle ally.

They were not far from the witch's house when they spied a lovely, small, spring-fed pond and drew up for refreshment. Irene dismounted in order to use the nearby bushes for a private function, while Xap, Xavier, and Zora went to the sparkling pond.

The hippogryph put down his beak and scooped in a mouth-

ful of the clear water, raising his head to let it trickle down his
throat, bird-fashion. He glanced across at Chem, making a flick
of the wing to invite her to join him, but she was waiting for
Irene, helping to shield her from the view of the males.

"If Xap says the water's good, it's good," Xavier said cheerfully. "Not that there was any question; you can see how green
it is around here. No dragons in this spring!" He flopped down
on the bank and put his mouth to the surface, man-fashion.

Zora, beside him, tripped over a rock and plunged headlong
into the pool. "Hey!" Xavier exclaimed, scooting back to avoid
the splash. "I meant to drink it, not swim in it!" He was smiling
good-naturedly.

Zora got awkwardly to her feet and trudged out of the shallow water. Her sunken eyes seemed to glow as she gazed at
Xavier.

"There's something odd about her," Grundy remarked. "Do
zombies glow?"

"Maybe when they're in love," Irene said facetiously as she
emerged from the bush. She would have been embarrassed,
too, if she had fallen in the pond!

"Love?" Chem asked. "You know, some springs—"

"Don't drink that water, Xav!" Grundy shouted.

Xavier paused, his mouth just above the surface of the pool.
"Why not? I don't care if she took a dip. It was just her bad
luck."

"Because it may be a love spring!" Irene said. "Look at
Zora!"

Indeed, Zora was gazing at the young man with such mute
adoration that no one could any longer mistake her transfor-
mation. It was the nature of love springs to cause anyone who
drank from them to fall hopelessly in love with the first creature
of the opposite sex he or she perceived thereafter. If the victim
already loved someone else, the new love was superimposed;
that person then had two loves, the most recent one being the
stronger. Love springs accounted for most of the crossbreed
species of Xanth, and there were many funny and tragic tales
of this. The effect of a love spring could not be changed by
lining up some more promising prospect and taking another
drink in his or her presence. That would only add yet another

love to the collection, making the situation even more difficult. Like death, love was practically irrevocable.

"The misfortune!" Xavier exclaimed in horror. "The curse that was meant for me! She got it instead!"

That made sense, Irene realized. Obviously the curse of the Furies *had* been slated for Xavier; he had been poised to drink, and only the zombie's accident had brought it on herself instead. This could have been considered coincidence—but the curse eliminated that explanation.

"What worse misfortune could there be for a zombie," Chem murmured, "than to fall in love with a living man?"

What, indeed! Especially a zombie who had suicided because of blighted love. Zora's love for the other man might have faded after she died, but that only left her more vulnerable to this new love.

"Maybe she could go to Mundania," Grundy said. But Irene knew immediately that that was no solution. It was true that magic did not work in Mundania—that land was extremely backward that way, and she often wondered how the inhabitants could stand it—so that any spell could be broken there. But Zora was not a normal person. She was a zombie, animated only by magic. She would be all-the-way dead in Mundania. So she was caught between hopeless love and death, and doomed to eternal heartbreak.

"Those Furies didn't mess around," Chem said. "They could hardly have inflicted a crueler punishment on a more innocent person."

No one could argue with that. They had agreed that Zora was the nicest of them all, already suffering unfairly—and now her grief had been intensified beyond reason.

"But they intended the curse for me," Xavier repeated. "For me to fall in love with a zombie." The horror of that intended fate was now coming home to him.

"We should never have gone near the Furies," Irene said. "Their punishments really do make people wish they were dead—perhaps even when they are already dead."

"But the water's supposed to be good!" Xavier said querulously. "Xap wasn't affected by it!"

"How about that," Grundy agreed. "I'll ask him."

The golem squawked at the hippogryph. Xap responded. Grundy laughed.

"What's so funny?" Irene demanded, shaken by what had happened. Compelled love was certainly no laughing matter! Suppose she herself had—

"It didn't affect Xap, because the first female he saw was Chem," Grundy explained. "And he was already in love with her."

Chem smiled, a little sadly. "Of course."

Irene understood the centaur's problem. Xap was one fine animal—but he *was* an animal. Chem was half human. She might dally with an animal, and even seek offspring by him— centaurs were notoriously open about such things, in contrast to straight human conventions. But love? Marriage? That was a more substantial matter. Males could fall in love readily, because their lives were not so much affected by it. They did not have to bear the offspring. Females were more careful, because their necessary commitment was greater. Chem would have to handle this in her own fashion and was surely competent to do so, as most women were.

Zora, however, was not competent. She had not been allowed to make her considered choice. An impossible love had been imposed on her. Irene didn't know any good way out of that. She had learned that zombies did have feelings, from her association with Zora. But when Zora had already suicided once for love, what remained for her?

"One curse to go," Grundy said.

Irene wished he hadn't reminded her. Zora had absorbed two curses of misfortune, one for Xavier, the other for Irene herself. Now they knew these curses did act on the zombie. What additional tragedy was slated for Irene—that Zora would inherit?

How could things possibly get worse for Zora than they were now? Irene felt the sickening certainty that they would soon find out. The curse of unrequited love was now on Xavier's conscience, thought it was not his fault; the next one would be on Irene's conscience.

"Make sure Zora understands what happened and why," Chem told Grundy.

"She understands," the golem said. "She sort of liked Xav anyway. He's a decent man, you know."

"I know," Irene agreed. Xavier was a much better man than one would have expected the son of a witch to be, perhaps because he did not let his mother influence him unduly. He preferred to go flying—and that, perhaps, had been his chief defense against corruption. The Furies had criticized him for neglect of his mother, but he was probably correct in that neglect. Some mothers did not deserve to be honored too much.

Again Irene reacted to what had happened. The Furies had planned to force Xavier into love with a zombie! The sheer evil of it appalled her. Now she was the one remaining to be cursed, and she knew it would be terrible, all out of proportion to her error—and that it would fall again on Zora. There was no way to view it that offered any positive aspect.

They moved on, but now Zora rode behind Irene. The others tacitly agreed that the zombie should not be with Xavier, who could only be embarrassed by her presence.

They came to a region they hadn't seen before, because a number of stone figures decorated it. Perplexed, Chem projected her map. "No—this is on our route. I thought I remembered it. See, my map shows us right on the dotted line. These statues weren't here before."

"Could be the work of Maw," Xavier said. "She collects strange animals and plants. She never collected no statues before, but she might start."

"These are very finely wrought likenesses," Chem remarked. "Look, there are even a number of insects." She picked one up and held it in the sunlight. It was a henroach, with every leg and two fine antennae perfectly sculptured in stone. "A very fine artisan made this."

"The elves, maybe," Grundy suggested. "Some of them are quite skilled. I can ask around—"

Irene spotted a figure walking ahead of them. It looked familiar. It was a tall, rather voluptuous woman. "I think I have another answer," she said, nudging Chem to trot closer.

The woman apparently did not hear them. When they were quite close, Irene called: "Hey, Gorgon!"

Slowly the figure turned. Chem suddenly balked, and Irene

had to hold on to keep her seat. Zora, less able to react, started
to fall. Irene grabbed her, looking down.

The zombie stiffened, her flesh congealing.

"Close your eyes!" Chem cried. "She's not veiled!"

Irene's eyes snapped closed before she raised her head.
"Gorgon!" she cried. "It's I, Irene! Put on your veil!"

"Why?" the Gorgon asked.

"Because otherwise you'll turn us all to stone!"

"That's right, I will!" The Gorgon agreed, sounding surprised.

"Of course you will!" Irene snapped, shaken by her near
escape. She had assumed—but assuming could be treacherous,
as the episode at the love spring had so recently shown. "Why
weren't you wearing your veil? You know you can't go around
barefaced!"

"I—forgot," the Gorgon said, as if remembering something
that might have been important a long time ago. "Very well;
I'm veiled now."

Irene pried open one eye, though uncertain whether this
would protect her if she saw the Gorgon's face. Maybe only
half of her would turn to stone! But it was all right now; her
friend was safely covered.

"How could you forget a thing like that?" Irene demanded,
still shaken.

"Well, I was just walking along, looking for something—
I don't remember what—when—it's all unclear. I didn't remember you, until—"

"A forget-whorl!" Chem exclaimed. "We're back in their
region! She got tagged by—"

"And forgot her mission!" Irene agreed.

"My mission?" the Gorgon asked, perplexed.

"To find and rescue your son Hugo!"

The Gorgon's mouth gaped under the veil. "Hugo!"

"And *we* forgot we were back among the rampaging whorls,"
Chem said. "Between her forced forgetting and our careless-
ness, we almost came to considerable grief. But her forgetfulness doesn't seem total, because her memory is coming back
as we remind her."

"A glancing blow," Irene agreed. "She must have brushed

the fringe of it, not getting a full dose. But the encounter was potentially deadly to us! I very nearly was turned to—" She broke off, remembering the zombie behind her. Zora had looked into the face of the Gorgon!

"Zora took your curse!" Chem said. "She has—"

Xavier and Grundy rode up. "Lucky you weren't stoned," the golem remarked. "I told Xav and Xap to stay clear when I saw what was up."

"Zora looked," Irene said dully. "She suffered the misfortune slated for me."

Xavier jumped down and lifted the zombie away from Chem's side, where she was half hanging. "She can't be dead!" he cried. "She wasn't alive!"

"The seeds of mischief sown by the Furies are deadly," Chem murmured. "We sought to avoid their curses, but only transferred them to the most innocent one among us."

The centaur was being kind. She had not been present, so she shared none of the blame. But the damage had been done.

"Wake, Zora!" Xavier exclaimed, holding the stiff zombie upright. "You don't deserve none of this! You never harmed nobody!"

"Yet there is a philosophical alignment," Chem continued. "Xavier's curse and Irene's curse—love and death—visited on the same person. The only cure for the one is the other. Zora isn't suffering now."

"The hell with that!" Xavier cried. "I won't let her die, not after what she done for me! Zora, come back!" And he took the zombie statue in his arms and kissed her on the mouth.

The others watched, saddened yet fatalistic, knowing that the man meant well but that the woman was doomed—and had been doomed from the time she absorbed the curses. The terrible Furies had had their way.

Then something amazing happened. The statue began to sag.

Irene stared. Stone couldn't sag! Even zombie stone crumbled or flaked away; it didn't really soften.

Xavier was still kissing her, holding her against him. The vital warmth of his body was almost tangible. And Zora was returning to her half-life.

"Look at that!" Grundy said. "The Gorgon can't stone zombies!"

Chem turned her human segment so her eyes could meet Irene's gaze. "Perhaps it is true. Zora was immune to the stare of the Python. She can't see very well, so perhaps it is like a veil between her and visual magic. She may have suffered only partial petrification—and she was not as solid as we to begin with. But—"

"There—there is a rationale?" Irene whispered numbly.

"If you were stone, or mostly stone, and the man you loved embraced you and kissed you and begged you to return—would you respond?"

Irene thought of herself becoming stone, and her husband Dor kissing her. "I suppose—if there were any way—any way at all—" Irene agreed faintly. "Love has power we hardly understand—"

Xavier broke the kiss. "I told you I wouldn't let her die!" he said.

Zora was flesh again. She stood stiffly, blinking as if her eyelids were heavy. Her body had been too loose before; now it was too firm. But she was more flesh than stone.

They could not argue with Xavier's claim, though Irene was uncertain which explanation had more to do with it. The Gorgon's face turned living people to stone—but a zombie was undead, a different matter. Yet some things did affect zombies, as they had seen.

"But what have you restored her to?" Chem asked. "A hopeless love?"

Xavier released Zora, who stood without difficulty, looking about her. She seemed more solid now, as if the Gorgon's magic had stiffened her decaying flesh to healthy flesh. She appeared more alive than she had ever been, ironically.

"I've been thinking about that," Xavier said. "About the good things she's been doing for us all. I'm not awful smart about women, but it sure seems to me a good zombie is better than a bad woman. This one is awful good—and you'd hardly know she's a zombie now."

It was true. Zora was still firming. Love and/or the Gorgon's magic had transformed her to something considerably more human than before. Her facial features had become both clear and animate, her body strong. She was indeed a woman, and not an unattractive one.

"But you—" Irene protested weakly. "You don't love—"

"I know where the love spring is," Xavier said. "I know what's right. Nothing to stop me from taking a drink—I was going to do that before. It's supposed to be my curse anyway. I never was one to let someone else pay my debts."

Irene's respect for him increased again. Xavier had a conscience and a rather clear notion of what was required. He had decided to honor his mother's wish that he settle down, and he had chosen the one to settle with. This was a strange and unexpected union—but it did make a certain sense. And it nicely reversed the double curse Zora had absorbed. "Good luck," she whispered.

Xavier turned to Zora. "Do you like to fly?" he asked.

"I do," she said clearly. Her teeth showed as hard and clear as polished stone when she smiled.

"That's a most artistic proposal," Chem murmured.

Xavier lifted Zora to Xav's back. It was evident she weighed more than she had, but his strength more than sufficed. Then he mounted the hippogryph behind her, putting his arms about her. "We'll take the seeds to Maw," he told Irene. "Zora's carrying 'em anyway, and I've got the feather. You folks can go on about your business."

"Thank you," Irene breathed, still dazed.

The hippogryph spread his beautiful wings.

"We shall meet again," Chem told Xap.

Xap nodded his beak, then pumped. He rose into the air, facing back toward the love spring.

"Your mother won't like this!" Grundy called after them.

"That's for sure!" Xavier called back, grinning. "But she can't stop me from being a dutiful son!"

They disappeared into the sky. Nothing more needed to be said. Irene felt tears in her eyes, and they were not those of grief.

Chapter 12. Glory Goblin

"I am the youngest and prettiest and sweetest daughter of Gorbage Goblin, chief of the Gapside Goblins," Glory repeated as she delicately chewed on the blackberries, grayberries, brownberries, guavas, and sugarplums Hugo conjured for her appetite. "I am in love with a wonderful creature."

"Love—that's poin-ant or peek-ant?" Ivy asked.

"Wonderfully sad," Glory said firmly.

"Love isn't sad," Ivy said, thinking of her family. She was glad for this chance to rest, since she wasn't used to walking the long distances she had covered in the past two days. "My father says love is fun, and my mother says it depends on the time of day."

Glory smiled. "They surely know. But you see, this is forbidden love. That makes it sad."

"How can love be forbidden?" Hugo asked. "My father says anything is possible with magic, except maybe paradox, and he's working on that."

"What is possible is not necessarily permissible," Glory said. "Love really shouldn't be forbidden. But after all, he's not a goblin." She bit into some more fruit. It was evident that when the goblin girl said "famished" she meant very hungry indeed.

"Well, my father says goblins are related to elves, gnomes, and dwarves," Hugo said. "They're of modified humanoid stock, he says. So they can interbreed if they want to, and when they run afoul of a love spring—"

"That's true," Glory said. "*Any* two species can interbreed

188

in Xanth, but this is generally not voluntary. Even if the individuals approve, others of their kinds do not. And some liaisons are expressly forbidden. I love a harpy."

Both children gazed at her blankly.

Glory sighed. "I see I'll have to explain. The goblins and harpies are enemies. The enmity goes back over a thousand years."

"You must be older than you look," Ivy said, perplexed.

Glory smiled again. She was extremely pretty to begin with, and when she smiled, the forest seemed to brighten. "No, I'm only sixteen. I mean the quarrel is ancient."

Ivy's brow wrinkled. "My father said something about a war a long time ago. He was there, when they were building Castle Roogna. A spell—"

Glory frowned delicately. "You really shouldn't fib, Ivy. You know he couldn't have been there."

"Well, he was in the tapestry with this big spider—"

"Oh, you mean he watched it on the magic tapestry in Castle Roogna! I have heard about that and would love to see it someday."

"I watch it all the time," Ivy said. "But I fall asleep before it gets interesting."

"I gather your father works at Castle Roogna."

"Yes, most of the time."

Glory shrugged, not really interested. "Well, once goblins and harpies existed in peace. They even shared caves. The goblins used the floors and the harpies used the ceiling perches. But in time, it got crowded, and the goblins complained about the droppings. You see, goblins sleep with their mouths open so they can snore properly, and—" She shrugged again. She did it very well. "The harpies got angry and put a curse on our males, making them ugly—well, really it was on the females, making them *prefer* ugly goblins. I understand it is much easier to apply a curse of perception than one of actual physical change—that's why illusion is so popular. Anyway, the girls stayed pretty, but the goblin men, owing to sexual selection— ugh! So the goblins got even for that by luring away all the harpy males—who, it seems, were partial to fully fleshed legs, unlike the chicken legs of the harpy females—until there were no males left and the harpies were all female."

Now Hugo's brow wrinkled. "All female? But how—?"

"I don't know exactly how they reproduced. Maybe they laid parthenogenetic eggs."

"What?"

"Harpies hatch from eggs," Glory explained patiently. "If there's no male, the eggs may hatch anyway—but only female chicks. Something like that. I'm not much for parthenogenesis myself; it's not a type of magic I understand. Anyway, they were all female, and mostly old and ugly and bitter, as perhaps they had a right to be. They were absolutely furious at us, though all the goblins had done was get even for what they had done to us. So there was war. All the goblins and our allies on the ground, against all the harpies and their allies in the air. In those days, the goblins and harpies were the most numerous creatures in Xanth and wielded the most power. But after the battle, there were not nearly so many of either, and true human folk became dominant.

"At least the curse was off, and the goblin girls liked handsome males again, and the harpies had a few males. But the damage took a long time to clear, because there weren't any handsome male goblins left, which made the girls understandably reluctant. There was only one harpy cock for every hundred or so hens, and all the hens were ugly and dirty, which made the cocks reluctant. So in eight hundred years, the numbers of goblins and harpies have hardly increased. Most goblin males are still ugly, and so are the old harpy hens. During that period they still fought one another, in honor of old grudges, but not so much, because there were so few—and the Gap Chasm interfered."

Stanley perked up his ears. He remembered the Gap!

"How could the Gap do that?" Hugo asked. "No one even remembered it!"

"That's the point," Glory said. "It's very hard to cross the Gap when you don't remember it. Especially when there's a dragon in it who gobbles anyone who tries to pass. So gradually, the goblins settled north of the Gap, the harpies settled south of it, and the warfare diminished. It was really the Gap that brought peace to Xanth."

Stanley snorted steam that swirled dangerously near her petite feet.

"And the Gap Dragon," Glory added quickly. Stanley relaxed. "Of course, the harpies could fly over the Gap, so there were some skirmishes—just enough to keep the blood feud alive—but mostly it was pretty quiet for several centuries."

Stanley might be satisfied, having established the importance of his office to the welfare of Xanth, but Ivy wasn't. "But you're across the Gap now!"

"True. But you see, the forget-spell has been breaking up—and anyway, my tribe lives right at the brink of the Gap, so we're partly immune to the spell. I used to sit on the ledge and look down into the Gap and watch the Dragon charge by, so big and awful. I could see the steam wafting up in frightening clouds."

Stanley puffed more steam contentedly. He was getting to like this goblin maiden, who certainly looked good enough to eat.

"But recently I saw that the Dragon was gone, so I knew I could cross." Glory peered at Stanley. "Is he really the Gap Dragon? He's so small!"

"Yes," Hugo said. "I dumped Fountain of Youth water on him, and now he's a baby Dragon. He's our friend now. I guess babies are nicer than monsters."

"That must be true," Glory agreed. "My people have always been nervous about your human kind, the full-sized folk, but you children seem very nice." She chewed some more fruit.

"I guess everyone's nice, if you know the person," Ivy said. "I like just about everything I meet, except maybe some clouds."

"Some clouds can be bothersome, especially the ones that rain on my hairdo," Glory agreed. "You must have been raised in a loving household."

"Isn't everyone?"

The goblin girl made her sad, peek-ant smile again. "Alas, no. My father is ugly and vicious, like most goblin males, and my mother was always afraid of him. Oh, I'm not saying Gorbage is a bad man; he *is* after all, my father. It's just his way. You see, though we goblin girls now prefer handsome and gentle men, they aren't very good fighters, and so they don't survive very well in our region. Gorbage is chief because he is violent and ruthless and tougher than other goblin men. He has been a good provider, but he just doesn't understand love. When my older sister Goldy came of age, Gorbage made a party of creatures escort her to the northern goblin tribes so she could trap a husband."

"But a pretty girl doesn't have to trap a man!" Ivy protested. "Not one as pretty as you."

"In Goblin-Land she does, unfortunately. That's part of what dismays me about it. And Goldy is not as pretty as I am, so it was that much harder for her."

"How could Gorbage make other creatures escort a goblin girl?" Hugo asked.

"He threatened to eat them if they didn't. He would have, too. One was an ogre, but the ogre had just fought the Gap Dragon—"

Stanley perked up again, interested, though it was evident he didn't remember this. Ivy wasn't certain whether this was because he had lost most of his memory when he lost his age, or whether the Gap Dragon had fought so many other monsters that he simply couldn't remember this particular spat.

"And the ogre had just climbed out of the Gap, lifting out a centaur, and was very tired, so he couldn't fight. That's a very rare state for ogres."

"But ogres eat people, too!" Hugo objected. "And they eat goblins and monsters and trees and dirt and everything! He should have gobbled up a tasty goblin girl."

"This was a funny ogre. He was with five assorted young females, so Gorbage figured if the brute hadn't eaten them, maybe he wouldn't eat Goldy either. It seemed like a good risk. No worse than going into battle or harvesting tentacles from a tangle tree. My father is very practical. He sent my sister with them, and it worked, because later we had news through the grapevine that—"

"My mother grows neat grapevines," Ivy said. "Some of them reach right to the top of the castle, and we talk to the grapes at each end, and the sound travels back and forth just perfectly."

"Yes, of course," Glory agreed, slightly annoyed by the frequent interruptions. "We have vines that grow well into Dragon-Land, and from there they connect to some of the northern vines, but often there is no complete connection because somewhere along the way some dragon has scorched out a section. Anyway, we learned that Goldy had snared a northern goblin chief and was moderately satisfied. That's how most goblins marry. But I am too romantic for my own good. My sister is tough; she's always able to do what is necessary. Not I; I am more a creature of fantasy. So when it came my turn to marry—" She broke off, grimacing, and such was her beauty that even that expression was impossibly cute. "I fell in love with a male who conformed more perfectly to my ideals."

"The harpy," Hugo said, showing his intelligence.

"Hardy Harpy," she said. "I was sitting one evening, dangling my feet over the brink of the Gap Chasm and thinking my silly thoughts, when I saw this bird flying down below me. Only it wasn't a bird, it was a harpy, and I was afraid because those harpy hens have the foulest mouths you ever heard. I put my hand on my knife in case it should attack me and I got ready to scream. I hiked up my skirt so I could run, but there was something different about this one. I couldn't smell the normally foul odor, so I lingered longer than I should have and suddenly realized that this harpy was young and clean and male. I had never seen a male harpy before. They remain rare and they don't go out much to mix with other creatures. I was so amazed I just waited there, marveling, my skirt held high."

She hiked her skirt a little to illustrate. Her legs were astonishingly shapely. "And he came and perched beside me and told me what pretty legs I had, so of course I didn't run away then. Goblin men's legs aren't pretty—they're all black and knobby and warped—and harpy hens' legs are even worse. I can certainly see how a harpy cock would be turned off by a harpy hen's claws. And he spoke the truth about my legs." She glanced down at them appreciatively, as well she might.

"But weren't *his* legs bird legs?" Ivy asked.

"Yes, of course. But males don't need nice legs. He had

such lovely wings, and a handsome face and manly chest. And he spoke with such gentleness and intelligence." She shrugged. "After that, he came to see me often, there at the brink of the Chasm, and in due course we fell in—"

"But didn't you get hurt?" Ivy asked, horrified. "The Gap's so deep—"

"Fell in love," the goblin girl continued blithely. "Oh, we knew it was wrong, for goblins and harpies are at war, and the war had started centuries ago because of just such liaisons as this. But we were so *right* for each other, we simply couldn't help it. We wanted to marry, but we knew we couldn't as long as I was bound to my tribe; the goblins would tar and defeather Hardy and then start mistreating him. So we could do nothing— and meanwhile, my father was looking for a way to get me north so I could snag a goblin chief and live in moderate declining satisfaction, like my sister. I knew I had to escape. Then the Gap Dragon left—and here I am, across the Gap, looking for my beloved. I hope I find him soon! If I do, then that will be the happy ending I promised we might have to this story."

"But the jungle is so big!" Ivy pointed out. "How can you ever find him? Xanth is so huge!"

"So I have discovered," Glory agreed. "My legs were made for looking at, not for all this walking! Hardy doesn't even know I'm coming; I just hurried across, not knowing how long the dragon would be gone."

"But if he doesn't know," Hugo said, "and you don't know where he is—"

"He said he lives near the mouth organ, so I am looking for that, but I fear I am lost. I can't find it anywhere and I've searched interminably."

That sounded like a very long time indeed. "What's a mouth organ?" Ivy asked.

Glory blushed prettily. "I'm sure I wouldn't know, and I hesitate to guess. But I've got to find it."

"Hugo can figure it out," Ivy said. "He's smart!"

Hugo, put on the spot, cudgeled his memory. "My father has books of pictures of things—monsters and plants—and I think there was one of a mouth organ. It's a big plant or animal or something, and it plays big, low notes you can hear for hours away."

"Then we can hear it!" Ivy said excitedly. "We can find it for Glory!"

"If we're close enough, and if it's playing," Hugo said.

"Let's listen!"

They listened, but heard no notes of any size.

Ivy refused to be discouraged. "Stanley can hear it!" she declared. "He's got good dragon ears!" She turned to the little dragon. "Tune in to the mouth organ, Stanley. Show us where it is."

But Stanley wasn't paying attention. He was sniffing the air as if trying to identify something odd.

"Hey, Stanley!" Ivy repeated imperiously. "Listen for the mouth organ!"

The little dragon perked up his ears and swiveled them about. It was evident that he had not considered tuning in on something this way before, but Ivy's presence and need made it feasible. Soon he caught a whiff of some sort of sound and pointed his snout at it, east.

"See? I told you he could do it!" Ivy said. "Now we'll find it for you, and everything will be just fine!"

"I certainly hope you are correct," Glory said uncertainly. "I just *have* to find Hardy!"

They walked east, over hill and dale, avoiding tangle trees and such. It was a fair distance, so they paused every so often to rest and snack. The sun was now high in the sky, trying to peer down to see what they were doing.

In due course, they could hear the organ themselves: ponderous, vibrating, authoritative notes that shook the very jungle with their power.

"It does sound big," Ivy said, and pressed eagerly on.

They rounded a large old tree and almost stumbled over a boy eating a bowl of polka-dot custard pudding. Startled, the boy jumped up, spilling his custard. The dots skidded around and rolled away, glad to escape the fate intended for them.

The boy was absolutely furious. His hair changed from yellow to raging red. "You—" he expostulated, and changed into a huge, hairy spider covered in red fuzz that was darkening to black. "Made," the spider chittered, and became a scraggly faun with black horns and hooves turning green. "Me," the faun cried, and coverted to a man with the green head of a snake. "Sspilll," the snake-head hissed, turning brown, and became a small, tan griffin. "My," the griffin squawked, and reddened into a raging ball of fire. "Lunch!" the fire roared, and yellow flames flared high. Oh, this thing was angry!

Hugo happened to be in the lead, so he took the main heat. "I'm sorry," he said. "I didn't see you. I can conjure you some nice fruit to eat instead—" He conjured a huge and pretty pomegranate and held it out.

The fire shaped back into the boy. "You offer a lutin mere fruit, you cretin?" he demanded, dashing it from Hugo's hand. He changed into a monstrous moth, hovering angrily. "I'll see you cocooned for this!" the moth fluttered. "I'll drive you to the flame! I'll punish all of you!"

"Oh, I love puns," Ivy said. "Pun-ish me first!"

"Stifle it in cotton, you brat!" the moth bawled, turning white. "I'll fix you! You shall never see Xanth again!"

"But we're *in* Xanth!" Hugo protested weakly.

"You shall be blind!" The moth vanished, and a monstrous eyeball replaced it. The eye was white, with ferocious blue veins crawling around it and a blazing red pupil at the front. From that pupil came a pale yellow mist, forming an expanding cloud. "Blind, blind, blind!" the eye repeated, speaking through the pupil.

"Do something!" Ivy cried, alarmed.

Glory drew her knife and stepped toward the eye.

"No, not you!" Ivy cried. "The mist will get you first!"

Stanley whomped forward, blowing steam. "Not you either!" Ivy gasped, catching hold of his tail to hold him back. "I don't want you to be blind! I mean Hugo!"

"Gee, thanks!" Hugo said, appalled. "I don't want to be blind either!"

"Conjure some fruit that will save us!"

"Oh. Yes." He conjured a pineapple.

"No, dummy! That will spread the yellow all around! Some other way!"

Hugo did not seem to react with the same pleasure to the endearment as she had. "But I can't—"

"Yes you can!" Ivy insisted.

The yellow was looming awfully. Hugo concentrated—and had an inspiration. A gourd-fruit appeared in his hands. "Look at this, lutin!" he cried, shoving it at the floating eyeball.

The eye looked, involuntarily, for that was its nature—and saw the peephole, and froze where it was, in midair. The yellow mist dissipated harmlessly.

Hugo set the gourd down carefully, and the eye tilted its gaze to watch its descent.

"What is that?" Glory asked, perplexed.

"A hypnogourd," Hugo said. "It's a sort of fruit, so I can conjure it, but this is the first I ever got right. I aimed the peephole at the lutin."

Glory laughed, relieved. "Of course! We have whole patches of such gourds in Goblin-Land. I just didn't recognize it out of context. What a clever way to nullify the eye monster!"

"What's a hypnogourd?" Ivy asked. She was only three years old and had seen a great many plants, but for some reason, her mother had never grown one of the gourd plants for her, so her education was not yet quite complete.

"It's a gourd with a peephole," Glory explained. "I should have recognized it instantly. Anyone who peeks in the hole is hypnotized, until someone moves the gourd away or cuts off his line of sight. It's a good, fairly harmless way to restrain a violent creature, though it isn't wise to leave anyone hypnotized too long, if you don't want it to be permanent."

"Let's get out of here before something happens to free the lutin," Hugo said nervously. "A leaf could fall and cover the peephole, or an animal could roll the gourd over. He'll be awful mad when he gets free."

The others agreed. They had never before encountered such a bad temper as that shown by this magical creature. They hurried on, leaving the veined eye and the gourd behind.

"I thought each person had only one magic talent," Ivy remarked thoughtfully.

"They do, dear," Glory said. "Goblins don't even have one such talent."

"But that lutin could change shape and do magic—he was going to blind us."

"That's right!" Hugo agreed. "How could he do that?"

"Maybe he was bluffing about the blindness," Glory said uncertainly.

"He sure didn't sound as if he were bluffing," Hugo said. "He might have had some kind of herb, or maybe some juice from a blindworm, to make us blind."

"Anyway, I'm glad you stopped him, Hugo," Glory said. "That was most intelligent, and you have a very useful talent."

Hugo flushed with guilty pleasure. He wasn't used to such compliments, especially from anyone as pretty as the goblin girl.

The organ notes became louder, until their booming was fairly deafening. There were many tones audible now, low ones and high ones, weaving in and out and around and through each other, forming a tapestry of sound. The effect was oddly moving, stirring subterranean emotions of pleasure, worry, and guilt. It was amazing what sheer sound could do.

"I wonder whether it knows how to play romantic music," Glory murmured.

"Why?" Ivy asked.

"Never mind, dear; it was an idle thought." But there was something about the way she said it that gave Ivy the impression it wasn't entirely idle.

Stanley looked around again, sniffing, questing for something he couldn't quite pinpoint. "Keep your mind on your business," Ivy chided the dragon.

At last they came in sight of the mouth organ. This was a structure the size of a tree, made up of mouths. Tremendous, roomy, toothy, ugly, ogrish mouths blasted out the huge low notes, while smaller, animalish mouths issued the middle-sized central notes, and tiny, pursed, ladylike mouths shrilled forth the small highest notes.

A figure appeared in the sky. It was a harpy. It cried a command, and suddenly the mouth organ silenced, deafeningly. Ivy almost fell over; she had been bracing against the sound, and now there was none.

The harpy swooped toward them. It was male, with beautiful wings and the handsomest face Ivy had ever seen.

"Glory!" the harpy cried.

"Hardy!" the goblin girl cried joyously.

He flew down to her, wrapped his wings about her like the folds of a cloak, and kissed her. The two were of about the same mass, but differently structured. Yet it did not seem strange at all that they should be in love, for each seemed more attractive than the other.

After a moment, the harpy drew back and hovered in air, his wings flapping with easy power. "Who are these?"

"These are my friends who helped me find you," Glory explained. "Ivy and Hugo and Stanley."

Hardy Harpy squinted at them. "They appear young."

"We are," Hugo said. "That's the best way to be."

"The dragon looks somehow familiar."

"He's the baby Gap Dragon," Glory explained quickly. "But he's friendly now. He tuned in on the mouth organ notes so I could find you."

"Must be all right, then," Hardy said. "I had noticed the Gap was oddly quiet recently. But why are you here, Glory? If I had known you were coming, I would have flown to meet you. As it was, I worried at your absence from the Gapside ledge; I feared you had fallen in, but I found no—" He broke off, not wanting to utter such a horror.

"I saw the Gap was empty, so I hurried across," Glory explained. "I was terrified. I didn't know the dragon had been youthened. It was my chance to get away from my father, before he made me marry some hideous and brutal knobby-kneed goblin chief."

"But you took such a risk, coming here!" Hardy protested. "There are so many dangers—dragons, griffins, even a bad-tempered lutin—"

"We've met."

"If anything had happened to you—"

"I just had to come," Glory said. "It was my only chance for happiness."

"True," the handsome harpy agreed. "Come to my perch, not far distant, and bring your friends. I will reward them with some pretty trinkets I snatched from a dragon's nest. Then, later, I'll tune the mouth organ to play something romantic—"

"Yes," Glory breathed.

Now Ivy began to catch on to what that meant. Kissing must be more fun to music!

Hardy led the way through the forest, flying low and slow so they could readily follow. A pleasant masculine aroma wafted out from his wings, quite different from the normal harpy hen stench.

Suddenly a net flew through the air and settled over them all. Before they understood what was happening, the five of them were bundled up in an awkward ball. Stanley's green tail was in Ivy's face, and she was standing on one of Hardy's wings, and Glory was sitting on Hugo's head. Hideous little men were charging from all sides, brandishing clubs. "Now we've got you!" one man yelled.

"Father!" Glory screamed, chagrined.

Stanley blew out steam, but this only made Hardy jump; the dragon's snoot was aimed inward instead of outward, so he couldn't steam the attackers.

Now Ivy recognized the creatures. They were male goblins. Each was so dusky as to be almost black, with a huge head, big flat feet, a bumpy round body, and a horrendous scowl. What were they doing here, south of the Gap?

That was answered directly by the goblin chief. "Now we've got the criminal harpy!" Gorbage exclaimed, grimacing in what was evidently supposed to be a smile of victory.

"That's redundant," another goblin said. "All harpies are criminals."

There was coarse general laughter. "Yes, birds of a foul feather," Gorbage agreed.

"And we'll hang him," a third goblin said, making a suggestive gesture of yanking up a rope and sticking out his purple tongue as if choking.

"Naw, he'd just fly away," another said. "We'll stab him!" And he made a gesture with a mock knife, as of guts being punctured.

"Better to club him to tar and feathers!"

"Force-feed him poisonberries!"

"Weight him down and toss him into a bottomless pond!"

They crowded around, leering, barraging him with horrible suggestions, each one worse than the others.

"Oh, Hardy!" Glory cried. "It's my tribe! They must have followed me! I didn't know!"

Suddenly Ivy realized what Stanley had been sniffing for. The goblins had been following Glory and the party all the time—not close enough for the dragon to identify them for sure, but still, he had been aware of something. If only she had paid more attention, instead of chiding Stanley for not sticking strictly to the mouth organ scent! She could have asked the dragon what was bothering him and had him tune in to it specifically; maybe they could have spotted the goblins and arranged to avoid them. Certainly they could have saved Hardy Harpy from this treachery! Now they were all in trouble.

At age three, Ivy did not have much experience with the cunning of angry creatures. But she was learning.

"First we must put this carrion on trial," Gorbage said. "We must make an example of him, so the rest of the birdbrains will know not to fool with goblins."

They untangled the captives one at a time, tying Hugo and Ivy with lengths of vine, wrapping Stanley securely in the net so he could hardly even wiggle, and knotting rope around the legs of Hardy and anchoring him to a stake pounded into the ground, so that he could perch but not fly. They left Glory free. She was, after all, only a goblin girl, pretty but helpless.

"Now we gotta do this right," Gorbage said. "We gotta have a jury-rigged verdict before we croak him. Who wants to be the jury?"

All the goblin hands went up. There were about a dozen of them, each one uglier than his fellows and more eager to do the dirty work.

"Good enough; you're the jury," Gorbage said. "And I'm the judge."

"But that's not fair!" Glory protested.

"Shut up," Gorbage told her mildly, and she was silent. It was difficult for her to oppose her father.

"Do something, Hugo!" Ivy whispered. "You're smart; you can think of something to save our friends!"

Hugo was pale and frightened; he had perhaps a better idea than she did of how much was at stake here. Notions of extreme violence tended to slide past Ivy's awareness because she had never been exposed to such concepts before. Hugo had lived more than twice as long; experience had given him a more sober perspective. He knew that Hardy was not the only one in present peril.

But he tried. "Hey, goblins!" he called. "You can't do that! My father says—"

"And who's your father, twerp?" Gorbage demanded.

"Good Magician Humfrey."

This made the goblins pause. They had heard of Humfrey. Monsters and kings came and went, but the Good Magician was relatively eternal.

"Can't be," Gorbage finally concluded. "The old gnome's over a century old. He wouldn't have any kids this age. Get on with the trial."

"You've still got it wrong," Hugo said determinedly. "You have to have a—a prosecutor and a defender, and witnesses and all, or—"

Gorbage swelled up like a toad with indigestion. "Or what, twerp?"

Hugo quailed before the challenge, but Ivy was sure he had the courage to continue, for he was her Night in Shiny Armor, even if the armor didn't show any more than Stanley's pedestal did. As it turned out, Hugo did indeed have the courage. "Or it doesn't count," he said firmly.

"Who says it doesn't count?" Gorbage demanded belligerently.

Again Hugo needed a boost of confidence, but Ivy's faith was strong, and so he had it. "The law. And people who don't follow the law of the land are crooks and thiefs and murderers and all-around bad folk—which I guess goblins are anyway."

"What?" the goblin chief exclaimed, brandishing his dark fist. "It's the harpies who are bad folk! I'll exterminate you, you smart-mouthed twit!"

"Yes, of course," Hugo agreed. "That's what murderers do, by definition."

Again Gorbage paused. He was cunning enough to see that he could not handily disprove the charge of murder by murdering his accuser. Hugo had verbally outmaneuvered him. "Okay, snot! We'll have a persecutor and deaf-ender and witlesses." He glared around, but there were no free goblins; all twelve were on the hanging jury. "But I have no more people!"

"Too bad," Hugo said. "Then you can't have a proper trial, and everyone will know you for what you are: a gutless murderer who kills innocent people dead."

"We'll have the trial!" Gorbage insisted, swelling to just this side of the bursting point. "You smart-mouth—you be the deaf-ender. And—and my daughter'll be the persecutor. Then the mur—the execution's all legal."

"I won't—" Glory began, but Hugo interrupted her.

"Yes, she'll do it," he said. "That's fair."

"What?" Glory shrieked.

"He's up to something," Ivy whispered to her. "He's very smart. You'd better do it."

Dismayed, the goblin girl was silent.

"Okay, now we got it," Gorbage said, grimacing smugly. "Persecutor, make your winning case."

Reluctantly, Glory went to stand before Hardy's post. Ivy saw her hand move toward her knife, but she didn't draw it. Any attempt to cut Hardy's tether would bring the goblins down on them in a savage horde. "I intend to—to prove to this dumb jury that the defendant is the handsomest, finest, nicest male creature alive, better than any ugly old knobby-kneed goblin—"

"Out of order!" Judge Gorbage ruled. "You're supposed to prove that this feathered freak is guilty of corrupting and polluting a fine goblin damsel and must be instantly put to death in the cruelest possible manner."

Stanley was quietly chewing on his net. He had separated several strands and was working on others. In due course he would be free—if he had time to complete the job without being noticed. Glory's eye fell on him and lighted with comprehension. A loose dragon could disrupt a trial long enough for a tether to be cut!

She walked to the side, attracting the goblins' attention away from the dragon. She was such a pretty girl that this was no problem; every jury-eye was riveted to her as she shook out her luxurious black hair and breathed deeply. "Yes, I shall prove all that and more," she said with new emphasis. "At great length. I call as the first witness the human child Ivy. Someone better untie her so she can testify."

"Oh, no you don't!" Gorbage cried. "No conniving goblin tricks here! She can speak well enough tied!"

Ivy walked up. Only her hands were tied. Gorbage glared at her. "You sniveling little snit, do you swear to blab the truth, most of the truth, and nothing much except the truth, or else?"

"Sure," Ivy agreed, interested in this procedure. She had never been to a trial before. Stanley chomped through another strand. "I generally do."

Now Glory took over. "Did you see this feathered freak here on this perch corrupting any innocent goblin girls?" Hardy winced but didn't squawk; he realized what was happening.

"No," Ivy said stoutly.

"What?" Gorbage demanded in high dudgeon.

"All he did was kiss her," Ivy said. "My father does that to my mother all the time, except when they think I'm looking."

There was a stir of ire in the jury. "Pollution!" a jury-goblin muttered.

Ivy's brow wrinkled. "I thought plooshun was bad water."

"That too, honey," Glory murmured, smiling obscurely. She adjusted her clothing, again riveting the jury. "I now call the defendant as witness."

"That liar can't be sworn in!" Gorbage protested.

Glory made a quarter-smile. "Is that true, defendant? Are you unable to swear?"

Hardy let out a stream of profanity that wilted the adjacent vegetation and sent wisps of smoke curling up from the post he perched on.

Glory's ears turned bright orange-red and her mouth caved in as if she had swallowed her teeth, but she turned to her father. After a couple of attempts, she managed to speak. "I don't understand a word of that, of course. Tell me, Father— is that or is that not adequate swearing?"

Gorbage hastily wiped a gape of incredulous admiration off his face. "Got to admit—that's one thing a harpy can do pretty well," he grudged.

"Very well," she said primly. "I am taking the judge's word that you have been properly sworn in. Defendant, did you ever kiss any goblin girls?"

"Only one," Hardy said.

There was another stir in the jury. "The cock confesses!" a goblin muttered. "Get the rope ready!"

"And what is your intent toward said girl?" Glory asked.

"To marry her and take her away from all this," the harpy testified.

Gorbage turned mottled purple. "The audacity of this cretin! Execution is way too good for him!"

"But, Father," Glory protested innocently, "you have always maintained that the only fate worse than death is marriage."

There was a stifled snigger from the jury. Gorbage glared, and the sound snigged out. "Get on with it!" the judge gritted.

"I trust I have made my case," Glory said with a certain demure smugness. "Now let the defender take over."

Hugo took the center stage, his hands still bound behind him. There was a faint crunch as Stanley separated another strand of the net. It was a tough net, but the dragon had strong teeth.

Ivy just knew Hugo would do a brilliant job in an impossible situation; already he looked handsome and confident, despite being bound. She saw several of the jury-goblins do double takes, as if seeing him for the first time; they had not realized how competent he would turn out to be. "Is there any law against harpy-goblin marriages?" he asked rhetorically. Famous lawyers were good at rhetoric, Ivy knew, though she wasn't quite certain what the term meant.

Gorbage and the jury burst out laughing. They rolled on the ground, expelling black tears of mirth.

"I gather, from this unbecoming levity, that there is no law," Hugo concluded suavely, just the way Ivy had known he would. A defender of his caliber could not be rattled by crude behavior.

"Indeed, historically there have been many such liaisons. Any of you could marry a harpy hen if you wanted to."

This set off an even more ferocious siege of merriment. Not even a cockatrice would care to marry a harpy hen!

"And so a goblin girl can marry a harpy cock if she wants to," Hugo concluded brilliantly. "There is no cause for a trial, let alone an execution. I therefore move that this court be adjourned and the defendant set free."

Suddenly the goblins were sober. "Outrageous!" Gorbage exclaimed. "Marry a harpy? Why not eat zombie refuse while you're at it?"

"But there is no law," Hugo insisted. "Therefore Hardy can't be executed for—"

"Yes he can!" Gorbage insisted. "For polluting and corrupting my innocent daughter!" The goblins of the jury applauded.

Ivy had to admit to herself that the situation looked bad, but she maintained confidence in Hugo's ability to handle it. Things always looked darkest just before the dawn; that was part of the script. And Stanley was now halfway free of the net. Before long he would be ready to fight, and she was sure he had built up plenty of white-hot steam.

"Very well," Hugo said smoothly. "I call the defendant as witness."

"Sure, the cock's already incriminated himself proper," Gorbage said. "Let the birdbrain do it some more."

Hugo faced the post. "Bird-br—uh, Defendant, has the subject of marriage between you and the goblin girl been broached before this date?" Hugo was sounding more like a lawyer as Ivy's confidence in him grew.

"Yes," Hardy said.

"Who broached it?"

"Well, actually she did. I mean, I would have asked her, but she asked me first."

Gorbage scowled but did not interfere.

"And you accepted?" Hugo persisted.

"Certainly. I was flattered. A pretty thing like her, with such lovely legs—"

Hugo turned to the jury, which was looking at the legs in

question. "Note who was doing the corrupting. *She* asked *him.*
So if one of them has to be executed—"

"No!" Hardy cried. "Don't try to incriminate her! I don't
want my freedom at her expense! She's the sweetest, most
innocent creature imaginable! She never corrupted anyone! I
surely am the guilty party!"

Gorbage nodded. "I couldn't have put it better myself."

Hugo eyed Hardy speculatively, as if the defender were a
dragon toying with trapped prey. "Are you denying your prior
testimony?"

The harpy was taken aback. "Well, not exactly—"

"Then you may step down." Hugo glanced at the perch and
rope. "Figuratively, of course. I call Ivy as next witness."

Ivy came forward again. She had been working at her bonds
but couldn't get her hands free.

"Who sought whom?" Hugo asked her. "Did the harpy go
to meet the goblin, in your experience?"

"Well, Glory said—"

He frowned competently. "No hearsay, please. What did
you actually witness?"

"Well, I saw Glory walking—"

"And did she seek out the harpy?"

"Yes, we helped her find him, at the mouth organ."

"So in your experience, she went to meet him, not vice
versa?"

"The vice is all his!" Gorbage cried.

"That is," Hugo clarified for the less intelligent goblins,
"she sought him, not the other way around?"

"Yes, but—"

"That suffices." Hugo turned to the jury again. "As you can
see, the harpy is ready to perjure himself to save the goblin
girl, but we have now established independently that she was
the one taking the initiative, not he. The defendant is therefore
innocent of the charge of corrupting, because he is in fact the
one being corrupted. You have no other choice but to let him
off."

The jurors looked uncertainly at Gorbage. "Ridiculous!" the
goblin chief exclaimed. "All that's out of order! The dirty bird
is on trial here; *he's* the one to be executed!"

"Oh, no he's not!" Glory cried. "I did it! I confess! I corrupted him! I'm the one to be executed!"

"As goblins," Hugo said smoothly, "you can dismiss the confession of a harpy, but you can not doubt the word of another goblin. Therefore—"

"Never!" Gorbage and Hardy said together.

Ivy knew the goblin chief didn't want to execute his own daughter; he wanted to make her marry a goblin man. Hugo and Glory had put him on the spot.

But Gorbage was cunning and unscrupulous, the very model of a goblin leader. "It is not for the persecutor or the deaf-ender to decide the issue," he proclaimed. "It is for the jury." He turned to the other goblins. "Jury—reach your verdict. You know what it is."

The jury-rigged goblins pondered momentarily, then caught on. "Guilty!" they cried.

"But that's not fair!" Hugo protested, losing some of his courtroom poise.

"Don't worry—we'll execute you, too, twerp, after we're done basting the bird." Gorbage turned to Hardy. "Deaf-endant, you have been found guilty of corrupting and polluting this innocent goblin girl. I hereby sentence you to be—" He paused, considering the most awful way to do it. "To be burned at the stake and roasted for dinner!" He turned to the jury-goblins. "Go fetch wood for the fire. We'll have a feast!"

The goblins dashed about, foraging for wood. "No!" Glory cried tearfully. "Don't do it, Father! Let him go! I'll do any-thing—"

"You'll marry a goblin chief," Gorbage told her. "Same as your sister did. After the bird's done."

Stanley had almost freed himself, but it looked as if he would be too late to help Hardy. The trial had not lasted quite long enough.

The goblins piled wood against Hardy's perch. In moments the fire was ready to be lit. Gorbage produced one of his treasures—a huge Mundane match. The Mundanes practiced very little magic, but this fire-lighting stick was part of what they did have. "Now who shall have the privilege of igniting the conflagration?" he asked dramatically.

"I'll never speak to you again!" Glory cried helplessly at her father.

Unfazed by this dire threat, Gorbage turned to her. "Ah, yes, the persecutor. Who is more fitting to light the fire?" He handed her the match.

"You're insane!" she cried. "I'll never—"

"Can you guess what we shall do to the bird before we croak him—if you don't?" Gorbage asked her.

Glory quailed. It was obvious that the goblins practiced terrible tortures. She couldn't let them do that to Hardy!

Ivy cast about for something to do to stop this, but she and Hugo remained tied, Stanley was not yet free, and the goblins were all around.

Glory approached the pile—and drew her knife. Gorbage, anticipating this, dashed it out of her hand before she could try to cut the rope that tethered Hardy. "You wouldn't be a goblin if you didn't try a trick like that," Gorbage said approvingly. "You'll make some chief real miserable someday. Now strike that match."

Glory's head drooped. Tears squeezed from her eyes. She found a rock and struck the match against it. The match burst into flame, hissing loudly. She hurled it into the pile of brush, where it ignited the dry leaves and moss set amidst the wood— and threw herself after it.

"No!" Gorbage cried, this time caught by surprise. "Get her out of there!"

But Glory had hold of the post, and already the fire was spreading through the eager brush. She intended to die with her beloved.

Ivy stumbled toward the fire, not knowing what else to do. She could not stop the flame; even if her hands had not been tied, she would have been largely helpless. Suddenly she was very much aware of the limitations of her age. Yet there was something—

Goblins were everywhere, screaming, trying to get rid of the fire. Glory, with goblinish cunning, had certainly found the way to foul them up!

Ivy fell into the brush, on the side not yet burning—and

there was Glory, her hand on Hardy's claw-foot, crying and clinging tight.

"You can do it!" Ivy cried, suddenly certain that love could conquer all. "You can save him somehow!"

Glory looked at her. Hardy looked down at her. Smoke wafted across, stinging Ivy's eyes, forcing them shut—and when it passed and she opened them again, tearily, both Glory and Hardy were gone.

Ivy blinked. She saw the vines that formed the rope that had tied the harpy's feet. Now they were tied about nothing—and untying themselves. In moments the vines dropped into the brush, empty. What was happening?

The goblins were staring, equally mystified. "Where's the bird?" one cried.

"Where's my daughter?" Gorbage roared. "Find them!"

Goblins scurried all around again, searching for the fugitives.

Ivy felt something. She was being hauled backward, out of the burning brush, before the flame reached her. Then hands were at her bonds, untying them, and soon she was free. But when she turned to look, there was no one there.

Hugo, standing beside her now, looked startled. His bonds were untying themselves, too! Ivy saw the ropes flip about and release their knots.

Stanley burst out of the net and came to join them. "Hey, the dragon's loose!" a goblin cried.

The goblins turned and charged, raising their clubs—and Stanley blasted them with steam, sending them reeling back.

"Run!" a voice cried. It sounded like Glory—but she was not there. "We'll distract them! You folk get away! You helped us, now we'll help you!

Ivy and Hugo and Stanley ran. Two goblins pursued them—but a fallen branch lifted itself up and tripped them. Then a flaming branch came from the brushfire and waved itself about menacingly.

Daunted, the goblins fell back; it seemed the inanimate was coming to life to threaten them! The trio made it to the shelter of a nearby tree.

"What's happening?" Ivy asked breathlessly. "I never saw magic like this before!"

"They're invisible," Hugo said, using his enhanced intellect to figure it out. "See, Stanley can hear them and smell them; he's not worried." Indeed he wasn't; the little dragon was grinning with all his sharp little teeth as he watched the burning branch set fire to the pants of one goblin. Since goblins did not wear pants, it was quite an effect.

"But goblins can't do magic!" Ivy said. "Neither can harpies!"

"Now they can," Hugo said.

"Only human people have magic talents," Ivy insisted. Then she remembered the centaurs. "And half-humans."

"Well, she's half human, and so is he," he pointed out. "Together they must have a talent—and it's invisibility."

Ivy realized that when she had joined the couple and willed them to save themselves, she had enhanced their hidden joint talent. Now, together, Glory and Hardy became invisible. Because no one could see them, they had been able to free themselves and Ivy and Hugo without interference.

Gorbage, no dummy—Ivy was beginning to realize the full meaning of that term—caught on at almost the same time. "It's them!" he cried. "See her footprints! There must have been some invisible wood in that pile, and the smoke got on them! Follow those footprints!"

"Invisible wood?" Ivy asked. "It looked visible to me!"

"Gorbage doesn't know about your talent," Hugo said. "So he figures there's some other agency. That's just as well."

The goblins oriented on the footprints. But then even these stopped. "He's carrying her through the air!" Hugo said happily. "I don't think he can lift her weight for long, but it should be enough to lose the goblins. We'd better flee before they remember us!"

They fled, hearing the uproar fade behind them. Then the mouth organ started playing again, drowning out everything else with its rich, mellow notes and harmonies.

"I'm glad Glory and Hardy got away," Ivy said when the party felt safe from pursuit.

"I'm glad *we* got away," Hugo said. "Gorbage was going to kill us, too!"

Ivy shuddered, knowing it was true. She always thought the best of new people, but she was learning the hard way that not all folk deserved that regard. They had walked into more than they expected when they met Glory Goblin! But it had been the right thing to do. Love had triumphed in the end, as it was supposed to.

The search, capture, trial, and escape had used up the main part of the day. They ate a supper of assorted conjured fruits, located some hammock trees, and settled down for the night. Stanley had some trouble getting used to a hammock, but enjoyed it when he mastered it. They slept in relative comfort and suffered only a few bad dreams.

Chapter 13. Hardy Harpy

They were down to four now—Chem, Grundy, the Gorgon, and Irene. This was easier, though the others had certainly done their parts. The Gorgon's memory was returning nicely, now that she was among friends. Irene's questions and comments acted to refresh what the forget-whorl had fogged. But Irene knew it had been a close call; if the Gorgon had passed through the center of the whorl, she would have been beyond recovery. And if Zora Zombie had not taken the curse intended for Irene, Irene herself would now be a statue.

"We can work together," Irene suggested to the Gorgon. "Grundy can ask the plants whether they have any news of either Ivy or Hugo, and when you learn Hugo's whereabouts, you can go directly there."

"That seems reasonable," the Gorgon agreed. She had wanted to join forces at the outset, Irene remembered; it might have been better if they had done so.

"The last news I have of Ivy is that she was in the Cyclops' cave," Irene continued. "So I'll just start looking for that. I have my ivy plant that shows she's still healthy, so I know nothing has happened to her yet. But the Muse said she was going to get into trouble soon. I want to find her before night, if possible."

"There is a goodly portion of the day remaining," Chem pointed out encouragingly.

Grundy queried the local flora and fauna. He was in luck; many of them knew where the dread one-eyed monster lurked. This entire region had been largely cleaned out of dragons and griffins because of the Cyclops' voracious appetite for meat. The smaller creatures appreciated that and felt the Cyclops was not such a bad fellow. But still they preferred not to encounter him directly, just in case.

Hearing that, Irene became even more eager to recover her daughter quickly. She didn't like taking chances either.

As they progressed, the references became more specific. It seemed that the Cyclops hunted only at night, but he was a terror then.

Either Ivy had escaped the Cyclops and was safe from pursuit while day remained, or she was still in the cave, perhaps trapped there. There was no separate news of her or of Hugo, to the Gorgon's disappointment. She looked worried under her veil. She did not have the assurance of an ivy plant that her son was healthy; and, considering Hugo's general backwardness and lack of an effective magical talent, Irene could appreciate her concern.

Then there was something new. Grundy paused. "I didn't know there was a mouth organ in these parts!"

"Mouth organ?" Irene asked.

"That's a natural musical instrument," Chem explained. "Part plant, part animal, part mineral. It has many mouths that sound separate notes. It's a rare thing, but it does occur in scattered locations and can attain considerable size. It is said to be very impressive. When it spawns, the little mouth organs can be plucked and played by hand, as they aren't big enough to generate their own wind. But handling stunts their growth, so few make it to maturity."

"It's hard to be a success if you're a plaything," Grundy agreed.

Irene cocked her head. Now she heard it, faintly, as from a fair distance to the east—deep, powerful, sustained notes, decorated by a pleasant, higher melody. "This one sounds mature," she said shortly. "Very nice. Some day we must visit it. But at the moment we have a more urgent mission."

"I'm not sure," Grundy said. "The organ is speaking, musically, and I can understand it because of its animate portion. It says there are goblins in the area."

"Goblins?" Chem asked. "That's unlikely. All the major tribes of goblins settled north of the Gap Chasm. There might be a few stragglers south, but not enough to cause any problems."

"The organ says a war party is here," the golem insisted. "It says that yesterday the goblins captured a male harpy, in the course of their raid into harpy territory. They were going to execute him."

"A male harpy—executed?" Chem asked. "That will instantly inflame the whole harpy species! They have very few males and they value them inordinately."

Now Irene took notice. "Goblins on the warpath—here? Ivy could run into them! What else does the organ say?"

"Nothing much. It's just alerting the harpies—that male hasn't been seen since last night—so they can form a battle wing and wipe out the goblins. There will be war, very soon."

"That's all we need!" the Gorgon said. "A resurgence of the old goblin-harpy war! My husband has texts delineating the atrocities of their ancient wars; Xanth is much gentler today."

"The Gap Chasm kept them apart for centuries," Chem said. "There are several bridges across it, but they are guarded by human folk who wouldn't let goblins pass. One of the bridges is one-way, so the goblins couldn't pass it anyway, and another is invisible, so they couldn't find it. The only practical way they could cross is *through* the Gap, and of course the Gap

Dragon—" She paused, a bulb flashing. "*That's* what the dragon did! It stopped the goblins from crossing, so as to preserve peace in Xanth! The goblin-harpy wars were the worst calamities in Xanth, apart from the Mundane Waves of conquest— and the Gap Dragon helped inhibit those, too! I'm sure it was no accident that Castle Roogna was built south of the Gap, and that most of the civilized settlements of men and centaurs were also south. Perhaps we owe, in this peculiar fashion, the survival of civilization in Xanth to the Gap Dragon!"

"So there was excellent reason for the Good Magician to spare the Gap Dragon, even if it was rampaging," Irene agreed, awed by the revelation. That was the last monster she would have expected to owe anything to.

"There is good reason for anything Humfrey does," the Gorgon said seriously. "He always did know what he was doing, no matter what others thought."

"He always did," Irene agreed. "But now the forget-spell is off the Gap, the dragon is gone, Humfrey can not act, and the ancient mischief is returning. We're in more trouble than we knew."

"King Dor will certainly have to act to nullify the goblins," Chem said. "But for the moment, this merely makes our mission more urgent. We must rescue the children quickly! There's no telling what will happen if they fall into goblin hands!"

They hurried on toward the Cyclops' cave.

Before very long, there was a raucous screech from the sky. Great ugly bird-shapes appeared. "Goblins! Destroy them!" an unlovely female voice screeched.

Great, gross harpies converged, descending from the sky, filthy talons extended. There were twelve or fifteen of them. Chem's bow was in her hands, but she withheld her shot, knowing that if she killed one dirty hen, the others would tear the whole party to bits. The Gorgon put her hand on her veil; *she* could deal with them all, if she had to.

"We're not goblins!" Irene cried, desperately trying reason before combat.

The leader-harpy hovered before them, peering. She had a hideous and filthy face, dangling, lumpy breasts, soiled tail feathers, and a nauseating odor. She was about as repulsive as a creature could get, not so much for her shape as for her lack of hygiene and her bad nature. "Why, so you're not!" the harpy screeched. "You made us waste all this effort for nothing! We'd better tear you apart anyway!"

"Let me talk to them," Chem said. "Be ready, Gorgon; we may still need you."

The Gorgon nodded, keeping one hand on her veil, ready to jerk it aside and glare about.

"Listen to me," Chem told the harpy leader. "We aren't goblins and we are not involved with them. We have no quarrel with you—but we do have power to defend ourselves, if you force the issue. Leave us alone and we shall leave you alone."

The harpies hovered in air made foul by their presence. The stench was assuming an awful intensity. "You can defend yourselves?" the leader screeched. "Prove it!"

"You wouldn't like that," Chem said warningly.

"You're bluffing!" the harpy screeched. No harpy seemed to have any voice other than the screech; too much of this conversation would give a person a headache.

"This woman is the Gorgon," the centaur said evenly. "One glance at her bare face will turn a person to stone."

"I don't believe it!" the harpy screeched. "Hatty, rip that rag off her face, then pluck out her eyeballs!"

A harpy lunged forward, spraying out small, soiled feathers in her eagerness to get at the eyeball tidbits. Irene kept her eyes on the harpy, not the Gorgon, as did the others of her party. She was aware, peripherally, of the Gorgon making a slight motion.

Then the harpy, Hatty, stopped in midair and dropped like a stone. This was only natural; she had become a stone. The Gorgon replaced her veil.

The other harpies flew down to look at their fallen comrade. Hatty was now an ugly statue that looked as if it had been too long under pigeons. Her calcified eyes gazed out in blind contempt, and her thin-lipped mouth was fixed in a perpetual scowl. Even a small drool of dirty spittle had frozen to stone on her lip.

"She's petrified!" a harpy screeched.

"Completely stoned," Grundy agreed. "You dirty birds can't say we didn't warn you."

"And who the smut are you, runt?" the leader screeched.

"I'm Grundy the Golem," Grundy said proudly. "I can talk to any living thing, even your kind, you nauseating hen, though I have to hold my nose. Who the upchuck are you?"

"I'm Haggy Harpy, leader of this motley flock," the harpy screeched. "We're looking for goblins. Who are those others?"

Again, Irene was cautious about identifying herself completely. "I'm Irene. I grow plants."

"And I'm Chem," the centaur said. "I make maps."

Haggy hovered, pondering, while her flapping wings wafted the smell of her past them. "Stoning—talking—planting—mapping," she screeched, totaling it up. "A pretty collection of talents. You creatures are lucky; not everyone has magic." She rotated to address the others. "Hannah, execute plan SA," she said. Then she spun in air back to Irene. "What are you doing out here in harpy territory?"

"I'm looking for my lost child," Irene said. "A girl, three years old. Have you seen her?"

"Anybody seen her brat?" Haggy screeched to the other harpies, who were milling about in some private pattern that continually wafted their foul odor past the party on the ground. Irene hoped she could keep from gagging.

There was a discordant response. No one had seen any lost human child.

"SSAAA!" Hanna Harpy screeched. Suddenly the harpies swooped in, acting together. Two carried a bag, which they dropped over the Gorgon's head before the Gorgon could get her hand back up to her veil. Others carried vine-cords, which they wrapped around the others. The action was so quick and treacherous that Chem did not have time to raise her bow.

"Grow!" Irene cried desperately at any plant in range. The grass under Chem's hooves shot up, and nearby trees put on new foliage, but there was nothing to interfere with the harpies. Naturally the confined seeds in the bag did not grow; that would have been a worse disaster than the harpies! In a moment all four of them were captive.

"Plan SA: Sneak Attack," Grundy said disgustedly. "I should have realized."

Irene cursed herself for the same oversight. Goblins and harpies were creatures largely without honor; she knew that. It had been folly to relax.

"Why did you dirty birds do that?" Grundy demanded of the harpies. "We did nothing to you, except for when Hatty forced the issue, and we had given you fair warning about that. You can fix her bad as new by carrying her statue out to Mundania, where the spell will be broken."

"We don't care about Hatty!" Hannah screeched. "Who cares about a harpy? We wanted you!"

"Because we can use your talents," Haggy screeched, satisfied. "Now we can track down those goblins faster!"

"But—but you can't just capture us and make us work for you!" Irene spluttered.

"Why can't we?" Haggy screeched reasonably.

"For one thing, we'll refuse to do your bidding," Chem said, swishing her tail in irritation.

"No bidding, you old biddy!" Grundy agreed.

"Oh, will you now?" the harpy chieftainess screeched. "Well, then, we'll just tear your stonemason friend to pieces, one piece at a time. We're due for a meal anyway." She turned in the air to face her subordinate hen. "Hannah, old cackle, let's see how fast you can get the first arm off that creature. Don't go near her hood!"

Hannah screeched with delight. "Hold her tight, hens! I don't want her thrashing about while I'm at work. That would spill too much tasty blood. Maybe I'll start with her gizzard; that's easier to claw out!"

The other hens converged on the hooded and bound Gorgon, sinking their filthy talons into her limbs, securing her for the ordeal. Irene knew they weren't bluffing; harpies really did like to tear flesh apart and cause anguish to feeling creatures.

"And fetch a basin," Haggy screeched. "So we can have a blood bath afterward!"

Irene's stomach tried to take flight like a harpy. No, they weren't bluffing! "All right! We'll cooperate." Irene said quickly. "Don't hurt her!"

Haggy Harpy screeched out a mind-rotting string of epithets. "Oh, you're spoiling our fun! Can't you wait until we've done with this one? She's a fine, healthy specimen and I just know she's got a lot of hot blood in her!"

"No, I can't wait!" Irene cried, in her desperation sounding almost like a harpy herself. "Don't touch her!"

"Oh, all right, spoilsport!" Haggy screeched. "I guess we can use her talent on the goblins as we planned. Hannah, you'll have to wait."

"Go suck eggs!" Hannah screeched back. She had been hovering, waiting for the others to secure the victim properly, exposing the Gorgon's midriff for the gizzard operation. "I want blood!" She launched herself at the Gorgon, talons extended, mouth gaping with lust for gore.

"Don't tell *me* to suck eggs, you bloated bag!" Haggy screeched, launching herself after her. She moved very swiftly; harpies had had many generations of experience snatching things, and could zip forward in the blink of a smudged eye.

The two collided in the air; Haggy lifted a claw and made such a swipe at the other that several greasy feathers were wrenched out of her tail assembly. Hannah spun out of control, sideswiped a tree, and landed on her back, her spindly chicken legs poking straight up. She screeched such an oath that the grass around her turned brown. Then she flipped over, and flapped up, leaving a smudge of discolor on the ground. She perched on a branch, shaking out loose feathers. Discipline had evidently been asserted in the normal harpy fashion.

"Now, this is what you'll do," Haggy screeched to Irene. "You'll grow us some blood lilies and a pitcher plant of gall for us to snack on, and the horse's rear will show us a map so we can guess where the goblins are, and the imp—"

"I'm a golem, not an imp!" Grundy said.

"—will ask around for the goblins," Haggy finished. "And if we don't find them by nightfall, we'll tear Stonestare up instead. That seems fair enough, don't you agree? I'll bet those little snakes on her head are mighty tasty morsels!"

Irene didn't even ask whether the harpies would let the party go if they found the goblins. Harpies didn't make positive promises, only threats. "You'll have to free my hands so I can sort through my seeds," she said. "I can't grow what you want if I don't have the seeds."

"We'll do it," Haggy screeched. "But if you grow any wrong thing, your hooded friend will be gutted before you can do anything else, and we'll make you drink the first blood."

"Unfair!" Hannah screeched. "You promised *me* first blood!"

"Oh, all right. We'll give you the blood, and stuff the first entrails into the captives' mouths," Haggy decided, being a fair-minded hen.

Horrified, Irene knew they had effectively prevented her from growing a tangle tree or anything else that would be useful against this awful flock. She opened the big bag of seeds and sifted through it, looking for the proper ones. She was in luck, for what that was worth; she found the items she needed. She dropped them to the ground. "Grow!"

The blood lilies came up and formed deep red bulbs, while the pitcher plant developed pitchers filled with liquid that would kill flies. The harpies snatched both eagerly and slurped them down messily. The dirty birds were even more repulsive when eating than when screeching.

While the hens were distracted, Irene consulted with Grundy. "Do you think you can locate the goblin band? Our lives may depend on it."

"I'll locate something," the golem promised. "I can start by going toward the mouth organ; since it has seen them, I know they were in that region."

"Good enough," Irene said. "And if, somewhere along the way, you get a chance to lift the Gorgon's hood—"

"You scheming females are all alike," Grundy said.

Irene smiled cynically. "Some day you'll encounter one your size, and she'll make you happy to be schemed into captivity—if you live through this present crisis."

"I can hardly wait." But the golem was momentarily thoughtful.

Soon the harpies were through gobbling their food. "Now get on it, imp!" Haggy screeched. "Find those goblins!"

Grundy jumped to the ground and made a show of questioning the local plants. Naturally none of them had seen the goblins. "That way," he announced, pointing in the direction of the mouth organ.

The harpies were so eager for blood and gore that they didn't realize he was pointing toward their own public-address system. "Map! Map!" Haggy screeched.

Chem projected a map of the region. It didn't have much detail, because the centaur hadn't seen enough of the local terrain yet. But it did show sufficient gross accuracy to satisfy the harpies that it was valid.

The harpies had to free Chem's feet so she could walk, but they left her arms bound, and one of them hovered near enough to attack her if she tried to bolt. They tied Irene's hands again and had her ride the centaur. They kept the Gorgon walking separately, another harpy screeching directions at her so she could find her way despite the hood. Irene was both saddened and angered to see her friend stumbling blindly, her hands bound, but she could do nothing about it.

They proceeded slowly north, constantly harrassed by the harpies, who wanted them to do the job faster. Then Grundy got a break—he intersected the trail of the goblins. Thirteen goblins were traveling southwest. There was no harpy with them.

"That means they killed him, sure enough," Haggy screeched. "We'll tear out their hearts and stuff them up their—" The rest became unintelligible, which was just as well, for the leaves of the nearest trees were turning brown and curling up. Harpies did seem to have a certain flair for that sort of thing.

Hot on the trail, the harpies spread out and became silent. They knew their screeching would instantly alert the enemy and put the goblins on guard. One bird flew high above the trees, trying to spy the new prey, casting her baleful glare hither and yon. And soon she succeeded.

She swooped low. "Straight ahead, on an island in a water table," she reported in a whispering shriek. "We can surround it. They think they're safe there, but they can't fly."

Irene realized that this was a typical mistake; creatures who could not fly had little awareness of the threat from the air until it was upon them.

"We won't take a chance," Haggy decided. "Thirteen against

thirteen—that's too nearly even. We don't want a fair fight, we want an easy slaughter. We'll make Stoneface look at them." They had it backward, Irene saw; they didn't realize that it was not the Gorgon's gaze that petrified people, but the sight of her full face. Irene was not about to correct their misimpression.

"But she'll look at us, too," another warned.

"That's right. Better not risk it right now. We'll bomb them instead. Get your eggs ready."

How the harpies carried eggs, Irene wasn't sure, but it seemed they had them somewhere. She also was not certain what good it would do to drop eggs on the goblins, unless the intent was to blind the enemy with the splats of whites and yokes.

The harpies flew into the sky, trailing small swirls of greasy feathers. "Oh, Hannah," Haggy screeched in an afterthought. "Now you can take care of these creatures here; they have become surplus."

"Goody!" Hannah screeched back. She looped about and flew toward Irene's party. She was slightly unsteady because of the recent loss of tail feathers but could maneuver well enough. Her hideous face gloated.

"Grundy!" Irene cried. But the golem was too far from the Gorgon to reach her before the harpy did.

Instead, it was Chem who leaped to the Gorgon's rescue. Her hands were tied, but she tried to use her teeth, bending to take a grip on the hood.

But Hannah did not come in that close. She banked, spread her legs, and laid an egg in midair. "Die!" she screeched as the missile slanted down.

"Watch out!" Grundy cried at the same time. "I just remembered what those eggs do!"

Chem lurched away from the falling egg, pushing the Gorgon down. The egg struck the ground beside them and exploded. There was a dirty boom, and brush and turf were blasted out, leaving a small crater.

The eggs really were bombs! Irene realized that the harpies probably ate pineapples when forming a battle wing to get the explosive ingredients. They really were prepared for war!

Grundy, unhurt, skirted the crater and reached them. He

climbed on the Gorgon's bagged head, tugging at the cloth. But it was tied on, and the cord was too firmly knotted for him to budge. Meanwhile, the harpy circled. Did she have another egg?

"No wonder they don't reproduce much!" Chem exclaimed. Grundy laughed. It would be hard to hatch a live harpy chick from an exploding egg!

But the peril wasn't funny. "Grundy, get me a seed!" Irene cried. "Hurry!"

The golem scrambled to her bag and fetched out a random handful of seeds. "Grow!" Irene ordered the handful.

The seeds sprouted immediately. Irene could, of course, grow plants with her hands tied behind her. But it was chancy starting a random sample. Those seeds could develop into anything, and the result might be harmless or negative.

A coral plant began to form coral on the golem's hand, and he hastily dropped the seeds. A sugar palm sent out a hand formed of sugar. Ironwood speared up, points already coated with rust because of their proximity to the water table. A saucer plant presented its dishes. A hunter's horn plant blew a loud note. Mistletoe nudged the earth with its toenail and fired off its seedpod. And a split rock plant dug its roots into the nearest rock and split it into two sharp-edged fragments.

Grundy jumped down and lifted one of those fragments. He brought it to the Gorgon's bound hands and started sawing.

But now Hannah Harpy was coming in again. Evidently she had another egg ready.

Chem projected a map. It showed a boulder where the people were, and people where a nearby boulder was. The harpy blinked, then corrected course and dropped her egg. It smacked into the boulder and broke it into a pile of rocks. Sand showered around them.

The Gorgon's hands came free. She reached up to draw the hood from her head, but the tie was at the back and did not yield to her fumbling fingers.

"Use the stone to cut it!" Irene ordered.

The harpy had realized that something was wrong. Chem's maps were good, but were not true illusions; a person could see reality through the maps when the proper effort was made.

Hannah looped about, ready to lay another egg on them, and this one would not miss.

"Here she comes again!" Grundy said. "And that old hen has blood in her grotesque eye!"

Irene was horribly sure that was true. But there was one chance. "Gorgon! If you can see anything at all—throw that stone!"

The Gorgon scratched the sharp edge of the stone across her face, ripping the bag in front of her eyes. Now she could see out, vaguely. She hurled the stone at the swooping harpy.

Her aim was good. The stone struck—and the egg detonated. The harpy had not yet released it.

The explosion was muffled. Truly appalling hail pelted them, and the stench was beyond belief.

Irene wiped the gook out of her eyes and peered up. There was nothing left of Hannah Harpy but a foul cloud of smoke. It was dull gray, tinged with streaks of blood-red.

"Hey, the prisoners are making a break!" another harpy screeched.

"We've got to get out of here!" Irene said tersely.

Now there was a clamor on the water table. The remaining harpies had attacked the goblins, and great and awful was the sound and fury thereof.

The Gorgon left the scratched hood on her head, so she could see out without having her deadly face exposed, and hastened to work on Chem's bonds. Soon the centaur was free. She took her bow and aimed an arrow at the sky; the first harpy who came close enough to lay an egg would be shot down.

Now the Gorgon came to Irene and undid her hands. Their party was ready to move, but Irene was uncertain. "The forest is too open; if we flee, we'll be vulnerable to attack from the rear. I don't want any of those eggs coming at my rear! We'd better take cover until it's safe."

Chem agreed. They moved onto the water table, which was a raised, level plain formed of jellied water with a solid crust. It was a blue-green level surface, and it sank beneath their weight slightly, forming a slow ripple.

On the far side of the table stood the goblin band, armed with clubs and spears and stones and scowls. The harpies were dive-bombing them, but the rain of thrown stones was thick enough to keep them too far away to score. Geysers of water shot up where the eggs missed their marks. The crust of the table was firm and flexible, but the explosions gouged out holes that took a while to reseal.

Three harpies detached themselves from the main formation and zeroed in on Irene's party. Irene plunged her hand into the seed bag and scattered the seeds she brought out. "Grow!"

The seeds sprouted in air and landed on the water table, where their roots delved down to find plenty of water for rapid growth. Leatherleaf ferns spread their leather across the plain. A gold-dust tree sent out a cloud of glittering gold dust. A foxglove swished its bushy tail and made hand signals with its glove. An amethyst plant grew purple crystals that sparkled in the sunshine. A balloon vine sent a cloud of colored balloons into the sky. A helmet flower produced several fine helmets in assorted sizes that Irene and the others harvested for immediate use in case an egg exploded nearby. A living fossil plant rattled its bones. And a water-ivy had a field day, spreading so quickly and thickly that it soon covered a sizable portion of the table. The vines and leaves became so big and piled on one another so thickly that they provided good cover for the party. The tabletop had become a thick jungle.

The goblins spied the jungle and charged toward it, recognizing the advantage of its cover. "Uh-oh," Irene said. "I didn't think of this consequence! Now we'll have goblins to contend with, too!"

Indeed it was so. When the goblins arrived and discovered that the jungle was occupied, they hurled some of their stones at these new targets. It had turned into a three-way battle.

The thick cover became a mixed blessing. Irene and her friends were hidden from the harpies, who wheeled and screeched their curses from above, ready to egg anyone who responded—but the goblins were also hidden from both Irene and the harpies, and she knew goblins were good at jungle combat.

A goblin appeared before Chem—but disappeared as she swung her bow around to aim at him. The thickly spreading leaves concealed too much!

A harpy spied the motion and zoomed down close and laid her egg. It detonated to the side, blasting out greenery that splatted green all around them.

A dark, gnarly hand grasped Irene's arm. She jerked around to look, not daring to scream because of the listening harpies, and came face to snoot with an ugly goblin.

The goblin opened his big mouth, showing his sharp yellow teeth. He lunged to bite Irene's leg.

She twisted her leg away, then kneed him in the ear. Ow! The goblin's head was undamaged, but Irene's knee was hurting!

"Don't hit their heads!" Grundy called. "They're hard as rocks! Hit their hands and feet!"

Irene stomped on one of the goblin's big feet, but the ground was so squishy that the foot merely sank into the soft water, unhurt. Then she grabbed one of the goblin's arms, wrenched it about, and slammed the goblin's own hand into his head.

"Owww!" the goblin screamed. "My hand's broken!"

A harpy heard his cry and circled, trying to pinpoint the source. She screeched a corrosive curse. Soon there would be an egg on both their heads! Irene knew she had to dispatch this creature quickly.

Now she moved her captured arm, the one the goblin's hand was grasping, and jammed that against his rock-head. She knocked the goblin's hand against his skull, and it was the hand that gave way. That made him let go. Then Chem got there and swept him away with a well-placed kick in the head. It didn't hurt the goblin the way a kick in the seat would have, but it drove him so far into the foliage that Irene was able to hide herself again.

"We've got to get out of this or we'll all be dead!" Irene gasped. She had not had much experience with this sort of combat and didn't like it at all.

"I think I'd better use my power," the Gorgon said, touching her head.

Irene sighed. "I suppose we have no reasonable alternative."

Then there was a stir among the wheeling harpies. "It's him! It's him!" they screeched.

Irene peered out through the foliage. All she saw was another harpy coming to reinforce the others. Bad news!

"Him?" Chem asked. "The male they thought the goblins killed?"

Now Irene realized the significance of this arrival. "Then they have no cause for war!"

"Oh, they'll fight anyway," Grundy said. "Harpies and goblins always fight one another when they get the chance."

"Well, they shouldn't do it while we're caught in the middle!" Irene exclaimed.

"Perhaps I can arrange a truce," Chem said. "The moment seems propitious, and I believe I have encountered the goblin leader before."

"Anything's worth a try!" Irene said. Her hands were cold and clammy, and she hoped she didn't look as flustered as she felt. She just wanted to get out of this battle and back on the search for her child.

Chem concentrated. Her map appeared—this time it was not a scene, but a huge display of letters: T R U C E. Simultaneously, the centaur called: "Gorbage! Gorbage Goblin!"

Few harpies could read, but the leaders were more educated than most. "Truce?" Haggy Harpy screeched, outraged. "Truce? Who says?"

And the goblin leader called back: "Who calls my name?"

"I am Chem Centaur," Chem replied. "I call for this truce because you goblins and harpies have no quarrel, and I want to show you this before you destroy your best chance for peace."

"Peace!" Gorbage and Haggy screeched together.

"We don't want peace!" Haggy continued.

"We want war!" Gorbage finished.

"But—" Irene protested, bemused.

"The old hen is right," Gorbage said. "We haven't had a good war in eight hundred years. It's long overdue!"

"That's for sure!" Haggy screeched.

The newly arrived harpy male swooped in. Now Irene could see that his face and feathers were clean and that he was, in fact, a handsome half-specimen of a man. "We shall talk peace anyway," he cried, and his voice, too, was unlike the screech of the hens. "We shall make truce and listen to the centaur, for centaurs are known to be fair-minded folk."

The harpy hens fluttered uncertainly, since they could not argue with the precious male. "If you say so," Haggy screeched grudgingly.

"Well, *I* don't say so!" Gorbage cried from his cover in the foliage. "I want to exterminate them all—beginning with that birdbrained cock!" He pointed at the male harpy.

A lovely female goblin appeared. "Then you'll have to exterminate me also, Father!" she cried. "I love him!"

A harpy-goblin romance? This was another surprise!

"A goblin tart!" Haggy screeched indignantly. "We'll bury her in eggs!"

"You certainly will not!" the male harpy cried. "I'm going to marry her!"

Irene was amazed. "It's true, then! No wonder these creatures are riled up! That's the most forbidden love, for them!"

"We'd *better* get a truce!" Chem said. "In a moment there'll be nothing but feet and feathers."

Irene felt in her bag for seeds. She found what she wanted: several wallflowers. She threw the seeds out in four directions, aiming and orienting each carefully. "Grow!"

They grew. One wall formed just behind Irene's party, expanding east and west, shoving aside the prior vegetation. Others grew to the sides, extending north and south. A fourth grew to the north, extending east and west. Soon they all intersected at the edges, making corners and forming a roughly square enclosure. Their walls thickened and gained height, with flowers on the top, until no one could see anything but sky from the inside.

"Chem, you face north and have your bow ready," Irene said. "Gorgon, you face south, with your hand on your veil—er, hood, or whatever. I'll try to watch the sky. Grundy, climb up on the wall and tell Gorbage and Haggy and the two, um, lovers to come in here under truce so we can talk safely. Watch out for thrown missiles."

"Gotcha," the golem agreed. He found handholds and clambered up the south wall.

"I hope you can apply centaur logic to this situation, Chem,"

Irene murmured. "If you can't persuade them, we're still in trouble." Her stomach felt weak; she didn't like the continuing tension of this situation. She knew her plants had gained them only a temporary reprieve.

"The logic is valid—if they will listen," Chem said. "But neither species is known for listening well."

Grundy reached the top of the wall and stood on it, a tiny figure. "Hey, stink-snoot!" he cried. "Come in here and show off your ignorance! You too, filth-feather!" Then he ducked as a rock flew by and an egg slanted down.

"I think you chose the wrong diplomat," Chem remarked. "Grundy thinks it's a challenge to be as foul-mouthed as the others."

"I should have known," Irene agreed ruefully. "I'll have to mediate this myself."

"You'll get your head bombed," Chem warned.

"Perhaps we can be of assistance," a new voice said.

Irene looked around, but saw nothing. "Who spoke?"

"We're invisible," the voice said. "We don't want to get shot or stoned."

"Invisible! Well, if you're friendly, show yourselves; we won't attack you."

Two figures faded into view—the male harpy and the female goblin.

"The lovers!" Irene exclaimed. "How—?"

"We discovered our magic talent," the girl said almost shyly. She was remarkably pretty. "Goblins don't do magic, and neither do harpies—not the way human folk do—but together we can become invisible." She moved to rejoin the harpy and they faded out again.

"Recessive genes, maybe," Chem said as the two reappeared. She glanced more closely at the girl. "You look familiar. I've seen a goblin girl almost as pretty as you—"

"My big sister Goldy," the girl said. "I'm Glory, the loveliest and nicest of my generation. And this is Hardy, the handsomest and best-mannered of his."

Irene introduced herself and her friends. "We're looking for my lost daughter—"

"Ivy!" Glory exclaimed. "The cute little child with the bone in her hair!"

Irene was astonished. "You met her?"

"She helped me find Hardy," Glory said. "Now I can see the family affinity. Her hair is a little green, while yours—"

"When she gets jealous, her whole face turns green," Grundy remarked, returning from the wall.

"A bone in her hair?" Chem inquired.

"She said the Cyclops gave it to her," Glory explained. "She was very helpful! She and Hugo and Stanley—"

"Hugo?" the Gorgon asked. "He's with them?"

"Oh, yes. He has such a wonderful talent!"

"But he can only conjure rotten fruit!"

Glory laughed. "You wouldn't say that if you knew him!"

"Well, I *am* his mother."

Glory gazed at her, perplexed. "You must have excruciatingly exacting standards! His fruit certainly seemed good enough to me! And he's so intelligent—"

"Intelligent?" the Gorgon asked.

"Oh, yes! And handsome—"

The Gorgon shook her hooded head, baffled.

"Stanley?" Irene asked, picking up on the other name.

"Stanley Steamer, the baby dragon. He's really very nice, too."

"Nice?" Irene repeated blankly. "The rejuvenated Gap Dragon?"

Glory smiled, and the wallflower enclosure brightened. "You're being humorous, right?"

"That must be the case," Irene agreed faintly. Something was certainly funny here, but not humorous. "How did you meet them?"

"I was coming south from the Gap, looking for Hardy, and I suppose I was lost, or at least mislaid. But the dragon located the mouth organ for us, and so we found Hardy—"

"And the goblins ambushed us," the harpy continued. "They put me on trial for corrupting Glory, but Hugo's brilliant defense acquitted me—"

"I just don't understand," the Gorgon said. "Naturally I want the best for my son, but I simply have to say that he was never brilliant or handsome or well talented. I wish it were otherwise, but—"

"It sounds as if his qualities have been improved," Chem commented.

"Ivy!" Irene exclaimed. "She's responsible!"

"That was my thought," the centaur agreed. "I suspect that her talent of enhancement is more potent than we knew. She has elevated Hugo to his full potential."

"But the dragon," Irene said. "The dragon should have become even more ferocious by the same enhancement!"

"Not if her talent is selective," Chem pointed out. "If it should, for example, enhance only what she perceives, or chooses to perceive, or wishes—"

"It would require Magician-level talent to make my boy a genius," the Gorgon said ruefully. "For a long time I hoped he would improve as he aged, but now he's eight years old and has shown no sign—"

"Eight? If he's not a genius, he's close to it," Glory said. "He picked up on precisely the right points!"

"Anyway," Hardy said, "Hugo won my case—but the goblin chief, Glory's father, reneged, and set up to execute me—"

"And I joined him in the fire," Glory continued, her eyes shining. "Ivy joined us, too—and suddenly we found our talent and were invisible. That made the difference, and in the confusion we were able to escape."

"Ivy's talent," Chem said. "*Much* more potent than we knew! That combined harpy-goblin talent of invisibility must have been latent. The stress of the situation and Ivy's power of enhancement must have joined to bring it out. Who ever would have suspected that a joint interspecies talent could exist?"

"Well, if half souls exist," Irene said, "maybe half talents exist too."

The centaur smiled. "Surely so! There is much we have yet to learn about the magic of Xanth! And it seems that Hardy and Glory are well matched, since their half talents match."

It occurred to Irene that it was possible that all goblins and all harpies had half talents of invisibility which could only be matched by the portion in the other species, so that this was not necessarily an indication of the compatibility of these two particular individuals. But there was no point in making that caveat; it would accomplish nothing.

"So we fled my father's band," Glory concluded. "And Ivy and Hugo and Stanley escaped, too, for the goblins were following our footprints. Hardy carried me part of the way, though I weigh as much as he does, and he couldn't lift me far. But when darkness came, we camped in a tree my father's band couldn't reach and got a good night's rest." She paused to blush delicately. "Part of the night, anyway."

"We gave them the slip," Hardy said. "But they kept casting about, searching for us, so we couldn't really relax today."

"We were getting pretty tired," Glory said. "But now, with the harpies—"

"We heard the commotion," Hardy said. "I recognized the screeching and thought I could reassure my people that the mouth organ's news was inoperative—"

"I believe I have enough of the picture now," Chem said. "But we can do nothing unless we get the leaders to negotiate."

"I can get my father to come in here," Glory said. "But he won't listen to reason."

"And I can get Haggy Harpy here," Hardy said. "All males are princes in Harpydom; she must come at my call. But she won't listen either."

"Fetch them in and keep them from fighting," Chem said, "and I will try to get through to them. I may not be as eloquent as you say Hugo was, but we may yet abate this war."

Goblin and harpy shrugged. Anything was worth trying. Then Glory climbed the south wall, flashing some remarkably well-formed limbs, while Hardy flew into the sky. There had been little commotion from either side during this dialogue, perhaps because neither could be sure where the present advantage lay.

"Father," Glory called from the wall. "You must come in here and talk to the harpy leader, under truce."

"Never!" Gorbage answered, his voice faint but ugly in the distance.

"Otherwise I just might throw myself to my doom," Glory said, making as if to jump off the wall. It really wasn't high enough for the fall to be fatal, but the bluff worked; Gorbage agreed to come in.

Hardy had an easier time. "Come down and negotiate," he told Haggy, "or I'll tell the Queen Harpy you suck eggs."

That cowed the hen. "I'm no egg-sucker!" she screeched, and flapped down to perch on the north wall.

Now both leaders were present, Haggy settling her blotchy feathers, Gorbage draping his knobby legs astride the south wall. Both glared at each other, and at anyone else in range. It was obvious that neither cared to be reasonable.

"First," Chem said, "I ask each of you to explain to your people that we are armed with accurate arrows and the stare of the Gorgon. Anyone who tries to storm this bastion will face the consequence." Gorbage and Haggy, knowing this was true, informed their parties. But neither showed any willingness to cease hostilities. Irene knew this was the main problem. Human folk would have wanted to find a way to avert bloodshed, but the goblins and harpies really did want to fight.

"For more than a thousand years, the goblins and the harpies have been at war," Chem said. "It started because of over-crowding and misunderstanding, and foul deeds were done on both sides. But King Roogna got things straightened away, and for eight hundred years the war has been quiescent. With the Gap Chasm and the Gap Dragon separating the parties, there has not been very much occasion for strife. But now it seems a romance has developed between the species—"

"I'll kill the fowl cock!" Gorbage cried. "Smirching my fair daughter!"

"That's 'smooch,' not 'smirch,' Father," Glory murmured.

"Listen, bulbnose!" Haggy screeched. "Your slut of a whelp of a daughter tempted him with her obscene legs, just like in the old days! She should swallow an egg sidewise!"

"What's wrong with her legs?" Hardy demanded.

"I'll egg her right now!" Haggy screeched, rising into the air. But Chem's arrow tracked her progress, ready to zing from the bow, and the Gorgon turned to face the harpy, her hand tugging at the hood. Haggy settled back down, muttering.

"Do you folk really object to interspecies marriages?" Chem asked.

"Of course!" Gorbage cried. "Why should we let miscegination pollute our pure goblin breed? My daughter will marry a goblin chief!"

"Never!" Glory cried.

"We have enough trouble preserving our species," Haggy screeched. "We don't need goblin sluts adulterating our stock! And most of all, we don't need goblins invading our territory and killing off our few precious males!"

"Well, keep those motley cocks away from our unspoiled maidens!" Gorbage yelled back. "You sure don't see our males going after your stinking hens!"

"They couldn't catch them!" Haggy shot back.

"Regardless," Chem cut in loudly. "We do have a cross-species romance here. And I think your objections are not well founded. Many of the creatures of Xanth are crossbreeds. The griffins, merfolk, chimerae, basilisks, manticora—and, of course, my own species, the centaurs. The harpies are an ancient crossbreed line; you should not object to further cross-breeding."

"Not the goblins!" Gorbage said. "We are of straight semi-humanoid stock."

"As are the elves, gnomes, and ogres," Chem agreed. "I think there is as much variation in the humanoid variants as in the crossbreeds. Would you prefer to have your daughter marry an ogre?"

Gorbage spluttered, while Haggy burst out in raucous laughter. "Marry an orgre!" she screeched. "Breed some looks and intelligence into your stock!"

"Listen, rotten-egg-brain—"

"My point is," Chem said, cutting their insults off again, "crossbreeds and humanoid variants should not be ashamed to continue the traditions of Xanth. Maybe in drear Mundania the species don't mix much, but Xanth is not Mundane. That's why Xanth is so much better! We creatures of Xanth have much greater freedom to—"

"Would *you* breed with some other kind of crossbreed, not a centaur?" Haggy screeched challengingly.

"The old biddy's got you there, horsy!" Gorbage cried. "*Would* you—?"

"Yes," Chem said. "If he were a worthwhile creature, and if there were mutual respect and appreciation."

"Centaurs aren't supposed to fib!" Haggy cried.

"Yeah?" Gorbage asked at the same time. "Like what?"

"Like a hippogryph," she answered.

Irene watched her, wondering how far Chem would go to make her point. Centaurs were relatively open about some topics that human folk preferred to keep secret, but her liaison with Xap was really no business of these foul-minded creatures.

Both the old and the young harpies looked at the centaur, surprised, as did the young and old goblins. It was evident that no one had anticipated this answer.

"Aw, she's making it up," Gorbage said after a pause. "There's no bird-horse to call her bluff."

"But there *is* one!" Haggy screeched victoriously. "He belongs to the witch's boy—"

"Xap," Chem said. "Who carries Xavier, son of Xanthippe."

Haggy's ugly mouth gaped. "She knows him!"

Gorbage was equally astounded. "She's really been with a hippogryph?"

"She must have been," Haggy screeched.

The two of them looked at Irene. "What do you know of this claim?" Gorbage asked.

"It's true," Irene said. "Chem traveled with Xap."

"Then she's worse than any of us!" Haggy screeched indignantly.

"She sure is!" Gorbage agreed.

The two looked at each other, startled. They were agreeing!

"Have you noticed," Chem said, "how few goblins and harpies there are, compared to what there used to be? And how many crossbreeds there are, and how vigorous they are?"

Now both goblin and harpy were sullenly silent.

"Did it occur to you that maybe your close inbreeding is weakening both your species?" Chem continued. "The straight human beings were losing power in Xanth, until they reopened the border and mixed with fresh new Mundanes. Human folk didn't want to do that, for they have always been afraid of the Mundane Waves, and contemptuous of the Mundane inability to do magic. But they did interbreed—and now the human folk are strong, and goblins and harpies are weak, when once it was the other way around. Before long, historically, you'll fade away entirely—especially if you keep killing one another off. You would both do better as species if you made peace and let your people interbreed, any who wanted to."

"Ludicrous!" Haggy screeched.

"Appalling!" Gorbage shouted.

Again they looked at each other, finding themselves in unsettling agreement.

"Let me show you something," Chem said. "You both know that neither goblins nor harpies have magic powers. That's another reason neither is prospering in Xanth now."

Mutely, they nodded.

"Please watch what Hardy and Glory do together."

"Oh, no, we won't!" Haggy screeched. "We're respectable creatures! We won't sit still for that kind of obscenity, will we, Gorbage?"

"Certainly not!" the goblin chief agreed emphatically. "We're decent, natural-law-abiding folk!"

The harpy spread her wings, and the goblin edged across the wall, both ready to jump down into the enclosure to preserve decency as they knew it. But the Gorgon turned to face one and then the other, her hand at her hood, and they settled back without further protest. Decency wasn't *that* important!

Hardy and Glory joined hand and claw—and disappeared.

Haggy almost fell off the wall.

"So that's how they got away!" Gorbage said. "I thought they found some vanishing cream or something."

"Together, they can do magic," Chem said as the two reappeared. "Together they have power that no other person in either of your species has. For the first time, goblins and harpies can compete with the human folk and the centaurs in magic. But only together. Apart, you are merely ordinary creatures, losing out to the ones who can do magic."

Haggy stared as the couple joined hands again and vanished. "What I wouldn't give for power like that!" she screeched faintly.

"Would you join with a goblin for it?" Chem asked.

"Never!"

"What—*never?*"

"Well . . ."

"But maybe you could see your way clear to let other harpies seek their magic, in whatever manner they wished," Chem said.

"Maybe. . ." Haggy grudged, looking as if she were tasting a stinkworm.

"And you," Chem said, turning to Gorbage. "Your older daughter married a goblin chief and got a magic wand that makes things fly. Your younger daughter has the chance to marry a prince and to do magic without the wand. Would you deny her that?"

"Well—" Gorbage said, looking as if the stinkworm had crawled into his own mouth.

"And what of their offspring?" Chem continued. "Maybe they will combine the best of both species. They could be winged goblins, able to fly like harpies without sacrificing their legs. Maybe they will have magic talents by themselves, as human folk do. Maybe they will make your line strong again, able to do things no other creatures can do. Your descendants may once again dominate the Land of Xanth. They may once again achieve greatness. Will you deny your daughter and your species that chance?"

Gorbage scowled. "I never thought of it that way." He was violent and opinionated, but he did want what was best for his daughter.

"So why not end the war and give your blessing to the union of these two fine young folk? It could be the dawning of a new age for your kind."

"Well, maybe, but the scandal—"

Glory jumped up and down, clapping her fine little hands. "That's his way of saying yes!" she cried.

"And you?" Chem asked Haggy.

"I don't have any power over any male of our species," the harpy screeched reluctantly. "I'm just a common fighting hen."

"Which is her way of saying yes," Hardy said. "All the old battle-axes are alike. If Haggy goes along, they all will, even the Queen hen."

"Good enough," Chem said, and Irene realized she was moving it along so the longtime enemies would not have a chance to change their minds. "Let's declare this interminable internecine war over and be on our way."

"Now hold on, horsefoot," Gorbage said. "Wars are not just stopped like that! Tradition must be upheld."

"Of course, I realize there will have to be conferences with the other chiefs and formal agreements made," Chem said. "But there's no reason not to start—"

"I mean there has to be a bash," Gorbage said.

"And engagements aren't just started cold," Haggy screeched. "There has to be a big flap."

"We need a whoop-de-doo!" the goblin cried.

"And a poop-de-poo!" the harpy agreed.

"Not on *my* head!" Gorbage said. He turned around on the wall and waved to his troops. "War's over," he bawled. "Come on in for the whoop-de-poop!"

Haggy flew up and screeched similarly to her flock about the doo-de-poo.

Soon goblins were swarming over the south wall and harpies were flapping over the north wall, ready to fling a wing-ding.

"I hope this is as positive as it's supposed to be," Irene murmured nervously.

"Don't worry," Glory said. "They'll fling a party like none you've seen."

"That may be what I'm afraid of." Yet this was bound to be better than war!

"Move it, human woman!" Gorbage exclaimed. "Grow some real party plants!"

"And make some music," Haggy screeched. "You can't match the mouth organ, but—"

Irene fished for a seed and planted it. "Grow!" she told it. The thing sprouted into a cactus with ridges up the sides and needles in every ridge. It brached into a number of shoots, some large, some small. When the plant reached sufficient size, it began to tootle.

"What is that?" Grundy asked.

"An organ-pipe cactus."

The notes deepened and richened as it continued to grow, until at last they were full, rich, organ sounds.

"We'll need dancing slippers," Glory said. "And hair-brushes, to pretty up."

Irene grew a moccasin flower, a hairbrush cactus, and, for good measure, a necklace plant so people could dress up.

"And refreshments!" Haggy screeched. Irene grew a pickle-weed.

"And perfume," the Gorgon murmured.

Irene wrinkled her nose, agreeing. Already the air was close with the fetor of the harpies, and the goblins were none too clean themselves. Irene grew several sweetly scented flowers, including some drops, which were really varieties of rose by other names, smelling as sweet.

"And everyone should sign the register," Hardy said. "But we don't have a—"

Irene grew an autograph tree. It had places for everyone to sign.

"And some party stuff," Grundy said, getting into the spirit of it.

Irene delved for some more seeds, and grew a fiesta flower, a rainbow fern, a good-luck plant, a silver-ball plant, a pearl plant, a live-forever plant, a love-charm plant, and a bag flower for the refuse of the party. Now the enclosure seemed appropriately festive, and the scent of the perfume plants was almost overpowering, enabling her to ignore the aroma of the harpies.

"Move it! Move it!" Gorbage cried, clapping his hands. "Start the bash!"

Hardy and Glory went to the center of the enclosure, where the surface of the water table remained clear except for a layer of carpet grass. The organ-pipe cactus blasted out louder music, and they began to dance. Hardy hovered in midair, his wings shining, while Glory whirled before him, again showing her pretty legs. Irene felt more than a tinge of jealousy; once she had had legs like that!

The two came together, wings and skirt swirling like sections of the same apparel, then flung apart, then came together again in a joint swing. Then they separated completely, going to the walls of the enclosure where the spectators were. Glory skipped across to reach out her hands to her father, bringing him grumblingly onto the dance floor. She was lovely and he was ugly, yet somehow the affinity of lineage was apparent. He stomped and she pranced, their feet striking the carpet in unison, and the dance was good.

Hardy flew to the wall where Haggy perched. "Move your tail, you abysmal old hen!" he cried. She launched into the air, sweeping a dirty talon at him, but he spun in place, and circled, making an orbit about her, and shoved her toward the center. She screeched an epithet that momentarily darkened the sun, but could not truly oppose the will of a male of her species. So she spun in air, joining the dance. As it turned out, she did know how; the two never touched the ground, but matched the beat of the music.

Irene smiled privately. It was evident that the bottom of the harpy male hierarchy ranked the top of the female hierarchy. Haggy screeched her protest, but she would have been affronted had Hardy chosen any lesser hen to haul in to the dance before her.

Irene had a bright notion. She delved for another seed, and found what she wanted. "Grow!" she said, flipping it at the north wall, where the harpies perched. It was a fumigation bush, which would quietly clean any harpy in its vicinity. She found another and flipped it at the south wall.

There were now four on or near the floor, dancing to the music. Harpy faced harpy and goblin faced goblin, making patterns, and it was heartening in the way that any dance was. This was indeed becoming a festive occasion.

Then the two couples separated, each person going out to fetch in another. Gorbage went to the wall to insult another harpy into joining them; Glory brought in another goblin; Hardy got a new harpy hen; and Haggy flapped over to challenge a new goblin. The four on the dance floor became eight. It was a multiplication dance.

Soon the goblins and harpies were all in the dance, and several were questing for new partners. A goblin came to claim the Gorgon, who was startled but suffered herself to be drawn forward. "But I can't see very well," she protested faintly through the hood as she went.

"Who needs to see?" the goblin demanded, moving into the

close ballroom embrace, his head coming up just about to her waist. "You petrify me!"

A harpy came for Grundy. She simply snatched the golem up and whirled with him in the air. Irene noticed that her feathers were now clean; the fumigation bush was working. All the old hens were looking better, now that their colors could be seen; they really weren't as old or ugly as they had seemed, though it would not have been fair to call them young or pretty.

Then Hardy himself came for Chem. "We crossbreeds must dance together!" he said. "I want to thank you for making a marvelous case!"

Finally Gorbage came for Irene. He was half her height and scowling horrendously, but he was now clean and ordorless and she could not refuse. The war had been converted to a party, and she wanted to keep it that way!

She whirled in the crowd, doing her version of the goblin stomp. Gorbage was a surprisingly good partner, for he had a sense of timing and motion. For an instant, she almost forgot that she was stuck in the jungle. "Hey, you got legs like my daughter!" Gorbage remarked, and she was embarrassed to find herself blushing.

"Want to know something?" Gorbage asked as he stomped in perfect time to the music, completely undisturbed about the difference in their sizes. "When I was dancing with one of those old hens, I did some high steps—and I swear my feet left the ground."

"Shouldn't they?" Irene asked, half bemused by the innocence of the remark.

"I mean I was flying—a little," he said. "I stayed up for two, three beats, instead of coming down on one. When I touched her, I had magic."

Irene paused. This was significant. "Are you sure? It wasn't just an extra high jump?"

"Sure I'm sure, maybe. But I could only get a little way off the ground without losing my balance, and nobody else noticed. I'm an old goblin; it's too late for me to learn good magic. But I guess the horserear was right—we *do* have half talents. And harpies have the other halves."

"That's amazing!" Irene said. This indicated that her private caveat about the significance of Hardy and Glory's matchup was not well founded. The talents did not necessarily align, and if a goblin with half levitation encountered a harpy with half invisibility—well, she wasn't sure what would happen then, probably nothing. So at least to some extent, there were proper and improper matchups, and Hardy and Glory were a proper one. That was reassuring.

"That's amazing!" Irene said again, remembering Gorbage. "It's a whole new horizon for your two species—and a new insight into the nature of the magic of Xanth! All this time, goblins have been fighting harpies when they should have been cooperating, so as to discover and use their combined magic. Now that can change. Never before has—"

"Well, we'll see," he said. "I can't say I like harpies, but I do like magic, and especially power. You human folk have had it too good, too long, because of your magic talents. Maybe now you'll have some competition."

"Maybe we will," Irene agreed, undismayed. This development had provided the warring factions the most powerful incentive to change their ways. Why try to kill a creature who might enable a person to develop a wonderful new magic talent? And if the goblins and harpies no longer warred, Xanth would be a safer place. Maybe both these species would become relatively civilized and would join the human and centaur folk as responsible societies.

Irene was really enjoying this wild dance now. Her dreadful initial vision, which had so appalled her at Castle Zombie, was being replaced by a vision of wonderful new things.

New shapes appeared above the enclosure. More harpies were arriving, attracted by the noise. Haggy flew up to screech the glad news at them. Her wings sparkled; now that she was clean and happy, she seemed to be a different creature.

"We'd better be on our way," Irene murmured as the dance broke up. "The day is getting on—"

They managed to make their partings and climbed over the wall. Haggy presented Chem with a whistle made from a hollow feather. "Blow this if you ever need harpy help," the old hen said.

Chem accepted it with due appreciation. Then they were on their way, leaving the celebration behind.

Chapter 14. Fire and Steam

They had been traveling northeast toward Hugo's home before encountering Glory Goblin and veering east. Hugo did some intelligent mental calculation and concluded that they ought to proceed straight north now to intersect their former route. That was better than walking all the way back the way they had come.

They took it easy, pausing to rest and eat, so progress was not rapid. Even so, Ivy was getting tired by the middle of the day and was wondering whether it would be in order to suggest an afternoon nap period. She decided to wait until someone else thought of it.

They crested a low hill and entered a clearing—and were brought up short by a sudden ferocious hiss. Alarmed, they looked about them.

There, switching his tail angrily, was a drake—a small, ornate, winged, fire-breathing dragon. They had unwittingly trespassed on his territory, and he was not about to let them escape.

The drake stepped toward them, still switching his tail. He eyed Hugo and Ivy, then slurped his tongue around his snout, obviously hungry.

"Maybe we can run away," Ivy said without much hope.

The dragon was small, but still far larger than Stanley.

Flying dragons tended to be lightweights, with large wings, and they could move much faster than a person could. Children afoot could never escape the drake.

However, there was a thicket at the side of the knoll. The plants were very thick there, which was, of course, why it was called a thick-it. "Maybe if we went in there—" Hugo suggested.

But though the drake massed much more than they did, his body was small in diameter. He could furl his wings flat back against his torso so that it was streamlined, and he could power his way through the brush in the manner of a snake. There was really no escape in the thicket.

"But we can't just let him eat us up!" Ivy protested with some justice, on the verge of tears. Her hand reached for the Cyclops' bone tied in her hair but halted; this was daytime, and Brontes would not come out of his cave.

Stanley stepped forward, huffing steam. He was perhaps a quarter the mass of the drake, and his wings were inadequate for flight, and he had no fire. It was plainly a mismatch, yet Stanley was ready to defend his friends.

"Oh, Stanley!" Ivy cried, clapping her little hands. "I forgot about you! Of course you can beat the monster!"

The notion was ludicrous, yet Stanley was ready to try, and it became more credible with Ivy's belief. A baby steamer could not hope to oppose an adult firebreather, but a baby steamer buttressed by the potent and subtle power of a Sorceress could indeed hope. But it would have helped had Stanley known about the support he had. As it was, he was indulging in an act of foolhardy courage.

Stanley placed himself between the children and the drake, his green body quivering slightly, his ears set back against his skull.

"You're so brave!" Ivy said enthusiastically. Stanley's shuddering stopped, his ears perked up, and he assumed a more confident stance. Ivy's belief in his courage had enhanced that courage.

"And your scales are so hard and strong," she said. Stanley's scales developed the luster of perfect temper and seemed to be thicker than before.

"And your steam is so hot," she continued. Stanley jetted a shot of steam that fairly crackled as it cut through the cool air.

"And your teeth are so strong and sharp!" Stanley grinned, showing surprisingly sturdy and sharp teeth.

"And you're so fast," she concluded.

Stanley launched himself at the drake with such suddenness and velocity that the larger dragon was caught still stoking up his furnace. Before the drake could react, Stanley's deadly teeth had clamped off the tip of his tail.

The drake was not one to accept such an indignity lightly. He roared, sending out a blast of fire that toasted Stanley's own tail. Stanley quickly retreated, getting out of the heat. Fire was not something to be cool about.

Now the fight was on. The two dragons paced about the knoll, maneuvering for advantage. Theoretically, a chomp on the neck could finish it quickly, but all dragons were well armored there; and, of course, it was almost impossible to get in a neck-chomp when the enemy's head was ready to shoot out a barrier of fire or steam. First the heat had to be abated.

The heat was not limitless. A firedrake normally had fuel for only a dozen or so good shots, while a steamer soon ran out of water and got dehydrated. Fighting fire with steam was hard work! So neither dragon squandered his resources. The trick was to set up the enemy for a telling shot, while causing the enemy's shots to be expanded uselessly.

Hugo and Ivy backed into the thicket, watching nervously. Neither thought of running away while Stanley distracted the drake; Stanley was their friend.

The drake fired out a white-hot jet. Stanley, swift to react, leaped high, letting the flame pass beneath him. Then, as he landed, and the other was inhaling for another shot, Stanley wooshed out his own spear of steam. It scored on a furled wing, and must have been hotter than the drake expected, for he jumped back and half unrolled that wing, cooling it.

Stanley made another lunge at the tail, but this time the drake was ready. His head swung about, ready to sear Stanley's head with flame. "Look out!" Ivy cried.

Stanley's head snapped about—but the jet of flame was

already on its way. All Stanley could do was shoot out his own steam, a desperate counterattack. Ivy cringed, knowing, despite her expressed confidence in Stanley, that fire was hotter than steam.

The jet of fire met the jet of steam—and just beyond Stanley's nose, the steam doused the fire. A cloud of smoke went up, the unburned fuel of the fire precipitating into a thick haze, and slowly the line of their meeting moved away from Stanley's nose toward the drake's nose. Steam was conquering fire!

The drake broke off the heat-duel and dived for Stanley's back. The jaws gaped and teeth closed above Stanley's middle set of legs. Ivy winced again. Such a chomp could cripple the little dragon and possibly cut him in half!

But the toughened scales held. The drake could not bite through Stanley's hardened armor. Then Stanley rolled over, and his claws came up and boxed the drake smartly on the snout, making him let go. Stanley had more legs than the other did, so at the moment the advantage was his, despite his smaller size.

They separated again. The fight was surprisingly even. The drake seemed perplexed; ordinarily it should quickly have disposed of an opponent a quarter its mass. But Stanley was a rare breed of dragon, one of the toughest and orneriest, and his power was enhanced by Ivy's talent. He was actually more formidable than he appeared.

The drake tried a new tactic. He unfurled his wings, spread them, and ascended into the air where Stanley couldn't follow. He wasn't fleeing—flying dragons had little room in their light skulls for brains, and what brains they had were cooked by the heat of their own fire, so these creatures didn't know when discretion was the better part of ferocity. The drake was simply attacking from a new direction. He looped about, aimed his snout, then shot fire down at Stanley's head. The object was to fry Stanley's brains, putting him at a slight disadvantage.

Stanley leaped forward, trying to escape the fire, for he was unable to bend his neck back enough to aim his steam at the enemy above. He wasn't geared for an air war. But the flame was too fast; it scorched his third-legs section. Ivy winced a third time; she saw smoke rising from the scales and knew that, no matter how hard they were, those scales couldn't stop the flesh beneath from getting burned. Indeed, Stanley was now limping, his tail dragging.

The drake gave a roar of victory and looped about for another pass. "Oh, Stanley's hurt!" Ivy screamed, feeling the pain herself. "We must help him!"

"But we're only children!" Hugo protested reasonably. "We can't fight a dragon!"

"Yes, we can," she insisted. "Stanley needs us! You're smart, Hugo; you figure out something. Now!"

Hugo sighed inwardly at the imperatives of women, but he was stuck for it. He concentrated, and discovered again that he was smarter than he thought. "Fruit!" he said, another bright bulb winking into existence above his head. "Chokecherries!" A fistful of dark red cherries appeared in his hand. He pelted the drake with them.

Several cherries bounced off the dragon's scales harmlessly. Even cherry bombs would not have hurt under these conditions. But then one landed in the mouth, which was just opening for another burst of fire.

Suddenly the drake was choking. He coughed, sending out a ring of fire, and bucked in the air. Clouds of smoke puffed out of his nostrils and ears, and he spun out of control.

But in a moment he recovered equilibrium and swooped back up before running the risk of crashing in flames. A single chokecherry was not enough to bring down a dragon.

Still, the distraction had enabled Stanley to get himself in order, and he was again ready to fight. He had found a stone and braced his foresection against it so that his body tilted upward. Now he could fire steam at the flying enemy.

But for the moment, the drake hovered out of range. Then, becoming extremely smart for his breed, he flew down at the far side of the knoll and clutched a smaller stone. He hefted this up, flew toward Stanley, dived, and let the stone go. It was a dive-bombing attack, and Stanley had to scramble away from his rock to avoid getting hit.

"Stanley needs more help," Ivy decided. "He's only a little dragon, after all. Throw some more fruit, but not the same kind."

Hugo was ready. He conjured a handful of berries and threw them. One struck the drake in the tail section as he was picking up the next stone. He quacked with outrage and almost flew into a tree, but was indignant rather than injured.

"What fruit was that?" Ivy asked, surprised.

"Gooseberries."

"Get something stronger," she advised. She had never run afoul of that kind of berry, but could see that it wasn't enough to put the drake out of commission.

Hugo conjured an alligator pear and hurled it. The pear clamped its serrated jaws to the edge of the drake's wing, annoying the dragon.

"Stronger yet," Ivy said, as the drake reached around to crunch off the paired pear jaws.

"I'll try currants," Hugo said. He conjured them and hurled a handful.

"But they're so small!" Ivy protested.

"Just watch."

She watched. One currant fell in the drake's ear. Another snagged against one of his wings. They were alternating currants; between the two, electricity arced, shocking the dragon.

That caused the creature to make a strategic retreat. Stanley, suffused with the spirit of battle, pursued. The drake, dizzy from shock, lacked the stability to get fully airborne and scurried with wings flapping down the far side of the knoll, Stanley hot on his tail.

"Stop, Stanley!" Ivy cried. "Now we can get away!" But the little green dragon did not hear her. He was hopelessly caught up in the rage of battle. This was, after all, what dragons were made for. He continued the pursuit, making cute little whomps in order to attain better velocity.

Ivy and Hugo followed, cresting the knoll. The far slope led down to a small, island-dotted lake, upon whose surface delicate mists played. It was very scenic, but Ivy just wanted to get Stanley away from it before he got in trouble. One never knew what was in jungle lakes.

The drake took off and swooped somewhat erratically along through the mist, inhaling deeply. His control system remained ravaged by the currants, but he was recovering. He managed to come to roost on the nearest island, almost crashing; his belly plowed a furrow in the turf, and a plume of smoke went up from his tail, but he squealed to a halt intact. There he rested, licking himself off.

Stanley hurried down to the shore, where he dipped his snout in the water and refilled his supply. He would have plenty of fuel for steam here!

Ivy dashed up to Stanley. "We must leave!" she cried. "Before the drake recovers!"

But Stanley shook his head no. He was tired, and his hind-section was scorched, and he still limped, but he wanted to finish the fight.

"Talk to him, Hugo!" Ivy pleaded imperiously. "Make him go!"

Hugo considered. "That may not be wise."

"What?" Ivy had trouble assimilating the notion that Hugo could side with the dragon against her.

"I think I understand Stanley's position," Hugo said, for he retained the smartness Ivy had perceived in him before. "He knows the drake will come after us as soon as he recovers, and will attack us from the air. As long as the drake has control of the air, we're vulnerable. So we have to stop him now, while he's in trouble. Only then can we travel safely."

Stanley nodded agreement. He had a certain insight into the ways of dragons, being of that persuasion himself.

"But you can't reach the drake," Ivy protested directly to Stanley. "He's on the island."

Stanley slid into the water and swam. Firedrakes didn't like to swim, but a steam dragon had to be at home in water. His body floated low, only the top ridge of scales projecting from the surface, along with his eyes and the tip of his snout.

But there was a stirring elsewhere in the lake. "Look out!" Ivy cried. "I spy an allegory!"

Sure enough, the allegory had mistaken the swimming dragon for another of its kind and was hastening to make a comparison. Ivy had seen a picture of an allegory in her magic coloring book; it was green and had a long snout filled with teeth, and it lived in the water, but it wasn't a dragon. It was—well, she wasn't quite sure what it was, but it was.

Stanley's head lifted and turned. He saw the allegory and blew out a worried puff of steam. He evidently did not know how to deal with a thing like this; indeed, few living creatures knew how to handle an allegory in its element. It was known that an allegory could turn a situation inside out without even touching it; that was this entity's magic.

"Get away from it!" Hugo cried.

Stanley obeyed, swerving toward the shore. But a relevant was just coming up to drink. The relevant was huge, with four trunklike legs and a nose so long it reached right down to the ground. Naturally, that creature liked to poke that nose in other people's business. Stanley wanted no part of it and swerved again.

But now he was traveling toward a hypotenuse who was basking in shallow water. The hypotenuse was enormously fat, with a huge mouth that opened into a triangle. When Stanley had turned and proceeded at an angle, and then turned to proceed at another angle, he had taken a line right toward the hypotenuse.

"Poor Stanley," Ivy cried. "Hugo, you must *do* something!"

Hugo obediently cudgeled his brain again. "I don't know what fruit can stop monsters like these!"

To make things worse, the drake had now recovered. He took off and circled, ready to fire down at Stanley's head. Stanley would be able to duck under the water, but he would not be able to stay down long, and the moment he came up that lance of fire would be coming at him. Ivy was not at all sanguine about the situation. After all, it was her dragon on her pedestal who was at risk. What would she do if anything really awful happened to him?

"Hurry up!" she cried at Hugo. "Only you can save him! Do something fantastic!" She knew he could, because that was the nature of Nights in Shiny Armor.

Prodded by that, Hugo concentrated and produced—a bunch of grapes.

Ivy had terrific confidence in Hugo, but even she had to harbor a small and unfortunate doubt about this. "Grapes?"

"These are the grapes of wrath," Hugo said proudly. "I

never was able to conjure them before. But they're dangerous to use. Are you sure—?"

The drake was diving toward Stanley, and the allegory and hypotenuse were closing in. "Use them! Use them!" Ivy cried.

"We may be sorry," Hugo said and hurled the bunch of grapes into the lake just as the drake was starting a lance of fire toward Stanley's nose.

Stanley ducked his head, avoiding the jet. But the fire passed through one of the bands of mist. The mist ignited, converting to flame.

The flame jumped to another patch of mist, then another. In a moment, there were columns of flame all across the lake.

The drake flapped awkwardly, trying to avoid the flame that appeared in front of him. The dragon breathed fire, but his wings were not fireproof. He dodged the nearest flaming cloud but had to continue swerving to avoid the other flames. The drake was no longer concerned with Stanley; he had his own hide to protect.

The other creatures were now in trouble, too. The hypotenuse quickly submerged, hiding from the fire, and the allegory swam swiftly away. The relevant trumpeted in fear and charged away from the lake.

A parody was just flying in. It had green wings and a squat, down-curving beak. "Wots this wots this?" it squawked and retreated in haste. "Polly wanna crackup!" This was not parody country at the moment.

But the rage of the mists was only the beginning. As the grapes of wrath sank into the water, the water became furiously agitated. It seethed and boiled. The surface became rough, ripples of emotion traveled across it, and soon it was making waves. The waves slapped at the fiery mists, and the mists heated the waves, turning their fringes to steam. This interplay only disturbed both forces further, and their angry efforts increased.

"Those are strong grapes," Ivy remarked, impressed.

"They come from a mean vintage," Hugo agreed. "I had to be sure to get the right ones, because if I conjured sour grapes by mistake, it wouldn't have worked out very well."

"Stanley's in trouble!" she said. "The waves—"

"I told you it was risky! I don't know any fruit that would help."

"Then find something else!" she cried.

Hugo looked around. "Ah—there are some string beans growing on the bank. We can use them."

"You're brilliant, Hugo," she said. And of course he was, now.

They harvested a number of beans and unraveled them. Each was formed of a balled length of tough string—too tough to be cut by any normal knife or bitten through by any normal teeth. They twined the strings into a longer, even sturdier cord and paid it out into the water. Hugo used a beanpole to push this cord toward Stanley, who clamped his teeth on it. Then they reeled him in, and the fierce waves couldn't interfere.

Stanley was all right, for he had been able to duck under most of the fires, but he was very tired. The day was now hot, because of all the fire, so they retreated from the raging, burning lake and sought shade beyond the next hill to rest in.

It was comfortable here beneath the spreading acorn tree, and no immediate threats manifested, so Ivy didn't even need to suggest a rest break. They all simply lay down and snoozed. Ivy lay with her head against Stanley's warm side, feeling most secure there. "You're a wonderful dragon for my pedestal," she told him. "You're just perfect." And Stanley got all steamed up with pleasure. Ivy was only echoing the kind of sentiment she had been exposed to in her own family, but her power extended it in a rather wonderful way.

Time passed quietly, like the calm before the storm.

Zzapp!

Ivy woke with a start. Something had passed close by, disturbing her, but she didn't see anything.

She got up. She *knew* there had been something, probably only a buzzing bottle fly, but she couldn't rest until she had placed it. This was her childish curiosity in operation, perhaps foolish, but quite compelling. After all, some of those flying bottles could be very pretty.

Zzapp! The sound was near the tree. She hurried to it—and discovered a small hole through its trunk. Odd—she didn't remember that! She could see daylight through it, for the hole was perfectly straight, or at least only a little wavy.

She went to the other side. There, an arm's length beyond the trunk, hung a little, loosely spiraled worm. She had seen similar things before, usually in the ground or in spoiled fruit, so she passed her hand above it to intercept the invisible thread on which it hung. But nothing happened. She checked all around it, to see if there were sidewise strands suspending it, but there were none of these either. What held it in place?

She poked the worm with her finger. It was medium-hard and fixed in place, not moving from her pressure. This was more curious yet! She got down to put her eye near it.

Zzapp! The worm was gone. She looked where the sound of it had seemed to go, away from her, and in a moment found the little worm again, hovering in midair farther out from the tree.

Ivy went back and woke Hugo, "You're smart," she said. "Come and tell me what I found."

Hugo grimaced. He would have preferred to sleep a little longer; being intelligent was not all that much fun when he had to keep using his brain to solve difficult problems. That was very much like work. But he got up and followed her to the place the worm hovered.

Zzapp! The worm was gone.

Hugo stared. His irritation ripened into horror. "My father said they were extinct!" he exclaimed.

"That cute little worm!" Ivy asked. She identified with cute things, quite properly.

"That's no cute little worm!" he said emphatically. "That's a wiggle! There must be a swarm."

"A wiggle?" Ivy asked blankly, wiggling her torso experimentally.

"The most terrible menace in Xanth," Hugo explained. "They destroy everything. See, this one has holed the acorn tree already! Don't stand in front of a wiggle, or it will hole you, too. We've got to get rid of it!"

"Stanley can steam it," Ivy said, unworried.

Stanley was now awake and had joined them. He sniffed the wiggle in its new location. The thing looked like no more than a tiny, twisted piece of stem, difficult to see at all from any distance.

"Steam it!" Hugo cried. "Destroy it!"

The little dragon shrugged and jetted out hot steam. The vapor surrounded the wiggle, cooking it in place. After a moment, the worm dropped to the ground, dead.

"That's a relief," Hugo said. "My father says it's been thirty years since the last wiggle swarm, and he hoped there would never be another. He says if the wiggles ever get out of hand, it won't be safe for any other creature in Xanth. I've got to tell him—" He paused, crestfallen. "But he's a baby now! He can't do anything!"

"But what do wiggles do?" Ivy asked, not quite understanding. She had not been around for the last wiggle swarming.

"Nothing. I mean, all they do is swarm. They just travel until they get where they're going, and then they swarm again, and everything has holes in it."

"Oh." Ivy didn't want her friends to be holed. "But we killed it, so it's all right."

"I don't think so," Hugo said "Wiggles always come in swarms, and—" He paused, listening.

Zzapp! It was the sound of another wiggle.

There was a swarm, all right. Xanth was in trouble.

Chapter 15. Lady Gap

"**D**oes your husband swear?" Chem asked Irene as they walked on toward the Cyclops' cave.

Irene was glad to take her mind from the goblin and harpy action just finished. "Dor swear? As in bad words? Of course not! Why do you ask?"

"Something the Muse mentioned. Clio is in charge of history, and she told me how she writes the official history books that cover all of what goes on in Xanth. But she said there's a lot to do, and because history doesn't remain still, she can never quite catch up. So when the time came to proofread the volume on Dor's visit to the time of King Roogna, she had another Muse do it. Then, later, when Clio looked at the book herself, she discovered errors—typographical mistakes that weren't obvious, so the other Muse hadn't realized. Only Clio, who was conversant with the material, perceived those errors—but by then the volume had been finalized, as she put it, and it was too late. Once a volume has been finalized in Parnassus, it can never be changed, even if it's wrong."

Irene had not realized that such a volume existed; Dor had never spoken of it, though she had known about his visit to Xanth's past. "And the book said Dor swore?"

"Not exactly. It was on—I think she said page sixty, about ten lines from the top—she's very fussy about such details—where Dor was talking to his sword. He was using this big Mundane body, you know—that was how he got into the past, by entering the tapestry-figure that was there—"

"I know about the tapestry," Irene exclaimed. "I'd like to see that book!"

"Why, there's a copy of it at home," the Gorgon said. She had at last removed the hood and was using her regular veil again. "Humfrey keeps a complete file. I read it when it was new. Fascinating story, full of barbarian violence and sex and gross stupidities. I love that sort of book!"

"Hmm," Irene murmured. "I begin to comprehend why my husband did not tell me about this. I believe I'll visit you after our search is over, so I can read that story."

"Dor's in trouble!" Grundy singsonged gleefully.

"I read them all as they appear," the Gorgon continued. "There was one about your journey to Mundania, and another about the ogres, and of course there was one about Mare Imbri. I can hardly wait to see how this present business is written up! And Humfrey mentioned getting an advance notice about a future volume that tells of Jordan the Ghost and his own visit to the tapestry, or something—"

"Hey, I know Jordan!" Grundy said. "He helped Imbri beat the Horseman in the Nextwave siege."

"What about Dor's swearing?" Irene asked, faintly nettled. She had thought she knew most of what was important about her husband.

"As I said," Chem resumed. "On that page, it is reported that his sword tells him he is undoubtedly crazy, and Dor says, 'Well, you're in my hand now. You'll do as I direct.' Or words to that effect."

"That's not swearing," Irene said. "You have to have a firm hand with the inanimate, or there's no end of mischief. Dor was simply establishing who was boss."

"But the text recorded it as 'Hell, you're in my hand'—an *H* instead of a *W*."

Irene grimaced. "You mean everyone who sees that text will believe my husband swore at his sword?"

"I'm afraid so," Chem said apologetically. "It seems a gremlin got into the works, and changed it the way gremlins do, and because of the circumstances of proofreading—"

"Oh, bother!" Irene said, irritated—and wondered whether that would be recorded as an obscenity, as the gremlin generated more mischief. But then she took heart. "Maybe not too many people will see it, so it won't do Dor's reputation too much harm. After all, *I* never saw it, so probably—"

"Oh, yeah?" Grundy cut in. "I happen to know that someone leaked copies of several of those texts to Mundania, including that one, so a whole bunch of people must have seen it!"

Black rage clouded Irene's vision, but she controlled herself so as not to give the golem satisfaction. "Not too many people who *count*," she amended.

"Oh," Grundy said, disgruntled. It was true that no one with any sense cared much about the antics of Mundanes.

"Maybe I shouldn't have brought it up," Chem said apologetically. "It was only one of a number of cases—"

"A number of cases!" Irene cried, outraged.

"They don't all involve Dor," the centaur said quickly.

The party marched on in silence. When they were about half an hour away from the Cyclops' lair, something else interposed. Some large creature was whomping through the forest toward them.

"If that's a monster, I'm going to grow a tangle tree!" Irene said, fed up with delays.

"If I didn't know better," Chem remarked, "I'd suppose that was the Gap Dragon. It's the only creature I know of that moves by whomping along."

"I saw what happened in the magic mirror," Irene said. "The Gap Dragon definitely OD'd on a Fountain of Youth water and became tiny. This is far too solid a whomping for that."

"Yes," the Gorgon said, remembering as she was reminded. "Humfrey and the dragon—both infants now. Lacuna is babysitting—"

"Well, it sure sounds like the Gap Dragon," Grundy said. "Better be ready to remove your veil, Stonestare, just in case."

The creature came into sight.

"The Gap Dragon! Irene exclaimed. "It *is* it!"

Indeed it seemed so. The dragon was full-sized, with bright metallic scales, three sets of legs, vestigial wings, and plumes of steam. It spied them and charged, shaking the ground with its whomping.

No time now to marvel at impossibilities! Irene fished for a seed. "I'd better sprout that tangle tree!" she said. "Or a strangler fig."

"No, wait!" the Gorgon protested. "I remember now! Humfrey said the Gap Dragon must not be hurt! It's needed in the Gap!"

Irene paused. "That's right. He did say that. It made precious little sense to me at the time, but now we know the Gap Dragon helps keep the goblins and harpies apart. Even if that wasn't the case, Humfrey always did know what he was talking about before, so we'd better heed him this time. But how can we stop that monster if I don't use my most devastating plants and you don't show your face?"

"That question makes me feel very insecure," the Gorgon admitted.

"Grow defensive plants," Chem suggested, worried herself. It was one thing to conjecture on the theoretical value of the Gap Dragon to the society of Xanth; it was another to watch that monster steaming down on the group. "Until we can slow the dragon down enough so it can listen to Grundy. Then maybe we can find out how it reversed the Fountain of Youth effect."

"Reversed the Youth!" the Gorgon exclaimed. "Oh, yes, we must learn that! I can get my husband back to normal!" She paused, considering. "Or maybe partway back. I'd like to know him at a comfortable age of forty or fifty, instead of over one hundred."

"The baby dragon was with the children," Chem said. "Now that it has reverted to adult status, I hope it didn't—"

"The children!" Irene exclaimed. But then her hand found the ivy plant she wore. It remained healthy. "No, the children are all right. At least Ivy is, and surely that means Hugo is, too, since they were together."

"Surely," the Gorgon agreed, relieved.

"Get on with the defensive plants, girls!" Grundy cried, seeing the dragon bearing down on them. It had been making progress all this time but had had some distance to go. Now it loomed excruciatingly large and fierce, the plumes of steam sweeping back along its long body.

Hastily Irene selected and threw down a seed. "Grow! Grow!"

she cried. How could she have stood here talking while the monster was charging?

Impelled by the double command, the seed fairly burst into growth. Irene was aware that her power had been slowly fading during her separation from her talented daughter Ivy, but she still had enough zip for this. The plant took firm root, developed a thick, gray-white stem, and spread out a globe of whitish leaves. Overall, it was not large or impressive; it was squat and low and showed no thorns or threatening flowers.

"The monster'll crash right through that!" Grundy said nervously.

"I doubt it," Irene replied. "Stand directly behind it."

The four of them placed themselves behind the bush. The dragon whomped right at it, shooting out a sizzling jet of steam. But the steam bounced off the leaves, coating them with moisture; they did not wilt.

Surprised, the dragon slowed. Ordinarily it would simply have crushed the bush underfoot, but it had learned caution about unusual plants. Some plants could defend themselves quite adequately. It moved into this one at reduced velocity.

And bounced off it. The dragon was shaken; the bush remained undented.

"Something odd about this plant," Chem said, understating the case somewhat.

"What *is* it?" the Gorgon asked, impressed.

"One you should recognize," Irene said. "A cement plant."

"No, I don't know anything about cement plants," the Gorgon said. "Plants don't have eyes, so can't see me, so can't be turned to stone by the sight of my face. Otherwise we'd have a handy way to foil the dragon; we could hide behind any bush and turn it to stone."

Meanwhile, the dragon had figured out that there was something funny about the plant and was circling around it, steaming angrily. Irene quickly tossed down several more seeds. "Grow!"

Ferns sprouted. "What can ferns do?" Grundy asked.

"These are chain ferns," Irene explained.

In moments the ferns developed metallic links, hooked up to each other, and formed a sturdy chain barring the dragon's progress.

But the chain was too low; the dragon sniffed it, pondered for a reasonable interval, then simply whomped over it.

However, Irene had already started more plants growing. Several amazon lilies lashed at the dragon's feet, striking with their small spears of leaves. But the reptile's feet were too tough to be hurt by these, and progress was hardly impeded.

But other plants caused more trouble. A firecrown landed on the dragon's head, heating it uncomfortably; a fishhook cactus hooked into several toes; a mountain rose grew in front, rising into a small red mountain, blocking the way while it continued to smell as sweet as its cousins by other names. A rattlesnake plant rattled, hissed, and struck at the dragon's nose; a star cluster heated the dragon's scales with a number of little burning stars; and scrub oak used little brushes to scrub at exposed anatomy. That merely tickled the monster.

"This small stuff is only slowing the thing," Grundy said. "You need stronger medicine."

"Well, I don't have any new seeds sorted yet!" Irene fussed. "I don't want to risk random seeds."

The dragon shook off the last of the nuisance plants and fired a jet of steam. Chem danced aside, but Irene felt the heat of the blast. The golem was right; she needed stronger stuff and soon, or they would be in deep trouble. But a tangle tree was too strong. She would have to gamble on some unclassified stock.

She nerved herself and threw out a random seed. "Grow!"

The seed sprouted into a huge tree that soon made everything else look relatively small. "Oh, that's a dwarf yew plant," Irene said. But the dragon simply whomped around it, undwarfed.

She tossed out another. It grew a number of cylindrical red fruits, and these exploded as the dragon passed, startling it. "A firecracker plant," Irene said, recognizing it.

A third plant looked like a fern, but it soon uprooted itself and walked away. "Walking fern," Irene said. "Oh, I'm wasting some fine seeds here! If only I had time to classify them, so I knew what they all were, I could do something effective!"

"Let me talk to them," Grundy said. "Maybe I can find a good one."

Frustrated, but unable to offer anything better, Irene let the golem put his little hand in the bag of seeds and draw out individual ones to query. She hadn't realized he could talk to seeds, but of course he could communicate with anything living. Still this took time, for he could only query one at a time, and the dragon was close.

Chem kept retreating, able to outrun the monster, but the Gorgon was afoot and having trouble. There wasn't room for her on Chem, along with Irene, Grundy and the bag of seeds; she was more solid than Zora Zombie had been. The dragon tended to go for whoever was closest. They had to get her out of danger, or she would be forced to lift her veil in self-defense and turn the dragon to stone.

Irene looked anxiously about. To the side was the base of a fairly steep slope covered with vegetation. That would be easier to hide in. "There!" she cried, pointing.

They hurried to the slope. Chem's legs plunged through the layered herbiage, seeking firm footing beneath. Vines and brambles abounded. The Gorgon had trouble, too. But maybe, Irene hoped, this would impede the progress of the dragon. Once it stopped trying to devour them, Grundy would be able to talk to it.

Chem reached out to grab the Gorgon's arm, helping her to scramble over the slope. "Oops!" the Gorgon cried. "My veil's snagged on a bramble! Close your eyes!"

Irene closed her eyes and looked away just to be safe. This was a very poor time to be without sight, but such a warning had to be heeded! She knew the others were doing likewise. She heard the angry hissing of the little snakes that were the Gorgon's hair; they didn't like being shaken up.

In a moment the Gorgon announced that her veil was back in place. Irene opened her eyes, looked back—and saw the dragon almost within steaming range. "Grow!" she cried to the vegetation between them and the dragon.

It grew. Oh, how it grew! The brambles become enormous and twice as tangly as before, and the vines threaded themselves into new layers of complexity. They twined up around the dragon, using it as support for their competitive rising toward the sun. In moments the dragon looked like a boulder clothed in vines.

The reptile didn't like this. It thrashed its powerful tail, snapping vines as if they were so many cotton threads. It steamed, making the green leaves wilt. It whomped forward, flattening multiple layers into one layer. The vegetation was no match for it.

"That's one tough dragon!" Irene murmured.

"The toughest," Chem agreed, struggling to stay out of steam range. She was panting, expending a lot of energy to move up the difficult slope, and so was the Gorgon. "I was (puff!) present when Smash the Ogre (puff!) fought it in the Gap Chasm nine years ago. (Puff!) It was an even contest."

"An ogre is stronger than a dragon, weight for weight," Irene said.

"In most cases," Chem agreed noncommittally.

The dragon made another whomp. Now it was within steaming range. It pumped up its body, making ready to issue the definitive blast.

"I've got it!" Grundy cried. "A dragnet seed!"

Irene snatched the seed as adeptly as any harpy might have. "Grow!" she ordered it, flinging it at the reptile.

The seed sprouted in midair. It developed into a broad net whose material glinted in the light like steel. This was no ordinary plant!

The net settled neatly over the dragon and dug its fringe roots into the ground on all sides. Irene had never seen a plant like this before; evidently there were some excellent seeds in the batch from the Tree of Seeds!

The dragon whomped forward, trying to brush the annoying net out of the way—and was thrown back by it. No strands broke. This was one plant the monster could not overpower by brute force.

Furious, the dragon reached out with a leg or two and clawed at the net. Still it didn't give. The dragon blasted out white-hot steam—but the net did not wilt or melt. The dragon chomped on the dragnet with its teeth, but the vines held.

"I think we've got it," Grundy said.

"Well, talk to it!" Irene snapped. This had been entirely too near a thing.

Grundy tried. He made a small roaring noise, which the

dragon ignored. They would have to wait for the monster to settle down.

They waited, glad for the chance to rest, and slowly the dragon's efforts abated. Soon it would listen to Grundy.

"Odd," the golem remarked innocently. "I didn't hear you thank me for locating the key seed, the dragnet."

Irene stifled further ire at his prodding. "Thank you so deliciously much!" she snapped. But of course Grundy's part in this *had* been essential; she did have to give credit where it was due, even to the most obnoxious person.

"I do so appreciate your gracious—" Grundy began, then paused, listening.

Zzapp!

Chem stiffened. "What was that?"

"What was what, silly filly?" Grundy asked, though obviously he had heard it, too.

"Probably my imagination," the centaur decided. "For an instant I thought—a historical phenomenon my father Chester told me about—"

"Who cares about history?" Grundy demanded. "We have a dragon to tame!"

"I'm not sure," the Gorgon said. "My memory remains vague in certain areas, but I remember Humfrey once describing a really bad threat—"

Zzapp!

Now the dragon froze, its ears perking up.

"Say—that dragon has two ears!" Grundy exclaimed.

"So it does!" Chem agreed. "That can't be the Gap Dragon! Smash the Ogre smashed off one of its ears; we used that ear to tune in on danger—"

"There are two Gap Dragons?" Irene asked, perplexed.

"I'll ask," the golem said. He made another small, steamy roar.

Now the dragon roared back.

Astonished, Grundy translated. "She's not our dragon."

"She?" Irene asked.

Grundy exchanged more roars. "She's the female of the species. She comes every so often to mate with the Gap Dragon, using a secret entrance to the Gap he doesn't know about."

"So she supposes!" Chem put in. "Once the forget-spell started breaking up, he remembered that exit, and the trouble started."

"This time, when she arrived, he was gone. So she set out in search for him. She can wind him from afar—but he's elusive."

"No wonder!" Chem said. "He's rejuvenated! Tell her that."

"No cure for the Fountain of Youth, then . . ." the Gorgon said sadly. "If this had been the restored Gap Dragon—"

Grundy told the lady Gap Dragon. She reacted with reptilian horror. Balls of steam drifted from her ears. "She wants to know how we expect her to mate with a baby," Grundy remarked with a smirk.

"I wish I knew!" the Gorgon said.

Zzapp!

Again the dragon reacted. Grundy inquired—and his little face sagged with horror. "She's heard that sound before! She says it's a wiggle!"

"A wiggle!" Chem said. "My dread has been realized. The worst possible threat to Xanth!"

"Yes, now I remember," the Gorgon agreed. "This is terrible!"

Irene was perplexed. "I think I've heard the term, but I don't really know anything about it. What's so bad about a wiggle?"

Zzapp!

Chem spotted two chunks of wood in the brush on the slope, picked them up, and stalked the sound while she talked. "The wiggles are tiny spiral worms that swarm periodically. Sometimes a century passes without an infestation; sometimes only a few decades. The last swarming was just about thirty years ago; my great uncle Herman the Hermit supervised the effort of containment, and lost his life in the process. It was hoped that the wiggle scourge had been permanently eradicated, but it seems not. Now we shall have to do the job over—and immediately."

"But all I heard was a little zap!" Irene said. "What's wrong with that?"

"That was the sound of the wiggle moving," the centaur

explained. "It hovers in place for perhaps a minute—it's variable, or perhaps each individual worm has its own typical frequency—then zips forward in a straight line, a variable distance, but not far at a time. It—"

Zzapp!

"Oops—it's the dragnet," Chem said. "Grundy, quickly—explain to the female Gap Dragon—"

But the dragoness had been paying close attention to the zaps. She had evidently been around for the last wiggle swarming, or perhaps the one before that, and knew how to deal with wiggles. She pounced on the tiny worm that appeared near her, crunching it in her teeth. Then she spat out the remains, making a lugubrious face.

"They taste terrible, I understand," Chem explained.

"But they can be crushed to death—if caught at the right moment." She grimaced. "Grundy, see if we can work things out with the dragoness. I fear we have a problem that's bigger than any of us."

The golem started talking to the netted creature, who listened attentively.

"So the wiggles travel in zippy lines," Irene said, irritated by her evident ignorance of something important. "What's wrong with that? Why kill an innocent flying worm that's just minding it's own business?"

"It's the *way* they travel," Chem explained. "They go through things, they leave holes. When they go through air, a vacuum is left behind; the 'zzapp' is the sound of that tunnel of vacuum collapsing. When they go through trees, the wood is punctured. When a person is in the way—"

"I begin to understand," Irene said, shuddering. "And there's no way to stop them?"

"Only by killing them," Chem said. "Their bodies are tough, yet can be crushed. I was going to squish this one between the pieces of wood, but the lady Gap Dragon chewed it instead. It's also good to put a wiggle between a rock and a hard place. However this was only one. Wiggles never travel singly; they're always part of a swarm of thousands, radiating out from a central nest. We must find and destroy that nest and must eradicate every individual wiggle who has already departed from it, because any one of them can get to where it's going, hibernate for decades, then form a new nest and swarm again. No one knows precisely what a wiggle is doing between swarms, but the life pattern of its species seems to resemble its individual one—mostly stasis, punctuated by sudden, calamitous movement. If too many wiggles escape, the next swarming could consist of many nests in different locations—"

"And all those zapping worms, punching through plants and animals and people, could threaten much of the rest of life in Xanth," Irene concluded. "Now at last I have caught up with you! We must organize a campaign for extermination!"

"We must indeed," Chem agreed. "I'm afraid this pre-empts our search for Ivy and Hugo, for now all of Xanth is threatened."

"Ivy and Hugo!" Irene exclaimed, stricken. "My vision—the terrible, unseen threat—*this is it*!"

The Gorgon was equally horrified. "If they are headed toward the swarm, not knowing—"

"Yet we cannot ignore the swarm itself," Chem insisted. "If we pursue the children now, the wiggles could overrun Xanth and be entirely out of control. The greater good requires—"

"Don't try to use reason on a worried mother," Grundy said.

"I'll do both," Irene said resolutely. "I won't let either Xanth or my child be doomed! But how can we best fight the wiggle menace?"

"All the creatures of the region must be summoned to help," Chem said. "Each must stomp or chew or otherwise crush or dispose of one wiggle at a time. It's a tedious and dangerous chore, for anyone near a wiggle swarm is apt to get holed, but there is no other way. And it must be done rapidly, because more wiggles must be pouring out of that nest every moment, and they don't wait for anything except their own mysterious imperative. How anyone can reach the nest without getting hopelessly holed is problematical, but it must be attempted."

"The female dragon understands," Grundy announced. "She's been around a long time. She's seen wiggles before. She'll help fight them."

"Will she stop chasing us if we free her?" the Gorgon asked.

The golem growled at the dragoness.

"How did they eradicate the last nest?" Irene asked in the interim.

"I believe they got a salamander to start a magic fire," the centaur said. "The fire burned inward in a constricting circle, destroying them all. But our chance of finding a salamander in time to do the job is not good; they're very rare and private creatures."

"I can grow a flame-vine—" Irene said.

"No, only magic fire will do it, as I understand it," the centaur said. "Ordinary fire might get a few, but could also burn out of control. Salamander fire burns anything and everything, which regular fire doesn't, but it is also one-way, so it is self-limiting. Both qualities are essential; otherwise we would do more harm than good."

"The dragoness says she'll spare us," Grundy reported. "She was after us only because she was hungry. She's been so busy searching for her mate, she forgot to eat—"

"I understand perfectly," the Gorgon said. "Tell her we'll help her find her mate, if she helps us now. But tell her also about the youthening—"

"Her mate is with my child," Irene said. "Our missions coincide."

"She agrees. But she's very hungry."

That was a problem. It was not safe for anyone to keep company with a hungry dragon! "I can grow beefsteak tomatoes for her," Irene offered. She fished out a seed. "Grow."

The plant burst into growth and soon fruited. The dragoness grabbed the beefsteaks as the Gorgon plucked them and tossed them to her.

Irene found an acid seed and planted it near the rooted edge of the dragonet. The acid ate into the net, dissolving the strands, and soon the lady Gap Dragon was able to crawl out.

Zzapp!

"Let me go after this one!" the Gorgon said. She followed the sound, located the worm, and put her face close to it. Then she lifted her veil, while the others averted their eyes. Grundy warned the dragoness, who also looked away.

The worm fell like a little stone. "It worked!" the Gorgon cried, dropping her veil back into place. "I can stone them!"

"Just watch you don't try it when one's about to zap!" Grundy warned. "You'd get holed through your face."

"I'll be careful," the Gorgon promised.

"Very well," Irene said. "Let's start organizing this. As I see it, we have three things to do. We have to fight the wiggles here, rescue the children—all three of them—and alert the rest of Xanth to the crisis. I think we can do all three at once, by splitting up our party. Gorgon, why don't you and the lady Gap Dragon work together here, stoning wiggles? She can carry you rapidly to and away from them, so you'll have the situation under control, and you can stone all the wiggles you meet. You can work better without the rest of us, because—"

"I understand," the Gorgon said. "I don't want a crowd of people around when I lift my veil!"

"But what about the dragoness' quest for the real Gap Dragon?" Chem asked.

"If she helps fight the wiggles here, that will free the rest of us to continue our search for the children, picking up their trail at the Cyclops' cave," Irene explained. "If we find the little dragon with Ivy and Hugo, as it seems we should, Grundy can tell him where to find the female dragon—so that will be all right." She nodded to herself. "You know, it becomes more plain why Humfrey said to preserve the Gap Dragon. There are interactions out here in the wilderness that we know little of, but that can relate intimately to the welfare of all Xanth."

"The total ecology," Chem agreed. "We ignore it at our peril. Everything relates."

Grundy explained to the dragoness, who nodded. She well understood the need and recognized that Irene's party could do a better job of tracking down the children more quickly than she herself could. Now that the edge had been taken off her hunger, she was a reasonable creature. Soon she and the Gorgon moved off, the dragoness' keen ears perked for more zaps. Dragons' ears were very special; she would locate more wiggles more rapidly than the others could.

"Now for the reinforcements," Irene said. "Grundy—we need you for translations, but now I think we need even more to get the word out about the wiggles. If we encounter the rejuvenated Gap Dragon before you rejoin us, we'll try to communicate with him somehow. Maybe Ivy has found a way. I'll grow an airplane plant you can ride to Parnassus, so you can tell the Simurgh. I'm sure the big bird will take it from there. Then you can return to us—"

"The Simurgh doesn't permit others to fly over Parnassus!" Grundy protested.

"It's a risk you'll have to take. Try to give your message the moment she sees you; then it should be all right. She's a pretty smart bird, and remember, she can read your mind. So you can think loudly as you approach: *WIGGLE! WIGGLE!*"

"Smart bird," Grundy repeated wanly.

Chem chuckled. Smart bird? The Simurgh was the most knowledgeable bird—and creature—of all time!

"You will do it?" Irene demanded, seeing his reluctance.

Grundy grimaced. "Yes. I'll try."

Irene grew the airplane plant. It sprouted stiff wings, an upright tail, and an airscope that sucked in air, heated it, and fired it out the rear, jetting itself forward. The plant wasn't large enough or strong enough to support any normal person, but Grundy was no normal person. He boarded the plane, and it took off with a whoosh of fumes. He was able to guide it by shifting his weight. "WIGGLE! WIGGLE!" he cried.

"Now let's get on to the Cyclops' cave," Irene said to Chem. "We have a good notion of its location. If we hear any wiggles on the way, we can destroy them. And let's hope Grundy rejoins us in time to translate for the Cyclops! We must tell him of the wiggle menace, and ask him where Ivy is. There are no normal enemies during a crisis like this."

Chem galloped. Irene was tense and worried, yet she experienced a certain exhilaration. Whatever threat the wiggle menace was, it certainly wasn't dull!

Chapter 16. Wiggle, Wiggle

"**W**e've got to do something," Ivy said.

"We can get stones or rocks and squish the wiggles as we find them," Hugo said. "But I think there are too many for us."

Zzapp!

"Here," Hugo said, conjuring two rockfruits. "Use these to smash it."

Ivy took the fruits, which fitted comfortably in her little hands, and stalked the wiggle. She found it and smashed the rocks together. "Ugh, squish!" she said, wrinkling her nose as she inspected the result.

"It's the only way," Hugo said, conjuring two more fruits for himself. "My dad says you can only really stop wiggles by destroying their nest. But anyone who gets close to it gets holed by the wiggles. He says that's how the Invisible Giant died. He was a big, big man, but the wiggles played eighteen holes in him and he crashed."

"Poor giant," Ivy said sympathetically. "I never saw him."

"No one ever saw him, dummy! He was invisible! So we just have to catch the wiggles as they come."

Zzapp! Zzapp!

"Oops, they're coming faster now," Ivy said.

"They do," Hugo agreed. "And they radiate out in a big circle that gets bigger and bigger. Maybe we better run."

"No!" Ivy said. "We must destroy the nest!"

"But I told you! We can't get close to it."

"We'll figure out how!" she snapped imperatively. She was

not aware of it, but at this moment she resembled her mother quite strongly, and not merely for the tint in her hair. "You're smart enough!"

This was of course an unfair assumption, but Hugo was used to it by now. He concentrated. It was amazing how smart he became when she insisted. "Well, we can't just walk up to it 'cause we'd get holed. Unless Stanley could keep steaming ahead and cook them in a channel—but no, he'd soon run out of water. We don't know how far away that nest is; it could be several hours' travel. Since nothing we know of can shield against the bore of a wiggle, any direct approach is doomed to failure."

Hugo was sounding more intelligent than ever before in his life, except when he served as defender at Hardy Harpy's trial. In fact, at this moment he resembled his father. Even Stanley, who really didn't have much truck with intelligence, sat up and took notice. But Ivy wasn't impressed. She wanted results, not dialogue. "Figure out a way!" she insisted. "You can do it if you really try—I know you can!"

"If we got there," Hugo said, "I suppose Stanley could steam the nest and cook the remaining wiggles. So the only problem is transportation. Now as I understand it, the wiggles radiate out on a plane; that is, they move out in a flat circle, not a sphere. They don't go up or down, just sideways. So it should be possible to approach the nest from above or below. Below is no good, for we can't tunnel through rock, but above—I wonder whether Stanley could fly there?"

Ivy liked this notion, which really was an excellent one. "Stanley, you've got wings!" she exclaimed. "So you can fly, can't you?"

The little dragon spread his wings and flapped them. He raised some dust and caused a gentle breeze, but could not get off the ground.

"Come *on*, Stanley!" Ivy said encouragingly. "I just know you can do it! Try harder!"

In response, the dragon pumped harder. His wings seemed to become larger and fuller and better webbed. For a moment his body lifted. Then it spun out of control and he plopped to the ground. Ivy's power, it seemed, had finally reached its limit.

"He's not a flying dragon," Hugo pointed out. "Those wings are vestigial. If he flew, he's probably crash and hurt himself."

Ivy considered that. She didn't want Stanley to hurt himself. She was very solicitous about pain. "Then find another way to fly," she told Hugo.

Hugo concentrated again. "I can conjure fruit-flies," he said. In his hand appeared a peach fruit-fly. It had fuzzy pink skin and two green leaves that flapped like wings. He released the peach, and it buzzed up and away.

"Can they carry Stanley?"

"No. They can only carry their own weight." Indeed, the peach was already laboring, for its leaf-wings were wearing out. Obviously it was not a power-flier.

"Then find another way," Ivy said insistently. "You're smart; you can do it. I know you can."

Hugo sighed. Intelligence was a mixed blessing, but he did privately enjoy being considered smart, and now he had become smart enough to realize how her talent worked. He could conjure good fruit because she believed he could. He was becoming handsome because she saw him that way. He was intelligent because she insisted that he be so. She was a little Sorceress; without her, he would once more be nothing. He was in a subtle but compelling manner dependent on her, and he wanted very much to please her. But he knew they could not safely fly to the wiggle nest. Was there some other approach?

He cudgeled his brain, but all it told him was that he had no answer. How could he arrange to accomplish the impossible? This group of three children simply lacked the resources to exterminate the wiggles.

Zzapp!

"I'll get it," Ivy said, grasping her rockfruits. "You keep thinking." She stalked the wiggle.

Zzapp!

There was another! Stanley went after it.

Hugo noted idly that the two wiggles seemed to be traveling on slightly divergent paths. Immediately his heightened intellect reasoned it out. Naturally the paths diverged, for the wiggles were radiating out from a common source. The farther they traveled, the greater their separation from each other became. It was an elementary matter to triangulate and estimate the location of the source, which really was not far from here. He and Ivy and Stanley could reach it readily—if they had any means of keeping from getting holed on the way.

He conjured a bunch of grape fruit-flies and watched them fly. Most of them were smaller than the peach and deep purple; their leaf-wings were much larger in proportion, which made them stronger fliers. A few were the opposite, being larger than the peach and bright yellow, with little leaves; they could not fly well at all. It all depended whether they were grape fruit-flies or grapefruit flies. Their differences in flying ability were a matter of elementary physics, which was the science of magic that Hugo was now beginning to comprehend. But the absolute weight that the small grapes could carry was no larger than that of the peach; by no stretch could the grapes support the weight of the little dragon.

Well, perhaps if Hugo could conjure grapes-of-wrath fruit-flies— No! That was definitely unsafe!

Several of the grapes spun dizzily and fluttered to the ground. They did not seem tired, merely confused. Others were unaffected. Why was this?

Hugo conjured a bunch of cherries. These had smaller but firmer leaves, and flapped more vigorously than the loose-leafed grapes, so they were actually stronger fliers. They pursued the grapes—and several of the former spun out of control, in the same place the grapes had.

Ivy returned, her rocks smeared with ick. "We got 'em," she reported with satisfaction.

The gist of a notion flirted with Hugo's consciousness. The fruit-flies—the wiggles—there was some connection, yet he couldn't pin it down. But he was smart enough to ask for the help he needed.

"Ivy, make me smarter yet," he told her. "Make me super-brainy-intelligent."

Ivy, like women of any age, did not properly appreciate the nature of her power. "Of course you're super-brainly-intelligent!" she said. "You're the smartest person in all Xanth. I just know it." And so she believed, now that she thought of it. Nights in Shiny Armor were supersmart, weren't they? And because she was a Sorceress, and had power that only Good Magician Humfrey would have believed—had he not been a baby—what she believed was mostly true. Hugo became almost too smart to be credible.

"The fruit-flies," he said, working it out. "They are being affected by an unseen agency that causes them to lose their orientation without physically damaging them. See, there go some more cherries."

"Cherries!" Ivy exclaimed, alarmed.

"No, these are cherry fruit-flies, not cherry bombs," he clarified. "These fly, they don't explode."

"Oh, goody!" She relaxed.

"But the disorientation effect is localized. There seems to be a region through which the fruits can not safely pass. And the nature of that region, judging from other small hints we have had, must be—a forget-whorl, of the kind my father described before he regressed to infancy."

"Is that bad?" Ivy asked, impressed.

"Yes and no. It is bad for us, for we must avoid it. Had we blundered into it, we should have suffered immediate amnesia." He knew about the whorls because he had been along when Good Magician Humfrey had told King Dor about them, back in Castle Zombie. With his present genius, he grasped their nature thoroughly. "However, we should now be able to use this whorl for our purpose, since it should have the same effect on the wiggles that it does on the fruits. This is not a certainty, but is a high probability. All we need to do is move that whorl over to the wiggle nest, and it will cause the worms to forget their purpose and perhaps forget even how to move. Then their menace will likely abate."

"Wonderful!" Ivy agreed. "Let's move it!"

"We can't even *see* it!" Hugo pointed out, now experiencing the necessary caution of a smart person. "And the thing is dangerous. It can wipe us out, too, as surely as if it had giant teeth. How can we move it?"

"You can figure out a way!" she said encouragingly.

Hugo sighed. Somehow he had known she would say that.

He concentrated again. "It seems there are a number of whorls, drifting generally southward from the weakening forget-spell on the Gap Chasm. They seem to have changed their nature, causing total forgetting instead of just Gap Chasm forgetting. I could probably work out a rationale for that effect—"

"Stick to business," Ivy said firmly.

Hugo sighed again. "These whorls seem to associate loosely with the Gap Dragon, or his rejuvenated state, perhaps because his exits from the Gap are through a convenient channel—convenient for the whorls as well as for the Dragon. Presumably the Dragon is at least partially immune to the effect of the forget-spell, having spent all his life within it. So it may be no coincidence that there is a whorl in this vicinity. But this suggests two things—that the whorls are to some extent affected by the prevailing winds and the lay of the land, and that Stanley may have more influence over them than other creatures do. If we assume this is true, Stanley should be able to move a whirl by fanning it with his wings and blowing along natural channels in the terrain."

Ivy clapped her hands. "I just *knew* you could do it, Hugo!" she cried joyously. "Now tell me what you said."

Hugo translated. "We can blow the whorl to the wiggle nest."

"Oh, goody! Let's do it."

They did it, after some further discussion and organization. Hugo explained that they should be safe from the on-zapping wiggles if they kept the whorl between them and the nest, for the wiggles would forget their purpose—assuming his conjectures were correct—when they entered the whorl and would be of no further threat. The three of them would have to stay together, not venturing out to destroy individual wiggles, as it would not be safe anywhere but behind the whorl. And Ivy and Hugo had to stay behind Stanley because, while the whorl might not hurt the dragon, it would erase the two of them if it touched them. This was a rather tricky, dangerous business.

But Ivy was not a creature of caution. She knew the wiggle nest had to be nullified, so she was bound to do it. Her mother would have had another vision, worse than the first, had she known what was contemplated here.

They proceeded. Stanley was in the lead, using his wings to fan the whorl. He could not fly, but he could generate a gentle, steady breeze that made the whorl slowly drift away. It did seem to respond to his breeze more than to the incidental passing natural breezes. Hugo was at the rear, conjuring bunches of flying cherries that he sent around and into the invisible whorl. The cherries that spun out of control showed where the whorl was; that was the only way it could be spotted. Ivy stayed between Stanley and Hugo, enhancing both their powers. It might have looked to an outsider as if she were doing nothing, but without her, Hugo assured her, neither he nor Stanley would have been able to perform. Both dragon and boy had enhanced intelligence and powers in her presence. The pedestal and the Shiny Armor needed constant tending now.

Hugo continued to triangulate the location of the nest by listening to the zaps of passing wiggles and performing rapid mental calculations. The zaps became more prevalent as progress was made. But it was not possible to approach the nest in a straight line, for there were trees and boulders in the way, and a hill that the whorl tended to slide away from, and a pond too deep for them to wade through. So they had to travel the contour, which meant moving the whorl sidewise on occasion.

This was a challenge. Stanley could blow the whorl directly forward, but sidewise travel meant he couldn't do that. The wiggles were zapping thickly out from the nest, preventing Stanley from moving to the side. He might be immune to the effect of the whorl, but he wasn't proof against the wiggles. They were stuck.

Ivy, of course, had the answer. "Figure it out, Hugo!" she cried, cowering as the zapping of wiggles became close and loud. *Zzapp! Zzapp! Zzapp!* "How can Stanley blow around a corner?"

Hugo cudgeled his brain yet again. Blow around a corner? Ridiculous! Only if he had a baffle—and he had no way to get one. There were half a dozen close zaps every minute now; he would be holed in short order if he ventured from the shelter of the whorl. As it was, he had to watch his flying fruits carefully, because a number were getting shot down by the wiggles. If he misread the position of the whorl by confusing holed fruit with forgetted fruit, disaster could follow!

Then it came to him. "Vectors!" he cried.

"Another menace?" Ivy asked, alarmed.

"No. Vectors are lines of force," he explained. "My father the baby was reading about them in a Mundane text once, while he was baby-sitting me before he got infanted himself." Hugo paused, smiling. "Now I can baby-sit *him*! If I ever get home." Then he returned to his concept. "Vectors are one of the types of magic that work in Mundania. Stanley's breeze represents one vector—pushing the whorl straight forward toward the next. The slope of the hill is another vector, pushing the whorl back. The vectors oppose, and therefore we can't make progress. But the slope isn't straight back; it's a little sidewise. So if we blow forward, and the hill pushes a little to the side, the net resulting force will be to the side."

"I'm glad you're smart," Ivy said dubiously. "It doesn't make any sense to me."

"I'll show you. Stanley, blow forward, steadily."

The little dragon flapped his wings, blowing forward at the whorl. The whorl moved a little, as shown by the falling cherries, then nudged to the right. As the blowing continued, the whorl moved faster rightward.

"It's sliding to the side!" Ivy exclaimed, surprised.

"Precisely," Hugo agreed. "This is slow but effective. As we make progress around the hill, the vectors will change, and we'll make better progress. We shall reach the nest—in due course."

It happened as he had foreseen. The curve of the hill made progress gradually easier. In addition, they discovered that by angling Stanley's breeze slightly, they could cause the whorl to roll or spin some, affecting its progress. They were getting better at this.

But the extent of the wiggle menace became evident as they rounded the hill and cut across the depression beyond it. Ivy looked back and saw the entire hill riddled by wiggle holes. Trees were tattered, and a few had fallen, their trunks so badly holed they collapsed. What an appalling number of wiggles!

Hugo glanced back, too. "Good thing we didn't try to fly," he remarked.

"Why?"

"Because now I see that a number of wiggles do, after all, travel upward," he said. "The holes do not form a perfectly horizontal plane; most holes are in a level line, but some are above and below. Some wiggles are angling upward or downward, and probably a few go straight up. If Stanley had tried to fly over the nest, he would probably have been holed so many times before he reached it that he never would have made it."

"Oooh, awful!" Ivy agreed with a shudder.

Zzapp! Zzapp! Zzapp! Now she was even more conscious of the concentration of wiggles. They were everywhere except right here, and the landscape of Xanth was devastated by their passage. She could see dead animals and birds, holed by wiggles. Even the ground was chewed up by frequent holing. The wilderness was becoming a wasteland.

But now at last the nest itself was in sight. It was a dark globe as tall as a grown man, perched on the ground beyond a ravine. There was a haze around it, which Ivy realized was actually the mass of wiggles hovering in the region, before zapping on outward. Most of them did hang in a plane parallel to the ground, making the nest resemble the planet Saturn—but of course this was much larger than Saturn, which as everyone knew was only a tiny mote in the night sky that never dared show itself by day.

Overall, the thing was awesome and horrible. How unfortunate no one had seen it while it was growing and destroyed it before the swarming started! But this was in the deepest depths of Unknown Xanth, where no one who was anyone ever went. So the nest had grown and grown, unmolested, perhaps over the course of thirty years. Now Xanth was paying for it!

It had taken time to skirt the hill and guide the forget-whorl this far. They were tired, for all three of them were children, and the day was fading. Still, there should be time to reach the nest, except—

"Hold up!" Hugo cried. "We can't go there!"

Ivy saw what he meant. The ravine was no minor cleft; it

was an abrupt, deep fissure in the earth, extending down into darkness. It was too broad for any of them to jump across and too deep to climb through. To the sides it leveled out somewhat, at the near edge; but the far edge remained an almost vertical cleft as far as they could see. They could certainly roll the whorl into this ravine—but if it sank to the bottom, they could never get it out again.

They halted, afraid to go farther, lest the whorl fall in. "What are we to do now?" Ivy asked dispiritedly. She was a creature of optimism and she believed in her friends, but the blank far wall of the ravine was a mighty pessimistic thing.

"Let me think," Hugo said.

While Hugo thought, Ivy's tired attention wandered. She wished she were home at Castle Roogna, watching the historical tapestry with its perpetually changing pictures. She could almost picture herself there, happily absorbing the yarns of the tapestry.

Suddenly she spotted a faint horse-outline. She recognized it. "The day mare!" she exclaimed. "I see you, Mare Imbri! You're such a pretty black, just like a shadow!"

And, as tended to happen in Ivy's presence, the object of her attention became more so. Imbri the Day Mare, who had brought Ivy's daydream, became clearer and blacker and prettier. She was now more perceptible than she had been.

"Hey, she can take a message to our folks!" Hugo said, his intelligence still operating. "We need advice about what to do now."

But the mare shook her head sadly, her shadow-mane flaring. She projected her thought into a dream figure of a nymph, and Ivy heard the nymph's voice faintly in her head, like a distant memory. "Night is nigh, and I can no longer carry dreams by night. I can not carry messages from one person to another; I can only bring thoughts *of* each other. I will have time only to hint to your folks where you are." And Imbri was off, racing against the suddenly looming night.

Ivy shook her head. They were still stuck! They wouldn't be able to see the flying cherries in the dark, and so the whorl would drift away, and then the wiggles would come through—

What were they to do? Their gallant effort was about to collapse into disaster. They didn't even have time to retreat or any way to bring the protective whorl with them if they did withdraw.

Chapter 17. Community Effort

They found the Cyclops' cave in late afternoon. The monster was asleep inside, with the bones of a recent carcass piled in the entrance. Irene would have felt dread for the fate of her daughter, but the ivy plant she carried still grew in health. Ivy remained well—somewhere.

"Be ready," Irene warned Chem. "I'm going to broach the monster."

The centaur nocked an arrow to her bow and stood ready.

Irene approached the cave. "Cyclops!" she called.

The creature stirred. "Ungh?" he inquired through a yawn. "Who calls Brontes?"

So the thing could speak the human language. Good. "Where is my daughter?" Irene demanded.

The Cyclops sat up. His big blue eye gazed out into the light. He saw Chem's arrow aimed at that eye. He blinked. "Daughter?"

"Ivy. She was with a little dragon."

The Cyclops brightened. "Sure, her, and dragon, and the boy. Nice visit, good fruit. Friends."

"All three are safe?"

"Sure. Nice children. We talk, tell stories. But they not stay."

"Where are they now?" Irene asked evenly, for her trust in monsters was small.

"They go home," the Cyclops said. "That way." He pointed northeast.

"But that's through the deepest depths of the unknown!" Irene protested. And, she added to herself, it was not the direction of the mouth organ where the children had interacted with the goblin band. Was Brontes deceiving her?

"Yes. Nice kids. I say I carry them at night, but they not wait. In hurry go home."

"They were all right when they left here?" Irene asked, still uncertain. This misalignment of direction bothered her. Once again, compulsively, she glanced down at her ivy plant. Of course the children were all right!

"They not wait for night. I not go out by day. The Sky—"

Chem lowered the bow. "I don't think he's deceiving us," she said. "He wouldn't be in a position to know about the goblins. The children must have changed direction when they encountered Glory."

Irene agreed. The Cyclops' story did, after all, align. "What about the sky?"

"My father the Sky—he strike me down, if—"

"Your father is in the sky?" Chem asked, approaching. "Is this a euphemism for—"

"He banish me, will strike down—"

"So you said," Chem cut in. "So your father *is* the sky, and he's angry with you. How long ago did you offend him?"

The Cyclops was at a loss. He started counting on his huge fingers.

"That many years ago?" Irene asked.

"Centuries," the Cyclops said, starting on his other hand.

"Centuries!" Chem exclaimed. "Your kind must live a long time!"

Brontes shrugged. "Sip of Youth water now and then; spring not far, for me. But not live long if I go out in sight of Sky!"

It was amazing how widespread knowledge of the Fountain of Youth was among the creatures of Xanth—while civilized people had remained ignorant. Yet this creature seemed unnecessarily restricted by his fear of the sky. "Have you ever tested it, this—this continuing animosity?"

"Not dare go out by day!"

"Look," Irene said impatiently. "There is a terrible hazard facing Xanth at the moment, and we need all the help we can get. Have you heard of the wiggles?"

"The wiggles!" Brontes exclaimed. "Many times, since time began! Very bad!"

"They're swarming again. If you don't come out and help us stop them, they may riddle this cave by nightfall. They're harder to fight at night, because you can't see them as well. So you may have to choose which chance to take—sky or wiggle."

"Must warn brothers!" Brontes cried. "Steropes and Arges are also at risk! Only found them last night!"

Irene wondered why the Cyclops hadn't found his brothers before, perhaps when the last wiggle swarm had passed this way. But probably they had been fighting different sections of the swarm, then retreated to their caves by day the way Brontes did. These semihuman creatures had funny values. "Do that," she said. "But first you must come out of that cave."

"But the Sky—"

"Forget the sky!" Irene snapped. "Come out here and see what happens. If you don't get struck down, you'll know it's safe. It's been a long time, after all."

The monster's big eye brightened. "True. Long time." He put a foot out of the cave, then hesitated as if thinking of something else. "But if Sky do strike—"

"Then you won't have to worry about the wiggles."

Overcome by this logic, though it seemed he reserved some small doubts, the Cyclops stepped out of his cave, cowering against the light, afraid a thunderbolt would strike him down. But as the sunlight fell on him, nothing else did.

"Evidently the sky has forgotten you," Chem said.

Brontes peered up, shading his eyes with a hand, amazed and relieved. "Long time," he repeated. "Oh, now I free my brothers, too! All fight wiggles!" He glanced about. "Not see as well as when Ivy-girl help. Where are wiggles?"

"Roughly east-northeast of here, we think," Chem answered. "We skirted the fringe of the swarm, and haven't pinpointed it yet. But it's not very far away—and getting closer all the time!"

"The kids!" he said. "Going right into it!" Then he charged off to the west, in quest of his brothers.

"He's right," Irene said with new alarm. "The children must be very near that swarm! Let's hurry!"

They hurried. Irene wished Grundy were still with them, for now the trail was fresh and the local plants would be able to confirm the route. But she could not wait for the golem to reappear. The threat of the wiggles made haste imperative.

As she rode, Irene began to daydream. This was unusual for her, as she was a practical woman; she had to make sure Dor didn't innocently foul up the kingdom. But now, at this time of the double tension of peril to her child and to all of Xanth, she found herself dreaming. She must be more tired than she thought.

She remembered how she had participated in the defense of Xanth from the last great threat, that of the Mundane Next-wave—which was, of course, now the Lastwave, but old thought and speech habits died slowly—and had herself been King for a while, since Xanth did not have ruling Queens. The final key to victory had been Imbri the Night Mare, now honored by a commemorative statue, who had given her physical life in the cause and now was a spirit of the day, a day mare, bringing—"

"Mare Imbrium!" Irene exclaimed abruptly. "It's you!"

And, of course, it was. Now she could see the faint shadow-outline of her friend, running beside Chem.

"I thought you knew," Chem said. "Imbri joined us several minutes ago."

"I'm not as alert to her as you are," Irene said, disgruntled. "You share your soul with her."

"True," Chem agreed. "But it is you she has the message for, except that she doesn't want to call it that."

"Well, let's have it!" Irene cried. "By whatever name!"

Now she was fully alert, and the day mare couldn't communicate with her directly. Chem had to translate, for the centaur's soul-affinity gave her a special understanding.

"Imbri says Hugo and Ivy and Stanley are safe, but—"

"Stanley?"

"Remember, Glory and Hardy told us. The rejuvenated Gap Dragon. They are safe, but need help. They're going after the wiggle nest directly."

"That's impossible!" Irene protested. "No one can approach a wiggle nest!"

"So we thought," Chem agreed. "But Imbri says they are using a forget-whorl as a shield, and plan to use the whorl to wipe out the nest. We must promise not to reveal that she told us this, because she's not supposed to—"

"I promise!" Irene exclaimed. "But how—a forget-whorl—"

"I believe that could be effective," Chem said. "If the whorl does to the wiggles what it does to most creatures, they will forget how to zap, and cease to be a danger to the rest of Xanth. I suspect this is a stroke of genius, though how they ever thought of it—"

"No one can even *see* a whorl!" Irene protested.

"It is amazing," Chem agreed. "Imbri says Hugo is locating the whorl by using flying fruit—"

"But all Hugo's fruit is rotten!"

"Not any more. Not according to Glory Goblin or Brontes the Cyclops. Imbri merely confirms that Hugo has perfected his talent, and is now a good deal smarter and handsomer than before. A woman has to be responsible."

"Or a little girl," Irene agreed. "I keep forgetting how much power Ivy seems to be manifesting."

"And the little dragon is fanning the whorl forward with his wings—"

"But the Gap Dragon's wings are vestigial! They're hardly noticeable! They can't—"

"They seem to have grown. I suspect your daughter has something to do with that, too."

The rest of the light dawned. "Only the talent of a Sorceress could account for all the changes we have noted!"

"A Sorceress," Chem agreed. "She was perhaps too close to you, so you didn't realize. Ivy will one day be King of Xanth."

"When my generation passes," Irene murmured, awed by the vision of it. This was more than she had hoped for!

Then common sense prevailed. "Three children can't take a risk like that!" Irene said. "We can't allow it! Those wiggles are the most deadly menace in Xanth! We've got to get them out of there!"

"We can't," Chem said. "Imbri reports the wiggles are so thick where the children are that no one else can approach."

"But—"

"All we can do is fight the wiggles where we encounter them, and hope that Ivy and her friends get through by themselves."

"But Ivy's only three years old!"

"And a Sorceress."

Irene stifled her reply, as it could only have debased a long friendship and would not have rescued her threatened child. She wanted a live daughter, not a dead Sorceress!

They had been moving along rapidly, covering much more distance in an hour than the children could have done. Guided by Mare Imbri's indication of the location of the children, Irene knew they were now very close.

They reached a grassy knoll. There stood a small flying dragon, a drake, somewhat bedraggled. Chem whipped her bow forward, arrow nocked; she knew better than to take any dragon for granted. If the drake launched itself in her direction, she would send a shaft through its eye before it got fairly aloft. Irene also reached for a seed; its effect would be slower than Chem's arrow, but as potent in the long run.

Zzapp!

Chem and Irene froze, trying to locate the wiggle. The drake lifted its head, spied the worm, and bathed it in fire. The burned husk dropped to the ground.

"I think we're on the same side," Chem said, but she kept her bow ready.

"We have intersected the swarm," Irene said with a sinking sensation. "And we haven't caught up to Ivy."

"And Imbri says we won't. The children are ahead, very close to the nest itself. A short distance geographically, but an immense one in the practical sense. We must fight the wiggles here, and hope for the best."

Zzapp!

Irene dismounted, perturbed. "I suppose so. But I don't like it. Those children—"

Chem found two stones and clapped them together experimentally. "You have to crush them hard," she said. "And quickly. We're going to be very busy now."

Irene dropped a seed. "Grow," she said in a no-nonsense tone.

The seed sprouted into a hairy toad plant. The hairy toads goggled their eyes about, looking for bugs. "Snap up the wiggles," Irene told the plant. The toads grimaced and threatened to croak, apparently knowing how bad wiggles tasted, but seemed ready to obey.

Irene found stones of her own and waited for the next zap. Chem was right; there was nothing else to do at this stage. She had done most of what she could do when she sent Grundy off to notify Parnassus. Now they just had to hold the fort, as it were, until competent help came.

The incidence of wiggles increased. The swarm was expanding, and it was obviously a large one. Chem and Irene found themselves retreating. They had to stay abreast of the outer perimeter, for any single wiggle that got past could start a new nest, in due course.

Yet Irene knew they were dealing with only one tiny part of what had become a huge circle. The wiggles were moving out everywhere, not just here. "We need help!" Irene exclaimed. "A *lot* of help, and soon!"

"Imbri has gone to notify King Dor," Chem said, stalking a wiggle. "She's decided this is so important she can justify breaking the rule about day mares and communications."

"And how fast will Dor be able to get here? It will be nightfall before this campaign gets truly organized, and then—"

"We won't be able to see the wiggles," Chem finished. "And by morning they'll be spread so far, we'll never get them all. I suspect that at some stage, some of them drop out, stop zapping, and settle down to hibernate; we have very little chance to catch those. So the battle may well be lost by morning, even if we do exterminate every wiggle that's still zapping. We can only hope Grundy gets help from the Simurgh."

"If only we could summon others here directly!" Irene exclaimed. "We—" She paused. "I'm a fool! We *can*! Didn't Haggy Harpy give you a—"

"Whistle!" Chem cried. "How could I have forgotten that!" She brought out the feather whistle and blew a resounding blast on it. "The harpies will be able to notify the goblins, too, and perhaps put out the news on the mouth organ."

There was a shuddering of ground behind them. Three huge Cyclops clomped up. Brontes had found his brothers and come to help.

"Spread out!" Irene called. "Each person take a section and destroy any wiggles that pass through it! We've got to get as many as we can before it gets too dark to see them!"

"We see well in dark," Brontes told her.

"Bless you!" Irene cried, relieved. This was a really useful contingent.

Now there were five of them, and they were holding up the advancing line despite the thickening of wiggles. Each Cyclops had a huge club with which he bashed each wiggle into goo. Irene had never dreamed she would be so happy to be so near such frightful monsters performing such violence! The ground rocked with their blows, but every crash meant another small victory.

It still wasn't sufficient. The wiggles were getting thick enough to represent a real danger to the people, for anyone standing in the path of a traveling wiggle would be holed, perhaps fatally. So far the folk had stood out beyond the fringe of the main swarm, running up only to smash the wiggles they spotted, but that was not efficient. If a person stayed within the fringe, he could smash only two or three in the time he otherwise smashed one—but how long would he last?

A huge creature glided in for a landing. It was the hippogryph, carrying a heavy load of three passengers. Irene glanced at them—and was surprised. "Xanthippe!" she exclaimed.

The witch dismounted and grimaced. "My son promised to get married tomorrow if I helped today," she said. "Besides,

I don't want my exhibits getting holed. So when I heard the Cyclopes charging about, and fathomed what was up—"

Zzapp!

Xanthippe marched up to the wiggle and glared at it. "Drop dead," she said. The wiggle dropped dead.

Good enough. "Find a place to the side," Irene told her. "We must englobe the swarm, if we can find the personnel."

"Will do," Xavier said. "Come on, dear."

Irene looked at the young woman with him. She was comely and unfamiliar. "Who's she?"

"My bride-to-be, tomorrow," Xavier said proudly. "Ain't she something special?"

"But—"

Zzapp! Irene was horrified to see a small hole appear in the woman's body. She had walked too close to the swarm, and been in the path of the wiggle!

But the woman paid no attention. "Wiggles can't hurt me," she remarked, and used two stones to crush the worm that had just holed her.

It was Zora Zombie—so much restored by requited love that she looked virtually normal! Her hair was now thick and black, her flesh was firm and healthy and quite pleasing in contour, and her eyes were clear. Even her clothing was good; she no longer wore decaying rags. But she retained her undead immunity to minor injury. It was as if she had regressed from months-dead at the time Irene had first met her, to weeks-dead when Irene's group welcomed her, to days-dead when she fell in love with Xavier, and now was only hours or minutes dead. She had evidently been a lovely young woman when she died.

"A live girl would be dead by now," Xavier observed, satisfied. "Ain't Zora great? No woman alive is better than her!" He leaned toward Irene confidentially. "She ain't cold, neither. She's warm, now."

"Yes," Irene agreed faintly. One part of her mind rebelled at the grotesque nature of the zombie, but that was being driven out by the beautiful nature of the restoration. It was a miracle of a sort—a good sort.

Then she had to attend to her own segment, for the wiggles weren't abating their onrush.

Other creatures arrived. Some were huge and strange, but Xanthippe seemed to recognize them. "You gi-ants get over there," she cried. "Chomp the wiggles in your mandibles and spit out the remains; they aren't edible. You ma-moths fly up and catch the ones just overhead. You gigan-tics scoot down under the leaves and catch any that are down there out of our sight. Watch out for your own hides; those wiggles may be small, but they're deadly!"

The strange, large creatures spread out and worked on the wiggles. Xap the hippogryph was also very effective, crunching them with his hard beak. He took up the section near Chem, who seemed pleased enough to have him there.

There was a screeching behind. Again Irene glanced back, since she used her ears more than her eyes to locate the wiggles—and saw three Furies. This could be real trouble!

Zzapp!

"A curse on you!" Tisi cried. The wiggle spun out of control and bounced off a tree, its power gone.

Another wiggle came through. "Woe betide you!" Meg cried at it. "What did you ever do for your mother, who zapped away her last energy in order that you might someday swarm?" She raised her scourge and whipped the wiggle out of its hold.

Irene relaxed. The Furies, too, had come to help. It seemed that all the normal creatures of Xanth were making common cause against this mutual threat.

As she worked, Irene continued to look around, spotting new arrivals. She saw the chocolate moose stomping wiggles with his sharp hooves—and next to him, a flock of ducks nibbled on other wiggles. Beyond them were several impossibly odd creatures with huge, hairy hands. They seemed, somehow, eerily familiar. Suddenly she made the connection. "The monster under the bed!" she cried. "You *do* exist—numbers of you!" And one of them waved. That was probably the one that had been stationed under *her* bed, before she had grown too old to believe in it.

Another odd thing rolled into view, stomping wiggles. Irene realized belatedly that it was a foot-ball. Everything was coming to help!

But now the sun was very low; night was stalking the land.

Some creatures, like the monsters under the bed, could function well in darkness, but others could not. If even a tenth of the wiggles got through, it would be eventual doom—and many more wiggles than that would escape in the night.

Then a truly monstrous shape came over the trees, darkening the sky farther. It was a bird, a roc, no, a—

GREETINGS, WARRIORS!

It was the Simurgh! Grundy had gotten through, and the eternal bird had left its perch on the Tree of Seeds and come to help!

PARNASSUS COMES!

"Oh, thank you, thank you, Simurgh!" Irene cried. "But it is almost dark, and many creatures will get holed—"

SEEDS OF LIGHT. And from the talons of the huge creature came a shower of tiny motes, each glowing like a little star. PERFORM, GOOD WOMAN, the bird directed.

"Grow!" Irene cried at them all. The stars grew, expanding into fat bulbs that radiated light everywhere. Some bulbs landed on the ground, illuminating it; others hung up in trees, casting wider flares. There were so many that the entire region became as bright as day. The problem of night was solved.

"Careful, Simurgh," Chem called. "Some wiggles travel high."

THEY WILL TRAVEL INTO MUNDANE SPACE, the Simurgh explained. NO HARM WILL COME OF THESE. AS FOR THE ONES BETWEEN—

A host of small birds appeared, evidently brought by the large one. Each had an outsize beak. "Those are pinches," Chem said, her centaur education operating again. "Just what we need!"

The pinches swooped about, just over the heads of the creatures on the ground and the ma-moths just above, and caught any wiggles zapping by in that region. They didn't bother with the really high wiggles, and now Irene understood why; only the low ones posed either a short-term or a long-term threat.

In the renewed light, Irene could see other arrivals. There was a big, friendly yak, talking wiggles to death; a bugbear was scaring them to death; and—

"Hiatus!" she exclaimed. "What are you doing on that carpet?"

The Zombie Master's son floated close. "I went out to help look for Ivy," he explained. "I didn't find her, but I did find the Good Magician's carpet, so I flew it home—and got the news about the swarm. So—"

"That's fine," Irene agreed. She was glad Hiatus had found a way to be useful.

Zzapp! A wiggle hovered close. Hiatus focused on it—and a big ungainly ear grew from it. Overbalanced, the wiggle fell to the ground, unable to maintain its course.

Still there were not enough creatures to complete the encirclement of the swarm on the ground. Her husband the King would not arrive with his forces for several hours, Irene was sure, and that would be too late; they had to contain the swarm while it was small enough to be containable. Every creature here was working loyally and hard, at considerable personal risk, but many more were needed.

Something huge slithered along the ground. It was the Python of Parnassus, come at the Simurgh's command. And behind him came a bedlam of screaming wild-haired naked women. The maenads! The big bird really did rule Parnassus!

The wild women spread out, enormously increasing the fighting forces. They seemed delighted with this task, smashing with glee at every wiggle that appeared.

Now the wild animals of this region were joining in, too. Every creature was quick to appreciate the need for action. Still, this was only one side of the swarm; on the far side, the wiggles could be spreading without hindrance.

But she had plenty to occupy her attention on this side! The skirmish line was advancing now, and the wiggles were thick. The sound of the *zzapps* was constant. Creatures were getting holed, and losses were mounting. Chem's flank was blood-flecked where a wiggle had grazed it, and there was a maenad on the ground, holed through the head. In death the wild woman was rather pretty, and Irene felt a pang of regret for her. This was no child's play!

Child's play—that reminded her all too forcefully of Ivy, there near the terrible center of the swarm, hiding precariously behind an invisible forget-whorl. How long could Ivy survive that, even if the swarm were eventually contained?

"What have we here?" Irene turned again—and there was the Zombie Master, animating the dead maenad. Now the losses of personnel, while painful, would not be critical; their zombies would carry on.

Steadily the line moved forward, the ranks closing tighter as they were augmented by other creatures. The wiggle swarm was now a magnet for the people and animals of Xanth, all coming to risk their hides and lives in this valiant effort. Irene realized that the Simurgh was broadcasting her powerful thoughts, summoning anything within range. The Simurgh well understood the menace of the wiggles!

Irene heard something new. It sounded like the beat of many hooves. She looked—and there at the fringe of visibility were many centaurs, each carrying two men. Dor had found a way to travel quickly, and now maybe they could complete the encirclement! Both men and centaurs would be effective against the wiggles, and if there were enough of them—

There were, it seemed, at last enough. Gradually the circle closed. The wiggles came even more quickly, but that was because this was closer to the nest. The creatures of Xanth were winning!

They forged inward slowly, abetted by the continuing light bulbs that showed every wiggle clearly. Not every ordinary bulb burned well and long, but the Simurgh had brought top-quality seeds for this occasion. The curve of the battle line became clear, showing more of the circle of closure. They had to maneuver to get past a lake whose surface was clogged with ash; something had burned on the water recently, taking some of the wiggles with it. Near that lake, a relevant was using its trunk to smash wiggles, and an allegory was crunching them in its teeth, and so was a hypotenuse, while a parody mimicked them. Irene was glad to see these creatures being of some help; she had never had much use for them before.

Now they were at the fringe of a rough plain beyond a low hill that was riddled by wiggle holes. What a mess the worms made of this land! Irene thought of the whole of the Land of

Xanth resembling this region if the wiggles prevailed, and shuddered. The swarm *had* to be contained!

The circle of closure became small enough so that Irene could see across to where the goblins and harpies held their front. They had, after all, responded to the whistle! The goblins were on the ground, lined up in military order, bashing efficiently. The harpies hovered above, holding stones in their claws to squish the elevated wiggles. The two groups held a major segment of the line and were, perhaps for the first time in over eight hundred years, cooperating with each other in useful work. In retrospect, it seemed that her encounter with the harpies had been fortunate, harrowing as it had been at the time.

And there, beyond a crevice, was the nest itself. Irene paused to gaze at the dread artifact. Here was the source of all this mischief!

Near it, this side of a crevice, was a small and odd group— a boy, a little girl, and a small, six-legged dragon. The children—at last! They seemed to have no protection from the wiggles, but they were safe behind their invisible shield, with tiny flying fruits buzzing around.

The wiggles were so thick between the children and the adults that Irene knew no one could reach the trio ahead before the entire wiggle menace was eliminated. There might be a channel, a place free of wiggles where the forget-whorl had blanked them out—but Irene couldn't see where that was and suspected that there was just enough variance in the paths of the wiggles to fill in that channel. Some wiggles might curve a little in flight, not being able to hew to a geometrically straight line. At any rate, it wasn't worth the risk, as the forget-whorl could drift the moment the children stopped guiding it, letting the wiggles suddenly through. The children were in sight, but hardly out of danger.

This seemed to be the limit of the contraction of the circle of closure. Any closer and it would be suicidal, because there would not be enough space between individual wiggles to allow a creature to stand. So they were at an impasse; they had contained the menace, but could not abolish it—and they were getting very tired.

They had to make a breakthrough soon, or their line would begin to collapse, and the wiggles would break out and win. All their available forces had been brought into play—and it wasn't enough.

Chapter 18. Hero Dragon

Suddenly there was light, as thousands of light bulbs rained from the darkening sky and illuminated the entire region. Ivy blinked, letting her eyes adjust to the new brilliance, and looked about.

The wiggles showed clearly, each casting several little shadows. They were so thick here that it would be risky to poke even a hand out from behind the whorl. But now there was no risk of that, for Hugo's flying cherries were also quite plain, defining the whorl. The three of them were safe; the onset of night no longer meant doom.

Beyond the immediate scene, the plane of the traveling wiggles extended out across the devastated landscape. Ivy thought she saw some winged shapes at the horizon, but couldn't be sure; they were too distant and too fleeting. She wondered who had sent the light bulbs; they certainly were useful!

But the children still could not reach the nest! It loomed there in the stark light, monstrous and deadly, like a giant pineapple in a process of a slow explosion. So near and yet so far, just across the crack! How could they cross?

Ivy squared her little shoulders and did what had to be done. "Hugo, think of a way to get across."

"You'll be a terror when you grow up," Hugo muttered.

"What?"

"Nothing. I'm trying to think." He furrowed his brow and thought. "We must fill in the crack," he concluded, his intelligence operating once again. "We must make a ramp, so we can walk across."

"Good idea!" Ivy agreed. "What do we fill it with?"

"I haven't yet worked out that detail," Hugo confessed.

"Well, work it out, before the bulbs get tired of glowing." She knew that light bulbs were notoriously unreliable, generally blinking out just when most needed.

Hugo concentrated again. He knew they couldn't leave the shelter of the whorl to fetch rocks, and if they scraped the ground they stood on into the crack, their position would soon be too low for them to cross. They needed something else— something available and plentiful. What could that be?

"Fruit!" he cried with inspiration as an especially bright bulb burst above his head.

"Fruit!" Ivy agreed, clapping her hands and dodging the falling fragments of the bulb. Probably a wiggle had holed it; if they holed too many bulbs, darkness would return. That was another reason to act quickly.

Hugo conjured a peach and tossed it through the whorl and into the crack. They heard a thunk as it struck bottom.

"We need more than that," Ivy pointed out. She was a practical girl, taking after her mother in that respect, and perhaps in other respects, too.

Hugo conjured several more peaches and threw them in. There were several more thunks from the unseen depth.

"Something bigger," Ivy suggested. "The biggest you have."

"That would be greatfruit," Hugo said after a moment's consideration. He conjured one—and the thing was so large it almost crushed him beneath its weight. He eased it to the ground, then shoved it forward. The thing rolled grandly into the crack and disappeared.

SPLAT! "That was a small one," Hugo said.

"Conjure some big ones," Ivy said.

"But I couldn't handle them!"

"Well, think of a way!" Ivy had little patience with excuses; she resembled her mother in that respect, too.

"Maybe if we make a channel—"

Zzapp! A wiggle holed the fringe of Ivy's dress. That was too close for comfort! "Watch the whorl!" she cried, alarmed and not a little annoyed about the damage to her dress.

Hastily Hugo conjured another bunch of winged cherries and watched them fly forward. Sure enough, the whorl had drifted to the right. The party shifted to get squarely behind it again.

Then they got to work on the channel. Stanley, perceiving the need, used his six sets of claws to help, and very quickly hollowed out a fine crevice.

Hugo used more cherries to verify the position of the whorl, making sure it was remaining in place, and then conjured the biggest greatfruit his enhanced talent could command. The thing was as tall as he was—a huge yellow sphere with a dimpled rind. It landed in the channel and rolled slowly into the crack. SPLAT!

After that, it was routine. One cherry-bunch, one greatfruit, alternating steadily, gradually filling the crack. After a while, the fruits stopped splatting and just bounced, and finally one rolled to the brink and balked. The crack was full!

They moved over, carefully, and deposited a few greatfruits to either side to broaden the ramp. They filled in with smaller fruits to even it out. Now at last they had their way to cross to the nest.

Ivy looked around—and saw in the distance a ring of people! Others had come to fight the wiggles! Mare Imbri had gotten through! But the wiggles were zapping so thickly that the people could not reach the nest. So it was still up to the three of them.

"Let's move across," Ivy said. "Keep a close watch on the whorl, Hugo. Stanley, blow it over the ramp."

The little dragon had been resting. Now he revved up his wings and fanned up a small gale. The whorl rolled to the ramp.

Hugo sent a steady stream of flying fruit aloft. Cherries flapped so thickly that they darkened the local region. A steady mass of them went haywire in the whorl and plunged into the crack, helping to shore up the ramp.

The whorl moved slowly and ponderously and invisibly to the center of the crack. They were doing it!

Then an errant gust of breeze passed by. It came from a small gray cloud that had drifted up to observe the strange activity.

"Oops," Ivy said, dismayed. "That's Fracto!"

Indeed it was. King Cumulo-Fracto-Nimbus, recognizing them at this instant and not giving so much as a wisp of fog for the threat to Xanth, since the wiggles didn't hurt clouds, now intended to blow up some trouble. He huffed and he puffed, at right angles to the direction of progress.

"Oh, no!" Hugo cried. "Another vector!"

The whorl nudged to the right. It started to move off the ramp. In a moment it would plunge into the depths of the crack and be lost—and so would they. Already the wiggles were zapping by close on the left, forcing Hugo and Ivy to squeeze to the right. Fracto grinned and heaved out another draft of chilling air.

"Blow it back, Stanley! Blow it back!" Ivy screamed.

But Stanley could not counter the vector of the wind without leaving the ramp himself—and the shelter of the whorl. His right three legs scrambled on the greatfruit rim of the ramp.

Then Fracto gave a nasty extra push, augmented by a dastardly roll of thunder, and the whorl moved to the edge and started to roll down off the ramp. Ivy screamed as the wiggles zapped thickly by the left side, forcing her and Hugo to the brink.

Stanley took the plunge. He scrambled off the ramp, slip-sliding down its sloping side. He got to the right of the whorl, braced himself, and flapped his wings vigorously.

The whorl slowed in its descent, paused, and nudged back onto the ramp, providing better cover for Hugo and Ivy. But the little dragon, off to the right side, was now completely exposed.

Fracto fired out a lightning jag of wrath. He took another breath, ready to blow out an adverse gale. Ivy saw that and pointed her finger in a perfect righteous fury. "Hugo—destroy!" she cried.

Hugo knew better than to argue with that tone. He conjured

a pineapple and hurled it with all his force into the hovering cloud. The fruit exploded with a dull boom, and Fracto fragmented. Straggles of gray fog scudded away; the King of Clouds would need time to recuperate. But the damage had been done. Stanley was in deep trouble.

Zzapp! Zzapp! Holes appeared in the dragon's wings. He winced but kept flapping. Now that there was no further adverse wind, Stanley's breeze prevailed. Slowly the whorl, defined by Hugo's renewed stream of cherries, moved across and onto the far side of the crack.

Zzapp! A wiggle holed Stanley's tail, for the dragon remained exposed. He yiped but kept flapping.

"Stanley!" Ivy screamed. "Get back on the ramp, behind the whorl!"

The dragon scrambled up. But as he did so, his wings paused, since he could not concentrate on two complex coordinations at once. The whorl slid back and teetered on the edge of the crack.

Stanley saw the cherries falling and knew what that meant. He stopped, braced himself, and flapped again, vigorously. The whorl resumed its forward motion, despite the opposing slope.

Zzapp! Stanley's neck was holed. Dark blood welled out and streamed down his scales. His head dropped, and his wingbeat faltered. The whorl began to backslide again.

"Keep going, Stanley!" Ivy screamed desperately. "I know you can do it!" But water was welling in her eyes in much the way the blood was welling in the dragon's neck. With a great effort, she compelled her own belief. "You're too tough to be stopped by worms!"

Perhaps in her maturity, Ivy's magic would have been enough, but she was only a child. Stanley tried to lift his head, but could not. Still, he flapped his wings as hard as he could. The breeze was off, since he could no longer see the guiding cherries, and the whorl began to go astray.

"Blow left! Blow left!" Ivy cried, and the dragon aimed farther left and pumped desperately, though there were more holes in his wings and his eyes were glazing. The whorl drifted back on course.

It wasn't sufficient. Stanley was halfway down in the crack, straddling the mound of fruits, while the whorl was beyond it. His draft was losing effect.

"Climb out quickly!" Ivy cried. "You can do it, Stanley! You can do it!" But she could hardly see him through her tears.

Hugo kept the cherries flying, knowing there was nothing he could do.

Stanley made his six legs move. His head dragged on the ramp, getting smeared with greatfruit refuse, but his long, low body moved. He scrambled awkwardly up the slope and out, leaving a trail of blood.

The whorl drifted back, impelled by the slight slope beyond the crack. The vectors never gave up!

The dragon made it to the edge just as the whorl did. "Flap, Stanley, flap!" Ivy screamed, horrified. Cherries were falling all around the dragon, bouncing off his green hide.

Stanley flapped. But he was now in the middle of the whorl and wounded; he had little strength remaining. The breeze he blew was not enough to do more than hold the whorl in place.

Hugo's smart mind was still working, and now he perceived a new strategy. "Hold your wings out!" he called. "Walk forward!"

The dragon heard him. Feebly, Stanley whomped forward, wings out, pelted by falling cherries.

The whorl moved with him.

"The forget!" Ivy exclaimed, remembering. "It'll make him forget! He's *in* it!"

Hugo looked at her, horrified. "Even if he survives the holing, his memory will be gone!"

The nest loomed close. Stanley saw it and gathered his last remaining strength for a final effort. All six legs heaved together, and he leaped, and sailed into the air—and landed on top of the nest.

The whorl was dragged along with him, settling around and into the nest.

The zapping of the wiggles faded at the center. They still moved outward outside the nest, but no new ones emerged. The whorl had made them forget, and so they had become harmless. The nest had been nullified, thanks to Stanley's heroic concluding jump.

The three of them were safe from the wiggles—and so was Xanth, once the ring of people got rid of the remaining wiggles. That was no easy task, but it was at least possible to do.

Stanley lay astride the huge nest, as if he were mounted on a pedestal, his blood dripping down around it to the ground.

"Oh, Stanley!" Ivy cried, rushing up to him.

Hugo grabbed her arm, whirling her around and holding her back. "No!" he cried. "Don't go into the forget-whorl!"

"Oh—the forget!" She nodded. "I don't want to be forgetted. Poor Stanley!"

One of the dragon's ears twitched. Stanley had always had excellent hearing, especially when he was mentioned; that was the nature of his ears. One eye opened.

Ivy clapped her hands. "Oooo, he lives! He remembers!"

"That doesn't necessarily follow—" Hugo said cautiously, his intelligence interfering with his emotion.

"Yes, it does!" she insisted. "It has to! Make it reasonable, Hugo!"

Hugo put his mind to work again. He could do some pretty impossible things when Ivy told him to. "Well, since he is the Gap Dragon and he has lived for centuries in the middle of the forget-spell that's on the Gap, we conjectured that he could be partially immune. But he could be completely immune, in which case—"

"Oh, yes! That must be it! He can't be forgetted!" She stood and looked at the dragon. "But he's hurt awful bad, Hugo. He's bleeding and everything! We've got to help him!"

Hugo knew there was nothing they could do at the moment. He looked about—and spied the Gap Dragon.

The what? Hugo blinked.

Then he saw, beside the full-sized dragon, the Gorgon. "Mother!" he cried, waving violently.

From the distance, the Gorgon made a familiar signal. "Cover your eyes," Hugo told Ivy. "You too, Stanley. Do not look. Mother is on the way. She will make everything right."

Obediently Ivy faced away and closed her eyes, and Stanley

relaxed into unconsciousness. He was a tough little dragon, but he was badly hurt.

They waited for some time. Then they heard something like pebbles dropping to the ground. "Mother's glaring at wiggles," Hugo said, figuring it out. "They're turning to stone!"

There was also a whomp-whomp approaching. "How can the Gap Dragon be big—and small?" Hugo asked, then answered his own question. "There must be another of the same species."

"A lady dragon," Ivy said with female intuition.

The dropping-pebbles sound stopped. "You may look now," the Gorgon said. "I am veiled."

Ivy opened her eyes and looked. The Gorgon and the dragoness were crossing the greatfruit ramp.

The Gorgon paused to turn and wave to the outer circle. "I have cleared a channel!" she called.

Another figure detached itself from the circle. It was a centaur, bearing a rider. Ivy knew who that would be.

The Gorgon completed the distance and picked Hugo up. "You get lost like this again," she said severely, "and I'll show you my face!" Then she kissed him through the veil. "My, aren't you handsome! Whatever happened to you?"

"Aw, Mom, it was fun!" Hugo protested. "But we've got to help Stanley!"

"Who?"

"Stanley Steamer," Ivy explained, indicating the little dragon. "He saved Xanth—but he's hurt!"

"Oh, yes, of course." But the Gorgon stood aside while the big dragon whomped up, sniffed Stanley, then opened her huge jaws and took him in her mouth. She lifted him down off the nest and set him on the ground.

"But the forget—" Ivy protested.

"She's immune too," the Gorgon reassured her.

A monstrous shape glided down from above: the biggest bird Ivy had ever imagined. It banked and flew away. A single feather drifted down.

"Thank you, Simurgh!" the Gorgon called. She picked up the feather, paused, and looked at Ivy through her veil. "I think it is better if you do this, Ivy," she said. "He's your friend, and it will work most effectively for you." She handed her the feather.

Ivy looked at the feather. It had seemed small in the sky, but it was as long as she was, now that she held it, but not heavy. "Do what?"

"Touch Stanley."

"Oh." Ivy took the feather and touched the tip to the little dragon's nose. "Like this?" she asked, perplexed.

"Wherever he hurts, dear."

"Oh." Ivy stroked the feather across the wound in Stanley's neck—and it healed immediately. "Oh!" she exclaimed, thrilled. She proceeded to touch the feather to every place Stanley had been holed, and soon the little dragon had mended completely. Once more he was able to hold his head up. "Oh!" she cried a third time and hugged him joyously.

"Hugo, how were you able to conjure good fruit?" the Gorgon asked her son, though her manner indicated she had an idea of the answer. This was the way of mothers.

"It's Ivy's fault," Hugo replied. "When I'm near her, I can do almost anything. I can even think straight. She's a Sorceress."

The Gorgon studied Ivy through her veil. "Yes, I believe she is."

"Just the way my father is a Magician," Hugo continued happily. Then he sobered. "Except—"

"He will be a Magician again," the Gorgon said. "It will take some time, of course, for him to grow—"

Another figure approached, seemingly careless of the remaining wiggles. It was a fairly pretty young woman Ivy didn't recognize. "May I help?" the woman inquired.

"Thank you, no," the Gorgon said, glancing at her in perplexity. "We seem to be in order here."

"Who is she?" Ivy asked. "Why don't the zap holes hurt her?" For the woman had several perforations.

"I am Zora Zombie," the woman said. "Holes don't hurt zombies, so I walked across in case there was anything I could do." She spoke with a slight slurring, as if her lips weren't quite tight.

"You don't look like a zombie," Hugo remarked.

"True love has almost restored me to life," Zora said. "And perhaps my spine was stiffened when I looked at your mother's face."

"That's why I didn't recognize you!" The Gorgon exclaimed. "You have changed so much—"

"I am what every zombie could be, if conditions were right, Zora said. "Now I can even do my magic again."

"What's that?" Ivy asked.

Zora smiled depreciatingly. "It's not very useful, I'm afraid. I can make creatures age faster."

"Age faster?"

"When I turn on my talent, any animal will mature two years in only one year," Zora explained. "But since no one in his right mind cares to speed up his life—certainly the man I loved when I was alive didn't—" She frowned, then set that aside as dead history. "So I never had use for it."

But the Gorgon perked up. "Could you make a baby grow twice as fast as normal, without harming him?"

"Oh, certainly," Zora agreed. "My talent never hurt anyone, except that most people feel that aging is the same as hurting."

"If you did it near Ivy, you could age a baby ten times as fast," Hugo said confidently.

"Ten times as fast!" the Gorgon exclaimed. "Zora, you must come to baby-sit my husband!"

"Certainly, if you wish," Zora said. "I always like to help people, especially older folk like my parents. But isn't your husband already over a century old?"

"He is and he isn't," the Gorgon said. "Believe me, you will be welcome at our castle! You and Ivy together!"

The centaur arrived. Ivy heard the beat of hooves and looked up, her arms still around Stanley's healed neck. It was Chem, and on her was—

"Mother!" Ivy cried, with tears of joy and relief. Now she *knew* everything would be all right. "You must meet my friend Stanley! He saved Xanth!"

"Yes, he did," Irene agreed, dismounting. "And in the process, he helped show us how to move the forget-whorls out of our way so no one else will be forgetted. We shall make a statue of him."

"No!" Ivy cried, gazing wildly at the Gorgon.

Irene laughed, patting Stanley on the head. "Not that way," she reassured her daughter. "We shall carve it from genuine stone, and set it beside the statue of Night Mare Imbri, exactly as I envisioned. It will be on a pedestal, with the words HERO DRAGON in the base. He will be famous." She glanced across at the full-sized dragon. "His place in the Gap will have to be filled by a substitute for a while, until Stanley is able to resume his duties there."

"Oh, goody!" Ivy said, clapping her hands. "He'll stay with me! Stanley is my friend!"

"That too," Irene agreed, getting down to hug child and dragon together.

Author's Note

The author wishes to thank a number of Xanth fans for their contributions of punnish notions for this novel. Roughly in chronological order: Paul Priu of the Isle of Illusion—the Football and the Baseball Diamond; Richard Hoffman—the Torment Pine; Bobby R. Bogle—the Trance Plant; Manuel Enriquez—Bed Bugs; Matt Mason—the Lady-Fingers Plant; Sean Logan correctly pointed out that the Time of No Magic in *The Source of Magic* should have abolished the Forget-Spell on the Gap Chasm; Alec Pontenberg—the Bumble Bee and the Armor-Dillo; Judy-Lynn del Rey—the Fountain of Youth, which just happens to occupy the same spot in Mundania as it does in Xanth, and the Gorgon-zola cheese; Freeda Scanlan—the game of People-Shoes; Liz Slaughter—the Chocolate Moose; Chris Carden—the Mouth Organ; Ben L. Geer, who didn't exactly send a pun but pleaded for more Xanth because it is his only link to reality (I know the feeling!); Bern "Pern" Eagan (evidently a refugee from another series—we do get all kinds here), who introduced me to his friend the Centaur of Attention, though that creature fled before I could capture him for this novel, being shy; and John Caporale, who sent me this plot summary: Dor and his friends use the Centaur Aisle of magic to cross over to the author's CLUSTER science fiction framework and explore for an Ancient Site. Sigh; I regret to report that the gulf between different publishers can be greater than that between genres; our heroes would never make it across unscathed. But this does show how much more imagination my fans have than I do.

And now it is done, and I think this is punnishment enough. Please, fans, don't deluge me with another squintillion puns; my mind may go up in smoke and I won't dare sneak any more of these volumes out of Xanth. Getting through Parnassus is difficult enough as it is. Also, please don't feel obliged to write me letters just because you feel I am neglected; benign neglect is vital to a writer. One month I answered over sixty letters and got behind on my novel typing. My publishers frown on that sort of thing, and such frowns can be as petrifying as the Gorgon's stare. Just read and enjoy and keep your groans about the worst puns to yourself so people won't stare at you. There will probably be another Xanth novel along in a year or so, not much worse than this one. In fact, if you read this one carefully, you'll have a better notion than I do what that one is about, but I'll give you title and description anyway: *Crewel Lye*, a Caustic Yarn about an Unkind Untruth.

Till then—

PIERS ANTHONY

About the Author

Piers Anthony lives near the North Village of Xanth. He and his wife, Carol, recently arranged to buy the Gap Chasm, after the Gap Dragon vacated it. His daughter Penny rides the night mare. His daughter Cheryl associates with ogres. His fans are elves who keep sending in more notions for Xanth revelations. This is the seventh Xanth history smuggled into Mundania; the earlier ones have been doing well in unmagical ways. The first one, *A Spell for Chameleon*, won the August Derleth Fantasy Award as the best novel for 1977, and the Spokane Public Library gave Anthony their Golden Pen Award as their favorite fantasy author in 1982. The fifth and sixth volumes, *Ogre, Ogre* and *Night Mare*, made the *New York Times* bestseller list. Of course no one in Xanth pays any attention to such things, but Mundania is a strange place.

Dear Reader,

Your opinions are very important to us so please take a few moments to tell us your thoughts. It will help us give you more enjoyable DEL REY Books in the future.

1. Where did you obtain this book?

Bookstore	☐1	Department Store ☐4	Airport	☐7		5
Supermarket	☐2	Drug Store ☐5	From A Friend ☐8		
Variety/Discount Store	☐3	Newsstand ☐6	Other_____		
			(Write In)		

2. On an overall basis, how would you rate this book?

Excellent ☐1   Very Good ☐2   Good ☐3   Fair ☐4   Poor ☐5   6

3. What is the main reason that you purchased this book?

Author   ☐1   It Was Recommended To Me ☐3   7
Like The Cover ☐2   Other_____
                                        (Write In)

4. In the same subject category as this book, who are your two favorite authors?

_____   8
_____   9
_____   10
_____   11

5. Which of the following categories of paperback books have you purchased in the past 3 months?

Adventure/		Biography	☐4	Horror/		Science	
Suspense	☐12-1	Classics	☐5	Terror	☐8	Fiction	☐x
Bestselling		Fantasy	☐6	Mystery	☐9	Self-Help	☐y
Fiction	☐2	Historical		Romance	☐0	War	☐13-
Bestselling		Romance	☐7			Westerns	☐2
Non-Fiction	☐3						

6. What magazines do you subscribe to, or read regularly, that is, 3 out of every 4 issues?

_____   14
_____   15
_____   16
_____   17

7. Are you: Male ☐1   Female ☐2   18

8. Please indicate your age group.

Under 18	☐1	25-34	☐3	50 or older	☐5	19
18-24	☐2	35-49	☐4			

9. What is the highest level of education that you have completed?

Post Graduate Degree	☐1	College Graduate ☐3	Some High		20
Some Post Graduate		1-3 Years College ☐4	School		
Schooling	☐2	High School	or Less	☐6	
		Graduate ☐5			

(Optional)

If you would like to learn about future publications and participate in future surveys, please fill in your name and address.

NAME _____

ADDRESS _____

CITY _____ STATE _____ ZIP _____ 21

Please mail to: Ballantine Books
                 DEL REY Research, Dept.
                 516 Fifth Avenue — Suite 606
                 New York, N.Y. 10036

F-17